PARTNERS

William Harrington

Seaview Books

NEW YORK

Manufactured in the United States of America.

First Edition

Designed by Tere LoPrete

Library of Congress Cataloging in Publication Data

Harrington, William, 1931–
    Partners.

    I. Title.
PZ4.H3112Par [PS3558.A63]   813'.54   79-67607
ISBN 0-87223-586-6

PARTNERS

Author's Note

This book is a work of fiction. There is of course a city by the name of Houston, and places and institutions mentioned in this book do exist. But the people of this novel do not exist; they are entirely fictional and not disguised versions of real people. Also, there are some businesses featured in this book. They are fictional, too. If the name of any person or business mentioned here is the same as that of any real person or business, that is an accident and contrary to my intention.

To Shannon, my son

PARTNERS

I

Teejay was in jail. She was locked inside a cell, behind heavy steel bars, and she was helpless. That was the worst part of it, the most frightening thing—to be abruptly *helpless*. Her head ached with the urgency of what she could not do: calls she could not make, people she could not confront, questions she could not ask, challenges she could not make. . . . She could do nothing to get herself out. Nothing. Each time she lay down and tried to sleep, she twisted with nightmares while still awake—tortured waking dreams of desperately important things not done—so she stood, tense and miserable, most of the night, leaning against the bars of her cell, nervously smoking, thinking, staring at nothing, waiting for tomorrow.

They had brought her in during the evening—too late for supper, as the matron put it—and the matron, called Bess, had checked her in and put her in a cell. Bess had chattered busily all the while, as she unlocked Teejay's handcuffs and as Teejay stripped. She admired Teejay's clothes as she took them from her and folded them into a paperboard carton—pants and a long, buttonless vest tailored of a sand-colored fabric made to look and feel like suede, a silk print shirt in warm colors. ("Bet that outfit's from Sakowitz. Set you back three hundred dollars, I bet. Goes awful nice with your red hair, though.")

Bess was businesslike and firm in spite of her chatter, and she was crisp as she ordered Teejay to bend forward and spread her nates with her hands, to open her anus for examination, then to sit on the edge of a table and spread her legs and press her pubes apart with her fingers. ("I'm sorry about this, but if you think girls don't try to sneak things in here in their assholes and pussies, I got news for ya.") Bess was sympathetic, too. When she ordered Teejay into the shower, she suggested that sometimes in the shower was where new prisoners had a little cry by themselves. Teejay had broken down and sobbed deep and hard under the noisy stream of water.

The sign painted on the brick wall outside the cellblock read "B" CAGE—WOMEN. ("I'll do ya a favor, Miz Brookover. Put ya in Nine with Janie Burke. Janie's a nice quiet girl.") Janie told Teejay she had been in "B" Cage, Cell 9, since May—eleven months and two weeks. She was asleep now, quite soundly, while Teejay hung wearily brooding on the cell bars and watched the dawn through the streaked windows.

The complex of locks and bars was exaggerated. If she counted right, she was separated from the streets outside by five heavily barred and locked doors. Six feet beyond the bars of her cell door stood the cage wall, and six feet beyond that was a gray-painted brick wall, with barred windows up so high she could see nothing outside but the sky.

The cell was tiny: six feet wide and eight feet long. Three walls were of heavy solid steel; the front was the barred door. The top was bars; the light—dead now—was a bare bulb in a wire basket, out of reach above those bars. The toilet was a stainless-steel bowl over which they had to squat; it had no wooden seat. A single tap let cold water into a smaller bowl above the toilet. Janie slept on the upper bunk. Teejay had the lower. The bunks hung on chains, and when the prisoners were not sleeping—or trying to—they folded the bunks to the wall, to make room to stand and move about in the cell. They put the mattress pads on top of each other on the floor, to make a place to sit.

The toilets stank. The women flushed them incessantly, but still they stank. The cage stank, too, of sweat on thirty or thirty-five bodies; also of old sweat in clothes and mattress pads, and of cigarette smoke. Teejay was not the only woman who was awake and smoking all night; all night the cigarette smoke drifted through the cage. They tossed empty packs out of the cells and out of the cage. The concrete floor was littered with paper and butts. All night long it was noisy. All night long she heard the cough and roar of flushing toilets, and staccato hacking, and spitting, and farting, and women crying.

Teejay was afraid. She was afraid of what it meant to be helpless. It meant she was absolutely dependent on other people, outside. And where were they? The truth was that they were where they would have been tonight anyway. The truth was that her being in jail was vitally important to nobody but her. The rest of the world was getting along perfectly comfortably tonight, and it would go on. And she, miserably imprisoned behind these bars, would stay imprisoned, help-less to do anything for herself, until other people found places in the busy hours of their lives to think about T. J. Brookover and do some-thing about her.

It was almost more than her sanity could survive. She was in control of herself all night—but only barely.

"All right. Right there. Hands on the wall. C'mon, hands on the wall. Above your head. Lean. *Lean, goddammit!*" Just outside the door with the word ATTORNEYS stenciled in black paint, Teejay leaned, letting the weight of the upper part of her body rest on her hands pressed flat against the wall. The tall black matron called Inez took time to light a cigarette while Teejay leaned, and then with the cigarette in her mouth she patted Teejay down—armpits, body, crotch, legs, anywhere the prisoner might hide something forbidden in the interview cubicle. She could take nothing in there but papers: her indictment, notes if she had any, nothing more.

For a moment Teejay was alone inside the interview cubicle, a room not much larger than a telephone booth and dim and dusty and lit-tered. It was divided from wall to graffiti-covered wall by a scarred oak table. She sat on a wooden bench. On the lawyers' side there was a dilapidated vinyl-covered armchair, all stained and split.

She sat wearily, awkwardly on the unyielding bench, clutching her faded, tattered gray wraparound smock to her body to prevent its fall-ing open. She was a lean woman, with long thin arms and legs and long slender hands, a high neck, a small head. It had been said of her, more than once, that she had the body and the spare, high-boned face of a classic ballerina. Her hair was deep, rich red. Lately she had worn it tied back, uncovering her ears and the lines of her jaw and neck; but now she had nothing to clasp it, and it hung loose almost to her shoulders. Her blue eyes were set deep now, behind the swelling of fatigue and tension. She glistened with perspiration.

A matron opened the door on the other side of the table and Lois Hughes came in.

"Teejay," said Lois solemnly. She pulled back the armchair and sat down. She did not offer to shake hands.

Teejay nodded. "Hello, Lois."

Lois put her softsided suede briefcase on the table and pulled a yellow legal pad from it. "You look like you had a bad night," she said.

"I suppose anybody's first night in jail is a bad night."

Lois Hughes scrawled something across the top of the legal pad. On her right hand she wore an old, yellow-gold signet ring, bearing the initial F—for Farnham, Teejay understood. Hughes was a good enough name; but in Houston, Lois Farnham Hughes counted as a Farnham —which was better. She was forty years old or so and was tall and well put together. Her face was large and open; her dark eyebrows were heavy, and her mouth was strong. She wore her dark brown hair thick and long, and this morning it was windblown. She was wearing a white blouse and a blue skirt of handkerchief linen, with a softly tailored tan jacket—Teejay recognized it as a Calvin Klein.

"I suppose that's your indictment," Lois said, nodding toward the document Teejay still clutched awkwardly. She took it and frowned over it for a moment. Then she smiled. "All the years I've known you as T. J. Brookover, I never knew your name was Tommy Jo." She chuckled softly. "I don't know what I supposed it was, now that I think of it."

"West Texas," said Teejay.

"Umm-hmmm," Lois responded, frowning again over the indictment.

INDICTMENT

THE STATE OF TEXAS

HARRIS COUNTY,   ss

IN THE CRIMINAL DISTRICT COURT

Of the term of April in the year of our Lord, one thousand nine hundred and seventy-eight.

We, THE JURORS OF THE GRAND JURY of the said County, on our oaths and in the name and by the authority of the STATE OF TEXAS, do find and present that:

TOMMY JO BROOKOVER, a.k.a. T. J. BROOKOVER, late of said county, on or about the 21st day of March in the year of our Lord one thousand nine hundred and seventy-eight, at the County of Harris aforesaid, did purposefully and unlawfully and of prior and premeditated malice kill, and destroy the life of, and murder one Benjamin B. Mudge, while the said Mudge was peaceably demeaning himself within the County of Harris afore-said, by procuring, employing, and causing one Kevin W. Flint to discharge a deadly weapon, to wit, a .38 caliber Smith & Wesson pistol at the said Mudge, thereby causing fatal injury and the death of the said Mudge.

Contrary to the form of the statute in such case made and provided and against the peace and dignity of the STATE OF TEXAS.

Signed: John William Hornwood   Signed: Fred T. Baker
         District Attorney   Foreman

Teejay watched Lois read the document, squinting as though she needed reading glasses. The squint was the only flaw in a cool professional demeanor. Glancing into Lois's open briefcase, Teejay saw white gloves—that she would wear when she went to lunch, no doubt. That was Houston style, *old* Houston style: white gloves for midday. Lois Farnham Hughes could be entirely comfortable conforming to an anachronistic Houston style—or just as comfortable not conforming. For herself, Teejay had been uncomfortable both ways.

She shrugged, and grabbed the jail dress with both hands, to drag it more securely around her. She had no underwear, and her loose breasts had shifted and opened the wraparound.

"You can get anyone in town," said Lois. "Percy Foreman . . . I haven't had much experience in the Criminal Court, you know. I've worked there, but—"

"I really want you to take the case," said Teejay flatly.

"Why?" Lois asked.

Teejay glanced down for a moment, briefly distracted by the sight of the bruises around her wrists. She had tugged and jerked on her handcuffs yesterday, and overnight two circular bruises had appeared. "Why?" she repeated rhetorically, quietly. "Well . . . For one reason, because you're a woman, and you have a reputation for fighting women's battles. I liked the way you defended that Galveston woman —what was her name?—that they wanted to disbar. One of the reasons for this prosecution—I'm convinced of this, Lois—is that I'm a woman; I'm an abrasive bitch in some people's estimation. They don't have the evidence to convict me of murder, Lois. I promise you that. What frightens me is things that aren't supposed to matter. I'm afraid they *will* matter."

"Nothing of what you're suggesting will have the slightest influence if Kevin Flint testifies you hired him to kill Mudge," said Lois. The statement was flat, bland. She confronted Teejay with her big, open face, showing her nothing but earnest concern, giving her nothing to read. "What will he do if they offer not to ask for the death penalty if he will testify against you? What will he say to save himself?"

Teejay frowned deeply and shook her head. "I don't think Kevin will lie. I don't think he'll give false testimony to save himself. But if he does, the argument is obvious, and I can't think of a better lawyer than you to make it."

Lois nodded soberly, and Teejay, studying her face, was satisfied she had been right in her evaluation, right in her choice. She had heard Lois argue in court, and it came out just like this conversation: understated, ingenuous, earnest; and whether it was honest and the product of her patrician self-assurance, or was an act, made no difference; it would make an effective defense with a dramatic contrast: Lois Farnham Hughes arguing for T. J. Brookover. If she could get her to take the case, now, it would be a quick small victory in the fight to get out of here.

"Do you intend to organize and run your own defense?" Lois asked. "Who's going to make the professional decisions? I want an understanding. Maybe you think you're a better lawyer than I am. Maybe you *are*. Anyway, you're the one with everything at stake. Can you really stand to let someone else run the defense?"

Teejay turned away from Lois for a moment, turned sideways on her bench, and drew three or four deep, swelling breaths to steady herself. "Look at me, Lois," she said very quietly. "I'm not any lawyer now. I'm a prisoner in the Harris County jail. I'm locked up in a place called 'B' Cage, upstairs; and it *is* a cage; and that's where I'm going to stay until you get me acquitted or they take me to the penitentiary, because they're not going to let me out on bond on this charge. I'm not allowed to have a *pencil* up there. I can't talk on the phone. I can't read a book. I can't write down a note, because I don't have a sheet of paper to write it on or a pencil to write it with. My cellmate keeps her lawyer's telephone number written on the inside of a torn-open cigarette pack. I'm going to live in a *cage* the next six months, or however long it is. I might like to run my own defense. But I'm not going to be running *anything*."

"I'm sorry," Lois said, professionally sympathetic but emotionally unmoved.

"It's hell," Teejay whispered. "I'm a lawyer, and I know all the glorious words and phrases about the rights of a person under arrest. But what good are the words, or the rights themselves, when they've got you in handcuffs and grab you by both arms and hustle you into a police car and haul you in? When they lock your cell door, Lois, all the beautiful words you know so very well and have thrown around so much suddenly haunt the hell out of you."

Lois nodded. Maybe she *was* moved.

Teejay rubbed her face. "Forgive the speech."

Lois tapped the tip of her gold ballpoint pen on her yellow legal pad. "I'll take your case, Teejay," she said solemnly.

Teejay met her eyes with her own. "I'm grateful," she said.

"What do you want to tell me about the case?"

"What do you want to know?"

"What *should* I know, right now?"

Teejay rubbed her eyes with the backs of her hands and smiled grimly. "The lawyer's old ethical problem, huh?" she said. "Do I want to know my client is guilty? Or would I rather not know? I can save you the dilemma, Lois. I didn't kill Mudge."

Lois smiled too. "Good," she said.

"I can give you a retainer. I'll have my partner, Frank Agnelli, write you a check for twenty thousand dollars."

"You don't have to do that," Lois said.

"I *want* to do it. And be sure you cash the check as soon as you get it. I'm being sued, you know. If somebody attaches my bank accounts, the check won't be any good."

"Is there anything you need?"

Teejay shrugged. "Anything. Everything. Whatever they'll let me have. Shoes. Toothpaste. Underwear. And books if they'll let me have them." She sighed and shook her head.

At nine o'clock a bell rang in the jail, signaling lock time, the hour when the prisoners had to enter their cells and be locked in for the night. In "B" Cage, most of the women got up reluctantly from the floor, where they had sat watching a smoky black-and-white television set outside the cage bars, and they wandered into their cells, cursing, shooting fingers at the matron, Bess. She was unlocking the control box outside the gate and would pull the levers that would send twenty cell doors sliding simultaneously in their tracks, shut, and would then drop the lugs that locked them. Teejay was there at the gate.

"Please, Bess—just this once. One goddamn time, *just one goddamn time!*"

She had heard nothing more from Lois Hughes all day, and Frank Agnelli had not appeared to bring the things she had asked for. Rationally, there was no reason why Lois should have returned or called, and there could be any number of valid reasons why Frank had not come; but she had spent all day waiting for something, anything, from one of them, and here it was lock time and she was not going to have any more word from outside before tomorrow, if then; and she needed to know what was happening, what they were doing, what calls there had been at the office, how Lois's firm had reacted to her taking this case . . . She *needed* to know!

"Bess . . ." she said weakly. "Honest to Jesus—"

"Miz Brookover," said Bess grimly, "You know I cain't give you special priv'leges. You made all the calls one woman is allowed in one day, and I special cain't let you make none after lock time."

Teejay glanced over her shoulder to see if any of the women were watching her beg. None were. All were in the cells but her. "You said it's hard, Bess. You said it. You said I've got a raw deal."

The control box was open, and Bess laid a hand on one of the big levers inside. "Miss Brookover," she said emphatically, "when I pull this handle, them doors is goin' to shut. If them doors shut with you outside, then you cain't git in your cell, and if that happens somebody is gonna come up from downstairs and take you to a disciplinary cell and I promise you, Miz Brookover, you ain't gonna like that."

Teejay swung around and walked the line of cells to number Nine, where Janie, her cellmate, stood gaping, wondering, and pulled her inside just as the rumble began and the cell door began to move. Teejay fell on her bunk as the door rumbled to a bump, shut, and the lugs thumped into place.

II

With her office door closed, Lois Farnham Hughes kicked off her shoes
and put her feet up on her leather-topped writing table. She had a
glass of iced ginger ale at her elbow, and as she listened on the telephone she remembered her drink from time to time, picked it up, and
sipped it quietly so her caller might not hear. The talk droned on.
She got a word in now and again. It was a conference call—Washington, Dallas, Houston—and even though she was impatient to be away,
it was a call she could not courteously stop.

She was tired. The blue linen skirt that had felt so comfortable and
cool in the morning felt like burlap now. She pulled it back off her
elevated legs. There was a little draft of chilled air from the air conditioner and it felt good blowing up her skirt, around her hips. She
shrugged her shoulders to flex her back.

"Not in Houston you can't," she said into the telephone.

She looked out the window. She wondered sometimes if there were
not someone in the Tenneco Building, or in some other building
around, watching her with binoculars when she put up her feet and
pulled back her skirt.

Someone tapped discreetly on her door. She dropped her feet to the
floor, pressed her hand to the telephone, and called, "Come in." It was

the late receptionist, with a telephone slip in her hand. She tiptoed across the floor and put her hand to her mouth in embarrassment when the parquet (which Lois had had laid over the office-buiding floor) squeaked beneath her feet. She put the slip on the table. It said, "Your father on line 4."

"Tell him I'll see him in thirty minutes," Lois whispered, glancing at her wristwatch.

The receptionist nodded and retreated, and when the door was closed again, Lois threw up her feet again. "Look," she said into the telephone, "this is all pointless until the SEC letter comes. I think we have to defer everything until we find out what's the SEC's attitude."

One of the other parties to the call spoke urgently.

"I think you should do that," Lois said curtly. "And after you do, we can talk some more." She flipped over the manila file folder that lay open on her table, to close it. She drained her glass of ginger ale. "Let us know. As soon as you have word."

She glanced around her table to see if anything needed to be locked up. She swung her feet to the floor and felt for her shoes. The wool of the Afghanistan rug under her table clung to her stockings. She had ruined five dozen pairs that way, she estimated.

She touched the receptionist's intercom number. "This is Mrs. Hughes. Did Mr. Farnham have anything more to say? . . . Okay, I'm leaving now. . . . Okay."

It was 6:30. It had been a long day.

Her father and her two children were at their table in the window overlooking the eighteenth green at Bayou Oaks. She saw them before they saw her—Daniel Farnham, her father, sitting tall and stiff on his chair, the flush on his face and bald head telling her he had played golf late in the afternoon, which, depending on how his game had gone, might determine his mood for the evening; Wendy, her daughter, honey-blond and tanned, in a sundress that bared her shoulders, self-conscious that she looked seventeen or eighteen, not fourteen; and McAllister John Hughes, Jr., her son, twelve years old, sitting slouched with his legs thrust as far under the table as they would go, his arm draped over the back of his chair. When they saw her coming across the dining room, her father stood. But Mac John, Jr., didn't. The child annoyed her every time she saw him; she loved him but she didn't like him. "Get up when a lady comes to your table," she said to him before she so much as said hello to any of them.

"Wendy and I are having our sherry," her father said.

"I'm going to have a martini," said Lois. "Honestly—"

"*Jake*," called her father peremptorily at the husky black waiter who had already seen that Lois had arrived and was waiting to be summoned. Her father snapped his fingers at Jake. When the man arrived, he said, "Mrs. Hughes will have a very dry martini on the rocks."

"More sherry, Mr. Farnham?"

"Yes. Two more sherries, please. Tio Pepe."

When he was in Houston— and he was most of the time—he dined on Thursday evenings with Lois and her children. He dined on other regular nights with her brothers and their families. It was said in town that he had recovered handsomely from his heart attack of three years before and from the death of Lois's mother two years ago; but Lois was not sure if it had been his bereavement or the postcoronary diet his doctor had imposed on him that left him thin to the point of looking hollow. He was six feet four inches tall, wore gold-rimmed spectacles, and rigidly disciplined the thin strands of his white hair to lie in parallel stripes across his sunburned, liver-spotted pate. For dinner he was wearing a light-blue jacket, white trousers, white shoes, a bow tie.

"Mac John stopped by and said hello," Wendy reported.

"He was drunk," snapped Mac John, Jr.

"Not really," said Wendy.

The boy shrugged. "Drunk enough."

"I was on a conference call, dad, when you called," said Lois, to change the subject.

"So your secretary said. Was it anything earth-shattering?"

"No."

"I had a call this morning I wanted to discuss with you," her father said. He looked up and nodded sociably but not warmly to a man who passed by their table and spoke to him. "What do you think of Dr. Walter Lindsay?"

"In what connection?"

"Two or three members of the hospital board want to promote him."

"Why?"

Daniel Farnham smiled. "My own reaction exactly. Why? I can't think of a reason, and if you can't, I'm not going to support any motion to do it."

Lois shook her head. "I can't think of any reason."

"They say he'll resign if we don't."

"That's *his* decision."

Her father tapped his fingernail on the menu lying by his glass. "They have some pompano tonight. I doubt if it's any good."

"Mac John *was* drunk," said Mac John, Jr., frowning.

"McAllister, I don't care if he was drunk or not," Lois said. "It's none of my concern and none of yours. If he's drunk when you go to see him, then we'll talk about it and worry about it. Otherwise, he can get as drunk as he wants, and God bless him."

Jake had brought Lois her martini, and now her father watched critically as she sipped from it—not, she knew, because he disapproved of the martini as a drink (indeed, he drank one now and again himself) but because he could not, literally *could not*, imagine anyone enjoying one made with the Tanqueray gin she always ordered.

He was distracted only for an instant and picked up the conversation where he had paused. The talk now was about recent acquisitions of the Museum of Fine Arts. "Since your mother is gone, I have no way to judge. I can't tell if those people are spending money like idiots or not."

"We have to trust someone's judgment," she said.

"I could always trust her judgment about whose judgment to trust," he said.

Lois smiled. "Maybe we should ease ourselves out," she said. "It was *her* interest. I'm afraid none of the rest of us has either the expertise or the enthusiasm to do it justice."

"Oh, I mean to extricate myself," he said. "But I mean to make a gift in her memory, and I'd like to think the money will be well spent. I'd like to think that people a century from now will look at the Mary Brady Farnham collection and marvel at what fine things were bought, not laugh to see how a memorial gift was dissipated on fads."

"We can never be sure of what another century is going to think," said Lois. "It's like my George Stubbs: prized a hundred years ago, scorned as syrupy junk fifty years ago, stashed away in an attic and forgotten as recently as twenty years ago, and now beginning to be highly valued again."

"Your mother," he said quietly, "had a fine aesthetic sense."

"In many things," said Lois. "In a husband. In a father for her children."

Three of them ordered the pompano, in spite of her father's fear, expressed to Jake, that it would be rubbery or tough. Mac John, Jr., ordered steak as always—well done, in defiance of his grandfather's exasperated frown. They had a chilled Rhine wine, a Rüdesheimer, with the fish. He referred to it as a Hock, which is what he called all Rhine wine. "A Hock. Well iced. There is nothing finer," he said to Wendy. "Although I suppose your brother would prefer a Mountain Dew."

"It wouldn't get me drunk, which is what she's getting," said the boy, laughing at the fourteen-year-old girl who, in fact, having had two sherries and now a glass of Rhine wine, had turned a little wide-eyed.

"Peace between you two," said Lois.

Lois looked out the window, at a foursome of golfers finishing a round on the eighteenth green. Golf had always impressed her as more a ritual dance than a sport, and she amused herself now contemplating the rigidly stylized poses of the putters. It would make a ballet, she had always thought. The steps were set, the costumes were fixed, even the facial expressions were prescribed. She smiled to herself and tried to ignore the petty contest between her father and her son.

"I'm beginning to think you can have the district, Lois," her father said. "Things are falling into line. They won't give it to you, but you have a fair chance to have it."

Her eyes swept back to him. "I haven't been thinking about it," she said.

"I have. And I've talked about it, to some people."

Lois lifted her hands and pressed her hair back from her temples. She shook her head. "I'm not sure I'm up to it," she said. "Sometimes I think I'd like to shrug off a few burdens, not take on more."

Her father smiled and chuckled. "That's precisely what you'd be doing, in my estimation," he said. "The Congress is a club. It's a form of retirement."

Lois grinned and saluted her father with her wineglass. "I don't think so. Not anymore. But we have time to think about it," she said.

He shook his head. "*Now* is the time to think about it. We may need to head some people off. Also, you may need to amend some elements of your act."

"Oh? Indeed?"

"Political elements. Not personal elements." He pushed aside with distaste his half-eaten plate of pompano and poured himself a glass of wine. "The black community, for example, doesn't feel you've made their cause yours. You could give them a bit more attention."

"How?"

"The same way you've taken on other causes. If you had given them half the attention you've always given to the business about juvenile delinquents, you'd have their admiration and support."

"They don't need me," Lois said acerbly. "They can call out legions of lawyers to fight their battles. But where's the NAACP for the kids in juvenile dungeons?"

"I wouldn't want to hear you quoted to that effect," he said dryly. "And to be perfectly cynical, kids in juvenile dungeons don't vote. Blacks do."

Lois put down her fork and knife, rubbed her fingers together thoughtfully over her plate, and after a moment said, "You can't be 'perfectly cynical,' dad. It's not in you. But let me change the subject. I've taken on a case today. Actually, it may have some small political significance."

"What now?"

"I'm going to defend T. J. Brookover."

"*Mother!*" gasped Wendy.

"In my judgment," said her father, "the court should not only acquit her but should award her a medal and a bounty. Whoever killed Ben Mudge performed an estimable service for the community."

"I'm glad you think so."

"That's not the way the district attorney thinks, is it?" Wendy asked.

"She can go to the chair if you don't get her off, huh?" said Mac John, Jr.

"You are right when you say the case has political significance," said her father. "I'm surprised you took it, actually. I'm not dismayed, but I am surprised."

"She's a woman," Lois said. "She put it to me that she's a woman and probably is being prosecuted at least in part because she is a woman."

"You know Bill Hornwood. He wouldn't be influenced by that."

Lois shrugged. "I don't know. Maybe not consciously . . ."

"Well, *is she guilty*, that's the point," Mac John, Jr., interrupted. "Did she kill the old boy or didn't she?"

Lois looked coolly at her son. "She says she didn't."

"Of course she says she didn't," the boy insisted emotionally. "*But did she?*"

"I don't know."

"Oh, Je——!" the boy exclaimed, turning his head away, shaking it.

"Did you see her at the jail?" Wendy asked.

"Yes. This morning."

The girl stared into her mother's face, intensely interested. "Is she anything they say she is? I mean, the *stories* . . ."

"What stories?" asked Mac John, Jr.

Wendy glanced irritably at him. "They say she's beautiful. Is she?"

"Well, she didn't look so good this morning, after a night in jail," Lois said doubtfully. "But she does have the reputation, yes, of being an exceptionally attractive woman."

"You're going to get to know her very well, aren't you?"

"Probably."

"*What stories?* Is she supposed to be loose?"

"Mac John, for heaven's sake!" Lois protested.

"Mac John," said Daniel Farnham, patient with the boy but firmly, by his tone, stopping him from saying anything further. "The woman is a lawyer, a very different lawyer from your mother. She has an ambiguous reputation. Some people think she is scrupulously honest; others are sure she isn't. Some think she is one of the best lawyers in town; others will tell you she is one of the worst. There have been stories of her bribing people to testify falsely—although nothing of the sort has ever been proved against her. She is an aggressive lawyer and has been very conspicuous. Your mother is going to see her name in the newspapers a lot over this one."

"The newspaper says she used to hustle drinks in bars," said Wendy very quietly.

"It doesn't say she hustled drinks," said Lois. "It says she once was a cocktail waitress."

"Well, there *is* a story . . ."

"I know there's a story. There are lots of stories. They have a way of proving untrue when you look into them."

"We can say she's led a colorful life," said Daniel Farnham with a sly grin.

"She's my client, and we don't say anything about her at all," Lois said emphatically to Mac John, Jr., and Wendy.

"She comes from a wretched background," said Daniel Farnham. "And I would judge she has not risen much above it."

III

1959–61

Tommy Jo waited on the front porch, sitting in the swing at first and then, driven from that by her rambunctious ten-year-old brother, sitting on the porch rail with one foot up, one touching the porch floor. Sometimes she rested her chin against her knee. She glanced down the road every minute or so—you could see two miles—and when she saw a car or truck coming, she watched it until it came by. Drivers waved. She waved. Some of them honked. If she turned and watched them go on west, she had to squint into the setting sun, but she could see the cars and trucks seem to waver and come apart, like images in an old mirror. It was the heat off the pavement that made them look like that. She had figured that out for herself.

It was too hot, and there wasn't any wind. Her sweat ran down her back, and in front it ran over the freckles between her breasts and on down to her navel. She was wearing her older brother's worn blue chambray work shirt. She had frayed the short sleeves and she wore it with only one button fastened and the tails brought up in front and tied in a knot. She was conscious of the way the tied-up shirt cradled her breasts, like in a loose brassiere. She was conscious, too, that her cut-off blue denim shorts were *very* short. Some of the drivers who honked at her didn't even know her. They just honked at the shorts and at the way she tied the shirt, and at her long dark red hair.

KER-SPANG! There they went again. Her father and her thirteen-year-old brother, and Billy Lee Mayo from down the road, were at it with their rifles again. They had piled up a backstop of pine logs to catch the bullets, and just about every evening somebody came around with a gun he wanted to show off. They talked guns at the supper table, and after supper they went outside, weather allowing, and shot at Magnolia Oil cans and bottles and sometimes at regular printed paper targets. Billy Lee would come, or someone else. They shot and they adjusted sights, and they swabbed out barrels with Hoppe's Number 9, and KER-SPANG! they went at it again.

Sometimes they invited her to shoot. She had a good eye. It irritated her brother that she could hit the red horse on the Magnolia can just about as often as he could. She liked to fill tin cans with water, to see the water fly when the bullet hit.

She had helped her mother with the supper dishes. Her mother was in the kitchen again now. Tommy Jo could hear her rattling around in the back of the house. She was making lemonade, probably, or iced tea, and they would sit here on the porch and drink it after the sun went down and it was too dark to shoot. Her little brother, swinging as hard as he could, heard their mother in the kitchen, too, and he frowned. Tommy Jo guessed the lemonade their mother was making frustrated his plan to beg their father to drive to the station in the pickup and get some bottles of pop from the cooler. It would also, she hoped, foreclose any plan their father had to drive on into town for a few beers.

Down the road a car approached. She saw it and at a distance judged it was a Dodge. It was the first Dodge that had passed since she came out on the porch—following four Fords, four Chevies, a Buick, an Olds, and seven pickups. The Olds had been black, beautiful. She didn't know anybody who had one—that is, she didn't know anybody well, to speak to, who had one. There was no dealer for them in La-Grange. She didn't know where you had to go to buy one; maybe all the way to Levelland. It was what *she* wanted: a black Oldsmobile convertible with red leather seats. She'd drive into LaGrange and all around Clayton County, before she drove away to someplace like Dallas or Houston, or maybe all the way to New Orleans, or the other way, to Los Angeles.

Her mother came out to the porch, hustled her brother out of the swing, and sat down. "Oooh," she breathed. "Looky yonder. Gonna rain." She pointed at a line of tall thunderheads building to the south and west. Tommy Jo had been watching them grow, hoping for the rain. Rain was money, her father said. It was just plain money. The cattle in the field across the road were watching the rainstorm build, too—in their silent, thoughtful way. Rain would put weight on cattle. That was how it was money.

Tommy Jo's mother was a young woman: in her early thirties. She wore a loose, shapeless, flowered cotton dress that hung on her like a worn towel thrown over a clothesline. In spite of it, she showed suggestions of a broad-hipped, heavy-breasted, still youthful figure.

"Is that a Buick comin' yonder?" she asked.

Tommy Jo shook her head. "Pontiac."

"Seems like they all look alike anymore."

The ker-spanging stopped out back. They would clean their guns now, and in a little while they would come to the porch. Her father, if he was in a good mood, would dance around the porch in his heavy shoes, playfully threatening to step on their bare feet, hers and her mother's. Then he would drop onto the swing beside her mother and ask which one of them had listened to the market report on the radio while he was out back. One of them always listened and remembered the numbers so she could tell him—cattle so much, hay so much, corn so much, peanuts so much. . . . It wouldn't make any difference what the numbers were; he would shake his head and say the Lord would have to provide, it was damn sure the land wasn't going to.

This evening it was different. Before the men came around from the back, a '46 Chevy came up the road and pulled in at their house. It was the reverend, come to visit.

He puffed up the porch steps, flushed and sweating, a medium-size man, middle-aged, wearing a wrinkled white shirt, loose at the collar, but with a maroon and yellow satin necktie knotted around his neck and tucked into his shirt: the Reverend Mr. Willis Baumgartner, pastor of the First Pentecostal Holiness Church of LaGrange. He was yellow-blond but nearly bald. His blue eyes seemed to shift behind his thick bifocals. As he reached the top step, he glanced at Tommy Jo and gave her a quick nod even before he spoke to her mother.

"The Lord be thanked for that," Tommy Jo's father said to the reverend as the first wind-driven drops of rain splattered onto the porch floor. The cool wind off the storm was refreshing, but the rain drove them indoors; and they sat in the living room: Tommy Jo and her parents and the reverend. They drank lemonade and nibbled chocolate cookies, and the reverend discoursed on the church: mostly on various members, the news of them.

"Well, I came out to talk about Tommy Jo, is what I came for," the reverend said at last, when Tommy Jo had begun to wonder if he would ever mention what she hoped he had come to talk about. "To say it flat out, I think you ought to send the girl to college."

"That'd cost a lot of money, reverend—which I haven't got," her father said flatly. "Besides, I'm not so sure it'd do her any good."

The reverend nodded. "Joe Bob, I wish you'd think on it, pray on it. Tommy Jo just graduated at the top of her high-school class, with never nothing but an 'A' grade all the way through school. The Lord made her somethin' special, Joe Bob, Miz Brookover; you just have to allow that: that she's somethin' special."

Joe Bob Brookover ran his hand down his ruddy, itching cheek. He shaved every other morning, and tomorrow was the morning, and the sweat itched in the stubble of his red beard. "Costs a lot of money, goin' to college," he insisted.

"Maybe not as much as you think. There's ways, you know, of coming up with the money. She'd work if she went."

"You've already talked about it, I guess," said Joe Bob.

The reverend nodded. "I suggested it to Tommy Jo, and she asked me to talk to you about it."

Tommy Jo's mother spoke. "She'd have to go a long way from home. She's just seventeen."

Joe Bob rose heavily from the couch where he had sat beside his wife, walked to a window, leaned on the sill with both hands, and peered out to judge the rain. "My daddy cain't read nor wrat," he said. "He used to think he wanted to, but *his* daddy would'a beat him if he caught him tryin' to learn. His daddy, my granddaddy, said it ruined a man's eyes, sittin' around starin' at the print in books, and he said no man that could call himself a man would make his livin' pushin' an itty-bitty pencil around on a piece of paper."

Joe Bob glanced back over his shoulder for a moment and chuckled. "When I was drafted in the army in 'forty-two, I hadn't finished the seventh grade—I mean, what with bein' in and out of school, runnin' around, workin'. What livin' I've made, I've made with my hands, and I ain't ashamed of it. I'm not opposed to education. Fact, I *respect* it. But I can't see where it would ever have he'ped me, makin' a livin' on the land in west Texas. I do hold one thing against education, which is that I think a lot of it's disrespectful to the Lord, and they teach a lot of ideas I wouldn't want a child of mine to have."

Tommy Jo watched and listened to her father reasoning out his solution to a problem, aloud. He did it often. It would be one of her memories of him. He was thirty-five years old, but he spoke like an aged patriarch, drawing on his experience, applying what he called his "lights" to what he knew, groping for an inspiration or an idea.

"Girl never talked to me about it," he went on. "I don't know how strong she feels about it. Still, it's the money that worries me the most. I just don't know where it'd come from. I sincerely don't know where the money'd come from."

"Where'd she have to go?" Tommy Jo's mother asked plaintively. "How far away?"

"I've got a college in mind," said the reverend, jumping on the chance to break into the conversation again. "I brought a paper about it, that tells about this college."

The printed brochure the reverend handed to Joe Bob described Calvary Christian College at Sweetwater, Texas. Tommy Jo had read every word of it three times or more. It said the students at Calvary worked on the farmland owned by the college, or worked in the kitchen, to help support the college. Some, it said, worked in town to earn some money toward their tuition. The faculty, it said, was well qualified to impart a higher education to students enrolled at Calvary Christian. Parents, it said, would prize the education their children obtained there.

The brochure carried the college's STATEMENT OF PRINCIPLES in boldface type:

> Calvary Christian College is a Christian institution of higher learning. It is a college of, by, and for Christians. Instruction at Calvary Christian College is based on the well-recognized principle that all any man or woman needs to know is beautifully exemplified in the Holy Revealed Word of God. A fundamental of Christian teaching, as practiced at Calvary Christian, is to improve a student's understanding of the ways in which God's word is made manifest in all His works. If a young man or woman understands that, he may mark himself "well educated."

It was exceptionally hot in May, toward the end of Tommy Jo's fourth semester. Calvary Christian College owned only one dormitory building, and first- and second-year students lived in several large houses around the periphery of the campus, rented to the college by a variety of landlords. Tommy Jo and her roommate, Peggy Sue Bradley, occupied a small room on the third floor of an old white frame house. Up there, under the roof, the heat of the sun accumulated all day and persisted into the night.

Peggy Sue sat on the edge of her bed and buttoned up her pajamas, each button, to the very top, no matter that the room was stifling hot and almost no air moved. Tommy Jo had come up the stairs from the bathroom and she tossed aside her towel and sat down naked. It amused her to see Peggy Sue turn her head away. She would not look at Tommy Jo naked.

"I—I want to share with you the beautiful thing the Lord has done," said Peggy Sue in the direction of the wall.

Tommy Jo stretched out on her bed. She was tired, as she was at bedtime every night. She worked in the college kitchen from 6:30 to 8:00. After classes, she worked in the afternoon at a hamburger stand in town. Evening prayers were compulsory—from 8:00 to 9:00. Her feet, especially, were tired, from standing four and a half hours on the tiled floor behind the counter at Kane's Burger Hots. "What's He done?" she asked.

Peggy Sue sighed. "He's shown me what to do. I mean, you know how I didn't come to college the first year after I left high school, because I wasn't sure if I should. Then the Lord told me to get an education. I understood then that He had a wonderful purpose for me. I didn't know what the purpose was, but I knew He had one. Now I know what His plan is. I prayed to God to reveal it to me, and today He did. Tommy Jo, the Lord wants me to be a doctor! I'm going to witness for Christ by healing the sick! I'm going to go to medical school."

Tommy Jo sat up. "Medical school? Where?"

"University of Texas, I suppose," said Peggy Sue. "Wherever the Lord directs me."

Peggy Sue stared at her feet. Tommy Jo could see tears in her eyes. She pulled the sheet up in front of her body so Peggy Sue could look at her. "I think you've got a big problem, Peggy Sue," she said quietly.

Peggy Sue smiled. "I've got nothin' *but* problems. It's gonna be such hard work! But I know the Lord will see me through."

"The first problem," said Tommy Jo, "is that you won't be able to get into medical school on the basis of your credits from Calvary Christian College."

Peggy Sue frowned and shook her head. "What do you mean?" she whispered.

Tommy Jo glanced down, then she looked into Peggy Sue's face. "Don't you understand this is a *Bible college?* Course credits from Calvary Christian are no good anywhere else. A degree from here is no good. Nobody recognizes it."

"What do you *mean* by that?" Peggy Sue whispered in shrill panic. "Who doesn't recognize. . . ?"

"*Nobody* recognizes," said Tommy Jo firmly. "With a degree from here, you can't do anything that requires a college education. You

can't teach in the public schools. You can't get into any professional
school. You can't do anything. The truth is, Calvary Christian is not
a real college."

"I don't believe that," Peggy Sue snapped angrily.

Tommy Jo shrugged. "Figure it out for yourself," she said. "Do you
think you could pass the entrance exams for a medical school? How
much biology can you learn here? How much chemistry? How much
physiology? How much psychology? How much math? Can you read
a foreign language? Huh?"

"We get a wonderful Bible education," Peggy Sue said defensively.

"Tell that to the entrance board at some medical school," Tommy Jo
said scornfully.

"This is a Christian college," Peggy Sue insisted. "We are guided by
the Lord."

"I've learned to be a competent waitress for a hamburger joint,"
said Tommy Jo. "That's my Christian education."

Peggy Sue was silent for a moment. Then she whispered, "If you feel
that way, why are you here?"

Tommy Jo's throat tightened. She nodded. "That's a fair question."

"Well, *why?* Why did you come here in the first place?"

"It was the only way I could get away from home, to get *any* education at all. And I had no idea how bad it would be."

"Then why did you stay, after you found out?"

"You can figure that out, can't you?" Tommy Jo said very quietly.
"How do I go home and tell my father and mother? How do I explain
to my father, who sold cattle off his land to send me here, that it was
a mistake? The Lord hasn't sent me an answer to that one."

"You've been dishonest, Tommy Jo!"

"Dishonest! What's dishonest is for a bunch of church yahoos to run
a fake college and take people's money and waste their time. My family
put money it didn't have into sending me here, and I've wasted two
years of my life, working my butt off, for *nothing*. I haven't got a college credit that will sell anywhere, and I haven't learned diddledy-
goddamn. And neither have you. Face it, neither have you."

Ten days later, at the end of the semester, she was called to the
office of the president and told that, in spite of her perfect record of
"A" grades, she would not be allowed to reenroll in the fall. ("We
think you are not sufficiently committed to Calvary Christian College.")

When she got home she found the Reverend Mr. Baumgartner had received a letter from the president. ("Besides that, Miss Brookover proved a troublemaker in the student body, intemperately criticizing the college to other students.") The reverend promised to leave it to *her* to explain to her parents that she would not be returning to Calvary Christian, and why.

She did not explain. She did not tell them. She found a summer job and let the weeks pass, waiting for some kind of opportunity to tell them. It was a dry summer. Maybe her father would say, some evening, there was no money to send her back for another year.

She worked at the Magnolia station. Mostly she worked inside, selling pop from the cooler, and bread and milk and .22 cartridges and shotgun shells and coal oil and flypaper and candy, but when Lee was busy with a lube job or changing a belt, she pumped gas and cleaned windshields. She wore cut-off denim shorts and shirts tied up in knots in front, and hardly a man came in the station who didn't have something to say about how good she looked. She enjoyed working at the station. She enjoyed talking with people who smelled of sweat and joked and laughed and swore. She was nineteen years old, and she drank her first beer that summer.

Lee was her cousin. He was twenty-two years old, a tall, muscular, handsome man. He wore tight Levi's, and a Stetson, and satin shirts with mother-of-pearl buttons, and he drove a Ford pickup truck with a rifle rack behind the driver's head. He drove Tommy Jo home every day at six o'clock, when his father, her uncle, came in to take over the station for the evening. Sometimes they stopped and picked up burgers and shakes and he drove her out along the river and they had an evening picnic. He got to picking up a six-pack of beer and a bag of ice, too; and sometimes they didn't go home until dark. It was all right. It had to be. He was her cousin, after all.

Since the sun was always setting when they had their picnics, they sat with their backs to it, on a bank overlooking a pool in the riverbed; and they kept quiet and watched the prairie dogs and jackrabbits and sometimes a coyote come to the pool to drink. Once Lee shot a wolf and once a rattlesnake. He always carried the rifle from the truck and had it beside him.

He touched her breasts. She let him do that. He wanted to kiss her, but she wouldn't let him, because they were cousins. But she let him lift her breasts in his hands and talk about them, tell her how pretty they were. "Ah never saw any so nass, Tommy Jo. Ah never did. They're the nassest things ah ever saw on any girl."

It troubled her a little that he wanted to touch her more and more as they continued to come to the river, and his touch grew firmer, more insistent, until he was kneading her breasts sometimes, not just touching. But he was good to her. It was Lee who had given her the job at the station, and he drove her back and forth, and he said if he went to the state fair, all the way to Dallas, he'd talk Joe Bob into letting her go with him. Anyway, she liked having him fondle her. He wasn't the first who had ever done it. But he was older and more confident. It felt good.

He talked about leaving LaGrange County. "Sooner or later," he said, "ah gotta move on, either that or spend the rest of mah laff here. An' ah don't wanta spend mah whole laff workin' in mah dad's Magnolia station. If ah had a girl lak you, if you wuzn't mah cousin and all, ah'd go in a minute. Ah'd go to Dallas, or El Paso, or somewheres. Ah really would."

She walked down to the water and stepped in, up to her knees. He followed in a moment and stood behind her. He put his arms around her and cupped her breasts in his hands. He kissed her neck.

"It's too bad you and I are cousins," she said. "But don't forget we are."

He put his hands on her shoulders and turned her around. "Sometams ah think ah could fo'git it perm'nent. Ah could, Tommy Jo."

"I couldn't," she said.

"Anyways, Joe Bob'd kill any man that—"

"He would. That's a fact."

Lee stepped back from her. Standing at the edge of the water, in Levi's wet to his knees, he frowned and shook his head. "Tommy Jo, do somethin' for me anyways," he said. "Jus' for a minute. Let me see your things—your titties. Open your shirt and let me see. Ah won't touch you. Ah been thinkin' 'bout 'em all summer. Jus' one tam, Tommy Jo, please."

She had begun to shake her head, but as he pleaded she changed her mind. "No man has ever . . ." she said. "You understand?"

He nodded emphatically. "Ah understand," he said quietly.

Slowly she loosened the knot in her shirttails, then pulled it apart. She pulled the one button out of its buttonhole. For a moment she stood with the shirt hanging loose, then in a quick, impulsive movement pulled the shirt open and bared her breasts. She looked down at them before she looked up at his face.

He stood in the water's edge, slack, his mouth open, and he looked and slowly nodded. He stared for the better part of a minute before he murmured, "Thank y', Tommy Jo," and turned and walked out of the water and up the bank.

She buttoned and retied her shirt and followed him.

Joe Bob Brookover died August 7. It was a week after he was beaten in a beer-joint brawl. They brought him home that night. He was staggering drunk, bloody, with an eye swollen shut—but elated. It had been a bottle-swinging free-for-all and he claimed he had broken the jaw of the man who had blacked his eye. He staggered around the house, claiming victory, laughing, spitting blood. The men who brought him home helped Tommy Jo and her mother to put him to bed.

He slept, but the next morning he was sick. He got sicker. It wasn't until it was too late to save him that they got him to a doctor and then to the hospital in LaGrange, where he died of acute renal failure. A blow across the back with a pool cue in the course of the brawl had damaged both his kidneys. He was so unmanageable a patient that it was not until he arrived at the hospital that he admitted to anyone that he had not urinated since the night of the fight.

When he lapsed into a coma and they had been told there was no hope he would recover, Tommy Jo's mother sat with her in the waiting room at the hospital and spoke of how he married her and of how Tommy Jo was conceived. She spoke in a low voice, for Tommy Jo only, in the midst of all the clan of Brookovers and Ameses gathered under the harsh, cold, waiting-room lights sitting solemnly on chrome and dark-green-vinyl chairs, smoking, crushing cigarettes on the brown linoleum-tile floor.

"He knew the draft was gonna take him," her mother said. "It was takin' ev'buddy in them days, in 'forty-two; and, way they talked, you couldn't be sure he'd ever come back. Lots of 'em didn't. Well, he told me he didn't want to go away and maybe get killed without never known what it was like to have a woman. I was just fifteen, but that's how he put it to me—that he didn't want to go off to war without never havin' been with a woman. I told him I didn't want it to be that way for him, either, but I couldn't let him have me without we were married. So he said, let's get married then. So we did. My daddy signed the papers for me. Daddy said it was somethin' we should do for Joe Bob, 'cause he was goin' off to the war.

"After he was gone, I wrote him letters, but the one where I told him I was goin' to have a baby got lost some way, so when he heard about you it was a surprise. But he was happy. He sent you a silk pillow cover from Hawaii. I can't think whatever happened to that."

Some of the Brookovers and Ameses said the man who hit Joe Bob with the pool cue had murdered him; but no arrest was made and no prosecution. They buried him and planted a flag on his grave, that he was entitled to because he was an army veteran. They said there was no way Tommy Jo's mother could afford to keep the ranch and try to work it without Joe Bob. They said she should sell it and the cattle and pay off what was owed and move into town and live with her Great-aunt Serena, whose house was too big for her anyway since her children were grown and gone. Tommy Jo's mother placidly accepted the family judgment and said that was what she would do.

It's really too bad, someone remarked, there won't be enough to keep Tommy Jo in college. Tommy Jo was struck by an appalling thought: that maybe this was how God had arranged for her not to have to explain why she wouldn't go back to Calvary Christian, and maybe it was her punishment. She was staggered, literally, by the idea. It was the evening after her father was buried, and while the others went to the graveyard to see that the grave had been smoothed over properly and to put some plastic flowers on it, she sat on the front porch, grieved that there was no ker-spang from out in back, and prayed. She asked God if he had punished her by killing her father.

Suddenly the utter insanity of the idea impressed itself on her, more forcefully than the idea itself had done. God, if He were good, wouldn't do anything like that. And if He had and He was not good, then to hell with Him! In a moment she shrugged off the Pentecostal Holiness Church and Calvary Christian College and all the murk and garbage they had preached at her for nineteen years. She got up from her knees, feeling clean. She decided when the family came back she would ask Lee to take her for a ride in the pickup truck. She'd like a cold beer, too.

They were at the river again. She had worked another week at the station. Everybody who came in, just about, told her how sorry they were about Joe Bob. It made her feel bad to hear it all the time, and she was glad at the end of each day to get away. Lee, out of some funny kind of feeling of respect he had, had taken her straight home every day but today; this day they had picked up a six-pack and some chips, and they sat on the riverbank the way they had used to do.

"Have you thought any more about leaving here?" she asked him.

His eyes fell, and he shook his head.

"Well? You going to or aren't you? You going to spend the rest of your life working in your dad's Magnolia station?"

Lee shrugged.

"Well, I'm leaving."

He turned toward her. "Where?"

"I don't know. But I'm not movin' in with Serena like my mother and the boys are gonna do. If I'd do that, I'd wind up marrying some fella that doesn't amount to anything, just to get out of that house."

"But where you gonna go?"

"Where *you* gonna go, if you make up your mind to go?"

He looked away, at the sky. "There was a fella in the station the other day, name of Baker, said if ah come to El Paso he'd gimme a job in a place he's got. It's a truck-wash place. They hose down big rigs, steam-clean engines, stuff lak that. Don't sound lak much of a job. . . ."

"You can find something else after you're there."

He nodded. "I s'pose."

"Anyway," she said, "jobs aren't hard to come by. I can find something. You can. It may be now or never."

He frowned and stared at her for a moment, his lips parted. "You talkin' 'bout you an' me goin' *together*, Tommy Jo?"

She nodded. "It'd be easier than going alone, wouldn't it? We can kind of look out for each other."

His frown deepened. "Jus' how you figgah we'd arrange things?" he asked.

She shrugged. "Any way you want it, Lee. Just about any way you want it."

IV

1960

They were in Kent, a ninety-minute drive down from London, on a Saturday afternoon in June. John Adams, the London representative of Flesselles et Frères, a Paris gallery, had brought her down here to spend a country weekend with the Polish sculptor Tadeus Kozichowski —which he had insisted was a high privilege, because Kozichowski received almost no one. Now they were in the walled, weed-choked garden behind Kozichowski's house, partaking of some cold roast beef, some bread and cheese, some relishes, and a pitcher of red wine, while Kozichowski and his assistant, Marjorie Singer, went on working.

Lois, who had heard the name Kozichowski only in some art class and could not identify him when Adams called to say he had arranged this weekend, had bought two books on twentieth-century sculptors and had studied them in her hotel room the past two evenings. She was surprised to see the sculptor working on a lifelike pair of figures. She had learned that Kozichowski's work was mostly abstract, some of it cubist.

"Eight or nine thousand pounds won't buy a Kozichowski today, you understand," Adams had said on the telephone. "He doesn't expect you to buy anything. I've done him a kindness or two, and he's reciprocating. It's a real privilege, though. He's one of the world's great, and he's a fabulous character as well. I know you will have an immensely enjoyable time."

The eight or nine thousand pounds Adams had referred to was $25,000 Lois had to spend on a gift for the Houston Museum of Fine Arts. It was the summer of her graduation from Wellesley, and her graduation present from her parents was a summer in Europe, traveling with a college friend whose parents had given her, too, a summer in Europe. On graduation day Lois's mother had announced she was placing $25,000 on deposit in a Paris bank, with which Lois could buy anything she wanted as a gift to the museum in her own and her mother's name.

("I can't wait to see what you buy. It will be a test of your values, of what you've learned, of what you are; and it will give your summer a purpose that will make it so much more exciting! Besides, I will acknowledge, I hope a taste of the world you are going to see will give you second thoughts about enrolling in law school this fall. There are so many more beautiful things you can do with your life!")

Adams, as the representative of Flesselles et Frères, had taken Lois in charge at her mother's request, to introduce her to the galleries and dealers and maybe some artists. He would advise her, but it was understood she was to make her own choice and take full responsibility for it.

"If dere are no red Indianss, I fill *not* go dere," laughed Tadeus Kozichowski, raising an emphasizing finger. "I vant to see *cowboyss* viss bowed lekss und—uh, big vite hats, und Indianss viss fedders. Iss it not, your Houston? Iss in Texass, yes?"

"Actually," said Lois, crisply defensive, "Houston is a quite cosmopolitan city. We have a fine symphony, an opera company, a really good museum of fine arts."

"Aghh!" scoffed Kozichowski jovially. "But iss no Indianss und cowboyss, you say? Vy should I go dere? Iss in Texass, de vorld's capital of crass."

"Tad, it's *Dallas* that's the world's capital of crass," said Marjorie Singer. She was an American, a New Jersey high-school art teacher, spending a summer studying with Kozichowski. "Anyway, you're embarrassing Miss Farnham."

"I apolochice," said Kozichowski with a courtly bow.

"Not at all," said Lois weakly. "It's quite all right."

She was acutely uncomfortable. She was dressed in a dark blue silk Coco Chanel jacket and dress, a white pillbox hat, white gloves, high heels, stockings; and she sat stiffly on a splintery oak bench, painfully conscious that she was overdressed.

Kozichowski and Marjorie Singer worked while they ate and talked.

They were smeared with grayish-white clay: their hands, their clothes, their faces. Between sips of wine, Kozichowski kept his mouth filled with water, which he spat freely onto the life-size clay model, to moisten the clay and keep it workable. He was a sixty-year-old, white-haired, muscular man. He kept on talking with animated gestures as he stalked around his clay model, spitting water, carving off clay, pressing on clay, cutting clay with his thumbnails, breaking off pieces, tossing rejected hunks into the weeds. Marjorie kept up with him, as intent as he was but not so animated.

On a wooden platform a foot or so above the ground, a Kentish boy, eighteen or nineteen years old, with a pallid hairless body, stood as the naked model for one of the figures of Kozichowski's sculpture. He ate, too, and though he held his pose, he worked beef and cheese out of his teeth with his tongue, tossed his head to throw his hair back off his forehead, and much of the time gazed placidly, curiously at Lois. From time to time he scratched, and often as not it was his crotch that itched; and he would casually push his penis and scrotum aside so he could scratch—never ceasing to work his mouth and never looking away from Lois for more than a moment. She tried not to meet his gaze or to stare at his big, blue-veined penis.

"Vonce I vass asked to make a monument for Dallas," said Kozichowski. "Something *beeg*. In Dallas, Gutzom Borglum dey should haff, to sculpt deir monument viss deenameet, so beeg dey vanted it. But I knew uff de town's *ee-fill* reputation, and I vould not go dere. I vunder, maybe I *should* have gone dere, eh, Miss Farnham?"

"You probably could have found your cowboys and Indians there," said Lois.

"In Dallas and not in Houston?" asked Marjorie Singer skeptically. "Aren't cowboys and Indians Texans, after all?"

"I wouldn't know," said Lois icily. "There *are* no *Texans* in Houston."

"Ha! Jesus!" laughed Marjorie.

"Very good!" exclaimed John Adams. "Very good, indeed. Carry on, Lois! Carry on!"

Adams was a diminutive but tautly built man, maybe forty years old, bald, with sharp, expressive brown eyes. He had an avidly cultivated public school–Oxford accent and manner. She had spent five afternoons with him before this weekend, touring London galleries. Her college friend did not like Adams or galleries and had accompanied them only once. Lois had become fascinated with Adams, with his polished self-confidence. The last two afternoons, after they'd seen some art, they had sat together in a bar for an hour or so, just for conversation. He had been protective of her in the company of aggressive art dealers; but this afternoon he was, perhaps, so comfortable in his own element that he failed to see that she could be uncomfortable.

"A great American, I tell you who," said Kozichowski. He had maybe sensed that they had talked too much about Texas. "Louie Armstrong. I heard him talk vunce, an interview. Dey ask him, 'You lak de seemphony? De oaperah? De classical? Or joost de jass?' He say, 'Oh, I lak it all, all dat. It's all *sooo pretty!*' I luffed dat statement. Vat he said expressed a great—how you say?—*esthétique.*"

"Well, whur do ya go to see the cowboys and Indians, then?" asked the Kentish boy, his mouth open in stupid sincerity. "Oy'd luk to see them."

Kozichowski spat water through his raucous laugh, and Lois did not have to answer the question.

Kozichowski asked Lois if she liked the work of Jacques Lipchitz. After that he talked about other sculptors. She could hardly respond. Most of the names meant nothing to her except as names mentioned in half-forgotten college lectures. Innocently, Kozichowski had speared her and left her squirming on the point of his conversation. Amiably he talked on, asking her questions, hardly hearing her mumbled answers. She was miserable—self-conscious and defenseless, and increasingly irritated with Adams for not helping her.

It was late afternoon—they had been in the garden for more than a couple of hours—when suddenly Kozichowski slapped the clay sculpture irritably and complained to Marjorie: "I cannot. De lekks. I cannot see de lekks widout de udder model holding onto dem."

It was true, what he said. Even Lois could see the problem. The sculpture was of two figures, life size or almost: a man and a woman, the man standing, the woman kneeling beside him with her right arm encircling his legs, drawing him to her, the two of them looking away into the distance or the future as if they had just been tested and had survived and now faced some new peril. But the Kentish boy stood erect. His legs were not distorted by the clasp of the female figure.

"*I cannot,*" said Kozichowski again, frustrated. "Marjorie . . ."

"Goddammit," said Marjorie Singer. She glanced hard at Lois, then at Adams, but she did not hesitate; she pulled off her clay-smeared shirt and skirt, her panties and brassiere, and in a moment she was naked. She climbed onto the model stand, knelt, and clasped the boy's legs in the posture of the clay female figure.

Gaping with surprise, the Kentish boy stared down at the naked Marjorie—a thirty-year-old, loosely fleshed woman with sagging breasts. His penis began to engorge. In a moment he had a full erection, his red, glistening-wet glans pushing out through his resisting, uncircumcised foreskin. His mouth fell open and his face turned red.

"Dennis, for Christ's sake!" Marjorie spat. She jerked away from him.

"Oy cahn't 'elp hit!" the boy wailed. "Wut kin I do?" He turned toward Lois, as if she especially should hear his appeal. His penis pointed at her like a swollen finger. "Oy'm sorry, miss," he said. Then he grinned and snickered. He shrugged. "Wut kin I do?"

Lois blushed deep red. "My God!" she whispered. She hid her face behind her hands.

Marjorie grabbed her clothes. She glared at Lois as she pulled on her skirt. "I'm not sure who's responsible for it, you or me," she snapped. "You're the one who hasn't taken your eyes off it all afternoon."

Lois began to cry. At first, for a moment, Marjorie laughed bitterly at her and Adams smiled and shook his head tolerantly; then they realized she was crying painfully, and they fell silent and stared at her. When she looked out from behind her hands, sucking a deep breath and holding down her sobs, she saw the Kentish boy first, staring in confused disbelief, then Kozichowski, frowning quizzically. Adams, his reserve broken at last, dropped his wineglass and rushed to her to help.

"I'm sorry . . . John," she said in quiet resignation. She stood at the window of a bedroom upstairs, looking at the rain beginning to fall on the narrow road that ran toward the village. "I really am—very sorry."

"Not *a-tawl*, dear girl."

"You must think—*Jesus Christ!*"

"Not a-tawl."

She sighed. "I come from nowhere. I'm not anybody. I've just graduated from what's supposed to be a good school, and I'm *ignorant*."

He stepped to her side at the window and touched her arm. "Not a-tawl," he said quietly.

"John," she said. She looked at his face. "Don't call me a dear girl, and don't tell me to carry on. You make me feel like an ass."

"If that is true," he said with quiet precision, "then it is *I* who am an ass."

She shook her head and looked out the window again. "It's not your fault."

"I'm not sure there is any such thing as fault to be assigned," he said. "That *was* an awkward scene down there."

She sighed. "There've been others," she said.

"Indeed? None of which *I've* been aware."

She looked into his face again. "Are you going to tell me," she asked, "you didn't notice how I ate the asparagus?"

He smiled. "Well . . ."

"I thought the Bordeaux tasted like old basketball socks."

He laughed.

"I never heard of Tadeus Kozichowski. I had to buy a book and read about him."

He laughed again. "So? None of this makes you ignorant."

"It makes me *feel* ignorant. I *want* to know about asparagus and vintage Bordeaux and—"

"Learn about them, then," he said briskly. "But don't feel inferior before you have it all learnt."

"Will you help me?"

He frowned. "We haven't much time."

"Help me as much as you can," she said. "Start by looking at what I've brought and telling me what to wear to dinner."

On the day before she was to fly from London to Paris, John Adams made a particular point of her setting aside the day to go with him on a drive in the country. He picked her up in his Austin-Healey, noting with satisfaction that the day was what he called fine, and he set out from London without saying where they were going. They drove with the top off the car, along country lanes north of London—she never really did know where. He stopped at two small parish churches, where he showed her examples of very old stained glass and some tomb effigies that he said were better than any in the cathedrals. They talked about things he thought she should be sure to see in France, and he said he would try to get away and meet her somewhere on the Continent in a few weeks.

He took her for lunch to an inn on a river where swans cruised in the millpond and the water still splashed over a mossy wheel. They ate roast beef and drank pints of dark beer, and after lunch they walked along the river.

"I'm going to miss you, you know," he said.

Lois nodded. "I'm sorry to be going, almost," she said.

He smiled. "You must never be sorry to be going to Paris. I wish I could come with you."

"I wish you could, too."

A couple passed them, walking along the river path in the opposite direction, and when they had passed, Adams asked her, "Did you dress as I suggested?"

She glanced at his face, then nodded.

"Good girl," he said, touching her elbow.

She had wondered if he couldn't tell without asking. She was wear-

ing a white linen blouse, an orange-brown skirt, a pair of dark brown
loafers—and nothing else: no brassiere, no panties, no stockings, nothing. ("Hats! Gloves! Brassieres with wires and bones in them! Rubber
panty girdles! Petticoats, slips, stockings . . . garter belts! My God,
girl, when you are dressed you are wearing twenty-four separate items!
I don't see how you can move!") She had been self-conscious all day,
particularly in the crowds in the hotel and on the London street; but
of course no one had guessed she was naked under her skirt and blouse,
and she had found a small, persistent excitement in it, and she was
glad she had done what he said.

On the road between St. Tropez and Le Lavandou, on a pine-
covered slope overlooking the Mediterranean, the French art dealer
Armand Flesselles kept a small white villa. Late in July, Adams caught
up with Lois in Florence. He handed her a set of keys to that villa,
told her Flesselles had given him the villa for the first weekend in
August, and suggested she spend the weekend with him there. "It's
that chance we've spoken of, to have some time together—more than an
hour or two in a gallery. You can bring the girl who is traveling with
you if you want."

Lois chose to come alone.

Saturday morning and again Sunday morning the Mediterranean
sunlight, reflected off the smooth water and diffused by haze, filled
the air with an intense, unnatural brightness. On the stone terrace
outside their bedroom the light was so bright it was painful. Inside
the white-walled room it seemed to have almost palpable presence, like
the light in a Vermeer, and those two mornings they lay long in bed,
savoring the quiet drama of the light. They were the best hours of the
weekend, the best hours of her summer.

Adams was not a memorable lover. He was too careful with her. But
she would remember the long hours lying on the bed, on the white
sheets, exposed to him as he insisted, enjoying the way he enjoyed ad-
miring her. He made her feel—as no one else ever did—that she should
be admired, that anyone who didn't admire her was insufficiently sensitive to the understated grace of her long, slender body. She even got
up and preened for him: high on the balls of her feet, her back arched,
unembarrassed. She never could do it before; she never could again;
but those mornings it was joyful, it was unforgettable.

The waterfront was crowded. They never went near it. He drove
her to a village in the forested hills, where they shopped in a market
for wine and cheese to carry back to the villa. Within a few kilometers
were village museums of art, but they did not even speak of art. Being

lovers was so new for them, they rushed back to the villa to be alone.

"John. . . ?" They lay on lounges on the terrace, on Sunday afternoon, taking the sun. He had concocted a mixture of *vin rouge*, lemonade, orange slices, and ice, and she had been sipping thirstily.

"Hmmm?"

"What do you think of a woman becoming a lawyer?"

He smiled lazily. "I'm sure I've not the faintest idea. I've never thought of it."

"I'm serious. Do you think a woman should be a lawyer, could be a good one?"

"Why not?"

"Well, my father thinks I couldn't be a good lawyer, and my mother wishes I'd do something more beautiful with my life. I've planned to go to law school this fall. I've applied and have been accepted."

"Then it's settled."

"No, not really."

"Why isn't it, if you've applied and have been accepted?"

"I'd like to think I've made a good judgment."

"You'd like someone to *say* you've made a good judgment."

"I guess so."

"All right. You've made a good judgment. Now tell me *why* you want to be a lawyer."

"My father is a successful businessman. Very successful. My two brothers are going to be, too. They're movers and shakers, as we say in the States. All three of them. My mother is a member of boards and committees. It's a family obligation. But I've always had the feeling my mother only *plays* at being a mover and shaker. She has a subordinate role, actually. It's the role that's set aside for the wives of successful men. I don't like it."

"Well spoken. So you've decided to be something more. Who can deny you?"

"My father and my mother and my two brothers."

Adams shrugged. "But you're going to do what you want to do anyway."

Lois nodded. "I guess so." She reached for his hand. "It isn't easy."

"Good," he said with crisp emphasis. "I should guess a great many other things have come *too* easily."

She made a salad for Sunday night's dinner, and they made omelets. They drank white wine—insufficiently chilled, because there was no refrigerator in the villa and no ice. He said she brewed better coffee than any European chef.

"Because I put eggshells in the coffee grounds. All us Texans do that."

"My God, you didn't!"

She laughed. "No. But you can't be sure I didn't put a little salt in it. We do that, too."

"*My God!*"

With the wine and the whiskey, sipped at all day and all evening, she was dulled and content. She could cope even with John's almost impenetrable self-possession. She had none of her own, but she was not intimidated by his.

"My father says French chefs invent great sauces to disguise the fact that the meat is not fresh or good."

"I guess your father is a philistine."

"No, a Democrat."

They went to bed early, made love quickly, and she went to sleep. She woke around midnight. He was not in bed. Startled, she got up to look for him. He was on the terrace. "It's warm. Too warm. I can't sleep."

The night *was* warm. Little air stirred. From the terrace they could see the lights of boats, fishing boats probably; and along the shore small fires burned at the campsites of young Germans and Swedes who came to the Côte d'Azur in August and camped wherever they could find space. Someone's radio was playing, and they could hear laughter intermixed with the music. Adams had pulled on his undershorts and sat looking out to sea, smoking. She had not seen him smoke before.

"Would you like something to drink?" she asked.

"A whiskey," he said.

She went into the house and poured two generous whiskeys. She stopped in the bedroom on her way back to the terrace and put on a pair of panties. Outside, she pulled a chair near John. She handed him his whiskey, and she sat silent and looked out at the sea as he did, sensing that he did not want to talk. They sat for some time, until the whiskeys were gone.

Finally Adams spoke. "As to whether or not you should become a lawyer . . . You should pursue whatever will let you own a place like this and spend as much time here as you can. You were born to it, of course, and—"

"*You* weren't born poor, were you, John?"

"No. But between my parents' spending habits on the one hand and the wars and the new taxes on the other, I have to struggle for what I have, and there's nothing left for this sort of thing."

She did not know what to say, and his mood did not invite conversation, so she looked out to sea again and waited for him.

"Ah," he said after a moment. "We should go back to bed. I'm afraid we have to end the idyll tomorrow. And rather early, too."

He started to rise from his chair, but before he could, she said: "I think before we go back to bed we should talk about something. We've put it off a long time."

"What's that?"

"I've got to spend my mother's twenty-five thousand dollars."

"You've seen some good things within that range," he said. "What have you chosen?"

"I haven't."

"But you must sooner or later, mustn't you?"

"Aren't you going to help me?"

He reached for her hand. "If you were the typical rich client I get, I would lead you to something, tell you to buy it, perhaps for more than it's worth, pocket my commission on the sale, and we would part happy—at least *I* would be happy. I'm not going to do it that way with you, Lois girl. You've got to choose for yourself."

"But—at least you can make a recommendation."

He shook his head. "No."

"Tell me about the Stubbs again," she said. "Why is it a good buy?"

He shrugged. "He was out of style for more than a hundred years. Even ten years back you could pick up a respectable example of his work for four or five hundred pounds. Today, if you get that one for seventy-five hundred or eight thousand, you'll have made a good buy. In another ten years it might be worth—God knows what. To my mind he was a better artist than Gainsborough or Joshua Reynolds."

"If I buy the Miró, you won't get a commission."

"Ignore that factor," Adams said firmly. "If you put a Miró in the Houston Museum of Fine Arts, you should have the city's gratitude."

Her choice in the end was between the two pictures they had discussed that night: a large canvas by the Spanish surrealist Joán Miró, a wash of color over which black and white shapes floated ignored by tiny faces attached to floating bodies; and a smaller painting by the eighteenth-century Liverpudlian romanticist George Stubbs, the portrait of a Whig squire and a huge, shining chestnut stallion in a cultivated rural landscape.

She chose the Stubbs. Her choice was influenced by two factors: first, and probably most important, that if her choice was not outstanding aesthetically, at least it was a good buy in a business sense, since Adams insisted a Stubbs was bound to increase in value; and, second, that from her purchase of the Stubbs, Adams would earn a commission of more than $2700.

The last week in August she took her father and mother to see what she had bought. It was at the London gallery of Flesselles, but Adams was not there. He had made it a point that he would not be there.

Her mother was pleased. "It shows a great deal of originality in choice," she said. "I expected something modern. I am surprised you should choose it. I am also surprised you could find one. It is also, I think, a most *conservative* choice. It—"

"Is it conservative to have spent almost twenty-two thousand dollars for *that?*" her father asked.

(In 1975, the Houston Museum of Fine Arts declined an offer of $265,000 for what was by then called "the Farnham Stubbs.")

They left for home September 7. Lois escaped from her parents for one afternoon, two days before, and spent it with Adams in his London flat.

"I could stay here," she said to him. "I think I could arrange it. They are so much opposed to my going to law school, I am sure I could get them to finance a year in Europe, studying art."

"Do you want to study art, more than to study law?" he asked. "I thought you were enthusiastically committed to the law and to the things you can do as a lawyer."

Lois lit a cigarette. She had started smoking again—having quit a year before. She was nude except for a pair of panties, and she sat in a chair facing him on the bed, in his surprisingly modest flat. "I could still go to law school—later," she said.

"But what is it you *want* to do?"

"I want to stay with you."

He lowered his eyes and nodded, as if he had expected the answer. "And do what?"

"Live with you," she said. "Make love with you. Learn from you. Become a little more like you. And who knows what might happen? We might be able, someday, to buy a place on the Riviera, like you want. If I were involved in art some way, like they want me to be, and if I were maybe married to a highly respectable English art dealer, I know they'd buy me a home in France—or anywhere else."

"There is an element of this I have missed," said Adams. "I don't recall I've heard you say you love me."

"I haven't heard you say *you* love *me.*"

"No. Yet you propose to live with me, perhaps marry me someday. I will say for it, Lois, it's the *boldest* thing I've heard you say since I've known you."

"Then you should like it," she said, smiling.

"But I don't," he said. "To be frank with you, Lois, you propose to throw yourself into an adventure—if I wished to be cruel, I might call it a postadolescent adventure—which I think will prove a quick disappointment to you and will be abandoned; and, to accommodate you in this adventure, you propose that I restructure *my* life completely. I think there's hardly one chance in a thousand that the adventure would wind up as you suggest: with you and me living on the Riviera in a villa purchased with your family's money, a pair of comfortable devotees of the fine arts, in love with each other and happy. The failure would leave me, I hope you see, in a ludicrous posture. I think it's a bad risk, dear girl, for you and me both."

V

Lois stepped off the elevator at the Houston Club. The men who had ridden up with her nodded and smiled at her and murmured something or other inaudible, each of them, before they hurried away to their different rooms and tables for a late lunch. Shifting her suede briefcase from one hand to the other, she stood for a moment in the foyer, taking the time to enjoy something she had long admired: the fountain the club had acquired and installed, graced with a copper sculpture of flying pelicans. It was an impressive piece of work and, in her opinion, insufficiently appreciated.

"Mrs. Hughes. Mr. Peavy is at his table. This way, please. Fine day, isn't it?"

Bob Peavy stood as she approached his table. (Robert Todd Peavy. Harvard Law, 1958. Partner at Stimson & Guthrie. Specialty: securities law. Within the past three weeks, newly serious speculation, not just in the *Houston Post* but in the *Wall Street Journal,* suggested he was one of two or three leading candidates for a place on the Securities and Exchange Commission.) Everyone's first impression of Bob Peavy was colored by his little round, gold-rimmed spectacles; and everyone immediately wondered why he wore them. Otherwise, he was tall and thin, somber-faced, blue-bearded. His hair had not begun to show gray, though he was forty-six years old. On the table before him was a glass showing in the bottom a couple of tiny melting cubes of ice and the red color of his last sip of Campari. The little green bottle of his Perrier water was beside the glass.

"I understand you were in court this morning," said Peavy.

Lois grimaced and shook her head. "Don't ask me about that."

"Oh, but I'm going to," he laughed. "But tell me about Tennessee first."

"They are amenable to a reasonable offer," she said. "I think they'll accept a reasonable offer. Let me warn you, though: They are very sensitive people, and if they see your offer as one iota less than reasonable, they'll back up on you and hold out forever."

"That's a negotiating ploy," he said, shrugging. "Very common."

"Suit yourself. The ball's in your court."

Peavy grinned. "So tell me about your morning."

Lois sighed and faintly smiled. "Criminal court's a pit. But you feel like a real lawyer when you work there."

"You couldn't drag me in with wild horses. Frankly, you look hot, and you have the appearance of a woman who could use a martini."

"I could use two martinis," Lois said. She sipped ice water.

"Your notorious client giving you a hard time?"

"Yes. Emphatically. Probably without meaning to. I don't know—maybe it's just Teejay. I didn't know her very well before she asked me to defend her, and I'm not sure if I'm just seeing facets of her personality or if I'm seeing her break down under the pressure. But right now she's very difficult to cope with. One minute she's cogent, telling you what she wants, in fact *demanding* what she wants, and the next minute she's in tears. Being in jail is very hard on her. She's frantic, and of course the judge denied her application for release on bond this morning."

"She didn't expect to be out on bail on a premeditated-murder charge, did she?"

"No, but she entertained some hope about it. She couldn't help that, I suppose. When the judge denied the motion and sent her back to the county jail, she broke down and cried. It was a tough scene. You'll read about it in tonight's paper."

"I didn't think I'd ever hear about that woman crying."

"Neither did Bill Madigan. For a moment I thought he was going to break down and cry, too."

"Madigan is your judge?"

Lois raised her brows high. "That's a good question. He said, publicly, from the bench, that he doesn't want to try the case. He said he knows her too well, and he said every judge in town does, too, and that an out-of-town judge should be brought in. But that's not what *she* wants. She knows exactly whom she wants. She wants Norma Jean Spencer."

Peavy laughed. "Christ! Does she want to be hanged?"

"She wants to be tried before a woman," said Lois evenly. "She wants to be defended by a woman and tried before a woman."

Peavy laughed again. Then his smile disappeared and he picked up a fork from beside his plate, and he frowned. "What's she have in mind, a novel defense? Or is she going to claim Ben Mudge tried to rape her?"

Lois shook her head. "I don't know what she has in mind for a defense—except that she vehemently denies she had anything to do with the murder of Mudge. She says Bill Hornwood is prosecuting, at least partly, because she's a woman—because she hasn't kept her place as a woman but she has shaken everybody's tree and rocked everybody's boat."

"Oh, Christ . . ."

Lois stiffened. "Don't be so quick with your 'Oh, Christ,'" she said acerbly. "She could have a point. How many times have you heard her called a bitch for something that, if you did it, you'd be called—"

"A son of a bitch," he interrupted with a self-congratulatory grin.

"There's a difference," said Lois soberly.

"I don't buy it."

"You don't buy it because you don't know anything about it, Bob."

He glanced around the room, still smiling broadly. "Are you going to tell me *you* suffer from male chauvinism?"

"Every day of my professional life," she said grimly.

"Really?"

She nodded. "My name is Lois Farnham Hughes. What firm do you think would have taken me in, in Houston in 1963, if my name had been Lois Smith or Lois Jones—or Tommy Jo Brookover? Even *with* my name, Childreth, McLennon and Brady was reluctant for a long time to put me out front where clients would see they were being represented by a woman."

"It's different now," he said.

"I'm glad you think so."

He raised a finger and opened his mouth to make an emphatic statement, but he was stopped by the appearance of the waiter bearing two fresh Camparis and a new bottle of Perrier water. When the waiter was gone, Peavy had reconsidered and had lowered his finger. "Still . . . *Norma Jean Spencer? Bunny Spencer?*"

Lois nodded. "She *demands* Judge Spencer. I left a call for Norma

Jean, for when she comes off the bench this afternoon. I'm going to make a personal plea for her to take the case."

Bob Peavy poured Perrier water over their Campari. "I'm glad it's your case, not mine. Tonight?"

She nodded. "Maybe a little late."

The assistant district attorney glanced at his watch. "Uh—if the Court please," he said. "Five minutes and we'll be finished with this witness."

Judge Norma J. Spencer nodded. "Five minutes," she said.

It was four o'clock. The court should adjourn, but the request for five more minutes was one she could hardly refuse, so she settled again into her high-backed chair, folded her arms, and assumed an air of attentive patience as the young assistant D.A. continued to question the aged black man in the witness chair.

"Where is Abdul Kaffar Hasi now, Mr. Washington—if you know?"

"He's doin' time for givin' me that bad check."

"At the time when Abdul Kaffar Hasi was in your store and gave you that forged check, was he alone?"

"No, sir. That fellow there was with him"—pointing at the defendant.

"*Objection!*" The defense attorney, a tall, bald, light-colored black man, stood and shook his head. "If the Court please, that is irrelevant and highly prejudicial. The defendant here has never been charged with having had anything to do with the crime the witness is talking about. Testimony that he was 'with' this Abdul Kaffar Hasi or was present when *that* man passed a forged check has nothing to do with *this* case and serves only to prejudice the jury against this defendant."

"If the Court please," said the assistant district attorney calmly, without rising. "Evidence that the defendant was present is admissible to show he was part of a continuing scheme or plan to pass forged payroll checks."

"*No, sir!*" complained the defense attorney angrily. "The testimony is that this defendant was 'with' this Abdul fellow, whatever that means. The witness has not testified this defendant was a part of what Abdul was doing."

Judge Spencer felt her mouth become dry. She felt beads of sweat form and begin to run down the hollow of her back. She was not sure how she should rule. What was the law? The courtroom was dead silent. She had to rule.

She licked her lips. "The objection is overruled," she said with as much firmness as she could bring into her voice. "The jury is instructed that the testimony placing this defendant at the scene of another crime is not to be considered as evidence that he is guilty in this case. You may consider it, however, as possibly showing a continuing scheme and therefore showing intent to commit the crime."

"*Your Honor, please!*" cried the lawyer for the defense. "In the first place, there has not even been testimony to the effect that this defendant knew this Abdul was committing a crime in Mr. Washington's store—"

"He might so testify, Mr. Johnson, if we can continue," she said sharply. (You had to be aggressive, or they would take control of your courtroom away from you.)

"Mr. Johnson can cross-examine," said the assistant district attorney. "I have no further questions of the witness."

The tall black lawyer stood silent for a moment, glaring at Judge Spencer. Whether by her ruling she had earned his contempt, or whether it was an element of his forensic technique, she could not be sure. He glanced at the jury, then at the witness. He scratched the back of his head. "Your Honor," he said evenly, "the prejudice to my client is so great, so irreparable, that I am compelled to move for a mistrial."

"The motion is overruled," said Judge Spencer quietly.

"Please note an exception."

"It is noted. The Court stands adjourned until nine-thirty tomorrow morning."

Whack! "All rise!" shrilled the bailiff.

As the spectators shuffled noisily to their feet and began to chatter, Judge Spencer grabbed her file folder, tugged her black robe more closely around her, and strode rapidly, with an air of purpose, toward the door. (This was part of the mystique of judgeship: the small, self-conscious drama of entering the courtroom, and exiting, in a grim, studied hurry.)

She put her robe in the locker in her office. Her bailiff, the short, dark, black man, David Berger, had followed her from the courtroom and now closed the locker door for her.

"The ruling there at the end was wrong, wasn't it, David?" she asked.

He nodded. "As I understand it . . ."

He had served as bailiff under three judges before her and had been watching criminal trials for twenty-seven years. He knew more of the law of evidence and trial procedure than most lawyers, and probably he was right.

"Goddamn your truthful hide," she said, smiling wanly, shaking her head. "Why can't you lie to me sometimes, just to make me feel better?"

David smiled. He picked up two pink telephone slips from her desk. "These calls came while you were on the bench," he said.

"Okay. Thanks, David."

The bailiff left, and she sat down behind the scarred, stained desk she had inherited from more predecessors than she knew. She looked at the telephone messages. One was from her husband, saying he would be in the parking lot at five o'clock unless she called to tell him not to. The other was from Lois Hughes. She frowned over that one. She thought she knew what Lois wanted. She put her glasses aside on her desk and rubbed her eyes. Reluctantly she picked up the phone and dialed Lois.

It was, as she had anticipated, a request that she take the Brookover case—put bluntly, firmly, personally.

"Okay, Lois. But you understand, the case has already been assigned to Judge Madigan."

"Bill Madigan said from the bench this morning he doesn't want to try it and is going to ask to have it reassigned. All you have to do is speak to him and to the assignment clerk, and it's yours."

"Thanks a lot, Lois. Thanks a whole goddamn hell of a lot."

"Can I tell Teejay you'll take it?"

"*Why,* Lois? For God's sake, why does she want *me?*"

"She thinks you'll be more sympathetic to her as a woman. That's what she keeps saying to me."

"If the evidence proves she killed that man, I might be the least sympathetic judge she could have."

"I talked to her in those terms. She says she'll take her chances."

Judge Spencer pulled across her desk the newspaper David brought in. Teejay Brookover was the subject of a front-page picture. The photographer had waited at the jail and had taken the picture when they brought her back, after Bill Madigan denied her bail. She was handcuffed. Her head was hanging down. The caption said she was crying. That was the trouble with the case: that every word of every day of the trial would be covered by the papers and television stations, in every grisly detail; and the judge, as much as Teejay Brookover, would be on trial.

"I know her," said Judge Spencer.

"So does every judge in town," replied Lois Hughes.

"Maybe a judge should be brought in from outside Houston."

"She wants you. I'm asking you to take it."

"I suppose this conversation at least verges on the unethical, Lois."

"You can refuse."

"No, I can't. You know I can't refuse you a favor, Lois."

"I know."

"All right. I'll speak to Bill Madigan. I'll take the case."

Teejay, with her dress hauled up around her waist, squatted over the small steel toilet bowl on the rear wall of their cell, and her cellmate, Janie, watched casually and kept on talking.

"You played with his cards, you played by his rules. Y'know? He never cheated. Y'know? But you had to play by his rules. He was a son of a bitch."

Teejay nodded. She had paid very little attention to anything Janie had said since they were locked in half an hour ago. They had heaved their bunk pads onto the floor, as they did every night, and Janie sat on one, with a game of solitaire spread out before her. She played only listlessly, more interested in talking than in cards, looked up ingenuously at Teejay—awkwardly half-squatted for a bowel movement—and went on chatting, gesturing, laughing. It never occurred to her to look away. When Janie used the toilet, Teejay made a point of looking away, out through the bars. Janie had been in jail so long, apparently she had lost any sense she ever had of privacy; she didn't have any and she didn't give any.

Janie was twenty-two years old, a little blonde with long straight hair and a vapid face. She had been in jail almost a year, while her lawyer obtained repeated postponements of her trial for killing her husband. ("We're going to beat it when we get to trial. Y'know? He's promised me. Maybe you know my lawyer.")

Teejay pumped the handle on the wall and a weak stream of water flushed the toilet inadequately. The stink filled the cell, though Janie didn't seem to notice. Teejay began to wipe herself, despondently wishing Janie would look away. She wobbled the flush handle again.

"I mean, Tommy Jo, did you ever hear of a rule that hearts beat spades? Y'know? I sure never did. I gotta grant him, if it was you that had the hearts, you beat his spades. He didn't change the rules to suit himself. Even so, he won more'n he ought to've. Y'know?" Janie laughed. "He was a funny son of a bitch."

Maybe noticing at last that Teejay was not responding to her, Janie looked down and played her cards; and Teejay finished wiping herself, flushed the toilet two or three more times, and pulled up her panties. She sat down on the other pad on the floor and leaned back against the bars of the door. On the floor within reach she had a little pile of things: two paperback books, a yellow legal pad and a ballpoint pen, a brassiere and a couple of extra pairs of panties, a carton of Winstons. She shook out a cigarette and offered the pack to Janie. Janie shook her head. Teejay lighted her cigarette. She smoked and stared vacantly at her bare feet.

Janie won her game of solitaire, then dealt and lost two games, shuffled her cards and dealt still another. "Tommy," she said quietly, "I been here a year, almost."

Teejay nodded.

"You been here a week."

"So?"

"Well—how long you gonna sit there and stare at your toe-toes? Don't you wanta play cards, or talk, or do some goddamn thing to keep from goin' nuts?"

Teejay shrugged.

Janie tossed down her hand of cards. "I mean, y' think I'm *interested* in that guy that said hearts beat spades? It's conversation, is all. You've got more to talk about than I've got. You've done a whole lot more in your life than I've done. Y'know? At least you've been on the outside the last year."

Janie picked up her cards again and, after she fanned them and looked at them, used them to scratch her eyebrow. "There was a woman killed herself in 'B' Cage six or eight months ago. Don't try it in here with me. I'll scream my head off."

"What makes you think I'd do that?"

Janie shrugged. "What other choices you got? You either sit right here until it works out—or that's what y' do. I figured that out a long time ago."

"Does that make it easier?" Teejay asked quietly.

Janie shook her head.

VI

1962

The fat woman beside Lois was eating a corn dog, which was a hot dog cooked in some kind of batter and served on a stick—served in the Cotton Bowl and maybe nowhere else in the world; Lois had never seen one anywhere else. The woman had swung the corn dog all around when she cheered, and twice it had passed under Lois's nose. That was how Lois happened to know a long black hair was entwined around the corn dog—which the woman was going to eat with the next bite if she did not discover it first.

"HOOK 'EM, HORNS! HOOK 'EM! YEEAAYYY! HEY, HEY, DARL RAWL! YEEEAAYYY!"

Lois watched. The woman had flipped grease from the corn dog, too. There were new grease spots on the white hat of the man in front of her and, indiscriminately, two or three spots on her own skirt. Lois had pulled violently away from her twice to avoid spots on her pink cashmere shirt or jacket. ("Ooops! Sorry, honey, sorry.") The woman was obese, redolently sweaty, flushed with heat and football fever, and cordially, enthusiastically drunk. And now she was going to eat a big hair.

She took a bite. She missed the hair, and Lois's smile diminished.

"C'MON, DARL RAWL! SEND IN MC CONNAGHEY! HEY! HEY! MC CONNAGHEY! HEY! HEY! MC CONNAGHEY!"

She stared popeyed at the corn dog for a moment, and Lois was sure she would spot the hair and pick it off. But she didn't, and now she opened her mouth, shoved in the rest of the corn dog, and pulled the bare stick from between her lips with a grunt of satisfaction. The hair was gone, on its way down her throat. Lois laughed. She could picture the thick black hair looped around the fat woman's tonsils.

"HOOK 'EM, HORNS! HOOK 'EM, HORNS! YEEAAYYY!"

Mac John nudged her. He pushed his pint over her paper cup and poured more bourbon over the little that was left of her ice. He winked. "C'mon, you son of a bitch! Don' let 'em—oh, kee-RIST!" He shook his head at Lois and pointed with dramatic helplessness at the field, where something or other—she had no idea what—had distressed him. He sipped bourbon. He turned and said something to Norma Jean Tyler, who sat on the other side of him; and she nodded and answered him—knowledgeably, since she knew all about football. Lois noticed how his eyes hung on her. The more he drank, the more he admired Norma Jean's legs and breasts.

"TWO BITS—FOUR BITS—SIX BITS—A DOLLAR! ALL FOR TEXAS STAND UP AN' *HOLLER!*"

The huge stadium was awash in hot, brazen sunshine, in screaming color, in garish noise, in beer and bourbon, and above all in flamboyant joy. The tiny, distant figures on the green field, in Texas orange and Oklahoma red, butting each other in their humorless struggle, were part of the gaudy pageant only in the same sense that the stars are part of astronomy. The football game was like the speck of dust that is the nucleus of a raindrop—there would be no raindrop without it, but it is diminished almost to insignificance in the middle of the self-generating something else that grossly outgrows it.

"HOOK 'EM, HORNS! HOOK 'EM, HORNS! HEY! HEY! ALL FOR TEXAS STAND UP AN' *HOLLER!*"

Lois stood and laughed. She did not shriek the way the fat woman did, or yell the way Norma Jean did, or bellow gutturally as Mac John did. However ingenuous the hysteria of the crowd, she withheld herself a little. She could enjoy herself and take part without letting herself be caught up entirely. And from her detached perspective, she remained an observer. This afternoon she observed the little blonde on the other side of Mac John. (They called her Bunny, usually.) She had for some time been intrigued by the duality of Norma Jean Tyler.

They had been thrown together. They were two of only nine women in the student body of the law school of the University of Texas, Austin. They were the only two women who had made law review. They

were not in the same class—Lois was a year older and a year ahead—
but they had inherited the limping law-school sorority and had been
told it was their obligation to keep it alive. They were thrown together
as a team for moot-court competition. They were thrown together
whenever a joint assignment was given in a seminar. Some of the men
called them the Brain Sisters: Big Brain and Little Brain.

"Mr. Evans, tell us how much formality this will needs in its
execution."

It was a seminar in estate planning. The problem was the writing
of a will with a marital deduction trust. Professor McKay was grilling
John Evans, a senior from Dallas who ranked second or third in the
class.

"The will," said Evans, "must be signed and acknowledged by the
testator in the presence of two witnesses who must sign as witnesses
in his presence and in the presence of each other."

"Uhhm-hmmm," muttered the professor. "Everyone satisfied?"

"*Three* witnesses," said Norma Jean Tyler.

"Three? Miss Tyler suggests three. Anyone want to try for four?"

Other men around the table smiled, but Evans shook his head and
said, "Two," sharply.

"Miss Tyler, the floor is yours," said Professor McKay.

Lois remembered how Norma Jean glanced uneasily around the
table. She remembered how she wiped her mouth with her hand before
she spoke.

"What if the testator owned property in a state that requires three?"

"The validity of a will is governed by the law of the state in which it
is executed," said Evans flatly.

"Miss Tyler?"

"An instrument that purports to convey title to real estate must conform to the law of the situs of the real estate," said Norma Jean. "The
way this problem is set up, the testator is supposed to be a millionaire.
So he might own a house in, say, Massachusetts. If he did, the will with
two witnesses would not convey title to his devisee."

"Mr. Evans?"

Evans leaned back in his chair and stared at the ceiling. "Objection
sustained," he said wryly.

That was one element of Norma Jean. She showed the other immediately after the seminar broke for the day, when she caught up with
John Evans in the hall and apologized, saying she hoped she hadn't
embarrassed him.

At the law school, Lois Farnham was the rich bitch from Houston:
the tall, not-bad-looking young woman you saw striding purposefully

toward the parking lot, her hair windblown, swinging her briefcase. She dressed well. She drove a Thunderbird. She was open, always ready to talk, to share a joke, to laugh; yet she kept a careful distance from you and left you feeling she had shown you a facade. She fascinated a good part of the law-school student body. With her brains and her father's money, she could make some young lawyer quite a catch.

Norma Jean Tyler was the one they called Bunny, because she was cute and petite and vivacious. You had seen her around the campus before probably, because she had taken her undergraduate degree, too, at the University of Texas. She was an Alpha Gam. They ran her for homecoming queen in her senior year. You might remember her on the Alpha Gam float in the 1960 homecoming parade, in the white fur bikini. Everybody remembered that. She studied in the law library a lot. She distracted people. They stared at her legs under the library tables, and sometimes when she leaned forward over a book, her boobs lay right on the table. You could buy her a cup of coffee. You could ask her for a date, in fact. She dated some guy on the football team, but not exclusively, and if you could get around her heavy study schedule, she would go out, and you would have a good time.

For the fall, 1962, issue of the *Law Review*, Lois wrote a commentary on the Connecticut contraceptive cases. She criticized the plurality of the justices as insensitive to the rights of women. Her comment was controversial, and it took a bit of politicking with the editors and the faculty adviser to get it published. In the same issue a case note on *Baker v. Carr*, the one-man-one-vote case, appeared above the name of Norma Jean Tyler. Other students had wanted to publish a note on *Baker v. Carr*, but Bunny Tyler's note excelled in the competition, and hers was published.

Bunny's father operated a gasoline service station on the southeast side of Houston. Lois drove her home for vacations. Bunny talked about her father, about his station, about people who came in and what they said and did, but she would not let Lois drive her to the station or to her home, not many blocks away; she insisted on taking a bus home from downtown Houston. Lois met Mr. Tyler once. She'd offered to drive Bunny back to Austin after the spring break, and Bunny said she could pick her up at the Rice Hotel. Mr. Tyler was in the lobby with Bunny. He said it was "a honor" to meet Lois, and he thanked her for being "so nice to my girl." He was a handsome, red-faced, muscular man, white-haired, wearing a double-breasted suit and a blue satin necktie. Lois noticed shreds of cigarette tobacco clinging to his lip.

"Gimme a T!"—"TEEEE!" *"Gimme a E!"*—"EEEEE!" *"Gimme . . ."*

Mac John was handsome. He had a strong, cleft chin, blue eyes under sun-bleached brows, sandy-red hair. He was trim and hard, in spite of his drinking and smoking. He played a good game of tennis. He swam. He rode. He had flair. Today he was wearing a dark green and white houndstooth-check jacket, midnight-blue slacks, a white shirt, a midnight-blue tie, aviator sunglasses—and he carried it off, it looked good. He had driven Lois and Bunny to Dallas in his Cadillac convertible, averaging almost a hundred miles an hour for the drive. They would spend the night, not in a hotel but in guest rooms at the Snapper Creek Country Club.

"We'll win the Southwest Conference," Mac John was saying to Bunny, "and *they'll* win the Big Eight; and then we oughta get a bowl game with each other and play this all over again to see who's national champion. But, shit . . ."

Lois looked away from them and ignored their conversation. It was easy to become annoyed with either one of them. Mac John was half drunk and talking nonsense; and Bunny, who didn't know he was drunk, was just the same, encouraging him, deferring to his stupid opinions, leading him on. Actually, as Lois full well understood, Bunny was not deferring to Mac John; she was deferring to his Cadillac and the rooms at the Snapper Creek Country Club and the country club party they were invited to tonight. If he had driven her to Dallas in a Ford or Chevy, put her up in a cheap motel room, and proposed to take her out on the downtown streets for the riotous night that would follow the game—the way she had come to the Oklahoma game before— she would have told him to shut up. It was an unattractive element of her character. She deferred to Lois, even, for a like reason.

On the other hand, her innocent wonder over the way they were spending this weekend—and her sincere appreciation for it—were irresistibly appealing. Mac John, before he began his drinking and became lecherous about her, had noticed this and had remarked on it to Lois.

"GET 'IM! GET 'IM! GET 'IM! OHH, JEEE-ZISS *CHRIST!*"

The room at the Snapper Creek Country Club overlooked two fairways, all juicy green and vivid white and deeply shaded. It was furnished with two double beds, two overstuffed chairs, a color-television console, a breakfast table with chairs, a writing desk. In the bathroom, the shower stall closed tightly and became a steam bath at the turn of a valve.

Bunny kicked off her shoes and stretched out on one of the beds. "It's first-class," she said. "You and Mac John know how to go first-class."

"Mac John does," said Lois. "He arranged it."

"Lois, if you don't mind my asking, where does Mac John's family get all their money?"

Lois, who had begun to undress, glanced quizzically at Bunny, not sure how the question was asked. "They stole it, I suppose—originally anyway."

"No, seriously," Bunny pleaded.

"I am serious. Hughes and Company is one of the biggest livestock brokerage houses in the Southwest. The family has some oil properties, too. But originally, I imagine, they were cattle rustlers, claim jumpers, confidence men, and maybe even train robbers—who knows?"

"You're putting me down," Bunny complained.

"No. I'm not putting you down."

"It's easy for you to talk like that."

"Bunny . . . Would you like to know where my great-grandfather got the money that—as you might say—established the Farnham family?"

Bunny shook her head. "No. It's private, and I didn't mean to pry."

"It isn't private," Lois said casually. She had taken off her pink cashmere suit and her blouse, and in a half-slip and brassiere she sat down and began to brush her hair. "My great-grandfather Farnham opened a saloon in San Antonio in 1867. That's a matter of record; you can read about him in the old newspapers and the old histories. We have a picture of him in an old local history of San Antonio. He was a huge man with an absolutely terrifying black moustache. My grandfather said he watered his whiskey. My grandfather also said he always kept a couple of girls in the saloon, who would go into one of the back rooms for a price.

"Anyway, that's how he made his money: as a saloonkeeper. He moved to Houston about 1891, and of course by then it was beneath his dignity to tend bar anymore, or keep a bawdy house, so he put his money in land and oil. There was never anything noble about the founding of the Farnham fortune, if you want to call it that."

Bunny cocked her head and looked at Lois with open, challenging skepticism. "It really doesn't matter how you got it, does it?" she said. Maybe Mac John's bourbon was the source of the thin edge on her voice. "The money does make a difference for you, doesn't it? You don't deny that, do you?"

"What difference do you have in mind?"

Bunny sighed. "It's the confidence you can have, I guess," she said, softening her voice. "I'm envious, of course. But you always know you can do what you want to do."

"Like what?" Lois asked.

"Go to school," said Bunny. "I've worked all the time I've been in school. I'm not complaining about that, but my dad has had to help me, especially in law school. He's the most wonderful man in the world, Lois, but it was never certain we'd manage it." She smiled. "He's going to be proud when I graduate."

"You're going to do all I'm going to do: graduate," said Lois. "You'll rank higher in your class than I will, too."

"Look at yourself sometime, Lois," Bunny said. The edge had returned to her voice and she faced Lois with an ironic smile. "You have class. It's *confidence*. You have confidence. And—experience. You've done things that are *wonderful*. It shows. It gives you poise. That's the word I was looking for: poise. You have poise."

"Which, if I understand you," said Lois in a brittle voice, "you think my family's money bought for me."

"I don't resent it," said Bunny quickly.

Lois put down her hairbrush. "You have poise yourself, Norma Jean," she said. "It's different from what you see in me and call poise, because we're different people with different styles. But you have it. I've sometimes envied *you* more than a little."

"For what, for God's sake?"

Lois smiled wanly. "I think you have enough self-esteem to figure that out."

A yard-high ice sculpture, the head of a longhorn, floated on an anchored raft at the center of the swimming pool, gleaming in the beam of an orange spotlight, surrounded by dozens of floating candles and scores of floating gardenias drifting on faint gusts that blew over the pool. The dining tables were on the terrace overlooking the pool and at poolside. Gentlemen went to the bar to fetch drinks to the tables for their ladies and themselves.

The place cards at their table read—MR. McALLISTER JOHN HUGHES—MISS LOIS ELAINE FARNHAM—MR. ROGER A. BLANCHESTER—MISS NORMA JEAN TYLER—MR. JOSEPH ROBERT BLANCHESTER—MRS. JOSEPH ROBERT BLANCHESTER.

The Blanchesters, she had learned only after reaching this table, were the origin of their invitations. Blanchester *père* was a friend and business associate of Mac John's father. What she had yet to figure out—and wanted to know—was whether or not Bunny was supposed to be Roger's date for the evening. Roger was thirty-five years old, the divorced father of three children.

Returning from the bar, Roger stumbled, or maybe pretended to stumble, just short of the table, and Bunny jumped up and grabbed two of his drinks. They sat down laughing. She handed bourbons with Coke to the two senior Blanchesters, still laughing; then she lifted her champagne glass and toasted Roger.

"Well!" said Blanchester, Sr., smiling broadly. "This is a nice party, isn't it? It's a lot of fun."

Mac John cast a smug glance at Lois. He was drinking bourbon on the rocks now, relaxed and smoking; and, having been drunk this afternoon and pretty much so again earlier in the evening, he looked sober now, and talked soberly, and in fact was having one of his better nights, when he was a witty observer of the same things she observed. He had danced four or five times with her and once with Bunny. He sent a tip to the orchestra with word that they should play a song she liked—"If Ever I Should Leave You."

"Norma Jean," said Mrs. Blanchester, "what do you think of what the Kennedys are doing to our country?"

Lois had often heard Bunny vociferously defend the Kennedy presidency in sharp arguments on the campus at Austin. Now she heard her say smoothly that she guessed she hadn't paid politics enough attention lately, being in law school and all. Lois glared scornfully, but Bunny only glanced innocently at her and smiled.

"There won't be much point in going to law school if Kennedy is elected again in 'sixty-four, then maybe Bobby gets a term or two after that," said Blanchester, Sr. "There won't be anything left of people's rights, or business, or anything else."

"You think so?" Mac John asked blandly.

"Mac," said Blanchester, Sr., earnestly, "do you realize that with eight years of this Kennedy we've got now, then eight years of Bobby, then eight of Teddy, we could have Kennedys in the White House for *twenty-four years?*"

"Well, I did realize three times eight is twenty-four," said Mac John with a grin, and he slapped Blanchester, Sr., lightly on the shoulder.

Blanchester, Sr., smiled and took a sip of bourbon.

In Roger Blanchester's car, later, the subject of Kennedy was raised again. Roger asked if they had heard the latest Kennedy joke: "If John, Bobby, and Teddy were on a boat and it sank, who would be saved? The country."

"How much of that shit do you believe?" Mac John asked Roger. The general subject of their conversation was Blanchester, Sr.'s, sincere conviction—as Roger described it—that the Kennedy presidency was ruining the country.

"Well . . ." Roger shrugged. "I'm strongly anti-Communist."

"I guess we're all that, aren't we?" Bunny said.

"Jesus," sighed Lois.

They were on their way to another party. Roger had said the country club party was stuffy and he knew where there was a *good* party. In the ladies' room, Lois had told Bunny firmly she was under no obligation to go to any party with Roger Blanchester, but Bunny had said she wanted to go. "I don't know how much money he's got or where his family got it," Lois had said sarcastically. "I didn't ask you, did I?" Bunny had responded with a grin.

Roger drove them to someone's handsome home, not more than a mile from the country club. He led them into the house and out to the patio and pool. The party had already begun.

No one was there who had not been at the country club. Six or seven couples who had become bored with the country club party had slipped away. Someone had asked Roger to bring his friends.

Their host—a man of thirty years or so whose name Lois did not catch—handed them all bourbon and 7-Up, without asking if anyone wanted anything else; and he said, 'Y'all know each other"—gesturing expansively toward the other guests—and hurried back to the bottles set up on a patio table.

"Don't mind Jack, he's loaded," interjected a young woman with a high voice and a high-speed eastern accent. "Hi, Rog. I'm Kathy, all. Take off y' coats and ties, fellas. Take off y' shoes, girls. We're all friends here."

"Hey," said Bunny to Roger, and she began to loosen his necktie for him. They had been walking hand in hand coming into the party, and were conspicuously a couple. He was fourteen years older than Bunny; his light hair was thin, and he had a protruding gut. But he did speak softly, deferentially, to her; and for her he had subdued the predilection to swagger that was his least attractive characteristic. She liked him, apparently.

"Sheet, Jack," a man said loudly. "That fallout shelter ain' gonna do you a *lick* o' good. Bomb falls, you take you fam'ly down in there, all the people ain' got shelters gonna beat you door in, to get in and try to save their lives, too."

Jack shook his head vehemently. "I got two riot guns stowed down there," he said.

"Jack, do you mean to tell me," asked a petite, pretty young woman sitting at a table nearby, "that if I bring my kids to that door and knock, you won't let me in?"

"Thelma, *I couldn't*," said Jack grimly. "I built that for *my* family. You can build one for yours."

"It's the most immoral thing I ever heard of," said Thelma.

"What the hell kind of a party's this you brought us to?" Mac John asked Roger.

Someone else—maybe someone who thought the same—put on a record and turned up the volume. A song by the Beatles echoed over the pool, and a couple began to dance. Roger and Bunny danced. Shortly someone switched off all the lights except the underwater lights in the kidney-shaped pool; and their host, Jack, stripped to his Jockey shorts and jumped with a whoop and a splash into the water. He was followed in a moment by Thelma, in her panties and bra. They treaded water side by side in the middle of the pool, laughing and sputtering and calling the others to join them.

"C'n see how this party's goin'," Mac John drawled to Lois. "You wanta sneak out?"

Lois shrugged. A sudden tug of vertigo she had felt a moment ago had told her emphatically she should stop drinking; and at the moment the thought of having to make some kind of excuse for leaving, and of having to drag Roger and Bunny away, too, since Roger was driving, and of having to enter a discussion of where they would go next, all seemed too burdensome to face. She sat down heavily on a redwood bench and gestured to Mac John to sit beside her. He sat and, misinterpreting her signal, began to caress the insides of her thighs. She clutched the bench and stopped the world's turning.

She watched another couple splash into the pool. The third couple was Roger and Bunny. Bunny swam a strong stroke, across the pool and back; then, turning over, she backstroked to where Lois and Mac John were sitting and faced them, grinning and swinging the water out of her blond hair. "Coming in?" she asked.

"I don't care," Lois said quietly. She did not really want to, but she would, because too often in her life she had been accused of being aloof and snobbish and injecting a cold, discordant note into moments when other people were having fun. (*From her childhood:* "Ham-Ham Farn-ham. Lois Farn-ham is a bad sport." Bad sport. It was a phrase she loathed.) She took off all her clothes but her panties and brassiere, folding the pink cashmere carefully on the redwood bench and pushing the bench further away from the edge of the pool. She slipped into the water. It was cool and pleasant and relieved the bourbon nausea.

She hoisted herself up out of the water after a few minutes and sat on the edge of the pool, her feet dangling. Their host, Jack, was stealing brassieres—she could see two hanging from the diving board—and he sneaked up behind her now and roughly unhooked hers. He ran off with a whoop and added it to the collection. Mac John's head popped out of the water just at her feet. "Relax," he said, and sank again. She shrugged again. Why not? The poolside concrete retained warmth from the sunlight that had beaten on it all day, and she savored the warmth coming up through her thin, wet panties to her bottom, and laughed when Roger chased their hostess, Kathy, around the pool, pulled off her bra, and hung it on the board. She accepted another bourbon from Jack.

Bunny was in the middle of every game, chased and kissed and fondled by every man but Mac John. She ran, her solid breasts bouncing. She jumped into the water. She jumped from the diving board. Roger, then Jack, then Thelma's husband, ran after her, and each caught her. She kept drinking. At the far end of the pool, almost out of Lois's sight in the dark, she plunged into a melee over Jack, who had been wrestled to the ground by Kathy and Thelma, who were trying to pull down his shorts. Bunny pushed in, managed to pull them off, and ran shrieking, waving them above her head. Jack, naked, ran after her, and when he caught her she threw his shorts over the high hedge, into the driveway. She giggled as he wrestled her down and pulled off her panties, and shrieked as he threw them over the hedge, too. He dragged her by the wrist to the bar and poured bourbon all over her. It burned between her legs, probably, and she broke loose and threw herself into the pool.

Roger, standing beside Mac John, laughed. "You brought a fun girl," he said.

"Damned if we didn't," said Mac John.

A few minutes later Bunny knelt naked beside Lois and whispered breathless in her ear: "Hey—you don't mind, do you—I—lost my pants?"

Kathy came around, saying there was food in the house and they should go in. They gathered around the Ping-Pong table, under the bright fluorescent lights of the basement game room, and filled plates with shrimp and potato salad and little sandwiches, and accepted more bourbon and 7-Up that Jack poured into paper cups—Jack and Bunny still naked, the rest wearing only undershorts or panties, all of them stumbling, spilling, giggling drunk.

"Y' okay?" Mac John whispered to Lois. She nodded, and he said, "Lemme know if you want to sneak out."

Lois was afraid. She had never been this drunk before: certainly never drunk and naked in a roomful of strangers. Realistically, she and Mac John could not sneak out; she was too drunk, and he was, too. Kathy put a record on the player, and she switched on two red-shaded lamps and switched off the fluorescents. Lois seized Mac John's arm. "Promise me one thing," she said in a hoarse, urgent whisper. "Don't let anybody else touch me."

No one else did. Some time later—she was not sure how much later—

Mac John took her upstairs and appropriated the master bedroom. He locked the door, and they slept four hours there. Before that, she had seen Bunny dance naked: a withdrawn, private but sensual dance, punctuated by staggering. Lois had seen her go upstairs with Roger, but she had seen her come back, too, saying Roger was asleep now. On the stairs, as Lois and Mac John went up, Bunny had stopped them. "Hey!" she had said, her charade of sincerity drunkenly exaggerated. "Jesus, *thanks* to both of you. Thanks for bringing me." Lois knelt on the bathroom floor and threw up in the toilet. Mac John was asleep before she came to bed.

In the morning Kathy served gallons of orange juice and coffee, and a few eggs, to half-dressed people. In the kitchen Thelma told Lois ruefully that Bunny had slept with Jack.

VII

November 22, 1963

Tommy Jo stood aside to let the waitress ahead of her shoulder by with her tray, then pressed up to the bar, between the stainless-steel rails that made a place for waitresses to come to the bar. She slammed her tray on the bar. "Hey, Gil," she called to one of the bartenders. "C'mon." She tossed her head impatiently. Lunch hour was hectic any day, but right now she had a crowd of strangers, men and women, at one of her best four-tops, crying for drinks and complaining already that service was not fast enough. If that four-top was going to produce any kind of tip at all today, she had to hustle drinks to them quick.

"Tough damn day, huh, Tommy Jo?" said the man on the barstool to her right.

She knew she did not know him, that he called her by name only because he had read her name tag; and she shrugged, glanced at him, and muttered, "Every day."

The man laughed and dragged on his cigarette.

"Hokay, Teejay," said the bartender.

"One Heineken," she said. "One Carta Blanca, one Forester on the rocks, one . . ." She glanced at her pad. ". . . Seven and Seven, one Cutty and soda."

"You got it," said the bartender briskly.

She nodded. She brushed a wisp of red hair off her forehead. The man on the barstool was openly staring at her, looking her up and down—making a straightforward, unsmiling appraisal. She looked at him.

"I don't think I've seen you here before," he said conversationally.

"I've worked here over a year," she said.

He picked up his martini and took his eyes off her to frown over it skeptically. "Well, I guess it's because I almost always have lunch in the dining room. I get to El Paso about once a month and always like to have lunch at the Casablanca, but it's almost always been in the dining room. I guess I'll forget the dining room and start having lunch in here."

The conversation was probably leading to a proposition. This kind of talk usually did. To discourage him, she pretended to study the figures on her check pad.

She heard a lot of propositions. The way she was dressed invited them. The dark green uniform of a Casablanca cocktail waitress exposed her shoulders and the tops of her breasts, pushed up and almost out of the bodice by a built-in boned bra; and the tiny suggestion of a skirt, puffed out with starched white ruffles, exposed her dark green panties and showed off her long legs in sheer black pantyhose. She heard twice as many propositions and collected twice as much in tips as she had ever heard and collected anyplace she had worked before.

"You a native of El Paso?" the man asked.

"I came here a couple of years ago."

"To get a job like this?"

"To go to school."

Gil began to put bottles and glasses on her tray, and she gave the man on the barstool a quick smile and turned away from him. She picked up the tray and began to work her way gingerly through the crowd.

"Hey!" yelled a man in the doorway. "Hey, turn on the TV, Gil! I'm hearin' on the car radio somebody in Dallas took a shot at Kennedy a while ago. May have got him, too."

With her cousin Lee, she had arrived in El Paso two years ago. They came in his Ford pickup: a long, silent drive down from LaGrange, during which both of them brooded over the hysterical scene precipitated by their announcement that they were leaving. They arrived in El Paso with almost no money. She took a job the first day in town, serving hot dogs and root beer at a drive-in. He tried the truck wash where he had thought he had a job waiting, to find no one there had ever heard of the man who had offered him the job—or maybe, as Tommy Jo suspected, he went to the wrong truck wash. Lee found a job, finally, pumping gasoline in a Magnolia station—the same thing he had been doing at home.

To save money, they had rented a room together, telling the woman who owned the house they were husband and wife. They had one bed and no option but to sleep together; but Lee would not have sexual relations with her. He was aroused by her, to the point of slavering; but more than touch her bare breasts he was afraid to do. "The Baable *says*, Tommy Jo! You're ma *cousin*. If ah screwed you, ah'd burn in hayul, an' so would you. Baable says y' not s'posed ta screw . . ."

She didn't really care. She had supposed they would rut in a rooming house bed, like two pigs, so long continent they would explode in sensual frenzy the first real opportunity they had. When he proved frightened, she was disappointed; but after sleeping in the same bed with him two nights, she discarded all idea of working to overcome his biblical scruple. He was not clean. He did not bathe often enough. He stank. She decided to find her own room and her own bed as soon as she had the money.

When they had been in El Paso two weeks, Lee abruptly telephoned his father. His father wired money, and Lee told Tommy Jo he was going home. He begged her to come with him. When he was convinced she would not, he gave her half his money—twenty-five dollars—and left.

She had found a better job, in a drive-in called Rancho Apache. One week she worked from 10:00 A.M. to 6:00 P.M.; the next week she worked 6:00 P.M. to 2:00 A.M.

Every night at midnight, Car 48, El Paso Police, stopped on the lot, and Rancho Apache provided free hamburgers and shakes for the two officers. Sometimes one of the officers in the car was Sergeant Coleman Bishop. He talked to her, joked with her. She thought of him as a pleasant, fatherly man—he was maybe forty years old. One night, several months after she met him, he asked her to dinner and a movie. She could not have been more surprised, but she accepted his invitation.

He picked her up at her rooming house (she had also found a better place to live) on the evening of her day off, which was Thursday. He was a compact, muscular man, gray-haired, deeply tanned. He told her during the evening he was divorced, that he was the father of two children, both of whom were in high school. He asked her to call him Cole. He drank straight bourbon, but sparingly. He like to tell jokes and must have had a thousand in memory. He took her to dinner and then to the movie *Lawrence of Arabia*. They had a drink in a bar after the movie, and when he returned her to her rooming house he kissed her on the cheek and asked her if she would go out with him again. She said she would.

Sometimes after that Car 48 picked her up when Rancho Apache closed and delivered her home. The word got around that the redhead was Sergeant Bishop's girl—which made working at night at Rancho Apache a good deal easier. She began to see Cole regularly. They went to dinner again, to other movies, to a ball game one Sunday afternoon; they took drives in his car, sometimes across the border to Juárez. He kissed her in the car and on the porch at her rooming house. He touched her hips and legs and breasts—always gently, even when she could see how fully aroused he was. But he never suggested they rent a motel room and go to bed.

One Thursday night when he was off duty, he phoned and said he would pick her up at her place and drive her to work. He said he would come an hour early, so they would have time for a sandwich and a beer. She had come home the night before in her Rancho Apache uniform—white vinyl boots, skimpy buff-colored shorts, a buff halter, a dark brown fringed vest, a white hat that hung down her back on a thong—so she could wash the halter and shorts; and, since she was on her way back to work when Cole picked her up, she came out on the porch wearing the uniform.

It was an unpleasant surprise for him, and it turned him moody. He'd had it in mind to take her to Western Steak House for a quick steak dinner, and he was disappointed that he couldn't. They ate instead at a drive in, and although he recovered his good humor and told her three or four funny jokes, she remained uncomfortable.

"You've been a real good thing for Cole," one of the other officers had told her only two or three nights before, when he took her home in Car 48. "Showin' you off, showin' he can date a good-lookin' young girl like you, it's done wonders for the guy. He feels better, he looks better, and his disposition is one hell of a lot better."

That was all right with her. She liked the idea that Cole was proud of her—or, more realistically, that taking her out made him proud of himself. She did not like what she discovered now: that showing off a drive-in waitress did not make him proud. She had thought she understood Cole, that he was a straightforward man, that the fun they had together was uncomplicated. This incident troubled her.

She did not expect to see him again for several days, but when Rancho Apache was ready to close, at 2:00 A.M., he drove into the lot and said he would take her home. He asked her if she had to go in, or could she sit and talk for a while in the car? She said she could talk, and he parked at the curb in front of the rooming house.

It was dark on the street. She could barely make out his face. He offered her a cigarette. She had begun to smoke a little, so she accepted a Winston and a light. He lit one for himself, too. During the business of taking out the pack of cigarettes, shaking them out, snapping the lighter, and so on, he said nothing. He sat with his back to the door on the driver's side of the car. She sat on her side. The windows were open. The smoke drifted out, and from a radio or record player in one of the houses across the street the faint sound of music with a heavy beat came in.

"I've been thinking about you," said Cole.

"What does that mean?" she asked.

"Well . . ." he said tentatively. "You graduated at the top of your high-school class. You went to college two years, even if it was only a Bible college. You're pretty and you're smart. So why do you work at Rancho Apache and live in a grubby rooming house?"

"What is this, a kick in the ass?" she asked.

"Thinking about you this evening, I decided you could use one," he said. "You can tell me it's none of my business if you want to, but Christ all fishhooks, Tommy Jo! You can do better than this."

She blew a stream of smoke against the windshield. "Where?" she asked quietly. "I can't do office work. I never learned to type. What *does* a girl do that's twenty years old and has the kind of education I've got? I get letters from my mother to come home. I could go home and marry some cowboy. I could marry some cowboy here—and live in some crummy house and make brats and spend the rest of my life getting fat and pimply. Is that what you recommend?"

"Do you like what you're doing?" he asked. "You think you can't do any better than what you're doing?"

"What're you talking about, Cole?" she asked. She took a drag on her cigarette and flipped it out the window. "I understand you don't like these shorts and these boots and all. Well, let me tell you about these shorts and the halter and the boots. *They make me money.* I could work in a nice indoor restaurant, in a nice black dress and a starched white apron, and take home fifty a week. Guys look at my legs—"

"They look at your ass," he interrupted.

"Okay, they look at my ass, then. And they leave tips. I make money. And living where I do, I don't spend money. Maybe I can save enough to do what I want to do. I—"

"What is it you want to do with this money you save?" he asked.

"Go to school, goddammit! What did you think?"

"Well, how much do you have saved, Tommy Jo?"

She sighed. "Not much. I've only been here eight months. But I'm not making it. I'm not making enough, not saving enough. So you tell me, Cole. Where do I make more?"

He put his cigarette to his lips, pulled on it, held the smoke in for a long moment, then blew it away unhurriedly. "I talked to somebody about that tonight," he said. "My brother runs a lumberyard," he said. "Lumberyard, building-supply store. He needs a girl behind the counter. Cashier. Bookkeeper. He'd teach you the job. He'd pay sixty a week to start, maybe seventy, seventy-five after you learn the job. And you don't have to live in a place like this. I can help you find a good place, on a good street, that won't cost you much more."

Tommy Jo looked out the window. "You and me," she said very quietly. "Is this supposed to make things different between you and me?"

"You wouldn't work nights," he said. "We could go out more often."

"And when we went out, I would be Miss Brookover, the cashier and bookkeeper at your brother's store; I wouldn't be Tommy Jo, the bare-ass carhop from Rancho Apache."

Cole sighed. "Which would you rather be?"

"I should be grateful, I guess," she said. "It's a little hard for me, because I didn't know before tonight you were ashamed of me."

"Tommy Jo—I'm no way ashamed of you. I want good things for you," he said heavily.

"Do you want to marry me?" she asked impulsively.

"Well—maybe," he said with ponderous sincerity.

"If my father were alive, he'd be younger than you," she said.

"You'd be embarrassed to be married to me, then."

"No. No. Let's don't cut each other up."

"I only want what's good for you."

"I'll think about the job with your brother. I really do appreciate your thoughtfulness, Cole. We'll talk about it some more."

They did not really talk about it any more. That very night, at three in the morning, she had soaked in hot water in the rooming-house bathtub that sat on clawed feet and she had searched the want ads for a different job. She drank a can of beer in the tub while she looked through the ads, and it was as she had said: For young women without secretarial skills, there were jobs in the factories, jobs as dime-store clerks, jobs as waitresses and barmaids, and not much more. She read one ad three or four times—for cocktail waitresses at the Casablanca. The age requirement was twenty-one or more.

Two days later, Monday, she went to the Casablanca and lied. She went wearing a dress, with high heels and stockings, and she told the manager she was twenty-two, newly moved to El Paso from LaGrange, Texas, so she could enroll at the university; and she was hired. Within two weeks, with her tips, she was earning seventy-five dollars a week. Within two months she earned ninety and ninety-five. She never talked to Cole's brother. He said nothing. He kept taking her out. She told him she was going to inquire at the university to see if she could enroll for courses in the fall. She said thanks, for the kick in the ass.

That fall she did enroll at the University of Texas, El Paso.

Gil, the bartender at the Casablanca, had switched on the television set above the bar, and immediately the troubled face of Chet Huntley appeared on the screen. The man in the doorway, who had said he'd heard the president had been shot, walked slowly toward the bar, staring at the screen.

". . . conflicting reports as to whether or not Vice President Lyndon Johnson has also been shot and wounded. One report says that the vice president was seen walking into the hospital. As to the president himself, the reports are sketchy and conflicting. On this point they agree: that President Kennedy has been seriously wounded, apparently in the head. The wound may even be fatal."

Tommy Jo had stopped in the middle of the room with her tray in her hands. She stared at the television set. For a moment, what the man was talking about on television intruded immediately into her life. President Kennedy . . . He was a remote figure. But—*shot?* She could evoke an image of his face more vivid than she could evoke of her mother. For a moment, that was reality: a street in Dallas, the president shot and hurt; and for a moment, the Casablanca—the room and the tables and the movement around her—was vague.

"Girlie . . . Uh, *Red* . . . If, uh, Kennedy's been shot, we *do* need a drink, now don't we?"

She was startled by the voice at the table, at the four-top where these drinks belonged. She looked down. The man was looking up at her, grinning. His face was friendlier, more tolerant, than it had been when he complained her service was slow a few minutes ago. She began to serve the drinks. She glanced around. Conversation continued all around the bar. Chet Huntley on the screen kept on frowning and saying something about reports being incomplete and maybe not reliable, but only the men sitting alone at the bar seemed to be paying him any attention. She put the Seven and Seven before the man who had spoken, the Carta Blanca before the woman to his left, the Cutty . . . and so on. She never put things down on tables wrong.

"You got pretty legs, Red," the man said to her. He nodded. "Pretty legs. Here's to you. Why don't you get another round ordered for us? Way it goes in here, these'll be gone before you get back."

She nodded, and walked toward the two-top at the window to see if Mr. Gonzalez needed another bloody mary. Mr. Gonzalez always had two bloody marys and a bowl of soup for lunch. He always read his paper and kept to himself. And he always left a dollar on the table.

"Another bloody mary, Mr. Gonzalez?" she asked brightly, as she always did. He smiled at her and nodded. "Do you hear the news up there?" she asked, glancing toward the television set. He frowned and nodded. "I can't believe it," she said. He shook his head again.

At the bar she recited her order to Gil—"One Heineken, one Carta Blanca, one Forester on the rocks, one Seven and Seven, one Cutty and soda, one bloody mary."

Chet Huntley's voice had taken on a strident tone. She thought she could see him tremble on the television screen. "The motorcade rushed out of downtown Dallas and to a nearby hospital . . . Parkland Memorial Hospital. Reports coming from the hospital describe Mr. Kennedy as bleeding and unconscious as he was carried into the hospital. Mrs. Kennedy was in the car with the president when he was shot, but we simply have no word at this moment as to whether or not Mrs. Kennedy was hit also. We're trying to find out, but the confusion around the hospital there is apparently . . . Well, it's very difficult to get accurate information. We keep trying. We'll report whatever we can. . . ."

The man at the bar, who had spoken to her before, touched her arm lightly. "It's unbelievable, isn't it? I mean, I thought we'd progressed in this country to where we're beyond that sort of thing."

Tommy Jo shook her head. She glanced around the room. Some people at the tables *were* listening—that is, were straining to listen, over the babble of conversation at most of the tables. She looked up at the television screen, at the stricken face of Chet Huntley, and she wanted to cry. She couldn't, here, and she wasn't sure why she wanted to; but *he*, up there on the screen, wanted to cry, too, and couldn't, and he did know why.

She looked at faces in the room—the tight, tanned face of an outdoor man, a cattleman probably, pinching his cigarette tightly between thin lips, squinting at the screen, studying the voice and the face, skeptical, contained; a woman, gesticulating with a drink and a cigarette, laughing, slapping up a flimsy but as yet unbroken barrier of centripetal talk to keep the separation between her and whatever in the world might jar her; one of the other waitresses, staring stupidly at the television screen, not because of what was on the screen but because *something* was on the screen, which was enough to hold her distracted; and Mr. Gonzalez, aged, full of knowledge, watchful, absorbing . . .

"Teejay?"

She glanced at Gil, who had put her drinks on her tray. She went to Mr. Gonzalez first, with his bloody mary, then to the four-top. She hurried back to the bar to hear what Chet Huntley was saying.

"More eyewitnesses are adding to what we know about the president—that his wound is in the head and very serious. Indeed, the phrase now being used on the UPI wire is 'serious and perhaps fatal' —and that wire-service bulletin comes from a reporter at the hospital in Dallas."

Tommy Jo wished she were not here, not here and not with these people. She wanted to be with someone she could talk to, like Cole or Professor Jarman or her roommate Kathy Lowe; she wanted to be with friends, so she would not have to contain in silence all she thought and felt.

". . . reports that a priest—two priests, actually—have come to Parkland Memorial Hospital and entered the emergency room where President Kennedy was carried more than half an hour ago . . ."

"Tommy Jo." The man at the bar was speaking to her: the man with the martini. She turned toward him. "Tommy Jo, do you ever, uh, go out after work? I mean, would you be interested in getting together later, like maybe for dinner or a show and so on?" The man was sober, expectant, waiting for her to answer, regarding her with cool, unmoving eyes.

She shook her head. "I can't, uh—I go to school. I have to study every night."

"One night off," he suggested, smiling. "We could have a really good time."

"Sorry."

Embarrassed now, the man shrugged resentfully and looked away from her.

She left the bar. She was responsible for other tables and she felt drawn to check them, to be doing something. To be doing something routine affirmed life. She went to each of her tables and was in the middle of the room when the tone of Chet Huntley's voice at last silenced everyone, and everyone stared at the screen.

"This is official. We do not have an announcement from the White House, but word has come out from the hospital—apparently reliable word—that John F. Kennedy, thirty-fifth president of the United States —is dead."

Tommy Jo wept. Standing in the middle of the silent crowd, where the funereal voice of Huntley at last reached every ear, she wept quietly—not from grief but from shock and bewilderment. And from fear. She shuddered with cold fear of death, of how powerfully it overcame life, how suddenly, leaving the living with empty hands, unable even to reach out for what it took from them. She had a sense of standing abruptly in next month or next year, that yesterday and today had been jerked away, into the distance, before she was finished with them. It was a fearful, gripping feeling: of loss and abandonment and disorientation.

A buzz of talk overrode Huntley. Tommy Jo looked around. She saw heads shaking, mouths open, eyes wide. She saw no other tears. She saw some smiles.

She stood near the four-top where the man had told her she had pretty legs. He looked up at her and saw the tears on her cheeks. "Hey, Red," he said cheerily. "Lemme tell ya somethin'. There's a saying that God looks out for little children, drunk men, and the United States of America. Well, you can believe it today." He smirked and toasted her with Seven and Seven.

VIII

Teejay could not sleep in jail. Janie could and did, and that gave Teejay the only privacy she had, her only chance to be alone. She spent hours awake, every night. When she was too restless and tense and too uncomfortable to lie longer on her bunk, she would roll off and stand at the cell door and smoke, and think. Miserable from the heat and damp with sweat, wearing only what she slept in, her panties, she leaned into the cool steel bars, sometimes hooking an elbow around a bar, sometimes resting one bare foot on a cross brace; she smoked and sometimes she cried quietly. She did not adjust to imprisonment. She remained frustrated and angry, and her helplessness was constant agony.

Lois came every other day now. She had obtained from Judge Spencer an order requiring the district attorney to give her access to Teejay's office files, which had been seized on subpoena the day she was arrested. She had conferred with Kevin Flint's attorney and had obtained an interview with Flint in the men's jail. Lois's chief concern remained Flint.

"How long have you known Kevin Flint and how well?" she asked repeatedly.

"He's a friend. He's been a friend for years. 1 don't even remember exactly where I met him. He's been around."

"Teejay . . ." Lois sighed. "I have to ask: Did you and Kevin sleep together?"

"Never."

"The district attorney thinks you did. He thinks that was the relationship."

Teejay shook her head. "Tell me something, Lois," she said, lifting her chin high. "Did you ever have a close friendship with a man and *not* have someone suspect you were sleeping with him?"

Lois opened her suede briefcase and pulled out a yellow legal pad already heavily scrawled over with notes. Teejay tugged at the hem of her faded gray uniform, trying to pull it down to her knees. She had noted the details of Lois's aqua-colored, full-skirted dress: meticulously styled, thoughtfully selected for Lois's long, angular body.

"Your relationship with Kevin Flint," said Lois in that flat, forthright tone that was so characteristic of her, "is not just a matter of scandal. It's a basic element of the case against you. If it were not for your relationship with Flint, you would not be in jail, I should think."

"I'm in jail, Lois," said Teejay angrily, "because Bill Hornwood is only one of the many people in Houston who are overjoyed to have me here. That's why I'm in jail."

"No," said Lois sharply. She tossed her gold pen down on the legal pad. "Every time I come to see you, you waste half our time talking about the way Houston hates you and wants to destroy you. I've sat and listened and haven't stopped you, because I understand how you have to feel. But your emotions, Teejay, are getting in the way of our building a defense for you."

"How can we defend?" Teejay demanded tearfully. "I'm convicted already. They've locked me up like an animal, and they're gloating over me!"

"*No!*" Lois barked. She slapped the table hard. "No. You are not in jail because you are being persecuted. You are in jail because you are being *prosecuted*. For aggravated murder. And they've got a case. I don't know if we can beat it. I can tell you one thing for sure—we can't beat it if you don't face it rationally. Two weeks ago you demanded I get Norma Jean Spencer to be your trial judge, and I got her. But that's the last time you contributed anything to your own defense."

"Okay, okay!" Teejay yelled. "To answer your original question, Kevin never fucked me. There's a goddamn *fact*. There's a fact you can work with. No emotion in it. It's—a fact."

Teejay's eyes were flooded with tears, and she blinked and squeezed them out to run down her cheeks. She glared at Lois accusingly, blinking and sucking in short breaths to stop sobs.

Lois stood and knocked on the inside of the cubicle door to summon the matron. "I'll come back tomorrow," she said. She picked up her yellow legal pad and stuffed it into her briefcase.

"Why bother?" Teejay whispered.

For an hour she hated Lois Hughes. Lois had the power to send her back inside the jail. With a couple of raps on the door, Lois had given the signal that sent her out for the humiliating body search and then back inside the locked doors and steel bars. Inside "B" Cage, she ignored Janie's invitation to join a card game and went inside their cell and sat down on her bunk. It was only ten in the morning; another day stretched ahead of her, during which she would do nothing. She had thought of some things she should tell Lois, but Lois had punished her for being emotional by sending her back inside the bars for another day. Lois would talk to her tomorrow, if she could control herself tomorrow. The telephone was outside. She could demand to be allowed to make a call. She could dismiss Lois and call in another lawyer. She could . . .

Instead, she left the cell and walked along the barred wall of "B" Cage from one end to the other, touching each bar idly with her fingertips, musing, considering. She lit a cigarette then and stood behind the cardplayers and watched. She declined another invitation to join the game. She paced up and down the cellblock. She did nothing.

Lois faced her on Wednesday morning as if Tuesday morning had not happened—professionally calm, vaguely smiling, her long, thick hair once more a bit windblown. She offered Teejay a cigarette. Teejay sucked hard on the cigarette and held the smoke down as long as she could. Her face was flushed. She gleamed with perspiration.

"One thing I need to ask you," she said to Lois. "What about the federal indictment?"

Lois turned up her palms. "I called the U.S. district attorney's office. No word. I can't help but think they're dropping the whole thing, but I can't get them to say so."

"I don't know if I could take it—to have another indictment handed in through the bars of my cell."

"I wouldn't worry about that. The feds have no inclination to pile it on you."

Teejay pondered for a moment, holding smoke in her mouth. "On second thought, it might be better for me if they did indict me. My motive for killing Mudge is supposed to have been to avoid the federal indictment, isn't it? If I'm indicted anyway, that weakens that idea."

"It's a thought," said Lois noncommittally, her attention on her yellow legal pad and her notes.

"It's a weakness in the prosecution anyway, Lois. Have you looked at the cases? What has anyone ever been sentenced to for violating the Interstate Land Sales Full Disclosure Act? Four years? I have a clean record. Chances are, if I had been convicted—which is a big if—I would have gotten a fine and probation. It's going to be hard to make out a case that I killed a man and risked life in prison to avoid a federal indictment for violation of Section 1703."

"On that conviction you'd have been disbarred," said Lois dryly, still looking at her notes.

"Financially ruined," said Teejay quietly. "Everything I ever worked for. But I've been broke before, don't forget. You and I are different on that score."

Lois looked up from her notes. "I suppose I can assume," she said, "there was no intimate relationship between you and Benjamin Mudge."

Teejay smiled ruefully. "The man was in his seventies. Ugly as a rattlesnake and with just about as much personality. He smoked cigars." She shook her head.

"Did he ever ask you?"

Teejay shook her head again.

"The detectives from the D.A.'s office are looking for the man in your life. I'm sorry to have to ask, but who are they going to find?"

Teejay frowned. "Nobody," she said.

"If that's so, that brings them back to Kevin Flint," said Lois. "And that means I've got to know more about your relationship with Kevin Flint."

Frowning deeply, Teejay ran her hand hard across her scalp, and with the other hand she pressed her cigarette hard to her mouth. "Recite it," she mumbled.

"What?"

"Recite the case again. I—If Kevin doesn't *testify* against me, I—"

"You don't see why he's so important," said Lois. "All right. To put everything in its proper frame of reference, let's recite it, point by point. First"—she ticked off the points on her fingers—"Benjamin Mudge is dead. Second, Kevin Flint killed him. Third, there is no apparent motive for Kevin Flint to have killed Mudge. He—"

"What about the money?" Teejay interrupted.

"Yes, ten thousand dollars in cash was found in Kevin Flint's apartment. But there is no reason to think he took it off Mudge. No one remembers Mudge carrying large amounts of money on his person, and he didn't withdraw any large amount from any of his accounts within the few days just before he was killed. In fact, he never withdrew more than pocket money from any account."

"He had sources of money all over," said Teejay.

"Not that anyone knows about," said Lois. "Anyway, four, *you* had a motive for killing Mudge. Five, you and Kevin Flint had some kind of close relationship yet to be defined. *Ergo,* you had Flint kill Mudge, or Flint killed him for you, for some reason."

Teejay sighed and ground out her cigarette in the black plastic ashtray on the table. "It's speculation," she said.

"Bill Hornwood is no fool, Teejay," she said grimly. "It's more than speculation, or he wouldn't have had you indicted. He won't come into the courtroom with a case that's ridiculously weak. That would be political disaster for him, and he won't bring a disaster on himself. So I keep asking you: What could Hornwood know about you and Kevin Flint?"

Teejay turned away from Lois and stared at the pencil marks on the wall of the cubicle for a moment. "What if he had some letters Kevin wrote to me? How much would that hurt?"

"What do those letters say?" Lois asked quickly.

Teejay turned toward her again. "Well, they don't say he killed Mudge for me. They were love letters. What if Hornwood got them?"

"Where would he have gotten them?"

"Out of my apartment. They had a warrant to search it."

Lois stiffened, drew herself more erect. "They would be disaster," she said somberly.

Teejay folded her hands on the table and leaned toward Lois. "Suppose he didn't find them but *you* did. What would you do with them?"

"What do you mean, what would *I* do with them?"

"I can tell you where they were. If Hornwood's boys didn't find them when they searched the apartment on their warrant, then those letters are still there. If I tell you where to find them, what will you do with them?"

"What do you have in mind?"

Teejay's eyes met Lois's. "You've got to burn them for me."

Lois shook her head. "I can't destroy evidence," she protested breathlessly.

"They are not evidence," said Teejay evenly. "Read them. They don't say anything about Mudge. They were written a long time ago. They're not part of Hornwood's case. In fact, he got his indictment before he got his search warrant, so if he has found them he got the indictment without them. All he could possibly use them for is to prejudice a jury against me. If they were read in the courtroom—Jesus, Lois, I've hung on those bars upstairs in the night, thinking about those letters, all that Kevin said. You've met Kevin now. He's a beautiful man, but he's a goddamn fool!"

"I can't destroy evidence for you," Lois said. "I might bring them here, to you—"

"I can't take in anything you bring me. I'm searched when I leave here to go back inside."

"You're a lawyer yourself, Teejay. You know what I can do and can't do," Lois argued.

"Get your hands on the letters and read them," Teejay said. "If you don't want to destroy them, put them back where you found them. Or if you don't find them, we'll know Hornwood has them; we'll know that much anyway. All I ask is that you don't be some kind of Girl Scout and think you have to turn them over to Hornwood."

Lois sighed heavily. "I won't do that. But ethics—"

"I know something about ethics myself," Teejay interrupted. "I took the same course you did. But you and I aren't sitting on some cute bar committee debating fine points of ethics, Lois. I'm asking you to do something that's maybe inside the rules and maybe out; it's questionable, but—"

"It's not questionable," Lois said unhappily.

"It might make the difference between my spending the rest of my life in prison or walking out of that courtroom free," said Teejay.

So it would look businesslike, Lois went to Teejay's apartment in the middle of the afternoon. It was in a brick building of only four apartments, in a middle-class neighborhood just north of Westheimer and just beyond the West Loop. She took the apartment key from her briefcase before she left the car, and wearing sunglasses and carrying the key in her hand she walked across the small parking lot and into the lushly planted little courtyard in the center of the four apartments. Teejay's was number three, and her name was on a card on the doorbell— T. J. Brookover. Lois tried the key, half expecting to find the lock had been changed. The key turned smoothly, and she opened the door.

She was intensely curious about how Teejay lived. She hoped to find clues to her character and personality in the rooms of this apartment. At first, just inside the door, she thought she was to be disappointed. The apartment was immaculate. It had been vacuumed, dusted; not a newspaper or magazine lay as clutter on a table; even the mail was being collected, and only one day's accumulation lay on the floor inside the slot. Someone was taking care of the place while Teejay was in jail. Lois was not sure Teejay knew that.

The living room was comfortably furnished. It had the look, though, of the parlor in an expensive hotel suite; it reflected, Lois felt sure, the taste of an interior decorator, not Teejay. The rose-and-white brocade couch looked new—looked at least as if no one ever sat on it. There was a numbered print on the wall above the couch. It was a good piece, but it looked as if it had been chosen to go with the couch.

Lois crossed the living room quickly. It was not where she was supposed to look for Flint's letters anyway. She entered a hallway and opened a door. This room was personal. It was Teejay's home office, conspicuously a lawyer's office, cluttered with lawbooks, note pads, open files. Whoever came in to clean had been told to stay out of here; the ashtrays remained full. Here, Lois felt an intruder. Teejay had expected to come back here, not to go to jail, and this room was exactly as she had left it. Except . . . Impulsively Lois pulled open a file-cabinet drawer. The files inside had fallen down and lay flat. The district attorney's men had taken many folders from this filing cabinet. She wondered if everything taken from here was on the inventory of things seized, a copy of which she had obtained by court order. A group of letters from Kevin Flint was not on that inventory. If the inventory was incomplete . . . She turned and hurried into the bedroom.

The ashtray was empty. The bed was made. Clothes were put away. The bedroom was exceptionally large, and—here was the revelation of character Lois had been looking for—it was filled with books. Books. Shelves. Every wall, from floor to ceiling, except for the doors and windows, was solid with shelves filled with books. Lois walked around the shelves, fascinated. College textbooks on business and economics. Books on art, on history, on food. Books on the assassination of President Kennedy, in a group. Biographies—political biographies, the biographies of film stars, of lawyers and judges, of presidents and presidents' wives, of artists, of kings: an eclectic gathering of biographies. History—most of it American, some of World War II. Fiction—a varied collection, some good, some bad. The shelves contained maybe six or seven hundred volumes.

Lois opened a double-doored closet. Teejay had a wardrobe as varied as her library. Of interest to Lois: pairs of blue jeans, cotton T-shirts, two or three pairs of jeans raggedly cut off for shorts.

The letters. "It will take a few minutes to get them," Teejay had said. "You'll need a screwdriver." Lois had brought a screwdriver, in her briefcase. She had brought something else, something Teejay had not suggested—a pair of surgical gloves. She was Teejay's lawyer and had every right to leave her fingerprints inside this apartment; but if any question should arise about the letters—whatever she might decide to do with them—it would be better if it could not be proved she had ever touched them. She sat down on Teejay's bed and writhed her hands into the powdered latex gloves. She felt melodramatic, comic-conspiratorial, but she had thought it through and decided, and she did not let acute self-consciousness override a rational decision.

She went into the bathroom and began hurriedly to remove the bottles and jars from the cabinet above the basin. She noticed that Teejay used the same cosmetics she did: Charles of the Ritz. Working as quickly as she could, she set the bottles on the Formica around the basin. She unplugged and set aside Teejay's electric toothbrush. When the cabinet was empty she was confronted, as Teejay had said she would be, with four large round screwheads. She began to unscrew them. She took them out one by one, feeling the cabinet loosen in the wall as each screw was removed. With all four screws out, she seized the cabinet in both hands and pulled it out of the wall. And there were the letters, lying on the two-by-four that framed the gap in the studs where the cabinet had been.

She put the cabinet back and put every jar and bottle back inside before she carried the letters from the bedroom. There were only two letters, in two different envelopes addressed to Tommy Jo Brookover at two different addresses, one in El Paso, one in Houston. One was dated 1966, one 1974.

The 1966 letter, Lois saw when she examined it more closely, was written on the stationery of the Oklahoma State Penitentiary at Mc-Alester. The handwriting was difficult to read.

Dear Tommy Jo,

I promised I'd write you, even if it had to be from a place like this, so here it is, a letter from a man damned ashamed of the letter paper he has to use and the place he has to write from. I don't want to talk about this. I don't think it should have happened, but it did, and I have to live with it. They say I'll be out in less than two years. I hope so.

I know you don't care if I write or don't. You don't believe anything I say. I want to tell you just the same how much I love you and will always love you and how important it is for me to love you and know that maybe there's some chance someday for me to make you love me too.

I'd do anything for you, Tommy Jo—anything to make you think better of me and love me. I want you to know, whatever happens to either of us, you've always got a friend. I love you. Don't think bad of me. Just let me love you. Don't write me here if you don't want to. I'll understand. I'll find you when I get out. Nobody will ever love you like me.

Your devoted,
KEVIN

The 1974 letter was written on a sheet of typing paper and mailed in a plain white envelope from Acapulco.

Dearest Tommy Jo,
  I get the word somebody has told you I'm down here arranging to fly a load of grass back to the States. Don't believe it. I'm no dealer. You and I have shared some good joints, but I've never been a dealer. I've never been into any deals with grass or anything else. I wouldn't want you to believe anything like that about me.
  I've loved every minute we've spent together lately. You've been such a baby doll! Even my big important lawyer lady that's knocking them dead in the Big H is still a baby doll and is always going to be a baby doll to me.
  Even if you won't marry me. I guess I've given up on that. Now that you're a lawyer and have such big plans, I guess you could never marry the likes of Kevin. And maybe you're right when you say neither one of us is the marrying and settling down kind. I guess as long as you don't up and marry someone else, I can't get too upset. I'd do anything in the world, change everything about myself, to get you to marry me. I'd do anything in the world for you, Tommy Jo. You know I would. Because I love you so much. Always.
  Keep healthy. Keep good. I'll be around when I get back.
  I love you as much as ever. That will never change.

Your lover,
KEVIN

Lois laid the yellowing typing sheet down on the other letter and the envelopes, on the bed; and for a long moment she sat frowning, nervously flexing her hands inside the latex gloves. The letters were exactly as Teejay had characterized them: not evidence that she had conspired with Kevin Flint to kill Benjamin Mudge, yet potentially disastrous if they were handed to the jury. The reference to smoking marijuana would prejudice almost any Texas jury. The idea that Teejay and Flint had been lovers for many years—which the letters strongly suggested, however much Teejay might deny it—would tip jurors not tipped by the marijuana. Surely the district attorney had other evidence that Flint and Teejay had been close friends for many years; but these letters would lend to any other evidence an element of life and intimacy. They were as damaging as Teejay feared.

Yet, what did they prove—in the strictly rational sense? Only that Flint and Teejay had known each other at least since 1966 and that their friendship had been more than casual. Of what legitimate value could they be to the prosecution? A prosecutor with a strict sense of decency wouldn't even put them in evidence.

The point was: How would a jury react to them? Rationally, they were nothing. Emotionally and potentially, they were Disaster.

Lois had a reputation for being slow and cautious about making decisions. She was known to weigh every factor endlessly before she acted on a conclusion; and even then the decision was apt to be a compromise, leaving her an escape if she had decided wrong. This formidable reputation missed an element of her personality: that sometimes she moved on reckless impulse. (Or, maybe, in truth, she had pondered and reached her decision before the event.) Anyway, those who relied on her conservatism sometimes erred—sometimes astoundingly, to their regret.

She stood, after thinking for a long moment about the letters. She gathered up letters and envelopes, and within two minutes the tiny bits of them were swimming in the whirlpool in the toilet and shortly disappeared into the pipes.

It was another element of her character, though not of her reputation, that Lois liked to have reinforcement; she liked to have a second opinion. Bob Peavy came home with her after the show at the Alley Theater, and after Wendy and Mac John, Jr., finally went to bed, they made Irish coffee and carried it to Lois's bedroom. As they sipped the Irish coffee, Lois told him about the letters and what she had done.

"I don't like to dump my problems on you, but I feel I have to have another reading," she said. "Don't tell me what the Standards of Professional Conduct say; I know what they say. Tell me what you would have done."

They sat together on a couch, facing the low table on which their glasses sat. He had put aside his jacket and his necktie; she had kicked her shoes into a corner of the room. They sat close, their hips touching.

Bob Peavy chuckled. "You want me to tell you I'd have done what you did," he said. "I can't say that. I don't think I would have. On the other hand, I stay out of the courtroom, and I've never represented a client like T. J. Brookover. I guess I should say that nothing more important than hundreds of millions of dollars has ever been at stake on my desk. I've never handled a criminal case. I've never handled a divorce or a custody fight. I've never arranged an adoption or challenged one. I've never done anything in the law that had to do with people. I work with dollars. So what the hell do I know?"

Lois yawned. "I feel like I've been one of two things today: a tough lawyer doing something to defend my client, or a despicable shyster destroying evidence in violation of every principle. I did it. It's over. But I would like to know what another lawyer thinks."

"Well," said Peavy. He stopped his glass short of his lips. "If I remember correctly, the indictment was a surprise to her. Right?"

Lois nodded. "She says she didn't know Flint killed Mudge. She didn't know he'd been arrested. The indictment was returned in secret, and as soon as they netted Flint, they went out and got her. She says she was utterly dumbstruck to be arrested."

"Okay," said Peavy. "If so, why did she go to such elaborate lengths to hide a couple of letters from Kevin Flint?"

Lois whispered, flushing, *"Jesus Christ!"*

"They must have been important to her," Peavy continued. "What's more, they're still important. She got you to destroy them for her."

"Jesus, did I destroy evidence for her?" Lois whispered.

Peavy shrugged and smiled. "I think you did."

"Then she's guilty as hell!"

Peavy's smile spread into a grin. "No. Not necessarily. Let me ask another question. If those letters were all that important, why didn't she destroy them herself, instead of hiding them? Baby, I think there're some complications in this case."

IX

1965

Tommy Jo peered over the bar, trying to see between the broad backs and through the smoke. On the pool table in the center of the room, $1000 was at stake, and dead silence had settled. The man with the cue—tall, thin, taciturn, intense—wore an out-of-style tuxedo with sharp satin lapels, and his thinning black hair was slicked down with shiny oil. He put his cigarette down on the table's edge. His eyes narrowed to slits. He lined up his shot quickly, decisively, and stroked the cue smoothly. The white cue ball darted across the table and sharply drove the lavender four ball against the rail. The four ball rebounded at an angle, crossed the table to the opposite rail, then rolled toward a corner pocket. It struck the ten ball lying near the lip of the pocket, and the ten ball dropped. The man picked up the black pea lying on the rail by his cigarette and turned it over to show the numeral 10 on the flat side. Casually he scooped up a pile of cash and pushed it into his jacket pocket.

"Goddamn!" someone muttered. Then a spatter of applause began.

The room was not crowded. It was a suite at El Abejorro, and no one was there who had not been invited. The man in the tuxedo—whose name Tommy Jo still had not caught—was a hustler from Chicago. Anyone who wanted to challenge him could challenge. He had

been brought to El Paso by a sports promoter named Tiny Half. Tiny
had hired Tommy Jo and another cocktail waitress from the Casablanca to work behind the bar. They wore black leotards and fishnet
stockings. They mixed drinks behind the bar; they did not carry them
through the suite. There were no tips, but the money was good. They
had time to smoke and sometimes to catch a glimpse of an interesting
shot on the table.

"That's how he makes his money," said a young man who had come
to the bar and noticed Tommy Jo watching the four-ball-ten-ball shot.
He spoke softly and grinned. "A man's a fool to bet money on a pea-
pool game with a hustler like that."

"What would you play?" Tommy Jo asked. The young man was
handsome, and his smile was appealing, and she didn't mind making
conversation with him.

"Nine ball, if I can get a game with him."

"He takes all comers," she said.

"He wants a lot of money," the young man said. "Let me have a
ginger ale."

The young man took his ginger ale and approached the table. The
hustler stood with the butt of his cue on the floor, smoking, sipping
from a glass, talking. He was negotiating another game. The young
man stood close to him. He was not as tall as the hustler, nor as thin.
He had curly blond hair and shifty blue eyes. He wore gray slacks and
a gray turtleneck shirt. He waited his chance to speak to the hustler.
Tommy Jo strained to hear what the two of them said. She caught parts
of their talk.

"Y' any good?" "Fifty says so." "Couldn't play y' for just fifty, son."
". . . guys'll back me maybe." ". . . don' care whose money we play
for, long's it's money."

They arranged a game. The young man put up his own $50, and
backers around the room—some of whom didn't even know him—put
$200 behind him. "One game of nine ball for two-fifty," the hustler an-
nounced.

Tiny, the promoter, racked the balls. The young man and the hustler
lagged for the break, and the hustler's ball stopped closer to the back
rail. He chose to break. He drove the cue ball ferociously into the rack
of nine balls and they scattered. None dropped.

The young man chalked his cue as he studied the table. He walked
around, looking nervous, studying. The hustler stood at a respectful
distance, heavy-lidded, attentive. Cigarette smoke hung like a sheet
in the air under the light.

The young man bent over the table and sighted along his cue.
Tommy Jo noticed how his tight gray slacks stretched across his taut

narrow bottom. He shot. The cue ball slipped between the six and eight and cut the yellow one ball into a side pocket. The cue ball rolled to the far end of the table, struck the rail uncomfortably close to a corner pocket as onlookers gasped, and rolled back down.

The cue ball rolled into a nearly straight shot for the two ball in the corner. The young man sank the two. The cue ball drew back with reverse English and struck the four and five, separating them. The red three ball was on the rail. He drove the cue ball against it gently, and the three skidded up the rail, across a side pocket, and dropped in the distant corner.

"Table's level," the young man muttered.

Tommy Jo poured herself a glass of ginger ale. She noticed that the young man's face was flushed now, and perspiration gleamed on his forehead. He lined up a shot on the lavender four ball. He stroked. The cue ball struck the four to one side and sent it rolling slowly toward the yellow-striped nine. The nine! The four almost stopped before it hit it. It cut the nine, which rolled away at a sharp angle, between the outreaching corners of a side pocket, where it fell quietly out of sight.

The hustler nodded and pushed the cash down the rail toward the young man. "Young fella's wasted his youth," he said with a faint smile.

The young man began passing out money, paying off his backers.

"Hey, double or nothin'," said the hustler.

The young man shook his head. "A hundred," he said.

"Aw, son. Can't hardly play pool for a hundred."

"I play with my money now, and that's what I've got."

The hustler's brows rose. He rubbed his pointed chin. "Well . . ." he shrugged.

Men crowded around the table, and Tommy Jo could not see any more. But she heard the hustler complain there wasn't enough money on the game. A dozen gamblers wanted to back the young man, now that they had seen him win. They pressed around, excitedly offering bets to the hustler. Suddenly they fell silent, and she heard the young man quietly explain that he was not going to play pool for other people's thousand-dollar bets unless they paid him twenty percent of anything he won for them. There was talk, some of it angry, and out of it they came to a deal: that he would play for fifteen percent of what they won on him.

He and the hustler played for an hour. He won some and lost some. She couldn't follow the talk about balls and odds and percentages, but when it was over she supposed he had come out a winner. He came to the bar, and she asked him.

"Ah," he said. He took a beer. "I got about six hundred out of it, I guess." She knew he was lying. His face was too bright with pride and elation for him not to know, to the dollar, how much he had won. He remained flushed and now a little high, a little up in the air; he even bounced up and down on the balls of his feet. His curly light hair fell over his red forehead. He grinned. He glanced all around to see how many were still watching him. "Hey!" he exclaimed to her.

She laughed. "I was pulling for you," she said.

"Then that's why I won," he said. "Here," he said impulsively, taking out his rolled-up money and pulling off a ten-dollar bill. "Your share." He laughed and pushed it across the bar to her.

"You shouldn't do that."

"Sure I should."

One of the gamblers called him away from the bar, and she did not hear his name.

He came into the Casablanca a week later, sat at the bar, saw her, and introduced himself. His name was Kevin Flint. The next time he came in he asked her to have dinner with him and she accepted.

"I'm selling an advertising-and-marketing idea," he told her over steaks and red wine. He explained sketchily that he would publish a business directory for El Paso, listing restaurants, shops, services, and so on; and anyone who bought one of these books for a dollar could obtain up to a hundred dollars' worth of gifts and discounts by presenting the coupons that would be printed with the ads in the book. Businesses that wanted to attract new customers would buy ads and agree to honor the gift and discount coupons.

Tommy Jo could not suppress a smile. "I've heard of those deals," she said quietly.

"Teach you about them at school?"

She nodded. "I'm majoring in business administration."

"What do they call them?" he asked, amused.

"Frauds," she said blandly, still smiling.

Kevin laughed.

"Do you make a lot of money on a proposition like that?" she asked.

He shrugged. "Depends on how many we sell. It isn't all a fraud, you know. It *could* work out."

"Do you pay a commission on sales of ads for your book?"

"Commission, salary, whatever."

"Could *I* make any money selling some?"

He shook his head. "I wouldn't let you. When it's all over, there'll probably be some complaints. I mean, we have to assume there will be some complaints. I won't be here to listen to them. You will be."

He shook his head. "No. Not a good idea."

He took her to a university baseball game and to dinner twice more —each time telling her his sales campaign was almost over and he would be leaving any day. He picked her up in a black Mercury convertible with Arizona plates, at the Casablanca after she finished work or at the apartment she shared with two other students. He said he was from Mississippi and that he had worked hard to rid himself of his accent. Traces of it remained, she told him—attractive traces in his unhurried and precise way of speaking and in certain archaic phrases he occasionally used.

She still saw Coleman Bishop. He took her out every other week. He came into the Casablanca one day at noon, in uniform, and sat at the bar and drank a Coke. He told her she ought to be careful what company she kept, that this Kevin Flint she was going out with had a criminal record. "Been arrested two or three times, charges of larceny by trick. Charges dropped all but once. He got sixty days and probation on the once they weren't dropped."

At dinner—this time Kevin saying he was leaving El Paso *for sure* in a couple of days—she regarded him with new curiosity. It was hard to imagine him in a police mug shot, being fingerprinted, being jailed, or any of that. It was so inconsistent with his insouciance. She did not appreciate Cole Bishop's having run a check on Kevin and having come to tell her what he'd learned. She did not like that at all.

She liked Kevin. Handsome, roguish Kevin. She liked the way he and she were stared at. He was handsome, and she knew she was beautiful; in common they took what advantage they could of being physically attractive. He dressed well. She had learned to dress. On their dates she wore long, soft skirts, light knit blouses; she wore little makeup, and she kept her long, rich red hair brushed out, smooth and lustrous.

"Tommy Jo . . ." he said to her hesitantly. "I really am finished here in El Paso. I'm going to leave. This time I really am."

"I'll miss you, Kevin," she said quietly.

"I . . . made up my mind to say somethin'." He paused and nodded nervously. "I have to say it, Tommy Jo. I can't leave without saying it. I gotta tell you, I think you're the finest person I've ever set eyes on. The plain truth is, I love you. I really do—love you, Tommy Jo."

She was not surprised, and yet she was shocked. She could not speak. Her throat was too tight. She reached across the table and took his hand.

"I—made up my mind I couldn't ask you to marry me, to give up goin' to school and all, to run off with me and live out of a car and motel rooms, like I do. Then I got to thinkin'. I decided that's not for me to decide; maybe you'd *want* to do it, and I should let you make up your own mind. If you want to, Tommy Jo, all I can tell you is, I'll spend the rest of my life doing anything I can do in this world to make you happy."

Three months later she went home to LaGrange. She and her mother had exchanged letters, but she had not been home since she and her cousin Lee left home in the fall of 1961. She did not want to drag home on a bus, like a defeated daughter coming to ask for help and she could not afford to rent a car, so she let Kevin drive her home in his Mercury convertible. He had left El Paso, as he had said he must, but ten weeks later he had come back. He looked good, wearing a blue blazer, white shirt, red and dark blue striped necktie, and gray flannel slacks tailored to hug his butt and crotch; and he stopped just short of the Clayton County line and had the Mercury washed. Kevin had as much of a sense of the dramatic as she had—in fact, more.

They planned to stay Saturday and Sunday. Kevin made a point of finding a room for himself across the county line, conspicuously not in the Motel Rancho where she took a room. He came to the motel to pick her up early in the morning, and he stayed with her all day. She had asked him to.

Her mother was full of talk. She had much to say, about people in LaGrange, her vegetable garden, the price of cattle, the rains that did not fall, and about how it was to live with Aunt Serena. When Tommy Jo told her she might graduate from the university with nothing but "A" grades, her mother nodded and said Serena's arthritis made her crabbier every day.

Kevin drove her around. They drove out to the ranch house where Tommy Jo had grown up, and she told him how she used to sit on the porch and count the cars that passed on the highway. They drove past her high school and past the Pentecostal Holiness Church. The school and church seemed newly shabby, as if they had not been maintained well the past four years. The men and women on the main street of LaGrange looked older and slower. They looked as if they were powdered with windblown dust, the same as buildings and trucks.

On Sunday, Aunt Serena had lunch for them. Some of the family came. A cousin of Aunt Serena's—no relation to Tommy Jo—was Earl Lansing, one of the three lawyers in Clayton County. Tommy Jo remembered him vividly. His reputation was for sly dealing. She could remember her father complaining that Earl had beaten so-and-so out of his property, so-and-so out of a good deal, so-and-so out of an inheritance. He had practiced law for thirty years, and he owned land he had taken as a fee, and cattle, and two or three houses he rented in LaGrange. He was a slight, gray, balding man with bad teeth and watery blue eyes, and he was the only man at the luncheon, except Kevin, who wore a jacket and a necktie. After lunch, when Aunt Serena had retired upstairs for her afternoon nap and Tommy Jo's mother was deep in conversation with two cousins, Lansing suggested that Tommy Jo and Kevin walk down the street to his office.

"Need a drink," Lansing said when they were inside his office above the hardware store and he had turned on the window air conditioner. "Figured you two would join me in somethin'." He had a small white refrigerator behind two filing cabinets. "Got beer, bourbon, Scotch, gin . . . What'll it be?"

Kevin took a beer. Tommy Jo let him pour her a Scotch.

Glass in hand, Lansing leaned back in his cracked old leather chair and lifted his feet to the corner of his desk. Prosperous, self-confident, at ease in the cobwebby, dusty clutter of his office, he was surrounded by a formidable defense against anything the town might elect to throw at him: a wall of mysterious heavy books, reinforced by stacks of threatening, official-looking papers. Tommy Jo formed and absorbed deep into her consciousness a vivid impression of him and his office.

"Understood you to say you're going to the university in El Paso," he said to her after they had chatted for a while about nothing much. "You doing well?"

"She's going to graduate with nothing but A's on her record," said Kevin.

"Summa cum laude!" said Lansing. He whistled. "Well, I guess I shouldn't be surprised. Her high-school record here was . . . But your cousin Lee came back here from El Paso, Tommy Jo, saying you were working as a drive-in waitress. I was disappointed with that. I expected you to do better."

She had not been aware he could feel disappointed with her or had any expectations of her. "Well, I—I had to get out of town and get started somewhere else some way," she said.

Lansing sipped from his glass. "Let me give you a little lesson in life, Tommy Jo," he said. "Never be reluctant to ask people for help. If you had come to me, I would have helped you get out of LaGrange and get started somewhere else on a better basis. Or suppose I hadn't helped you—suppose I'd told you to go away and don't bother me. What harm? It couldn't have hurt to ask."

"I didn't know," she said quietly.

He nodded. "Of course you didn't. That's the point. What's your major?"

"Business administration."

"Ah . . . And what are you going to do after you graduate?"

She sighed. "I don't know for sure. In fact, I don't know at all."

"With a degree in business administration, a young woman is apt to wind up a secretary," he said. "That's the way a lot of businesses are going to look at you. Another word of advice: When you go out to interview for jobs and they ask you how many words a minute you type, you tell 'em you *don't* type and *won't* type."

Tommy Jo grinned. "The 'don't' part will be the truth, too."

"Seriously," said Lansing. "They'll want to make a secretary of you, because you're female. You'll have to find an enlightened and thoughtful guy who'll see beyond that one fact. That's the way it is in business."

"Are you telling me four years of college isn't worth much?" she asked.

He shook his head emphatically. "I'm not telling you that. I don't mean to discourage you. I just want to give you a realistic picture of what you'll be up against."

"Suppose I went to law school," she said impulsively. She was surprised to hear herself say it. She had never thought of it until they came into this office.

"Ah . . ." said Lansing with a broad smile. "Then you'd have a *profession*. You could tell 'em to shove their typewriter up their backside. I don't want to *promote* law school to you, Tommy Jo; but I will tell you, that certificate you hang on your wall that says you're a doctor, lawyer, dentist, whatever—a professional—that's your declaration of independence. Whatever that says you are, they can never take away from you. You work here, you work there, that certificate, that license, that's worth a lot."

"How would I find out more about law schools?"

Lansing shrugged. "Talk to your faculty adviser. Go see the school. There're a few scholarships, I suppose. Check it out. Check it out, Tommy Jo."

X

Late Tuesday afternoon, one of the women in "B" Cage stabbed another and killed her. It happened while the women were eating their final meal of the day. Teejay was sitting hunched in silence over the compartmented tin box into which her food had been ladled through the cage bars. She was eating with a spoon, the only utensil allowed. The meal was unsalted spaghetti with a few crumbs of gray hamburger, unbuttered but long-boiled and mushy lima beans, unbuttered white bread. Janie was on the floor, and an older woman, a shoplifter named Murdock who had befriended the two of them, was sitting on the floor just outside their cell. Murdock, who always ate fast and finished first, had begun to talk and was saying something about another jail where she had served time, when the woman in the far end of the block stabbed her cellmate.

Teejay heard the actual blows of the knife and the agonized scream that immediately degenerated into the resigned, gurgling moan of the woman dying. Teejay clapped her hand to her mouth and smothered a cry of shock. With a shrill yell, Janie jumped up and rushed out to see what was happening. An alarm bell began to ring deafeningly, and suddenly the cell door slid across in its track and clanked shut. Teejay was locked inside the cell, and Janie was locked out. Women ran through "B" Cage, yelling. They began to throw dinner boxes and tin cups. Murdock grabbed Janie and wrestled her to the floor, trying to shield her. Teejay clung to the bars. She smelled smoke. There was a fire in one of the cells. She screamed.

The first deputies who trotted into the jail wore gas masks. Afraid of tear gas, Teejay backed away from the cell door and stood slack, cowering, and sobbing in the middle of the cell. Then other deputies and Houston policemen came in; and immediately "B" Cage was subdued without tear gas, under the menacing barrels of their riot guns. The alarm bell stopped clanging, and an angry bullhorn voice ordered all prisoners to stretch out on their bellies on the floor with their arms extended in front of them.

Teejay dropped, first to her knees, then to her belly, and stretched the way they were ordered. For the next half-hour she knew only what she could hear and what she glimpsed from the corners of her eyes: the arrival of the emergency-squad men and their protracted, futile ritual of an attempt to revive the stabbed woman; the seizure of the woman who had killed her, hustled out of the cellblock wailing that the matrons had pinched her with the handcuffs that pinned her arms behind her back; the removal of the body at last, on a wheeled cot; the relaxation of tension among the deputies and policemen, who milled about casually after a while, smoking, talking, making crude jokes about the women who lay on the concrete inside the bars, afraid to move to relieve their cramped muscles, thwacked by the billies in the hands of the matrons if they did.

Teejay cried quietly part of the time. There was nothing to do but cry.

The men left. Houston policewomen came in, carrying riot guns too, and formed an orderly line with their backs to the brick wall, their guns facing the cage. The matrons opened the cells and ordered all prisoners out. They ordered all prisoners to stand and face the barred cage wall. Then they ordered them to strip and to toss their clothes outside the bars. In a minute thirty-five women, young and old, thin and fat, black and white, stood naked in a rigid line touching the cage wall, their hands tightly clasped behind their heads. This, the matrons announced, is a shakedown.

They shook down the cells first. Women who turned to look, to see what was happening in their cells, were prodded back with the matrons' billies. The matrons tossed contraband through the bars, where it lay on the floor at the feet of the policewomen. They found two more knives. They found marijuana and a variety of capsules. They found money. The found a pint of whiskey. Teejay wondered how women smuggled things like this into the jail—where she had been unable to find a way to bring in even a cigarette they didn't know about. From her cell they threw out her ballpoint pen. She recognized it as it clattered across the floor. It was a weapon. She could not cry, not anymore. She stood weak, her lips apart, her eyelids heavy: enduring.

In the cell, locked in some three hours early, Teejay and Janie were spent and quiet. Janie had not suggested pulling the mattress pads to the floor and folding up the bunks. They lay on their bunks. Janie tossed and did not sleep. Teejay, lying on her back and facing the stretched springs of Janie's bunk two feet from the tip of her nose, tried at first to sleep. She could not. Tense with confused and overlapping emotions, she could not sleep or cry.

Lois had been in that morning. It was easy to resent Lois: always so well dressed, so briskly confident—Lois, who was sipping her before-dinner drinks somewhere and would soon sit down in candlelight to wine and good food. She had become demanding. She was trying to reconstruct the Lago Aguila business. Her questions were tough.

"Why did Mudge come to you? He had been represented by Todd and Graybar for years. Why did he bring this business to you?"

Teejay did not like the question—because she did not like the answer. She had tried to evade at first: "Why not? Don't you think I was lawyer enough to handle a deal like that?"

"That's hardly the point, is it?" said Lois evenly. "Todd and Graybar represented him on everything else. Why did he come to you with this one proposition? Didn't you wonder?"

"Confidentiality," said Teejay. "Or secrecy, if you want. He thought the lots at Lago Aguila would sell better if his name were not associated—"

"I'm sure he was right about that," Lois observed wryly.

"If . . ." said Teejay. "If Todd and Graybar did the legal work, Mudge's involvement would be obvious." She shrugged. "Anyway, I asked him just what you are asking me, and that's what he said."

"Turning the question around then," said Lois, "why did you take him as a client? He had a filthy reputation."

"That didn't seem to bother Todd and Graybar," Teejay snapped aggressively. "Would it have bothered your firm? Or are only lawyers in firms of less than a hundred lawyers supposed to worry about things like that? Lago Aguila was a forty-million-dollar business proposition. It was a breakthrough for me. Why shouldn't I take it? Can you say you wouldn't have?"

"I don't think Todd and Graybar would have exposed themselves to the risk of the federal indictments you risked. I *know* Childreth, Mc-Lennon and Brady wouldn't," Lois said coldly. "In fact, I'm beginning to think that what Mudge wanted was for you to front and take the fall. Didn't you suspect that?"

"I suspected it," Teejay conceded quietly. She nodded. "But it didn't have to go sour. It didn't have to produce indictments. I knew the odds —or thought I did, anyway—and I took my chances."

"A murder rap wasn't one of them," said Lois, eyes on her notes.

"Christ, no."

"All right," said Lois quietly. She frowned. She drew her lower lip between her teeth. She was wearing a pantsuit that day—unusual for her—and her long, blank, honest face showed unusual concern. Her demeanor suggested the physician who must confess to his patient that the cytology lab has found cancer cells. "There are three federal indictments," she said. "They will be returned by the grand jury. If —God forbid—you should be convicted of murder, they will be dropped. Otherwise, you will be offered an opportunity to plead—"

"Followed by disbarment," Teejay interjected.

"Probably. Anyway, two will be for violations of the securities laws in the manipulation of the stock in Futures Dynamic Corporation. The other will be for violation of the Federal Land Sales Full Disclosure Act, in the fraudulent prospectus for lots at Lago Aguila. Others will be indicted. Luiz, Glencoe . . ."

"If Mudge were alive . . . ?"

"He would be indicted," said Lois. "He didn't get around this one."

"He could have," said Teejay bitterly. "He could have held it all together, and nothing would have happened."

"That's optimism, Teejay," said Lois. "Anyway, I want to go over the Lago Aguila deal with you, to be sure I have it all straight in my mind. So . . . You formed the corporation in 1976—Lago Aguila, Incorporated. You personally owned one hundred fifty shares, and all the rest . . ."

"Luiz owned one hundred fifty, too."

"All right," said Lois. "Roberto Luiz, one hundred fifty. And—"

"The rest of it, the other ninety-seven hundred shares, was bought by Futures Dynamic Corporation," said Teejay.

"Why Futures Dynamic?" Lois asked. "You got yourself in trouble with Futures Dynamic. Why did you have to take it over?"

Teejay sighed. "Mudge wanted Lago Aguila to be owned by a publicly held corporation. Futures Dynamic was a shell. All the company had was a small building and some patents that paid royalties. It met a small payroll and paid a generous salary to Glencoe, but it had paid only ten cents a share dividend since 1968. We made a proposition

to the stockholders—we would invest two million dollars in Futures
Dynamic stock, and Futures Dynamic would invest the two million in
the stock of Lago Aguila. Futures Dynamic would become a land-
development investment company. The stockholders were overjoyed."

"The federal indictment," said Lois, "will charge that you and Glencoe and Mudge deceived the stockholders of Futures Dynamic by failing to tell them that Lao Aguila was a highly speculative venture, that
if it failed they stood to lose not just the two million dollars of new
capital but their corporation—lock, stock, and barrel. The indictment
will also charge that you failed to tell the stockholders that Glencoe,
who was recommending the deal to them, was already on your payroll. And finally the indictment will charge that you concealed from
the stockholders that one man, Mudge, was gaining control of their
corporation."

"None of which would have made any difference to them if Lago
Aguila had made money," argued Teejay.

"All of which, if true, violates the federal securities laws," Lois rejoined, "and exposes you not just to a fine but to a prison term if you
are convicted. Frankly, Teejay, it was a typical Mudge manipulation;
and if someone hadn't shot him, the SEC would be ecstatic at the
chance to nail him at last."

"I very much doubt they *would* have nailed him," Teejay said bitterly.

Lois nodded. "Because he had a defense, didn't he? He was going
to say you were his lawyer and you advised him all these things were
legal, and all he did was follow your advice. Right?"

Teejay nodded. Her face was shining red, her eyes wide.

"I've read the letters he sent you. 'On your advice, Miss Brookover,
I authorize . . .' 'With your assurance, Miss Brookover, I will proceed.
. . .' He was papering the files, building a defense just in case he
needed it."

"Yes," said Teejay.

"All of which is one hell of a fine motive for killing him," said Lois.
"Which is what makes Hornwood think you did."

"I won't deny I'm glad someone killed him," said Teejay.

The evening was interminable. Janie did not sleep, except for a few
minutes now and again; she lay above and tossed and twisted. She
jumped down and used the toilet and climbed back up again—without
a word. Teejay dozed once or twice, but not for more than a few minutes at a time. The jail became noisy again. Women yelled obscenities
through their cell bars at the matrons pacing around outside the cage,

glaring in at them. Reporters came through and stared in.

The news that federal indictments would be returned had not distressed her as she had thought it would—and certainly not as Lois had thought it would. Confinement brought with it a certain stark simplicity that put things in a bright, contrasty perspective. It was something Lois could not understand—that she, Teejay, could not have understood a few weeks ago. She had learned to concentrate on what what was important—which was only one thing.

She had been confident when she was brought in here, in April, that she would spend six months, or whatever time it took, in jail, would go to trial and be acquitted, and then would go out to cope with federal charges, an effort to disbar her, or whatever came. Now she was not so sure. Acquittal was *not* a certainty. Even if Kevin did not testify against her—and she remained confident he wouldn't—still she might, conceivably, be found guilty of murder. Being charged with deceiving the stockholders of an almost-defunct corporation, or with preparing deceptive statements about the value of subdivision lots, was petty. People in jail claimed being in jail made them wise. She had been scornful, but they were not entirely wrong. They knew what was important.

The lights went out at eleven as always. The jail quieted a little. Teejay was awake and anticipated a night awake. She lay for a while, listening for Janie's small, quiet snore; and even though she did not hear it, she rolled off her bunk and stood at the bars the way she had done too many hours now, too many nights. She leaned into the steel bars and lit a cigarette.

Lois, behind her easy facade of cosmetics, coiffure, and couture, had no idea what this was: to be locked behind the unyielding bars of a jail cell—just as she, Teejay, had had no idea of it a few weeks ago. The difference made Lois hard to take, a little. She worked within a different reality. She—

"Teejay?" Janie whispered. She rolled off her upper bunk, dropped to the floor, and moved to stand beside Teejay at the bars of the cell. Teejay handed her the pack of cigarettes and the matches, and Janie lit a cigarette.

"Did you know Marcia?" Janie asked. She referred to the woman who had died.

Teejay nodded. "I talked to her once in a while."

"Niggers . . ." Janie whispered regretfully, shaking her head.

"No, it's not niggers," said Teejay. "It's this place. You and I could get that mad at each other."

Janie shook her head. "Not me," she said. "Not with you, Teejay.

You're some kind of different person. You're not the kind that belongs in here."

"Who belongs in here?" Teejay asked bitterly.

"Teejay . . ." Janie put her hand on Teejay's, on the crosspiece of the cell bars. She sighed loudly, then spoke in a low voice. "I killed my husband—"

"*Don't tell me!*" Teejay interrupted in a shrill, urgent whisper.

"I want you to know," Janie said in the same low, confidential voice, but with determination to speak. "I shot him. I don't even know why anymore. My lawyer keeps delaying my trial. He says maybe we can beat it. He knows we can't. I know it. I'm going to get a life sentence, Teejay."

Janie looked away, through the bars. She dragged thoughtfully on her cigarette and stared at the brick wall outside the cage. Teejay put her arm around Janie, impulsively, for a moment; then she withdrew it. She shook her head.

Janie glanced up at her. "I'm scared the same thing is going to happen to you," she said.

"I appreciate your thinking about it," Teejay said soberly. "You're a friend, Janie."

"I read about you in the papers," Janie went on. "Doesn't it bother you? Aren't you scared?"

"I'm scared to death," Teejay whispered.

Janie nodded. She moved half a step closer to Teejay until her hip touched Teejay's; and she slipped her arm behind Teejay, around her. "Jesus— Maybe I can help a little," she whispered.

"Teejay—" Janie tightened her arm around Teejay, pulling her a little off balance and closer to herself. "I mean—look, we're two people. We can't help but be close to each other. We haven't got anybody else to be close to. You know? Tell me to shut up if you want to."

Teejay shook her head. "I won't ask you to shut up," she said quietly.

Janie touched Teejay's cheek. "Do you know what I mean?"

Teejay nodded.

With the tips of her fingers Janie caressed Teejay's cheek and jaw and throat. "This is a god-awful place," she whispered between clenched teeth. "Nothing good ever happens to you in here. But—a little something can. Just for a little while, you can feel good. Let me—"

"Janie, I don't think we should."

"Let me," Janie said in a low, urgent voice. "Don't tell me no."

Teejay frowned and slowly shook her head, but Janie put her hands to both Teejay's cheeks and reached up and kissed her on the lips. Teejay did not pull back. Janie kissed her again, touching Teejay's lips with her tongue.

"Teejay—" Janie whispered. "C'mon."

Janie tossed her cigarette through the bars. She took Teejay's and tossed it, too. Moving abruptly, she grabbed the mattress pad on Teejay's bunk and heaved it to the floor. She knelt on it and took Teejay's hands and pulled her down. She pushed Teejay onto her back; and, hurrying, she pulled up Teejay's dress and began to tug at Teejay's panties.

Teejay's first strong impulse was to pull away and stop Janie, but the excitement of her body diffused her will. It was like being drunk; she was not able to organize a response. She did not want Janie to do what she was doing; but she did want it, too. She was afraid of what Janie was doing; but it was exhilarating. She wanted to think, to decide if she should accept what Janie was going to do; but the sensations monopolized her consciousness, as if all the power in her had run down to where Janie was touching her. She had to lift her hips to let Janie pull down her panties. She lifted them. It was almost involuntary.

She lay yielding on her back, not looking at Janie but looking up through the ceiling bars of the cell to the pipes and cobwebs in the shadows above. Janie pressed her legs apart. Janie kissed the insides of her thighs, then she pressed down and began to lick the smooth parts inside her pubic hair. Teejay had never known anything like it before—either the experience or the surge of feeling it generated. Any little remaining power of decision she had about it was gone immediately. Janie pressed in, until when Teejay looked down she could see only the top of Janie's head between her thighs; and Janie's blond hair lay over her legs and belly. She felt Janie's tongue reaching into her. It found her clitoris. Teejay gasped. Shortly she had a raging orgasm, then a second, then a third before Janie slipped away and lay with a cheek on Teejay's leg.

Teejay reached down and caressed her head. "God, Janie . . ." she whispered. "My God . . . !"

XI

1966

Lois was pregnant. The baby was due in about six weeks, as she calculated. She experienced heavy pregnancies, becoming big and awkward; in the final two months it was difficult to move and she tired easily. Even so, she was in the courtroom.

It was juvenile court. No spectators were allowed. She sat at a table with her client and his parents—a middle-class family whose fifteen-year-old son was charged with breaking into a carry-out and stealing two six-packs of beer—facing Ellis Keiler, a juvenile-court referee appointed by the judge to conduct these hearings. Keiler sat behind a desk, not on a raised judicial bench. A Houston police officer was testifying. A caseworker questioned the officer. No one from the district attorney's office was present. There was no court reporter. Although Lois had asked for it, no record was being made.

"Now," said the caseworker—a plump, gray woman. "When you picked up Gerald, what did he say?"

The police officer shook his head gravely. "He said he done it. He asked me to take it easy on him."

"No!" protested the boy. "I asked you to take it easy. I never said I—"

"No you don't!" yelled the referee. "You don't contradict the police

officer in *this* courtroom. You just shut up, Gerald. You're in big enough trouble as it is, without showing disrespect."

Lois seized the boy's arm and whispered to him urgently to be quiet and wait until she cross-examined. From the corner of her eye she watched Keiler, the referee. He was a sixty-eight-year-old man, loosely fleshed; the red of his apple cheeks had almost disappeared now in the hot pink flush of his anger. He stared at her.

"Uh—" the caseworker stuttered. "Uh, you say Jerry told you he did break into—"

"Yes'm," the officer said. "He admitted he done it but said he was just a young feller and I should let him off maybe."

The boy sadly shook his head.

"Now, I told you to cut that out, Gerald," said Keiler angrily. "I won't have you sitting here calling a police officer a liar."

"I didn't say anything," the boy protested in a shrill, frightened voice.

"You shook your head," snapped Keiler.

"If the Court please," said Lois evenly. "I—"

"*Mrs. Hughes,*" said Keiler, pointing a finger at Lois, "you are here as a concession and a favor. Now, don't try to tell me how to run this hearing or how to make this boy show respect. I have a lot of experience with that, and I can handle it."

"It was not my intention to try to tell you how to run the hearing," said Lois.

"Good," said Keiler. He looked to the caseworker. "Anything more?"

The caseworker shook her head.

"Fine, then—"

"If you please, I have a few questions for the witness," said Lois.

"Oh, no you don't," said Keiler quickly. "You're not turning this hearing into a trial. You're not cross-examining."

Lois lifted herself to her feet. "This young man has a right to counsel," she said. "He has a right to my effective participation in this hearing."

Keiler shook his head. "This is *juvenile* court. This is not a trial. This is a hearing to determine if this boy is a delinquent. This is not a criminal proceeding."

"Since you have the power in this proceeding to impose penalties as severe as those a criminal court can impose, I am curious as to what the difference is," said Lois.

"*Sit down, Mrs. Hughes,*" Keiler ordered. "Juveniles brought before this court for delinquency hearings have no right to a lawyer, and that's the law. You're here because you called Judge Landsittle and asked to be let in, and he was kind enough to do you that favor; but he told me I didn't have to let you turn this hearing into some kind of circus, and I'm not going to. If I hear any more from you, I'll put you out of here."

Lois tossed a pencil on the table. It clattered across the table and fell to the floor. "I don't think I'd try that if I were you, Mr. Keiler," she said. She stood for a moment glaring at him, with her hands on her hips. Then she sat down.

Keiler stared back at her. He rapped on the table with his knuckle as if with a gavel. He looked down at the open file before him and began to mumble, only half audible. "Information is enough. . . . Find that Gerald Crow is a delinquent child. Released on probation in custody of his parents. Report to caseworker as she requires. That's all."

Mac John had developed a bit more paunch over the past few weeks, Lois noticed. He stood at the window, and she saw him in silhouette against the light from the lawn, which made it more obvious. She wondered if her mother, who was regarding him quite thoughtfully, had noticed it, too, or was studying the way he drank his whiskey. Mac John had ceased to pretend he was interested in her father's conversation, and he was watching something outside. She and her mother were as much withdrawn as Mac John was, for that matter, and she made a point of looking up at her father and smiling, as if she had followed every word he said.

He was talking about Vietnam. He stood by the fireplace, which at this time of year was filled with yellow flowers, and spoke with animation. He was enjoying himself. He held a crystal glass of Tio Pepe and sipped with conspicuous enjoyment of that, also. Lois was sipping the sherry, too—as a concession to her pregnancy. Her mother had whiskey and water.

"I think the Rivers was a good buy," said Lois's mother. She nodded toward the unframed canvas sitting on an easel—a painting by Larry Rivers, a multiple portrait in which indistinct, yet perceptively drawn, faces looked out from a wash of colors.

"I'd like it better if he'd finished it," said Daniel Farnham.

"I'd like your monologue on the war better if you'd finish it," said Mary Brady Farnham.

Daniel Farnham tossed off his sherry at a gulp, as if irritated; but Lois saw his faint smile as he swallowed. Her mother regarded him quizzically for an instant, her face a mask of bland ingenuousness; then she picked up the silver bell from the coffee table and rang for their houseman.

Mac John had turned from the window and frowned apprehensively. Lois smiled at him. She wished he could learn to appreciate these exchanges between her mother and father. To her they were lessons in domesticity, an example of how two disparate people could accommodate themselves to each other. Ever since she had understood them this way, since she was very young, they had been a source of security for her. Her father and mother gently—and sometimes not so gently—trading words was a part of her life in the same way this room was.

This familiar room: the furniture that had always been the same—brocaded couches, leather armchairs; the fireplace generously filled with flowers most of the year; the graceful antique mantel clock that always ran but never kept time; the Cézanne and the Degas in gold-leaf frames to either side of the fireplace. It was a gracious room, but lived-in, even to the point of showing a tatter here and there. Her father drank Tio Pepe and made a point of being scornful of any other sherry; her mother made her own point by drinking whiskey before dinner. These things fit together, all of them. Lois told Mac John he had to notice all of them if he really wanted to understand her.

"I believe we would like another round of drinks, Sinclair," said Mrs. Farnham to the house man.

Lois was not confident, actually, that Mac John wanted to understand her. He showed no interest in probing her personality. She was what he wanted in a wife, he was content with her, and he expended none of his demonstrated powers of perception on her. He didn't have to. His marriage was a success. His wife was a stimulating partner, an ornament, a complaisant lover; she was fecund, and she was an apparent heiress to a considerable fortune. Success in marriage had come easily to him, as had success in business: in part by inheritance, in part through his own doing. There had been no difficulty, no challenge.

She wondered about that, wondered if he was not bored with the easiness of it all. He was bored with his business. He showed no sign of being bored with his marriage, but she wondered if he did not hide it. They were satisfied with each other. That was their marriage, in a word; and as she sipped her sherry and allocated half her attention to her mother's and father's ongoing verbal sport, she wondered casually how much challenge satisfaction could survive. Was there any depth to it?

Dinner was served. They went into the dining room—her mother on Mac John's arm, she on her father's. Sinclair and his wife served: whitefish in a wine sauce with seedless grapes. Her father called for an iced "Hock," which Sinclair had ready and served immediately.

The lights were high; Daniel Farnham disliked eating by candle-light. He also disliked saltshakers, and their salt was before them in crystal cellars. Bradys—Mrs. Farnham's Carolina ancestors—stared pop-eyed out of stiff primitive portraits on the dining-room walls. Cross-conversations shot back and forth across the table—Daniel Farnham talking to Mac John about beef prices and golf, Mary Farnham talking with Lois about flowers and art, each pair aware of the other pair's conversation and injecting a comment into it from time to time. Sinclair and his wife watched the table attentively and served without being told.

"Dad," Lois said when their plates were nearly empty. "There's something I want to do—politically." She had waited for a chance to raise the subject, and now she raised it in a voice that stopped other conversation.

"Uhmm," said Daniel Farnham through a sip of wine. "And what is that?"

"I want Fred Landsittle's ass," she said. "He's nothing but a political hack. He staffs that court with his cronies, none of them competent. They run a kangaroo court. And that's where the kids get their first impression of the law and the system of justice. Aside from the arbitrary, self-righteous things they do in individual cases, Fred and his cronies destroy the respect young people might have—"

"Hear, hear," said Mac John.

"Ellis Keiler again?" her father asked dryly.

"Yes, Ellis Keiler again," Lois admitted grimly.

"Why couldn't you be satisfied by simply getting rid of Keiler?" her father asked. "That could be done easily enough."

Lois shook her head. "Fred Landsittle would just appoint some other crony. That's what all his referees are, and half his caseworkers—cronies, incompetents, courthouse hangers-on, hacks. And he doesn't even know the difference. He was a hack himself, and he was re-warded for a lifetime of loyal errand running by being elected to a judgeship that's a mile beyond his depth."

"Haven't you just described the majority of the judges in Texas?" asked Mac John.

"No, I've just described about twenty-five percent of all the judges in the United States," said Lois.

"I'm reluctant to spend political credit on merely knocking down a juvenile-court judge," said Daniel Farnham.

"It's important," said Lois. "Juvenile courts generally are bad. They have too much arbitrary power, and some of them use it viciously. But this one . . ."

"Who do you have in mind to take Fred's place?" asked her father.

"A woman," said Lois.

"Not yourself, I hope."

She smiled. "No. I was thinking of Constance MacInroth." She shrugged. "Anybody but another political hack."

Mac John summoned Sinclair to pour him another glass of wine. He grinned at Lois. "What's the old saying in the law? The one you quoted to me? 'If you can't win on the facts, attack on the law; if you can't win on the law, attack on the facts; and if you can't win on either, attack the judge.' Do I have it right?"

"Something like that," Lois conceded briskly, allowing only momentary distraction from her argument. "But why is it that we build elaborate procedures to guarantee the rights of adults on trial, yet send our kids into kangaroo courts? Why—"

"Just how do you propose we put this proposition to the Democratic party of Harris County?" her father interrupted quietly. "What do we say to Tom Hertford?"

"We tell him we've paid our dues to the Democratic party of Harris County for many years and have asked for very little—"

"We've asked for and got a good deal," her father said. He had his last bit of fish on his fork, poised before him. "Our political activities and contributions have been an investment."

"Tell Tom your daughter practices law in Landsittle's court and is afraid the dear, loyal old fellow is about to become a major embarrassment, by reason of senility," said Lois sarcastically.

Mac John grinned again. "The propriety of all this—the ethics of it, if you will—I find extremely curious. Is this how lawyers win cases? By their political influence?"

"How else?" snapped Lois irritably. "You use what you've got."

As her family had done—she could have reminded Mac John—to get her into Childreth, McLennon & Brady, three years ago. The firm had been influenced by certain persuasive facts: that it was counsel to the Western Banking and Trust Company, of which Daniel Farnham was chairman of the board; Farnham Oil, of which he was president; and Sovereign Development Corporation, of which his son, Lois's brother, was president. The firm was influenced at least as much, probably, by the fact that it did *not* represent Partridge Gas Transmission, Incorporated, or Gemini Broadcasting Company.

Lois had been reluctant. "It isn't what I went to law school for," she had protested.

It was a weak argument and had never had a chance of prevailing against the combined pressures brought by her father and Mac John, and even by her mother.

—"You want to move and shake the world? Well, by God, young lady, that is where it is moved and shaken: in the big, prestigious firms, where they've got brains and muscle and know how to use them."

—"Anyway, honey, what else you gonna do? I mean, if you don't go into a firm or join the law staff of some corporation, what are you going to do—open an office on the street?"

—"Whatever it is you want to accomplish, Lois, I should think you would be reluctant to surrender one of your best advantages: the position and influence of your family."

From the day three years ago when she first sat down at the old desk in her little associate's office, Lois was recognized as someone special and different from the other associates of the class of 1963. Childreth, McLennon & Brady recruited top graduates from the best law schools all over the country. At eight and nine at night, young Harvardians and Michiganders in white shirtsleeves sat at library tables, squinted wearily into beige-bound lawbooks, and scribbled pinched notes on big yellow legal pads. They carried papers to the courthouse. They toted partners' briefcases. They conformed to the unwritten and scoffed-at, but rigidly followed, dress code of Childreth, McLennon & Brady—dark-colored business suits, white shirts, conservative striped neckties, laced black shoes; associates to hang up their jackets and work in their shirtsleeves until the date of their second anniversary with the firm. (That Ted McCadden, the most senior partner, regularly appeared at the office in gray tweed jackets, charcoal-gray slacks, and black loafers was an envied sign of his specially exalted status in the firm. Only two or three others would have risked the displeasure of the management committee.)

For Lois, none of this quite worked. It was never clear in the first place just what you told a young woman to wear to give her the appearance of a shirtsleeved clerk. In any event, she worked directly for Ted McCadden, in an office not far from his, and took work assignments from him only. She did not work at night or on weekends. When McCadden left for the day, never later than 6:30, he would stop at her office and ask if she was going down on the elevator. She was the only junior associate in the firm ever to have appeared in court on behalf of a client during the first two years; she was allowed to take the juvenile-court cases in which she was especially interested—the only cases of that kind the firm had taken in many years.

When Judge Fred Landsittle was informed the Harris County Democratic Executive Committee would not endorse him for renomination and reelection to the juvenile court but would sponsor and endorse a candidate against him, he was bewildered and announced his retirement.

Lois received a note of congratulation from Bunny Tyler. Bunny was still at the university. She had graduated from law school, at the top of her class, the year after Lois. She had stayed to take a master's degree in law, then to teach a year. Now, she went on to say in her note, she wanted to enter the practice, and she suggested she would like to come to Houston and meet Lois and Mac John for dinner some evening. Lois was scheduled to take maternity leave from Childreth, McLennon & Brady within the week, and she called Bunny and invited her to have dinner at home. She would have something brought in, she explained, and would feel more comfortable spread out in her own living room than sitting erect on a chair at a restaurant table.

"I try to discourage the name Bunny," said Bunny. "It's—uh, you know—I want to practice law. It isn't dignified. It doesn't suggest a good lawyer."

She was tanned, and her blond hair shone against the skin of her deep-colored cheeks. Her body was more taut. Mac John admired her, as he had before—conspicuously; and she coquettishly accepted as many drinks as he offered and was shortly relaxed.

"Who's the lucky guy?" Mac John asked her. He pointed to the engagement ring she wore.

She grinned. "You remember Hal Spencer? He was playing football the time when we went to the Oklahoma game. He's in law school now."

"Going to form a partnership, you two?" Lois asked.

"Only the domestic kind," said Bunny.

Lois was uncomfortable. She was carrying the baby low and heavy and was beginning to think it might come two or three weeks early. She sipped Tio Pepe, only half a glass, while Mac John and Bunny drank bourbon and found a great deal more humor in the small quips they traded than she could discern. Their dinner had been brought by a caterer and was in the kitchen. Bunny had volunteered to heat and serve it. Lois was grateful for that. She only dreaded having to sit at the table to eat it.

"I'm surprised you don't stay in teaching," Lois said to Bunny. "You certainly have the qualifications for it, and I'd think it would make a pretty attractive career."

Bunny shook her head. "I can't stand the goddamn appropriateness people find in it."

"Huh?" said Mac John quizzically.

"Oh, it's just so *appropriate*," Bunny sneered. "I'm a woman, so I really must be a nurse, a secretary, a waitress, or a goddamn teacher. I really *must* be. Isn't that what I must be?"

"Jesus, Bunny . . ." Mac John laughed.

"She's right," said Lois.

"Besides," said Bunny bitterly, "young men with blue beards and strong cleft chins can't live with the idea that someone with good tits and legs could know more than they do and could teach them anything. I get propositions—"

"Sure you do," said Mac John. "What the hell?"

"I do, too," said Lois grimly.

Mac John frowned. "We haven't talked about that," he said.

"Do you get them?" Lois asked him. "Do you get propositions that you pop up to a hotel at lunch hour for a quickie?"

He grinned weakly and shook his head.

"Are there openings at Childreth?" Bunny asked. Her voice was pitched with a sudden urgent quality, of which she was maybe not aware. "I think I can show pretty good qualifications."

"That would be a tough proposition, Bunny," said Lois.

"I graduated number two in my class," said Bunny. "I have an advanced degree in estate planning. I've taught a year."

"They'd treat you like a piece of shit," said Mac John. "Why would you want to take an apprenticeship? That's what they'd give you."

"It's the big world," said Bunny simply. "Teaching isn't."

"It comes back to that with you, doesn't it?" Lois said.

"I've never been anything but honest with you about that," said Bunny.

"Are you asking us to do this for you?" Mac John asked.

Bunny looked at his face for a short moment, then at Lois's. "It never hurt anyone to have someone around who owes you everything," she said.

XII

1967

Norma gasped as her memorandum flew toward the coffee table, typed papers fluttering wildly. It struck a coffee cup on the table and stopped short of falling to the floor. "If I accept your conclusion," said John Finley between clenched teeth, shaking a finger toward the fanned papers, "our client Harrison is out a hundred ninety-seven thousand dollars."

"Mr. Finley," Norma said in a thin, strained voice, "I just don't see any way around those two sections of the U.S. Code, plus the Munsey Trust case."

"Norma," he said, pretending at least that his patience was extended to the breaking point, "I know what the goddamn law is. I wanted you to *find* me a way around it. Munsey's a bastard of a case. There've gotta be cases that distinguish it."

"I looked for them," she said.

"Did you find the Central Bank case?"

"Yes, sir. It's cited there," she said, nodding toward the memorandum.

He grabbed her memorandum off the table and impatiently flipped the pages. Norma—she had succeeded in discouraging the two or three in the office who remembered her as Bunny from calling her that—clasped her hands tightly and watched him read. He had a grim reputation among the young lawyers at Childreth, McLennon & Brady, as a short-tempered, demanding perfectionist: the firm's intellectual heavyweight, with no patience for work that did not meet his standards. He was fifty-five years old. Bristling black eyebrows, entangled with the gold frames of his glasses, exaggerated the fierce stare he fixed on the world. His complexion was ruddy. Only a few narrow strands of his black hair crossed his red pate. He suffered some defect, some insufficiently healed injury of his left hip, walked with a limp, and carried a stout wood cane. She had written one other memorandum of law for him, and she had known what to expect when she reported to him. He was hurried, blunt, abrupt.

"When the Emery creditors—including Harrison—compromised the claim against the Post Office Department, they made a damn fool mistake," Finley muttered, not necessarily to Norma. "They should have held out for every last damn cent the post office owed on the prime contract, then let the IRS have its setoff against that. The short of it it," he said, looking suddenly into Norma's eyes, "the goddamn government's welshing on the settlement."

Norma nodded. "Yes, and it can get away with it, too."

"Why?"

"Because the statutes say it can. The government always has an unconscionable advantage when it's collecting tax money."

"Umm-hmm," he agreed quickly. "So where's my argument around it, Norma? You're going to write my brief. What're you going to say?"

"I—Mr. Finley, I don't know."

He shook his head in disgust and tossed her memorandum again. This time it slid across the glass top of his coffee table and fell to the floor. Norma hurried to kneel and gather up the sheets, which had now come unstapled and scattered.

"*Miss Tyler*," Finley growled somberly. His face darkened. "Get up. I may from time to time lose my temper and fling something on the floor; and when I do, you do *not* get down on your hands and knees and pick it up. I—" He had reached for the cane, which always stood within his reach, and he began to stab at the loose sheets and flip them toward him with the rubber tip. His breath was a little short as he reached. "I will not be shamed out of my—right to lose my goddamn temper."

Norma smiled as she sat down again on the couch beside him and stacked the papers she had retrieved. He did not concede the hint of a smile in return. He stabbed papers and flipped them impatiently. Leaning to reach for a sheet, he balanced himself suddenly by planting a hand heavily on her knee. When he sat erect again, he kept the

hand there for a moment, just at the hem of her gray tweed skirt; and
when he lifted his hand, he paused and patted her leg three times.

"We can win this case, young lady," he said, still short of breath,
"if we put our minds to it. If we don't win it, we'll give it a damned
good shot."

Norma nodded. She waited for him to explain how.

He tossed his cane to the far corner of the couch and slammed the
sheets of paper he had gathered down on top of the ones she had
stacked, leaving the dozen pages of the memorandum in no particular
order. "You see," he said, "it's only the professors—and maybe the
law-journal boys—who entertain the fancy that the law's a fabric of
logic. The judges have guts inside them, just like other people; and
it makes a judge uncomfortable, way down deep in the gut, to have
to decide a case so that it screws some innocent party out of what
he's honestly entitled to.

"So there's your argument. What you've got to do for me is write
me a brief that will convince a few judges that Harrison Electric
Company's an innocent party that installed a lot of electric wiring in
a government building and earned its money honestly—and now is
being screwed out of it because an oddity of the law gives the government an unconscionable advantage over other creditors. Okay?"

"I understand," she said.

He nodded. He glanced at his watch—it was after seven, she knew—
and sat silently regarding her for a moment that was for her uncomfortable. He did not smile; she had never seen him smile; and now,
seeing him stretch and flex his left leg, she concluded that something
she had suspected during past conferences with him must be true:
that his hip gave him constant pain.

"Where do you live, Norma?" he asked.

"I have an apartment out west."

"Do you have a car downtown?"

"I take the bus."

"Well, I sometimes stop at a place out Westheimer and have a drink
on my way home. Like to join me? I'll drive you home after."

The place on Westheimer was called the Corona Lounge. Finley
was greeted by the bartender and by one of the waitresses, a leggy
redhead in an abbreviated Irish-green leotard, and he led Norma by
the arm across the pink-lighted room to a booth in the corner, out of
sight of the not-very-many customers who were drinking quietly in
other booths and at the bar. He asked her to sit so she would be to
his right when he slid into the booth beside her and his bad hip

would be on the outside. She had little view of the lounge as her eyes adjusted to the light. The music was not loud, and the girls in leotards did not dance. Most of the men she could see were wearing jackets and ties. The waitress in the green leotard took their order immediately and quietly and hurried away to the bar.

Norma was apprehensive of Finley, more than she had been before when she had to face him in his office and justify her memorandum to him. He had driven out Westheimer in a buzzing little Porsche, weaving skillfully and aggressively through the traffic—which she had found surprising, considering how much he had to work the clutch with the leg she guessed was painful. He steered with both hands high on the wheel. But when he stopped for lights he took the opportunity to caress her legs. All the way he had chatted—inconsequentially but still unsmiling and crisp—about the law and other cases he had on his desk; but at one light he had pushed up her skirt and run his hand over the sleek sheer nylon of her pantyhose, and he had cocked his head and admired her legs—all casually, without interruption of his description of a problem of evidence. Now, here in the booth in the Corona Lounge, he had started again—his hand was between her legs, and his fingertips stroked the insides of her thighs.

"Communication, Norma," he said. He still spoke with the intensity he used in the office, as if it were impossible for him to relax. His only concession to being in a happy-hour bar was that he had taken off his gold-rimmed spectacles and laid them on the table, and he had rubbed his eyes. "Half the problem of arguing a case is just communicating your ideas. Half? More than half. When you read judicial opinions in cases you've argued, you find the judges didn't *reject* your arguments; they just missed them. They didn't examine your ideas and decide you were wrong; they couldn't—they never understood your ideas. I'm talking about good judges, too, not stupid time-servers." He rubbed his eyes again. "It's discouraging sometimes, damn discouraging."

The waitress came to their booth with their drinks. Finley looked up and talked with her for a moment, asked her how she was. Norma could not hear exactly what she said—she was soft-spoken—but she said something about Childreth, something about a case. Obviously she knew exactly who he was. Norma studied her Irish-green leotard, which was cut in a narrow V that barely covered her crotch, swept in high curves up over her pelvis, exposing her bare legs and hips as high as her waist, then curved down behind, leaving half of each buttock naked.

Finley had whiskey on the rocks. He lifted the glass with his left hand and kept his right on Norma's legs. He asked her how she came to know Lois Hughes.

"We were in law school together."

"She spoke very highly of you in the partnership meeting when she sponsored you."

"I've heard she did," said Norma cautiously.

"She said we shouldn't take you in just to have another woman in the firm. She said you are damn sharp. In fact, I put in an order for you right then, to do some work for me."

"She's given me a wonderful friendship. I hope I can live up to it."

"Bullshit."

"Huh. . . ?"

He glanced away from his whiskey, to her face, then back. "I said bullshit."

"I guess I don't understand," she said weakly.

Finley turned, to be more nearly facing her. He looked down at his own hand and he pushed her skirt up her legs a little more. He caressed the inside of her thigh, firmly. "Tell me something, Norma," he said, with the first suggestion of animation in his voice. "It's Norma Jean, isn't it? Tell me, Norma Jean, just what is it you want in this world? I mean, short of the lyrical three wishes. Within your reach in some practical sense, what do you want?"

Confused by the turns in the conversation, Norma hesitated, searching for an answer. She started, then stopped. She was distracted by his hand on her leg. She drew a breath, found voice. "I want to make partner at Childreth, McLennon and Brady," she said. She met his eyes with hers. "I want that—for a beginning."

"Ah," said Finley dully. He picked up his glass and sipped whiskey. "Well, do you think you're good enough? Only about half the boys and girls who come to us make it, you know. Are you a good enough lawyer, do you think?"

"I hope so," she said. That wasn't strong enough. She amended. "I *think* so."

"Think you've got the ability . . ." he mused, nodding.

She thought she was hearing cues. Maybe he was trying to prompt her to say *yes*. That was it, flat. "Yes. Yes, I really think I have."

He rested his elbow on the table and propped his chin in the palm of his hand. His fingers resting in one formidable black eyebrow half covered his one eye, and he regarded her with condescending curiosity with the other. "Okay," he muttered, nodding slightly. "Then why this bullshit declaration of your gratitude to Lois Hughes—who's done nothing for you but toss you a few crumbs that cost her nothing? And why don't you tell me to keep my hands off your legs?"

"*Mr. Finley—*" she began in an angry, voicy whisper.

"Kind of inconsistent, isn't it?" he interrupted. "I mean, if you've really got the ability . . ." He took his hand from her leg and picked up his glass.

"Why'd you bring me here?" she whispered shrilly. Blushing, her eyes hard and sharp, she glanced across the room to see if the girl in the green leotard was watching and would see her anger. "Did you bring me here so you could feel my legs? Or did you have something else in mind? I can't follow this conversation. It doesn't make sense."

"Why don't you tell me to go to hell?" he asked casually.

"You *know* why I don't."

"Why?"

"Because I work for you."

He shook his head over his whiskey. "You don't have to let me put my hand up your skirt because you work for me. Even the little secretaries we hire, right out of high school, know better than that. I couldn't help but wonder . . ."

"How far I'd let you go? Is that what you wanted to find out?" she whispered, leaning toward him to confine their conversation to their booth.

He had taken a chip of the ice from his glass into his mouth, and he sucked on it and formed his next words awkwardly around it. "Uhmm-mmmm. How far *would* you go, Norma?"

"For what?"

For the first time, Finley smiled. He gulped down the chip of ice, and his smile broadened into a grin. "That's honest," he laughed. "I like that. Okay. Now I know what I wanted to know."

Norma let her shoulders slacken. "I don't think you're very fair to me," she said disconsolately.

"You have *nice* legs," he said. He put his hand inside her skirt again. "And you're a pretty good lawyer. Take my advice, though, if you're going to play the office game—keep your pious declarations of gratitude toward Lois Hughes to yourself. Don't get yourself too much identified as her protégée. You'll probably make partner. You'll make it the way most people do. Nothing to be ashamed of. Personally, I'm a little disappointed, but that's all right."

"Disappointed. . . ?"

His chin still rested in his hand. He had taken his fingers off his eye. He turned down the corners of his mouth and shrugged. "I'm always looking for the one who'll say, 'Fuck you all, I'm so goddamned good you've *got* to make me partner, whether you like me much or not.' It's a fantasy maybe. . . ."

"Is that how *you* did it?" she asked.

"Well—I like to tell myself I did."

The waitress brought their second round of drinks. She distracted

Finley for a moment. As she walked away he watched her uncovered
nates rhythmically twitching. When he turned his attention fully to
Norma again, he reached down with both hands and pushed her skirt
up as far as it would go, until it was stretched tight over her hips,
uncovering her legs almost to the crotch of her pantyhose.

Norma glanced around the lounge. No one but Finley could see
how she was exposed. He stared. She did not push down her skirt.
She picked up her drink and asked him how Harrison Electric had
come in the first place to agree to the settlement the government was
now welshing on.

The waitress in the green leotard was Teejay Brookover. She had
noticed what Finley was doing to the young woman in the booth, and
she was amused. He was John T. Finley, one of the senior partners
at Childreth, McLennon & Brady; and Childreth was one of the best
firms—by its own account *the* best—in Houston. Finley came in from
time to time. She was always glad to see him; he would leave as much
as five dollars for a tip. This was the first time he had ever brought
a woman here with him.

Teejay was a law student at the University of Houston, in her second year, and she had welcomed opportunities to have moments of
conversation with John T. Finley—although she had never told him
she was a law student. In another year she would be looking for a
place in some law firm, probably in Houston, and it seemed wiser
that Finley not know that the girl in the skimpy leotard, showing her
hips and backside bare for tips, was studying law. In fact, no one at
the Corona knew she was a law student, and only one other law student knew she worked at the Corona Lounge.

Alan Merimac was the one who knew. She lived with him.

She had suffered through a grim first year, working as a waitress in
the dining room at the Warwick Hotel, living in a graduate women's
dormitory, and struggling through the hardest course of study she
had ever encountered.

"Miss—uh, uh—Brookover, tell us about the case of *Countess of
Salop v. Crompton.*"

"This was a case in the Court of Queen's Bench, in 1599. What happened was that the plaintiff leased a farm and farmhouse—"

"Was this really a lease, Miss Brookover?"

"They called it a lease. Today I think we'd just call it a tenancy at will. The plaintiff had the right to put the tenant out at any time."

"Go on."

"The tenant was careless about the fire in his fireplace and let the house burn down. The plaintiff brought an action for waste, and—"

"Waste. What's waste?"

"When a party having less than a fee damages the property. I mean, he damages the reversion."

"What does it mean in the Countess of Salop case?"

"Well, she owned the house, and she was entitled to have it back after the expiration of the tenancy. If it burned down—"

"Who had the fee, Miss Brookover? And who had the reversion?"

"The Countess of Salop, the plaintiff. She was entitled to have the house back after the expiration of the tenancy. But the tenant negligently burned it down, and she sued him."

"And the form of the action was. . . ?"

"Trespass on the case, for waste."

She glanced around the classroom. Half the students watching with skeptical eyes were relieved that the redhead had been stuck with this damned, mysterious old English case with its turgid prose about common-law writs and capricious rules; and the other half were jealous that Fenlow had called on her for it and that so far she was surviving his questions.

"How'd it come out, Miss Brookover?"

"The plaintiff lost. The court held that the action did not lie."

"So. Does that make any sense to you?"

"No, sir. No sense at all."

"Why not?"

"Well, it seems to me the owner of the house ought to have some remedy against the tenant who negligently burned it down."

"In simple justice, hey, Miss Brookover?"

She ventured a smile. "Justice is not very often a consideration in real-property law," she said.

A nervous titter went around the room. Professor Fenlow conceded a wry smile. "Especially not the real-property law of sixteenth-century England," he agreed. "All right. But does the decision in *Salop v. Crompton* really leave the landlord with no remedy?"

She frowned over her handwritten brief of the case. "I—don't think the court suggested any."

"What about trespass?"

She shook her head. "Crompton was a tenant."

"Was he, any longer, after he negligently burned the house?". . .

She had graduated summa cum laude from the University of Texas, El Paso; but her first set of law-school grades included two B's. After those grades were issued, between fifteen and twenty percent of her class dropped out. By the end of the first year, one-third had dropped out—or flunked out.

With the survivors, she could already carry on conversations other people could not understand. They had been very quick to draw around themselves the first veils of a professional mystique. They sat over coffee and excluded other people by their talk about *Hadley v. Baxendale, McPherson v. Buick, Erie v. Tompkins*, the Slaughterhouse Cases, the Rule in Shelley's Case, fee simple, fee tail, reversions, remainders, Gobitis, Miranda, Brown, grantors, grantees, bailors, bailees, pretermitted heirs, relicts, the Rule Against Perpetuities, trover, replevin, scienter, res ipsa loquitur, *Baker v. Carr*, tenancy by the entireties, hereditaments . . .

"It is not," Alan said, "an insuperable intellectual challenge. It's just that there's so damn *much* of it, and so alien, you literally have to *immerse* yourself in it."

She and Alan were two years older than most of the other students in their class: she because of the two years lost at the Bible college, he because he had spent two years in the army, fourteen months of it in Vietnam. She liked his maturity, his soft-spoken, self-confident presence. He was six-foot-four, taut and hard-muscled, with broad shoulders. His face was strong, deep-lined around the eyes; he had a long, sharp nose, and his mouth and smile were wide. He wore his blond, bristly, curly hair long, covering his collars and lying on the shoulders of his jackets.

They met in the law library, where both of them studied afternoons. Both of them worked: she as a waitress at the Warwick Hotel at that time, he as a driver for a bank, delivering processed checks and other documents from branch banks to the central office, every business-day afternoon. They had the same reputation among their classmates: for being intense, sober students, withdrawn and not much fun. When they were tired, they took breaks for coffee, together. They became friends.

They found time to see an occasional movie together, to sit an hour in a bar afterward and drink beer and talk. One Sunday evening he suggested she go to his room and spend the night with him. She went. A few weeks later he asked her to share an apartment with him. They could afford more room and better amenities if they shared, he said. She agreed. They found an apartment, the second floor of a white frame house near the university. They had a living room and a kitchen. They had one bedroom, one bed.

That Sunday evening when she went to bed with Alan, she was a virgin. She did not tell him, and he did not realize it. She went to bed with him with the thought that it was an experience too long postponed, an innocence too long continued, and Alan was a big, clean, healthy, kindly man: a good partner for her first time. She would always think she had been fortunate in him. He was direct and honest and cheerful about sex. What he wanted was uncomplicated: only to shove his big penis into her as often as she would let him; and he made love with an appealing ingenuousness, in the assumption that her body responded to stimulation with the same simple sensations that his did. That he was wrong did not make her less fortunate in him.

She discovered about herself, to her surprise, that her drive was not as strong as she had supposed it would be. After a few weeks' introduction to her own sexuality, she found herself surprisingly comfortable with it. She could accommodate Alan. It was easy and pleasant. But if she went a few days untouched, she did not develop anxiety. She liked what she could do. She was glad she had learned she could do it. But she was not driven to it.

She and Alan did not fall in love. She was surprised by that, too. But he never told her he loved her. And she, with the imprisoned Kevin always in her consciousness, subdued a few excited impulses to declare love to Alan and then settled, as he had done, into bland acceptance of their arrangement. When Alan told her he did not approve of the job she took at the Corona Lounge and particularly of the leotard she would wear there, she could tell him quietly, without emotion, that it was presumptuous of him to suppose she asked for his approval.

XIII

Ronald Steen was appointed to defend Kevin Flint against the charge of having murdered Benjamin Mudge—appointed by the court because Flint said he was without the funds to pay an attorney for his defense. Steen was maybe thirty-two: a tall, slender man with black curly hair and a thick black moustache. His brown eyes swam behind the heavy lenses of his horn-rimmed glasses. He had asked for a conference with Teejay, and three of them—Teejay, Lois, and Steen—sat around a small conference table in a dingy, dirty-green-painted room on the ground floor of the jail. An air conditioner rattled in the window, but the room was stuffy and hot, and Steen sat in his white shirtsleeves. Lois looked cool in a blue and white summer dress. Teejay's gray uniform was limp with perspiration. She smoked with a hurried air of impatience and watched Steen shuffle his notes.

Steen extracted a Xerox of a document from his file. "When Kevin was in the Oklahoma State Penitentiary, he applied for permission to write letters to you. Since you were not a member of his family and were not his lawyer, he had to have permission to put you on his letter list. He had to state the relationship, and he wrote on the form that you were his 'girl friend.' He didn't list a family. You were the only person on his list."

"I didn't know that," said Teejay.

"How many letters did he write you?"

"Just one."

Steen nodded. "That's what he says. It was the only letter he wrote in the thirty-odd months he was there. And he only received one—from you."

"Poor Kevin."

"Did you ever repay the hundred dollars?"

"What?"

"The loan, the hundred dollars. He says that's why he put you on his list, why he wanted to write you: to ask you to repay a hundred dollars he lent you in El Paso, so he'd have a little money for candy and shaving soap while he was in the pen."

"Oh." Teejay glanced at Lois. "No, I couldn't send him the money. I was working and going to school, and I didn't have it."

Lois sat at the table after Steen had gone. Teejay stood and was looking out the window.

"What's between you and Kevin Flint, Teejay?" Lois asked. "He lied about that letter; and when Ron told you what his lie was, you picked it up and ran with it. What don't I know?"

Teejay looked down at Lois, at that long, solemn face, an archetype for thoughtful sincerity. "Kevin doesn't want it known that he wrote me a love letter—the love letter, incidentally, that you read before you destroyed it. What is it you don't know? You read the letter."

"Why did he lie to Ron about it?"

"Why do you think? To protect me. He doesn't want Hornwood to know he wrote me a love letter. He thinks it would hurt me."

"To protect you . . ." Lois mused, frowning. "Teejay, I have to ask —just what is he protecting you *from?* And why? Teejay, he's going to Huntsville *for life,* if he doesn't go to the chair. You've said all along you could depend on him not to testify against you. What's your hold on him, Teejay? Is that man so deeply in love with you that he'd go to the chair to protect you?"

Teejay sat down in the chair immediately facing Lois across the table. "You're my defense counsel," she said quietly. "I can tell you anything and they can't make you reveal it. All right, then. Kevin loves me. He's loved me for thirteen years. He's a crazy man about it. As for me . . . I guess I've never loved him. But you can't just ignore a man that . . . Could *you?* I'd do just about anything to get him out of the mess he's in. Do you have any suggestions?"

"No, but I've got a question," said Lois. "Are we sending this man to the chair by holding back things we maybe know? I'll be frank with you, Teejay. I couldn't go that far with you. I'd pull out as your counsel. I'll get you someone else, someone good—"

"Lois," Teejay said in a clipped, controlled voice between tight, white lips. "Let's suppose something, just for the sake of discussion. Let's suppose I demand you take me into court tomorrow morning, and suppose I stand up and confess to the murder of Benjamin Mudge. Since the evidence is incontrovertible that Kevin killed Mudge, I'd have to confess that Kevin and I conspired to kill him. Now—what good would that do Kevin? He's saying he killed Mudge in a robbery, which is aggravated murder, murder in the first degree. Would he be any better off if it came out that he killed Mudge for me, maybe that I paid him to do it?

"No, Lois. The truth is that Mudge was a client of mine, involved with me in a stinkin' illegal deal, and Kevin, who is an old friend of mine, killed him; and out of that, Hornwood thinks he sees a connection—mostly because he'd very much like to find a connection.

"Two horrible things have happened to Kevin. It's amazing that he keeps his sanity. The first thing is that he committed a crime—why I don't know—and by some stupid accident got caught; and the second thing is that, because he has been known to care for me, I've been charged with being involved in his crime. Kevin hates that. He'll lie or anything else to show I didn't have anything to do with it. It's all up with Kevin, and he knows it. He's trying to protect me. It doesn't make anything worse for him. Everything is as bad for him already as it could possibly be."

It was hot in the jail. Electric fans ran outside the cage bars, but they blew only hot, damp air through the cage, and the women sweated and stank. They were allowed two baths a week. Teejay hated to smell herself. Worse than that, she itched. The matrons yelled at them every day that the jail rules required them to keep their uniforms on; but most of the prisoners tossed the gray dresses and sat listlessly on the concrete floor, sweating in yellowing and sometimes tattered pants and brassieres. Teejay knew she would be no cooler for taking off the dress. Generally she kept it on, sometimes allowing it to fall open like a limp gray kimono. At night inside the cell, where the fans did not move the air, she and Janie sat on their mattresses, played cards endlessly, and talked, stripped to their panties.

Teejay had been afraid at first that the other prisoners, then the matrons, would find out she and Janie were loving each other in their cell after the lights were turned out; she was afraid the matrons would separate them, put them in different cells. Then she found out no one cared; if anything, the matrons encouraged such relationships—they made the prisoners more tractable. She put no barriers between herself and Janie after that. They made existing in jail a little easier for each other, and that was justification enough for anything they did.

On the day when Teejay met Ron Steen in the conference room of the jail, Judge Norma Spencer was the guest speaker at the quarterly meeting of the Harris County Methodist Adult Fellowship, held at the Lamar Hotel. The chairman of the meeting introduced her—

"It is my pleasure to present to you a woman who has in every way devoted herself to service—service to her family, to her church, and to her community. Serving now in her fifth year as judge of the criminal district court of Harris County, Judge Spencer has established a clear record for being anything in this world but soft on crime. She is one of those rare judges who believe that when the law says 'you shall not,' then *you shall not*—and if you do, you will suffer the consequences."

The chairman was interrupted by applause.

"More than that, Judge Spencer is a faithful and active member of her church—which I must reluctantly confess is the Presbyterian—"

The chairman was interrupted by laughter.

"She has taught both adult and juvenile classes of her church's Sunday school. She is a member of the county council of the Girl Scouts of America. She is a past president of the Harris County Council of the PTA. She is an active member of Doris Leach Farragoe Chapter, Order of the Eastern Star, and has served a year as Ruth and a year as Esther—and those of you who are Masons or Eastern Stars will know what that means in terms of time and dedication. She is an active member of the American Association of University Women. She is a member of the American Bar Association, the Texas Bar Association, and the Harris County Bar Association, and she is active on committees of each of those associations. She is a member of the American Judicature Society, a group organized to improve the administration of justice in this country.

"She is—well, you can see she is not one of those who sits back and waits for others to do things. But with all this, she is a devoted and supportive wife to Harold Spencer, one of the leading attorneys in Houston, and she is the mother of two lovely children, a boy and a girl. To be with us this evening she has given up a Little League ball game, where I am sure Harold, Jr., will hit a home run. Anyway, his daddy is there to see it, and we are privileged to have as our speaker a woman who makes her life a constant example of Christian witnessing. I am honored to present JUDGE NORMA SPENCER."

An hour after her speech she sat down at a table in the bar at the Warwick Hotel, with the Reverend Mr. Charles Sharp.

"I can't stay," she said. "One drink."

"Relax," he said. "With the Roman collar here and the cross hanging around my neck, we could check into a hot-sheet motel and it wouldn't cause gossip."

"I'm not thinking about gossip," she said.

"Hubby and the kids," he laughed. "God, Bunny, I couldn't believe it! Are you by any chance active in the American Automobile Association and the National Geographic Society?"

"Don't be an ass. And don't get the name 'Bunny' started again."

"Judge Norma Spencer! I almost didn't come. I had no idea Judge Norma Spencer would be Bunny Tyler. It's worth the trip from Dallas."

"What'd you think I'd be doing—still riding around on sorority floats?"

"Oh, it's not the judgeship," he said, gesturing. "I have no doubt you're well qualified. It's that other stuff. Order of the Eastern Star? *Bun-ny!* Teaching Sunday school? Jesus!"

"If you're going to be something good, you have to do the things that get it for you. Don't *you?* Don't you eat a lot of chicken dinners—rubber chicken and yellow gravy—'*Reverend*' Sharp?"

"Sure, and it hasn't done me any good, has it?" he admitted, patting his protruding belly.

Norma shrugged. "Who stays young? Peter Pan?"

"You're a little heavier," he said thoughtfully, looking critically at her. "You'd still look good in a bikini. You ever wear one anymore? When'd you start wearing glasses?"

She shrugged again. "You still have a seven-inch whang on you?"

He grinned. "As it was in the beginning, it is now, and ever shall be."

Norma laughed. "Chuck, you pagan son of a bitch, whatever possessed you to become a preacher?"

His grin disappeared. "I rationalized that the chance to do something good was more important than the bullshit. By the time I found out how wrong I was, I was stuck."

She frowned. "You're never stuck."

"To break out of it, I'd have to be divorced to start with . . . give up my kids . . ." He shook his head. "Anyway, I'm good at it. I preach a hell of a sermon."

"The church long ago ruled," she said quietly, "that the efficacy of the sacrament is independent of the character of the priest. You probably save a lot of souls."

"Yes, and I have a lot of testimonials to prove it," he said bitterly. "Anyway . . . So you finally married Hal. Did he ever grow up?"

"No. He's still a Longhorn."

"One of Houston's leading lawyers."

"Drop it, Chuck. He's a scrivener. He's a fine man, with a lot of wonderful qualities. But a first-rate lawyer . . ." She shrugged and smiled. "He's a good father."

"So am I."

"I'll bet you are. Don't put yourself down."

"Bunny," he said urgently. "You and I. For old times' sake."

She shook her head. "I know I'd enjoy it. But there's too much at stake."

"Listen," he went on, leaning toward her, his voice thinning. "There's a play called *Same Time Next Year*. Have you seen it? About the couple who meet for one weekend a year in California? Once a year they get away to a remote and private place and—"

"I've seen it."

"Well, then. You and I."

She shook her head again.

"Talk about the soul, Bunny! God, what it would do for the soul!"

"Chuck, no. Too much at stake."

"I've got as much at stake as you. But I've got the guts. Or maybe I should put it another way: that I've got the *need*. I'd come back a better man. You'd come back better, too."

"Listen to me, Chuck," she said quietly. " 'Cause I'm not going to say this very loud. My dad, who is a beautiful, wonderful man, is a filling-station operator. I, Norma Jean Tyler, his daughter, am a judge of the Criminal District Court of Harris County, Texas. And I'm not yet forty years old. My dad is so proud of me—it would kill him if I did something stupid enough to throw it away. It'd kill me, too—because I didn't get this judgeship as a gift. There are people I've pleased to get this, and I've got to continue to please them. All I'd have to do is be found shacked up in a motel somewhere—with a Methodist minister, for Christ's sake!—and—"

"It's that important to you," he said curtly.

"Of course it's important to me. What the hell'd you think?"

"Okay. What do you drink, judge?"

XIV

1968

"You remember my daughter, I expect," said Mary Farnham to the tall, tuxedo-clad man.

The tall man was Lyndon Johnson. He separated himself from a knot of laughing men and women and bowed to Lois. "I'm not the one to forget who's the prettiest girl in Harris County," he said. "How are you, Lois?"

"Very well, Mr. President," said Lois. "I hope you're the same. And I hope you're enjoying the party."

"Miz Farnham," said Johnson, "with your kind permission, I'll ask your daughter to dance."

They danced in the hall outside the living room, on the waxed parquet floors, to the music of a string quartet playing on the balcony above. He held her firmly, but he danced lightly and with easy confidence. She could smell on his breath the two or three drinks he had had, and she could feel in his body that he was relaxed and comfortable. She was glad. She admired the man, and always had, and she felt he was entitled to moments of comfort, in the company of friends. She was pleased, too, he had known he could always be comfortable here, in the Farnham home, in Houston.

"You have two children, I believe," he said in her ear.

"I have a girl four years old and a boy two," Lois said.

"I read in the newspapers that you're also a tough lawyer."

Lois looked up into his eyes and smiled. "I hope so," she said mischievously.

What the president had read in the newspapers were stories about the Dyersburg case.

Edward Dyersburg died in 1957, leaving an estate of more than $11 million in trust for the benefit of his invalid wife and his three children. By his will he appointed two trustees and ordered that they should be able to act only jointly. One trustee was his son, Robert Dyersburg, and the other was his accountant and longtime friend and business adviser, John Shapley. The trustees were to administer the trust so as to "support my said wife during her lifetime in the manner and style to which she has been accustomed during our joint lives of recent years, and specifically my said trustees shall receive and pay all her bills, pay all taxes which may become due, and generally so manage the trust funds so that my said wife need not concern herself with bills and taxes or other financial problems." The trustees had the power to continue the investments made by Edward Dyersburg during his lifetime or to liquidate those investments and make others, as they might judge would benefit the estate.

Under the provision of the will which required the trustees to act jointly, Robert Dyersburg and John Shapley established joint accounts at Gulf Security Trust Bank. Their deposit agreements with the bank specifically required both their signatures on every check written on the trust's checking account.

During the life of the trust—from the death of Edward Dyersburg in 1957 to the death of Mrs. Adelia Dyersburg in 1967—more than eight thousand checks were written on the Dyersburg Trust checking account. Of these, two hundred eleven carried only one signature: that of John Shapley. With those two hundred eleven checks he embezzled $231,814 from the trust.

Tina Dyersburg Scott was a friend of Lois's and came to her for advice. Tina and two other grandchildren of Edward Dyersburg retained Childreth, McLennon & Brady—and specifically Lois Hughes—to recover the money embezzled from the trust.

Shapley did not have it. He had spent the money.

"Let me set forth the facts for you, in one-two-three order," said the frowning Gil Bradshaw irritably, jamming his right index finger rhythmically on the conference table. He was attorney for Gulf Security Trust. The president of the bank sat to one side of him, the chief

trust officer to the other. "Your clients' loss—assuming the alleged loss
occurred—is the result of misappropriation of funds by Mr. Shapley.
Gulf Security Trust is in no way responsible for that. Mr. Shapley was
authorized to write checks—"

"No, he wasn't," Lois interrupted. "Mr. Shapley and Mr. Dyersburg
jointly were authorized to write checks. But the bank honored two
hundred eleven checks signed by Mr. Shapley alone. Not only that,
the bank sent the canceled checks and the monthly statements only
to Mr. Shapley, in spite of the fact that it was a joint account."

"Mr. Shapley had been Mr. Dyersburg, Sr.'s, accountant for many
years," protested the chief trust officer. "He always reconciled the
statements."

"Well, it doesn't make any difference," snapped the lawyer, Bradshaw. "If Shapley embezzled money from the trust, that is between
Shapley and the beneficiaries. There is no liability whatever on the
part of the bank, and I for one am more than a little surprised to find
myself sitting here discussing it."

"Let me put the law and facts straight for you, Mr. Bradshaw,"
said Lois forcefully. "I'll do it in the one-two-three order you favor.
First, the Dyersburg Trust deposited funds in your bank. *Second,* the
bank accepted those funds and agreed to hold them and to disburse
them only as authorized in the deposit agreement. *Third,* the bank
honored checks totaling $231,814 which did not have the required
signatures. Gulf Security Trust was negligent, and it breached its contract with the Dyersburg Trust."

"Mrs. Hughes," said the president with a condescending smile,
"you seem to have little comprehension of banking procedures. Do
you really suppose we can run signature comparisons on the hundreds
of thousands of checks that—"

"Mr. Bronson," she interrupted. "I don't care what your procedures
are. You entered into a contract whereby you committed yourself not
to release funds from the accounts of the Dyersburg Trust except on
two signatures. If it was not practicable for you to check those signatures, then you should not have contracted to do so. But you did
contract, and your bank then breached the contract two hundred and
eleven times, resulting in damages to the trust in the amount of
$231,814—plus interest accrued since the checks were honored."

"Interest!"

"Interest. As of today, the total claim against you is . . . $287,764.98."

Bradshaw smiled bitterly. "So you expect Gulf Security Trust to
make good on Shapley's embezzlement."

"No," said Lois. "I expect Gulf Security Trust to pay the damages sustained by my clients as the result of its negligence and breach of contract."

"It is your intent to sue us, I assume."

She nodded. "Unless you pay without suit."

"You may be sure we will not do that."

The district court entered judgment against Gulf Security Trust for $304,556—the interest had continued to accrue.

"We all regret your decision not to run," Lois said now to the president.

He smiled faintly but did not otherwise respond. Instead, he made an abrupt turn, as if he meant to dance away from Wright Patman, who had nodded to him from the bottom step of the stairway to the balcony. He held her close and plainly savored the touch of her body on his.

For Lois this big, long-eared man was a great president, and she was deeply resentful of the crazies hooting on the streets and the yapping politicians sensing blood and cynically moving in to hurt him. They had never given him a fair chance. They had hated him from the beginning. She loved him. He was the only president in her lifetime in whom she had confidence. She had written to him, saying so. She would like to say so now, but she sensed he wanted to dance, not talk. She looked up into his face and smiled. He squeezed her hand.

"We'll have to dance again. That was too short," he said when the music stopped.

"Whenever you like," she said.

People crowded around them, and conversation began again. Even a forceful man like Johnson could not control the social play around him. In a moment Lois found herself separated from him. Visibly sullen, she watched the crowd push in around him. She resolved to dance with him again.

Lois set a martini aside, with ice cubes still swimming in gin. She felt suddenly that she'd had too much to drink. She looked at herself in the long mirror across the room and took a moment to study an image that never entirely pleased her—tonight an image of a tall, dark-haired woman in a yellow silk cocktail-length dress: a woman a little long in the tooth, in her own judgment. She commended herself, anyway, on not growing matronly the way Bunny seemed to be doing. If Mac John's eye had begun to wander, it was not because she had deteriorated. She was still the woman he had married. She would be thirty years old in a few months. She was not the overdressed girl John Adams had laughed at, then slept with, in London; she had matured since 1960, and maturity had improved her self-confidence; but she was still the lanky, long-striding, introspective young woman Mac John had married in 1963. She had not cheated Mac John out of his young wife; she had not let herself deteriorate.

"D' you really think we should let all these welfare women drop one brat after another onto the taxpayers?"

The intrusion was by their life-insurance agent, Mel Penland, the early-middle-aged son of an insurance-agent father and so a partner in the biggest agency in Houston.

"Go sober up somewhere, Mel," she snapped viciously at him.

Penland retreated angrily. Lois retrieved the martini she had set aside.

He had referred to the Muriel Sampson case. Muriel Sampson was a Negro welfare mother. She had four small children and was pregnant with a fifth illegitimate child when she was convicted of making false statements to a welfare investigator to obtain higher payments. A judge of the criminal district court had given her a choice: spend six months in jail on the conviction of welfare fraud, or submit to a tubal ligation so she could not bear any more children. She refused to submit to the surgery and was sent to jail. She was free now on a habeas corpus obtained for her by Lois Hughes. The case was on appeal.

Part of Lois's argument to the court had been quoted on television as well as in the newspapers: "It seems so reasonable a proposition: to sterilize women who give birth to a succession of babies destined to live their lives on public welfare. Yet, if the Court please, I hear no suggestion that men who father a succession of illegitimate children should submit to vasectomies. Why must the burden of this eminently reasonable solution to a social problem fall on the woman? Why not on the man equally? Indeed, Your Honor, does the Constitution allow anything less than the equal sharing of this burden? Or has my client been denied the equal protection of the laws?"

Childreth, McLennon & Brady did not like identification with the Muriel Sampson case. Lois appealed it in her own name, not in the name of the firm. She had been abused by a succession of drunks at a succession of cocktail parties—essentially in the terms used by Mel Penland—and she had no patience left and little sense of humor on the subject.

She looked at herself again in the mirror across the room. She stiffened her back and lifted her chin high, and stared. She owed herself more than she paid. She owed herself a debt of self-confidence withheld. That was the most difficult thing for her: her own self-image. Sometimes she took stock of herself, of her life; and, rationally, there was nothing wrong. She did well. She was more than the rich man's daughter her father wanted her to be, more than the understated ornament Mac John wanted; and if she was not all she wanted to be herself, at least she was more, better, than others expected.

Sometimes she fantasized a trip to England, to find John Adams, with whom she had corresponded in a desultory way over the years. In her letters she never told him anything intimate, never expressed to him what she supposed, really, she could express to him and receive more understanding than from anyone else in the world. She imagined two weeks in London, sleeping with John Adams in his modest flat, parading naked for him: having from him the appraisal for which she hungered. She could accept it better from him than from anyone else. If John Adams said she had failed, was nothing, she could throw over the whole damned thing—husband, children, career, whatever else anyone supposed she had. But she expected he would not pronounce that kind of judgment. He would admire her. He would like her better than he had before. He would, in her fantasy, tell her he would have accepted gladly her old proposition if it had come from the mature and improved young woman he saw now.

"Lois." This intrusion was by John Finley, red-faced, intense, carrying a glass in one hand, clutching his cane in a desperate grip in the other. "I am grateful to be invited here tonight. I will be more grateful if you will concede me a moment's private conversation."

"No crisis, I hope," she said in a flat, dull voice. "Yesterday was my day for crises. Today is the day for catastrophes. Debacles tomorrow."

John Finley, his fierce black brows bristling, smiled and nodded. "On catastrophe day, the catastrophe is that I am about to lose my grip on my cane and fall on my nose. I was hoping you might sit down with me somewhere for a moment. I seem not to know many people here."

She gestured toward the door. They could step out on the terrace, and she, too, would welcome the moment. "Why not?" she asked. "I think you know everyone. The invitation list includes no accidents, no aberrations; if you are on it, you belong here."

He showed her an apologetic face, but he did allow her to open the door; and he stepped out into the warm April night, she following. He sank immediately into a wicker armchair.

"Where's your protégée?" she asked.

"Whom do you have in mind?"

She slugged the last of her martini, regretting she had not thought to pick up a fresh one before she came out with him onto the moonlit stone terrace. "The onetime Bunny. Norma Jean."

"I would have supposed she was *your* protégée."

"My relationship with her is somewhat different from yours."

He sipped casually from his glass of whiskey. "God, let's hope so," he said.

"Are you going to propose her for partner?"

"I'm going to ask you to do that for me," he said quietly.

"I'm not going to do it," said Lois. "She works for you. Anyway, I brought her into the firm. She's got to impress someone besides me, sometime."

"She has impressed me," he said.

"So I've heard."

Smiling faintly, staring directly into her eyes from the gap between his bristling black brows and the wide frames of his spectacles, he chuckled under his breath and said, "Don't believe everything you hear."

Returning his smile, Lois tipped her head to one side and said, "All I've heard is that she impresses you as a capable lawyer."

"She's ambitious as hell," he said solemnly, punctuating the remark by taking a large swallow from his glass.

"Is that the same as capable?"

He sighed. "She's smart. Her lapses of judgment are destructive, though."

"For example?"

He hesitated, then shrugged. "Why'd she want to marry that oaf Spencer?"

Lois smiled. "Don't you understand that? He's one of Darrell Royal's football players. He thinks that will carry him a long way. She thinks so, too."

"He should have opened a restaurant," Finley grumbled.

Lois laughed. "Don't discount the value of being a handsome couple. Spencer is one gorgeous hunk of man, and I would assume Norma Jean will be Bunny again after she has the baby. A couple like that only needs one brain between them, and Norma Jean can supply that."

"Things like that don't get you anywhere in a firm like ours."

"Really? Are you saying you made Norma Jean your protégée because she's the best young lawyer in the office?"

Finley frowned. "You assume too much. The office assumes too much." He struggled to his feet. "She *is* good. She's smart."

"Then she has nothing to worry about, has she?"

Planting his cane for balance, he took a step toward the door. "She has plenty to worry about," he muttered.

"I think Mac John has left," her father said. "I never did find him."

"Where's the president?" she asked.

"In the library. He met with some people in there. The meeting is over."

She walked in, into the awkward end of a political session, where three men—one smoking a cigar—clustered around Lyndon Johnson and muttered and nodded grimly. "Mr. President," she said firmly, "you promised to dance with me again."

Johnson smiled. "I promised," he said.

"You will excuse us, gentlemen," she said to the three men. "I'm going to offer the president a brandy before we dance." When they had filed sullenly out, she grinned at him and added, "Or some champagne, or some sippin' whiskey, or just the dance."

He smiled broadly. "I'll take the brandy and then the dance," he said.

She suggested a deep leather chair, by a gesture, and when the president settled in the chair she sat on the ottoman in front of him.

"I'm being a naughty girl," she said. "I've had a crappy evening, and I guessed you had, too, so I followed an impulse to isolate you from all the people who are here to see you and have you all to myself for a minute or two. And I promise I won't speak a single word about anything important."

"Why, Miz Hughes," he drawled. "Anything you may choose to say will be impawtint to *me*."

The president sighed comfortably and settled more deeply into the big black leather chair that was a favorite of Daniel Farnham's. He took a crushed cigarette pack from the inside pocket of his tuxedo jacket. He lighted a cigarette with a paper match. She remembered reading that he had once smoked heavily but had quit after his heart attack. He closed his eyes now and inhaled tobacco smoke. To her it was a distressing gesture of resignation.

"I remember when I first met you," she said. "I was just nine years old. It was at a big political barbecue, during your first Senate campaign, in 1948."

Johnson grinned. "Your daddy brought you to hear the speakin', did he?"

She nodded. "You were the chief speaker. I guess it was my introduction to politics."

"I understand your brother's interested in running for Congress."

Lois shook her head. "He's interested. My father is interested in his being interested. But between you and me"—she shook her head more emphatically—"Dan is no politician. He has no sense for it."

"He lacks something more important than that, as long as we're talking to each other off the record," said the president, nodding as he spoke. "He seems to want to be a congressman just to be a congressman. I can't figure out anything else he wants. And that's not enough."

"My father pretends to be cynical. Dan really is."

Johnson shook his head. "He won't go far on that. A man has to have something more in him than that."

"I agree," she said.

The president's mood brightened suddenly. "Now, on the other hand, I hear *you* have causes you believe in. You're the one that should run. I'll come down here and campaign for you."

"I'll take you up on that another year," she laughed.

"You may regard that as a pledge to be redeemed," drawled Johnson.

When they had drunk their brandy and coffee, they danced again.

XV

1968

The top was down on Teejay's little red Falcon convertible, but she
was stuck in heavy traffic, and the sun was bright and hot, and her
sunglasses slipped down her nose. She stopped for the light at Westheimer and Post Oak. A Houston police cruiser pulled up alongside in
the center lane. She glanced apprehensively at the cruiser and at the
two policemen inside: big, suntanned fellows wearing oversize sunglasses, looking all around them, self-consciously playing their role.
Teejay glanced nervously at the traffic light, then at her rearview
mirror, then at the light again, then at the mirror again—until finally
nervous compulsion forced her to turn her head and look squarely at
the police car.

The officer in the right seat grinned. "How ya doin', Red?" he greeted
her.

Teejay smiled and shrugged.

The green arrow cleared traffic for left turns and the cruiser swung
decisively into the intersection and hurried south on Post Oak.

Teejay drove on west, slowly in the creeping, rush-hour traffic.

She had had the car about three months. She had bought it off a
used-car lot and had insisted on the convertible in defiance of Alan's
scornful insistence that convertibles were not safe and that it wouldn't

be cool anyway, top down or no, driving in city traffic. He was wrong. It was cool, at night at least; and she enjoyed it, driving with the rush of air around her. She enjoyed just driving, in fact: just having her hands on the wheel and driving where she wanted to go. He could not understand why she would go out and drive to nowhere in particular for no better reason than that the car was hers and she could drive it anywhere she wanted to. Alan was an intelligent man, but insensitive.

After fifteen minutes more in the heat and fumes of traffic, she turned off Westheimer into the parking lot at the Corona Club. (It was the old Corona Lounge, where she had been working for more than a year, but changed at the beginning of the summer to a semiprivate club, open to whomever bought a $10 membership.) Parking at the rear of the lot, where employees were supposed to park, she carefully locked in the trunk of the car a paperbound copy of the Internal Revenue Code, a volume of tax-court reports, and a folder filled with notes—her materials from a seminar on income taxation she was taking this summer at the law school.

She entered the club through the front door, using her own plastic membership card to work the coded electric lock. "Hey, Tommy Jo!" Regulars in the club raised their glasses to her and called to her as she walked through. She went behind the bar. Cal, who was the owner of the club, was tending bar; but she was bartender in the evening, and before she changed her clothes she always reviewed with him the inventory of liquor on hand, then counted with him the cash in the register before she assumed responsibility for it. Also, he told her who would be working. He would be in the club most of the night, but when he went out, she was in charge.

She went to the storeroom behind the bar to change her clothes. Stripped to her panties, she dried the sweat off her body with a towel, then dusted herself with talcum powder. She pulled on a pair of silver lamé pants—so tight she had to tug and writhe to pull them up her legs and over her hips. She stepped into silver shoes and bent to buckle the straps around her ankles. She stood then before a mirror propped up on some empty liquor cases and brushed her long red hair smooth, down her back and over her bare shoulders. This was her costume: the silver pants and shoes and nothing more. She had been working topless since the lounge became a club at the beginning of the summer.

"Do you make much money working topless?" That was usually the first question. The second would be: "Does it bother you? I mean, does it embarrass you? Was it hard to get used to?" Almost always it was a man who ordered a mixed drink who asked. Most of the evening she poured beer and bourbon, and most of the men essayed a weak joke or two, then sat and silently stared at her. A man who ordered Scotch or a martini would usually try to make conversation, timidly at first, then he would ask his questions. The answer to the first was that she made a lot of money; she had made more than $1900 in July, adding tips to wages. The answer to the second was that it did not bother her and it never had. On the contrary, she enjoyed it. Alan told her she was an exhibitionist.

"Sure. Why else would I do it?" was her answer to the man sipping Cutty and soda. She had discovered that they liked to think she was shamed and had to force herself to bare her breasts because she badly needed the money.

"You're very pretty. Does it bother you to—like, I mean—show your-self like this?"

She lowered her eyes and smiled. "Of course it does. But the money is really good."

"Well, you're by far the prettiest girl I ever saw working topless."

That was what Cal said, too, and he acknowledged that she had been the major factor in saving the business from closing. As the Corona Lounge, it had slipped badly. It had had nothing to distin-guish it except the high-riding leotards the waitresses had worn; and when other places around town went topless, the leotards were no longer much of an attraction. Cal was nothing but a west Texas bar-tender migrated to Houston to try to make a bigger buck, and to save his business he had done all he could think of to do—go topless, con-vert to a club to keep the law off, talk his very prettiest girl into work-ing topless behind the bar, and let the other girls double as waitresses and go-go dancers. The other girls, assorted hard- or vacant-looking types, worked in little bikinis, and each one took her top off only when she did her stint on the dance platform across the room.

He had offered Teejay a share of the business. She had been tempted to take it, but decided having her name on it as part owner could be-come an impediment to her admission to the practice of law if any-thing bad ever happened in the place. Instead, she took a guarantee from him. He paid her $200 a week as a wage and guaranteed two hundred a week more in tips. Only the first week they opened as a topless club did he have to make up a part of her guarantee.

"The point about you," a man in jacket and tie had said to her one night, "is that you have a certain *dignity*. You just don't look like the kind that you usually run into doing this kind of thing. Besides, you can talk."

She was careful about her conversation—careful not to have anyone learn she was a law student. Even Cal didn't know that. She called herself Tommy Jo, and she practiced at giving Tommy Jo a character Teejay did not have. She spoke with the west Texas accent she had grown up with and had since taken pains to overcome. She wore lipstick. Teejay didn't. Teejay, in fact, dressed more conservatively of late and wore her hair tied tightly behind her head. She thought there was a good chance that even if one of her fellow students happened to come into the Corona Club, he would not recognize her.

"I suppose you get a lot of propositions."

She shrugged. "I been working in bars ever since I was old enough, and I've always got propositions. The only difference is, now they offer more money."

"I'd go a couple hundred myself."

"I've been offered five hundred."

"And?"

She shook her head firmly. "No way. That's a different business. I'm not in that business."

"Does it offend you that guys ask?"

She smiled. "No. Y' can't blame a man for trying."

In July she bought Alan a cashmere sport jacket. "Jesus, Teejay, it's great—it's wonderful. But—why?" "Because I can afford it and you can't," she told him. "That's the result of exhibitionism."

Also, it would pay for her law office, her desk, her chairs, her bookcases, her typewriter, her library. She had all but concluded she would not be accepted in any established firm. She was a woman. She would graduate from an undistinguished law school. No one was going to do her any favors. She found a certain romantic attraction to the idea of hanging out her shingle in the tradition of Lincoln and Herndon. She was finding more and more a piquant flavor in the dusty, cobwebby traditions of the profession. She was intrigued with the idea of opening her own independent law office. But it would cost money.

She had some money. Over the years she had learned to live cheaply and to save. Some of her money was invested in treasury bills, bought for her and held for her by the Bank of the Southwest. The treasury bills were absolutely secure and paid more interest than any savings account. She read the *Wall Street Journal* every day in the school library and keenly watched the market in treasury bills. They came in thousand-dollar denominations, and from time to time she would call the bank and order a bill, paid for with money transferred from her savings account.

She kept some cash in a safe-deposit box and some more hidden in a suitcase in the apartment she shared with Alan. She never confided to Alan that her suitcase contained some four thousand dollars. That, and the cash in her safe-deposit box, was tip money she had not reported on her income-tax returns. During the past six years she had never reported more than half her tip income. Her thought was that she worked too hard and sacrificed too much for her money to be compelled to hand it over to the government to waste and steal. She paid the taxes she could not escape, and no more.

"Tommy Jo," drawled one of the bikini-clad waitresses who had no customers at her tables and was sipping a beer at the bar. "Y' boobs startin' t' droop any, y' think? I mean, from hangin' out as much of the time as whut they do?"

Teejay shook her head. "No," she said coldly. "Not at all."

"What are they, Tommy Jo? Thirty-eight?" asked a young man in an open-collared shirt drinking successive beers from the bottles.

She shook her head again. "Not quite."

When she moved in with Alan she had started taking the Pill for the first time in her life, and to her surprise her breasts had grown about an inch. Because she was high-necked and slender and carried herself with erect posture, her heavy breasts looked bigger than they were. Although they were firm, they were pendulous and swung and bounced as she hurried at her work behind the bar. She was a better show, just serving drinks or wiping off the bar, than the girls on the go-go platform, Cal said. Actually, her most generous tips were from men who sat at the bar at quiet hours and talked with her. They stared thoughtfully at her nipples, sometimes frowning, and, except for the inevitable questions about how much money she made and whether her seminakedness embarrassed her, they talked and never mentioned her breasts.

"Whut ah'd lak t' dew," one beery, crew-cut cemetery-lot salesman told her on a night in July, "is go up there t' Shy-cago t' th' Democrat convention with a couple buddies a mine with some ball bats and knock a few a them hippie heads. Ah mean, we'd give them Shy-cago cops a little backup and show them screwballs whut real Americans think a *them*."

Alan bought a membership in the club and stopped in a few nights, late, to drink and chat with her at the bar shortly before the club closed; but he could not stand the talk of some of the customers, and he stopped coming. He did ask her one night if she had ever thought of joining any of the protests of that summer of '68.

"I have important things to think about," she had said. "Like finishing law school, passing the bar, opening an office. Important questions like whether or not to work topless here, when you tell me I shouldn't. I leave little problems like how to run the country in the hands of little people like Lyndon Johnson and Hubie Humphrey and Tricky Dicky Nixon."

"Don't you think about the war?" he asked abruptly, lifting his beer bottle and tugging beer.

"Yes," she said. "And I'll accept your judgment. You were there."

"It's easy to be sophomoric," he said soberly. "It would be easy to say: By God, I went, so you have to go, too—like some college boy rationalizing a fraternity initiation." He shrugged. "I went partly in the thought that, because I did, later guys wouldn't have to. But here we are, still at it and no closer to winning it than we were when I was there. It didn't seem futile when I went. I can understand how it seems so now."

"My little brother is there," she said.

"You never mentioned it."

"I don't talk about my family. They don't talk about me. I get a letter two or three times a year."

"You think your little brother ought to come home?"

She nodded. "I don't think it's a good deal. I never said anything, because I knew you'd gone and I didn't know what you'd think if I were critical of it. But I don't think he's fighting for anything. I don't think there's any purpose to it anymore."

"Well, you ought to say what you think," Alan said. "This is a country where what people think counts, you know."

Teejay smiled. "Who'd listen to the opinions of a topless bar girl?"

Early in September, on a Wednesday night, she opened a fresh bottle of Dewar's, and when she turned back toward the bar, twisting the pouring spout into the throat of the bottle, she came face-to-face with Kevin.

"Tommy Jo," he said grimly.

She recognized him, but he had changed. He was thinner. His curly blond hair was cut short. He was wearing a conspicuously cheap, ill-fitting, light green sport shirt. The skin of his face was stretched tight over the cheekbones and jawbones, and it was ruddy and shiny, as if it had been scraped with a straight razor by a rude country barber.

"Kevin . . ." she whispered.

"You ain't the easiest person in the world to find," he said.

"How long have you been out?" she asked, standing close to him so she could talk out of the hearing of others at the bar.

"Six weeks, about," he said. "Seems like they thought my record wasn't so good and it'd be a good idea to keep me. They tossed me back on my first parole hearing. I was promised when I copped that I'd only have to do ten, twelve months. I wound up doin' twenty."

"I'm sorry, Kevin," she said very quietly. "Was it bad?"

"I did some of it on the roads, some of it in the cow barns."

She had drinks to serve. She opened a beer for Kevin and worked briskly to pour whiskey for the orders brought by two waitresses. She watched him. While she worked, he drank beer and stared unhappily at the array of bottles behind the bar. She saw him curtly halt a man's attempt to open a conversation with him. His arms were heavily muscled and he was deeply tanned. His forehead was longer; his hair had thinned in front. He had lost his boyishness. He was a damaged, sullen man.

"I've jumped parole already," he told her when she had another moment to talk with him.

"How did you find me?"

For the first time he smiled. "I haven't got dumb," he said. "I'll tell you, though, I expected to find a lady lawyer, not a barmaid workin' half naked."

"I'm going to be a lawyer very soon," she said. "In the meantime, I'm making a lot of money. Do you need a loan?"

He shook his head. "You're livin' with a man. Gonna marry him?"

"No."

He sat at the bar and drank three beers, waiting for moments when they could talk. After midnight, business slackened. She pulled her stool over to where it faced him, sat, and lit a cigarette. She was not wearing the silver lamé pants that night, just a pair of white stretch pants, skintight, with white wedge shoes. One of the liquor suppliers had given her a necklace: a gold sunburst medallion on a chain; and the medallion, the size of a silver dollar, hung between her breasts. She crossed her legs and inhaled smoke from her cigarette.

"What do you plan to do, Kevin?" she asked.

He did not answer immediately. He sipped thoughtfully from his glass of beer, his eyes soberly and speculatively fixed on her bare breasts. "I couldn't do what they had me set up to do," he said. "I mean, what the parole had me set up to do: workin' in a factory. You know me, Tommy Jo. I can't do that kind of work unless they got a gun pointed at me—like they did for thirty months. That's why I jumped it already."

"You think they're looking for you?"

He shook his head. "What's Oklahoma care about one small-time con man more or less? Course, if I was to get picked up for any reason—and I mean *any* reason—they'd flop me right back to McAlester." He looked up, into her eyes. "That's why I've changed my name. Say hello to Jim Hedwig. I've got a fake Ohio driver's license in the name of James O. Hedwig of Cincinnati. I'm going to be Hedwig, for a while anyway."

"And do what?" she asked.

He grinned—the old, roguish grin. "I've got a couple of ideas. I'll get a scam going."

"If you get in trouble again, they'll take your fingerprints, and—"

"I know," he interrupted.

She got down from the stool and went to the end of the bar to take a drink order from one of the waitresses. She opened three beers and sent the girl on her way, and she came back. She retrieved her burning cigarette from the ashtray on the bar and perched again on the tall stool.

"You changed, Tommy Jo." It was an accusation.

"Almost three years, Kevin." She shrugged. "What'd you expect?"

"You're twenty-six, aren't you?"

She nodded.

He glanced around the club. "Men come in here to see what a real woman looks like. You were somethin' of a little girl yet in El Paso. Now . . ."

She tried to lighten the conversation. "You like me more? Or less?"

"I don't love you any less."

She had hoped he wouldn't say it. She lowered her eyes and stared at the smoke curling off the tip of her cigarette.

"Don't be afraid I'll get in your way," he said.

She looked up. "What's that mean?"

"I didn't come here to talk to you about us gettin' together any other way than we ever did," he said. "I gave up a long time ago any idea you and I were goin' anywhere together."

Teejay sighed. "So did I," she said.

"You did think about it, then?"

She nodded.

He smiled faintly. "Well—that's somethin', anyway." He grinned. "Hey," he said. "What would you have done, back in El Paso, if I'd asked you to drop out of school and marry me and run off with me somewhere in that black Mercury I had?"

She ground out her cigarette and blew away the last breath of smoke. "I might have done it," she admitted.

He raised his chin and nodded curtly. "Yeah, and been sorry for the rest of your life," he said in a harder voice.

She nodded. "Probably," she said quietly.

"Anyway," he said, "I've loved you a long time. Maybe you loved me back, just a little. I mean, if you—Did you ever, Tommy Jo? Did you ever love me at all?"

Teejay frowned. "Sure," she whispered. "Sure I did. More than just a little, too."

"Now?"

It was the question—the confrontation—she had dreaded. She had rehearsed an answer. She had an answer ready. She could not use it. "Why not?" she said quietly. "What's changed?"

"Would you drop out of law school and marry me and come east with me?"

She shook her head. "No."

"You can be damn sure I won't ask you," he said. "Or let you if you wanted to. Talk about bein' sorry the rest of your life!"

"Let's don't talk about it."

He stared for a moment into his glass of beer, then decisively pushed it away. It was a gesture she had seen many times: the abrupt decision to stop drinking. He clasped his hands before him on the bar and began to talk quietly, flatly, as if he were talking to himself and only letting her listen.

"You're the only person I ever met," he said, "who could keep up with me, keep right up with me. I'm smarter than most of the race of mankind, Tommy Jo. I know it's true. They don't wise up to me. They can't keep up with me. Except you. You're as smart as I am, maybe smarter, and you have a stubborn streak up your back that's absolutely scary." He unclasped his hands and clasped them again, nervously, staring at them. "You're going to do better than I am. I've outsmarted myself a couple times. Anyway, I haven't got the discipline you have. You're going to beat the world, Tommy Jo."

She shook her head. "I don't know, Kevin. . . ."

"It's the biggest reason why I love you," he said. "You and I are different from each other, but we're more alike than maybe you think and very different from most of the world. I'd never stand in the way of you goin' where you're goin'. That's what I meant when I said not to worry about me gettin' in your way. I'm proud of you. I'm proud to have anything to do with you. I'm goin' to be a whole lot prouder, though, when you put your clothes on and open that law office."

XVI

On their bunk pads spread out on the floor of the cell, Teejay and Janie lay clutched together, naked and sweating but with their arms tightly clasped around each other. Janie wept softly, and Teejay, with tears in her own eyes, gently nuzzled her and whispered in her ear. It was their last night together. Tomorrow Janie would be transferred to the Goree unit of the Texas State Prison system, to begin serving the sentence imposed on her yesterday in criminal district court.

Her trial had been quick and simple, lasting only two and a half days. The jury had found her guilty of killing her husband; but, to her surprise, and Teejay's, and even to the complete surprise of her own attorney, the jury had defined the crime as murder in the second degree, not premeditated murder. She would be eligible for parole in less than ten years. The verdict was great good news for Janie and a rare stroke of luck. Yet, as she said, it was unrealistic: The promise of release from prison after ten years was something out of another life, one yet to be lived; and reality right now was that she was leaving the jail in the morning, leaving the only friend she had.

She had not cried until now, after midnight. They had talked earnestly all evening, and after the lights were out they had made love with special fervor. Then they had lain together and talked more, and suddenly Janie began to cry.

"It's because I love you, Teejay," she whispered. "You're my only special darlin' and I love you."

"I love you, too, Janie," Teejay whispered in her ear.

Janie stopped crying and lay breathing heavily against Teejay's shoulder, and Teejay began to pat her hip, rhythmically, reassuring.

At first Janie had not used the word "love." She had used loving words about the gratification in what they did together, but never the world "love." Then, sometime after Teejay learned to reciprocate, to return the sensual pleasure Janie gave, Janie began to whisper occasionally that she loved Teejay. Yesterday and today, she had declared, ardently and repeatedly, that she was in love with Teejay and no one else in the world was important to her. No one else in the world, she said, cared if she lived or died; but if Teejay cared, that was enough; she didn't need anyone else.

Teejay had firmly withheld the word until tonight. Tonight she could not hold it back any longer. With Janie clinging to her, kissing her, tearfully insisting she loved her, Teejay was incapable of withholding a human response. She had told Janie she loved her too. She had repeated it, not urgently, but gently, to comfort Janie.

In a sense it was true: She did love her. Janie was a giving person, an innocent giving person, who had seen that Teejay needed warmth and the erotic touch of another human being and had given all she could of herself, without reserve. She had made love to Teejay every night for more than a week before Teejay was able to return it—without complaint, without insisting that Teejay do for her what she did for Teejay. Teejay had learned to do what Janie did; and now, with this semi-literate, vapid little blonde who had murdered her husband, she had shared a carnal intimacy she had never even approached before, with anyone. And because Janie was such an innocent and so giving, and because of what they had done together, she did love her, at least in some sense, and it troubled her.

When Janie was taken out of jail to go to her trial, she was allowed to have her hair done and to make up and dress as she wanted. She had had her blond hair teased into an unstylish high bouffant, and she wore shiny pink lipstick and a faint pink eyeshadow to match the hot pink of her pantsuit. Teejay watched through the cage bars as Janie was led out, bouncing stiffly in high-heeled sandals, carrying a cigarette between her lips.

Teejay had watched her, thoughtfully. Her thought was that she knew the taste and smell of every private part of that pink-suited young woman. Her tongue had touched all of her flesh. She had done with her what she had always thought was loathsome—what *was* loathsome. She had shared with her what she had never expected, never intended, to share with anyone. With Janie. With that one, there—the one in the cheap pink pantsuit, the grotesque makeup, and the teased hair. Teejay had walked away from the cage bars, back to the cell, burdened with her thoughts. Now, lying on the cell floor, holding the naked Janie to her own naked body, kissing her, the thought came back: *This was her lover?*

Yes—or maybe no. Tomorrow she would be gone. It would be easier then to think, to decide, to know. Now she held Janie close and nuzzled her throat, comforted her, and accepted one more hour's half-escape from the harsh ugliness of the jail.

The next morning at ten they took Janie away. She was dressed in her pink pantsuit and her high heels. She had put on a little lipstick, but had done nothing for her hair. She was handcuffed, and her hands were secured at her belly by a loop of chain around her waist. She stopped at the bars where Teejay stood.

"Goodbye, Teejay," she whispered.

"Goodbye, Janie."

Teejay took possession of the upper bunk in the cell. She lay on it for an hour, smoking, staring up through the barred ceiling at the dusty pipes above. She suppressed an impulse to turn over on her stomach and cry into the blanket. It was better for her—she had firmly decided days ago—that Janie would not be there anymore.

She had committed too much to Janie. The trouble was, Janie was part of being a prisoner in this jail, and what they had done together was part of that, too. Outside, they would not have become friends. Outside, they would not have been lovers. (Unless they had been impelled by a latent predilection for a homosexual relationship: something Teejay would not believe of herself.) The trouble was that, in here, inside the jail, Janie had dragged Teejay's attention to her existence as a prisoner. Janie had contributed to the frightening retreat the world had been making. Teejay resented any attention she had to give to this place: to things like getting a uniform that was not ragged, like the food they ate, like small adjustments in the way the matrons set up the fans, so that some cells got a breath more air than others— all the petty conditions of existence inside this wretched place. She had studied Janie: Janie had learned to live here; she had adjusted to it. Teejay did not want to. She did not want Janie to teach her to endure. She did not want to adjust. She needed to focus absolutely on getting out of here. Janie had distracted her. She was better off without Janie.

It was frightening how much the jail had become the center of her existence and how remote everything else seemed, in spite of her resolution that it should not be so. Frank Agnelli, the young lawyer who worked for her and had been trying to keep the office running since she had been in jail, had come in a few days ago, embarrassed and tentative, to tell her the office was producing little income and that he saw no alternative to letting one of the secretaries go, also dropping some lawbook subscriptions, and otherwise cutting costs. He had thought she would be distressed. She had supposed she would be, by having to face such a reality. But she was not. She had only shrugged and told him to use his best judgment.

Lois had arranged for her apartment to be disassembled. Her furniture had been moved to a storage warehouse. Boxes of her personal things were stacked in her office. Again, Teejay had found it impossible to care very much. She would care some other time, not now. It was frightening to know that she would have been more interested, more involved emotionally, in news that a better television set was going to be set up outside the cage bars or that something was going to be done to make the jail toilets flush more vigorously.

She had gained a little weight. It showed especially around her cheeks, around her jawbone. The jail food was starchy, and she got no exercise. She could not wash enough, and her complexion had suffered. She found pimples on her face from time to time. She felt the jail was damaging her. She had been in jail three months. She wondered how she would look in three or four months more.

Lois brought the word that a date had been set for her trial. "Monday, November twenty-seventh—the Monday after Thanksgiving. Norma's setting aside three weeks for it. Okay?"

Teejay nodded, but she frowned deeply. "Four more months in jail," she said resignedly.

"I'm sorry," Lois said. "I didn't press for an earlier date. We need the time."

"Have they set a date for Kevin?"

"Oh, yes. I meant to tell you. A month earlier. Actually, Bill Hornwood wanted to try your two cases together. Judge Spencer—Norma—said no. I had told her we couldn't stand that."

"You've talked with Kevin," said Teejay.

Lois *had* talked again to Kevin Flint. She had arranged to meet with him and his lawyer, Ronald Steen. Because the three of them could not meet comfortably, smoking, in one of the interview cubicles in the jail, the sheriff had allowed Flint to be brought out of the jail to sit with Steen and Lois in a deputy's office, on condition that Flint be chained to a chair. They had met at ten. Steen and Flint were already in the office when Lois arrived, and Flint was indeed wearing a pair of leg irons that were attached to the heavy chair in which he sat by a length of chain and a padlock.

It had been Lois's immediate judgment when she met him before that Flint was one of the handsomest and most personable men she had ever met. He was a well-built but not conspicuously tall or muscular man, probably in his early forties: ruddy of complexion, as though he had found in the jail some window by which he could sit and take the summer sun, with curly light hair that had backed up from his shiny red forehead. His smile was fascinating, engaging. It involved his whole face. He smiled easily. He sat poised and at ease in his chair, showing no embarrassment over being chained to it. A cigarette burned in an ashtray at his elbow, but he ignored it and sipped Coke from a can. He was manifestly conscious that he was a handsome man. His blue denim jail coveralls were unbuttoned at the top, exposing his chest and the curly hair on it.

"You call her Teejay," he said. "I always knew her as Tommy Jo. I love her. I always have, for a long time. But I was never married to her, never slept with her. I guess the way she looks at it, probably, is that I'm her friend. I hope I'm her friend. I always meant to be her friend. But I love her. I've never known anybody I've admired as much as Tommy Jo."

"Kevin," Ronald Steen interrupted, "we've set a ground rule or two for this meeting. Mrs. Hughes has agreed nothing you say can be quoted. What she wants is background."

Flint shrugged and picked up his Coca-Cola can.

"Mr. Flint—" Lois began.

"Call me Kevin. And it's, uh—Lois?"

She nodded. "Right. As I understand it, it will be your testimony, if you're asked to testify, that Teejay had nothing to do with the death of Benjamin Mudge. Is that right?"

"Right. Absolutely."

"You're going on trial for killing Mudge. What's your defense?"

Flint's smile disappeared. He shook his head. "Ron's tryin' hard, but we don't have one."

"This is off the record," Steen interrupted firmly.

Lois nodded. "That's understood."

"There was never any reason for them to bring Tommy Jo's name into this," Flint protested.

"Well, let me ask you this, then," said Lois. "When's the last time you talked to her? Or saw her?"

Flint shook his head. "I don't know, exactly. I didn't see her very often. It's been six months, I expect."

"Three months or so before you were arrested?"

"Yes."

"The prosecutor's going to ask a question like this: If you were in love with this woman, how does it happen that you didn't see her very often?"

"It was just—kind of frustration to see her," said Flint. "I had to accept it a long time ago that she would never marry me. She had her life all planned when I met her: what she was goin' to do. Runnin' around with a guy like me was just something she did for fun, for a little while. Really makin' an arrangement with me—like, I mean, marrying me or living with me—wasn't part of what she had in mind. I don't mean to say she was cold. She was just what you might call realistic.

"You know, I hadn't known her very long when I had to go and do two and a half years in the penitentiary in Oklahoma. That probably fixed it. Any ideas she might have had, that fixed it. She was goin' to be something in life and not live hand-to-mouth like I did, like her family had done, and gettin' tied up to a convict or an ex-convict just wasn't any part of her plans. I accepted that. I understood. I wanted things to work out right for her. Sometimes I wished I didn't love her. But I always did. Nobody else ever compared to her."

"Other women?"

"Sure. I've had lots of girls—and did with 'em what I never did with Tommy Jo. But they didn't compare. It would make you sick to compare." He smiled. "In my line of life, you don't have many chances to meet somebody like Tommy Jo."

"When you did see her, Kevin, where would that be? In what circumstances?"

"Different places," he said, lifting both eyebrows high. "I'd call her, go see her."

"Only once or twice a year?"

"More than that. I used to see her every month or two."

"But where?"

"Dinner. I'd go to her place, and she'd fix dinner. Sometimes we went out. We liked steak and wine. But I'll tell you: We tried to stay away from places where anybody'd know us. She had a good name as a lawyer. I'm an ex-con, a hustler, a guy with about as bad a name as you could get. She never said it, but I knew she had a problem about bein' seen with me, and I took care of that problem for her. I made sure we weren't seen."

"Did you ever stay the night at her apartment?"

"Never. I've never had sex with Tommy Jo."

He spoke with an unembarrassed, calm gaze into Lois's eyes. She made a note: He would be an effective witness. His face was mobile; it followed his emotions, or rather, probably, the emotion he meant to signal. Teejay had described him as a confidence man. It was easy to see how he could operate as one.

"You aren't thinking," said Ron Steen, "of denying that Teejay even knew Kevin, are you?"

Lois shook her head. "No. But the more distance we place between them, the better it will look for her."

"I'll testify I saw her once a year, maybe twice," said Kevin ingenuously. "It wouldn't be smart for me to swear I *never* saw her, because your district attorney might come up with a witness that saw us together eating somewhere."

"What did you tell the police about it?" Lois asked.

"Nothin'. I stood on my rights and didn't tell 'em anything about anything."

"Do I understand you're offering to lie from the witness stand?" asked Steen.

Kevin grinned and shrugged. "By the time Tommy Jo's trial comes up, I'll be under a death sentence, or a life sentence," he said. "You think they'll indict me for perjury, too?"

Steen shook his head unhappily. "As your counsel I advise you not to lie," he said.

"If you don't want to hear about it, why don't you wait outside?" Kevin asked casually.

"Now, wait a minute," said Lois. "I'm not asking you to lie, either."

"All I want you to do is tell me how to help Tommy Jo," Flint said firmly to Lois. "That's what you're supposed to do, isn't it? You're her defense lawyer."

"It won't help her if you are caught lying," said Lois.

Kevin grinned again and shook his head. "I'm not gonna get caught, lady."

Lois's impulse was to remind him that he did sometimes get caught. But he could destroy her client, with one misplaced word, and it would not be wise to test his emotional stability. "I simply mean that you and Teejay must not contradict each other," Lois said, staring at her pen poised over her note pad.

"We won't if you do your job."

Lois looked up. "Do what?"

"Tell me what she wants me to say," said Flint blandly. "Tell me what she's going to say. Tell her what I'm going to say. We can't get together and plan the testimony, so you have to carry messages."

"He lies, Teejay. One lie after another," Lois complained. "I couldn't tell him I read your letters—and destroyed them for you. But I *know* he didn't write you from the Oklahoma penitentiary to ask you for money. In the letter from Mexico, he wrote about smoking pot with you—which was the biggest reason why I tore up the letters and flushed them down—but he tells me he never smoked pot himself and thinks you never did either. You can't believe a word he says."

"You could if you didn't know better," said Teejay.

"Meaning what?"

"Meaning a jury would believe his testimony."

"Are you asking me to call a witness I know is going to lie?"

"Are you telling me you've never done it?" Teejay asked aggressively. "Are you telling me you never used a witness you knew would slant the facts his way, or outright lie, for that matter? How about a client? Did you ever sit in court and listen to your client lie to the judge and jury? Did you ever sit at a negotiating table and listen to a business client lie?"

Lois pushed her chair back from the table. She folded her arms. "Tell me something, Teejay," she said. "Just how much lying is it going to take to get you acquitted? What would happen if everybody told the truth?"

"I might just wind up with a life sentence," said Teejay flatly. "On the basis of circumstantial evidence . . . prejudice . . . Hornwood will do everything he can to prejudice the jury. Marijuana . . . The idea I had a love affair with Kevin . . . Anything . . ."

Frowning, Lois flipped through her notes again. She sighed and shook her head. "Incidentally," she said suddenly, "do you know a lawyer in Dallas by the name of Alan Merimac?"

Teejay nodded. "We lived together when we were in law school. Does Hornwood know about *Alan*, for Christ's sake?"

"Yes. Merimac has been interviewed by investigators from the district attorney's office."

"My God—"

"He called me from Dallas to tell me. I think he's another one who would be willing to lie for you if it would help you. Did he know you once worked topless? It was about the time when you lived with him, wasn't it?"

Teejay nodded.

"He told the investigators you worked as a waitress at the Warwick Hotel."

"I did work there for a year."

"Well—that's all he told them."

Teejay smiled. "Alan—"

"Men in your life," said Lois. "Merimac is pretty respectable. He's trust officer at First Bank in Dallas. Are there any others the investigators might know about?"

"I have my friends," said Teejay.

"Are there any I need to know about?"

"I don't think so."

Lois pushed back her chair once more. She clasped her hands before her and regarded Teejay with a conspicuously thoughtful mien. "Sex life, Teejay," she said after a moment. "I'm sorry I have to ask. Anything I need to know?"

Teejay shook her head.

Lois tapped her pen nervously on her pad, making a pattern of dots. "There is a story going around," she said in voice so controlled it was artificial in sound, "to the effect that you and your cellmate have developed a—strong attachment for each other. I'm sure that can't be introduced in evidence, but—"

"*Where is this story going around?*" Teejay demanded angrily.

"A couple of courthouse reporters have heard it. Hornwood knows it. Nobody will publish it."

"Prepare a libel suit and have it ready to go if they do."

"Truth is the perfect defense to libel," Lois said.

"No. *Proof* is the perfect defense to libel. No one could prove—"

"And it comes to that again," said Lois. "Truth versus proof. What *is* the truth, Teejay?"

"Every goddamn word they've said is the truth," Teejay muttered, shaking her head. "And every goddamn word is impossible to prove."

"*For Christ's sake!*"

"You try it sometime, Lois," Teejay growled angrily. "You get yourself locked up in a cage sometime, like a goddamn animal, and you see what you feel toward someone who offers you a little human sympathy, and you see how you express it. That's what it is. That's what it amounts to. Anyway, it's over. She's been sentenced."

"I don't care what you've done. All I'm interested in is your defense."

"I know that. She says I'm the only friend she has in the world. Maybe *she's* the only one *I* have."

"No," Lois said quietly. "I signed up to be your defense lawyer. But I do care personally about—I do care, Teejay."

Teejay said nothing. She only stared at Lois. Tears streamed down her cheeks.

When the time came to be locked in, she was locked in alone. She read for a while. She took off her dress and bra because of the heat and sat in her panties on the pad from the lower bunk, on the floor. Her eyes watered—maybe from the smoke in the cell, maybe from nervous tension—and she put down the book and spread a game of solitaire. She played listlessly, listening to the murmur of conversation in nearby cells.

After five games, she lifted herself heavily from the floor and stood pressing her hips against the bars. "Hey, Murdock," she said. Murdock was the shoplifter, the beefy older woman, Janie's friend, who shared the cell to the left.

"Hey, princess," Murdock answered.

"Suppose we could, uh, lay out a game of cards on the floor?" Teejay asked humbly.

"Possible," said Murdock. The steel wall that separated them was less than an inch thick, and if they sat in the corners of their cells, on the floor, they could play cards on the floor outside the bars.

"I'd appreciate it," Teejay said.

"Yeah. You miss Janie, don't you?"

Teejay nodded; then, realizing Murdock could not see her, she said, "Sure. It's tough, being alone."

"You're learning," said Murdock.

They spread a game of gin on the concrete floor outside the two cells, and Teejay, leaning against the steel wall and the heavy, close-set bars, played cards with Murdock, though she could not see her. They played for an hour.

XVII

1969

She heard Mac John in the bathroom, vomiting. Lois rolled over, glanced at the clock. Four in the morning. He gagged deep and the vomit splashed into the basin. She lifted herself on an elbow and watched him for a moment through the bathroom door. He hung over the basin, his pale, hairy bums lifted, his extended scrotum swinging between his parted legs. He choked, and the vomit burst from his mouth. He moaned.

Once she would have gotten up and gone to the bathroom and offered him help. She had done it many times. Now, she settled back on her pillow and closed her eyes. He had drunk his whiskey, and now he was heaving it up. Nothing she could say or do would make it any different.

Before she went to sleep again she heard him rinsing out the basin. She heard him shake aspirin tablets from the bottle and heard him run water in a cup to wash them down. She heard him splash aftershave lotion on his face and hands to cover the sour smell on his breath. When he returned to the bed, she pretended she was asleep.

At the breakfast table he poured vodka into his orange juice.

They had breakfast alone, before the children woke—never anything more than pastries, coffee, and orange juice. When Sally came at 8:30, she would fix the children's toast and cereal, or eggs and bacon. Sally would take care of the children all day.

Lois switched on the small television set on the breakfast table to watch the news on the "Today Show." "It's our night to have dinner with my father and mother, you remember," she said.

"Thursday, yes," he said with no enthusiasm.

He was dressed. His jacket and tie were lying on the couch in the library. She was wearing a short yellow nightgown and mules. She had brushed out her hair before she came down, but she would dress for the office only after Sally came. It was their long-standing morning routine: for him to shower first and dress and come down to make the coffee; for her to lie in bed until he finished his shower and then to brush out her hair and put on a fresh nightgown for breakfast. They never talked much. They looked at the paper and turned on the television set. He would leave before she did. She would watch him back out of the driveway. Finally, she would return to the breakfast room, finish her coffee and the newspaper, and be ready to go upstairs as soon as Sally came.

Their lives downtown were filled with variety: demand, challenge, even with crisis. Some nights one or both of them came home wrung out, exhausted. It was too easy, then, to compress life at home into comfortable, prosaic routine, to accept boredom because it was not demanding. Mac John drank too much. He played golf too much. He threw himself too much into their Saturday parties. It was because he was bored; but when she tried to talk to him about it, he would shrug and change the subject. He seemed to accept the round into which they had fallen: hard, purposeful days and dull, purposeless nights and weekends. She did not accept it. She thought about alternatives. If he did, he would not talk about it.

It troubled her that she did not love her children as much as other people seemed to love theirs. Wendy Anne, who was a pretty little girl of five, was easy to love, and Lois did love her; and Mac John, Jr., three, was a romper, loud and infuriating, but appealing, and she loved him, too. But not enough to give up all the rest of her life for them. Other parents she knew justified their every shortcoming with the litany that the children required this, the children needed that, and parenthood demanded total devotion. It didn't. She could not understand people who destroyed their own lives for their children; she had decided before her own were born that she would not do that; and she was scornful of those who did. Mac John was demonstrative with the children. He hugged them and bounced them around. She loved them no less, she thought, because her own demonstrations of affection were more subdued. Still, the people who subordinated everything to their children, plus Mac John's boisterous demonstrations, made her wonder if she were not merely rationalizing and if it were not true that she loved the children less than Mac John did and less than other people loved theirs.

Right now, for example, she had fifteen minutes before Sally would come—time for her to take the children to her bed and to cuddle with them, or time to play with them, let them romp and yell around her. She wouldn't. She never did. Sally would get them up and dress them while she was in her own bathroom, bathing and dressing for the office; and when they were dressed and sitting at the breakfast table, and she was dressed and ready to leave, she would come down and sit with them for a few minutes, talk to them, before she left for the day. They would run shrieking to her when she came home tonight. She would be tired, and she would have to dress them for dinner at her parents', and she would likely be curt. Was it possible to be loving and curt?

She was thirty years old, and it was a cliché to be dissatisfied with your life when you were thirty. She was determined not to live a cliché. Still, it was another cliché to live the way she did.

It was a quarter to ten when she stepped off the elevator at Childreth, McLennon & Brady. Carrying her leather briefcase, she strode briskly to the reception desk.

"Mrs. Hughes—" the receptionist said breathlessly. "The partners are meeting in the big conference room. They want you to come in immediately, before you take any phone calls."

She put her briefcase in her office, just the same, before she went to the conference room. It was not the morning for a partnership meeting, and as she walked along the hall she saw that many doors were closed. Partners were in their offices, not in the conference room. There was a hush over the whole office, something ominous.

"Lois—" said Ted McCadden. McCadden, the senior partner, sat at the head of the table in the conference room. Others stood around, staring out the window, drinking coffee. It was not a meeting. "Sit down, Lois," McCadden said.

She sat, glancing quizzically at her partners, most of whom now stared at her.

"Lois—" said McCadden. "Succinctly put, John Finley shot himself last night."

It was a shock: literally a blow that felt like a sharp jab to her body. "*My God!*" she gasped.

McCadden licked his lips. "He was dying of cancer."

"I didn't know that."

McCadden shook his head. "I did. A few of us did. He didn't want it told."

Finley—hobbling with his cane, wincing now and again. He had always been in pain. A mind so incisive, aggressive . . . To think of him taking his own life . . . Maybe it was his final, dreadful, relentlessly rational decision.

"Uh—I suppose Norma Spencer has been told," Lois said.

"Yes. We called her at home so she wouldn't come in."

"So she wouldn't . . . Why not?"

McCadden interlaced his fingers and stared at them briefly. "I suppose she will have some emotional reaction."

"Don't we assume a good deal?"

"Do we? You would know better than I."

Norma had decided to go to the office after lunch. McCadden on the telephone at eight o'clock had suggested she take the day off, but she could not accept the implication behind the suggestion, and she could not easily explain to her husband why she should take a day off just because the senior partner for whom she had worked had shot himself. A half-day to compose herself was perhaps understandable. A collapse would not be.

Anyway, she was not going to collapse. For a moment, after McCadden's call, she had sat down, stunned; and for a few minutes she could not stop crying. It was only because of the shock: to know that a man she had talked with as late as six last evening had gone home and killed himself within two or three hours—without having shown the least sign of such an intention. It was a shock to know that a man who had come to figure so large in her life was suddenly gone, suddenly did not exist any longer. For a moment the whole world had spun and shaken.

Hal was sympathetic. He offered to stay home himself, to be with her. Hal was good about things like this. Hal was a wonderful man for taking a woman in his arms and offering her sympathy, offering her help. A huge man—he weighed some two hundred eighty pounds—it was his unthinking, natural reaction to express his love, his sympathy with hugging, lifting, carrying. He expressed many emotions the same way: with vigorous, meaty handshakes, ebullient slapping on the back, clutching shoulders, laughing nods, great broad smiles.

He had done well by her this morning. His warmth had been a comfort. But she had insisted he go on to his office. Her father's sister—Aunt Madge—had come as always, to be with the children until one of them came home. She had not told Aunt Madge why she was at home. She had told her she had a headache and would go to the office as soon as she felt better. Madge had brought a pot of tea to the bedroom, insisting it was better than any pill for sinus headache, and had left her alone.

She had lain in bed, inside a closed bedroom door, thinking of John Finley. She had much to think about.

Without him she might not be able to stay at Childreth, McLennon & Brady. He had become her sponsor, her protector. Others did not like that. The firm had grudging respect for Finley, but few of his colleagues liked him. Whether he had chosen her for a protégée or she had chosen him to carry her upward made no difference; either way the other lawyers saw it, they resented her special, personal relationship with Finley.

He had taught her more about lawyering than she had learned in school. Six months ago he had won a case by arguing from the placement of a comma in the Constitution of Ohio. If the comma was where the attorney general of Ohio said it was, then a convincing argument could be made that a new section of Ohio tax law was constitutional—which would cost Finley's client half a million dollars. If that comma was on the other side of the word "provided," then a persuasive argument for unconstitutionality was available.

In the printed books, the comma was where the attorney general said it was. It was there, plain and simple.

"But it makes the goddamn sentence ungrammatical," Finley argued to Norma. "Those old boys in the days when they wrote these things didn't write bad grammar like that. They cared about things like commas in those days."

He sent her to Columbus, Ohio, to look at the original Constitution of Ohio—written with pen and ink on sheets of parchment. The parchment was kept rolled up in a huge copper tube in a safe in the office of the Ohio secretary of state. The secretary of state—Brown was his name—handled the parchment lovingly, as if it were one of the Dead Sea Scrolls, but he was cooperative and pleased to show it.

Sure enough, the comma was not where it appeared in every printed version of the Constitution of Ohio. It was where Finley said it should be.

He was never patient. He was scornful of people who did not follow the turns of his logic. He did not have the time, he said, to wait for fools to understand. She had known what he meant about not having time. She had known about the cancer. She had known about his pain, too. It had made it easier to have respect for him. Indeed he didn't have time. She had known for a year.

She had never spent a night with him anywhere. She had married

Hal not long after she began to be intimate with Finley. Two days a week, on the average, she went out for a drink with Finley when they left the office, and half of those times they went to a room in the Lamar Hotel. She was always home by nine, and Hal never suspected she was doing anything but working late. He understood what big law firms required. His own law practice was so far from the precincts of Childreth, McLennon & Brady, in every sense, that there was no chance he would stumble on the fact that his wife spent a couple of hours on a hotel bed with a senior partner at Childreth, on the average once a week.

She had not agonized over what she did with Finley. She had rationalized it early and had lived comfortably with that rationalization. They had been honest with each other. She understood he wanted physical gratification, and he understood she wanted his sponsorship in the law firm. They had not exploited each other. . . .

By eleven o'clock even going to the office after lunch seemed too long to stay out. She left the house and was at her desk before noon. She noticed that conversations stopped as she walked through the halls.

"If the Court please, I move the prosecution be dismissed. No crime has been proved."

The judge—his name was Crowe—peered over the tops of his half-glasses. "I beg your pardon, Miss Brookover?"

"Your Honor, no crime has been proved. My client is charged with obstructing a police officer in the performance of his official duties. It has not been proved that my client did anything of the kind."

"We have lots of cases like this, Miss Brookover."

"If Your Honor please, I would like to argue the point."

Teejay's client was a thirty-nine-year-old black man. Sitting at the table, he watched the courtroom proceedings with apprehension and sullen hostility. A month ago he had been found sitting in his car in an alley, about midnight. He had his motor running. His lights were off. A police car entered the alley, and the black man began to drive away. The police stopped him. When they asked him his name, he told them to go to hell.

That was his offense. When they asked his name, he told them to go to hell; and thereafter he simply sat in his car, arms folded, and refused to talk. The officers called for a backup car. When it arrived, four police officers opened the black man's car, seized him by the arms, and pulled him out. He did not resist. They handcuffed him, put him in a police car, and took him to headquarters. There, when they searched him, they found his driver's license and other identification. He was not drunk. He was carrying no weapon, no narcotics. He had not even been illegally parked. After some discussion in his presence, they charged him with obstructing them in the performance of their official duties.

"As is obvious to the Court—although it may not be so to Miss Brookover—" the police prosecutor impatiently argued, "the refusal of this defendant to answer the lawful questions of police officers clearly obstructed them in the performance of their official duties. I can think of hardly any clearer instance of obstruction. Four police officers—at least two—could have been engaged in far more important activities during the hour and a quarter they spent taking this man in and finally discovering his identity. Refusal to answer the lawful questions of a police officer has always been regarded as obstruction of an officer in the performance of his duty, and we prosecute many such cases."

"That is true, Miss Brookover," said the judge. "Defendants are often brought before this court for impeding an investigation by refusal to answer questions."

Teejay smiled and nodded. "I know that, Your Honor," she said. "But let me point out that, carrying this line of reasoning to its end, you could charge every suspect who refuses to confess with obstructing a police investigation. If a suspect refuses to confess, police officers are required to spend time investigating the crime, trying to find other evidence of his guilt. If he will not confess, they must then appear in court and testify about the crime: another waste of their time, another obstruction of their performance of more important duties. I—"

She was interrupted. "*Your Honor!* Are we to sit in this courtroom and hear an argument that people are under no obligation to answer lawful police inquiries? Does Miss Brookover seriously want us to believe he was within his rights and was guilty of nothing when he refused to extend to two police officers even so much cooperation as to tell them his name?"

"I do indeed, Mr. Perry. I suppose I need hardly point out that if this defendant had in fact been guilty of some crime, he would have had a perfect right, under the Fifth Amendment to the Constitution of the United States, to remain silent in the face of police inquiry. Your Honor, does Mr. Perry mean to argue that an innocent man has less right than a guilty man?"

"This Court will rule," said the judge abruptly, authoritatively, "that the mere refusal to answer a question put by police officers—as distinguished, incidentally, from misleading an officer by a false answer—does not of itself constitute the offense of obstructing an officer in the performance of his lawful duties. Accordingly, the case against this defendant is dismissed."

In the hall outside the courtroom, the big black man grinned at Teejay. "I guess I got me some lawyer," he chuckled.

"How about paying your lawyer the other twenty-five dollars?" she said crisply.

"Sure," he said. He dug the cash from his pocket. "It wuz worth every cent of it," he said, "to hear them *po*-lice dudes put down."

She had taken the bar examination in March and passed with no trouble. As soon as she was sworn in, she had opened an office—on Louisiana Street, south of the freeway, in a one-story frame building that housed a barbershop and a dry cleaner as well as her law office, the three establishments lined up along the sidewalk. T. J. BROOK-OVER—ATTORNEY AND COUNSELOR-AT-LAW it said in black letters on the big front window she had covered with a curtain. She was her own secretary still, and when she went to court, as she had done this morning, her office was closed, with a sign on the door saying BACK AT 11:00. This was her fifth month. In the first four, her fees had totaled $940. They paid the office rent.

It was where she had had to go. The few interviews she'd had with lawyers established in offices and practices had been curt and cool. She was a woman, graduated from a law school not particularly distinguished; she had no family or other connections. They suggested she find a job in government. Two firms insisted on knowing how many words a minute she could type. One firm openly expressed surprise that she should even inquire. ("You mean *here?* You mean you want a job with *us?*") She quickly decided the job search was demeaning and that she would open her own office at any sacrifice.

She found the vacant storeroom on Louisiana Street. She could park her red Falcon behind the building and drive it uptown to the courthouse. She bought some carpet—cheap, because it had a flaw in it. She bought used furniture from a liquidator. She had letterheads printed—not engraved. She bought a new leather briefcase.

It was the year of miniskirts, but she kept her skirts at her knees, tied her hair behind her head, wore no makeup, and played her young-lawyer role with all the artifice she could muster.

She was confident. She discovered immediately that her knowledge and skills as a lawyer were entirely adequate to cope with the little business she got—and, more importantly, to cope with her fellow members of the Houston bar. Some of the older lawyers welcomed her and offered her small helpful suggestions. Others tried to bully her. Her confidence was tested.

"Miss Brookover, you may not realize this, but it is customary in Houston for the attorney for the seller of a piece of property to provide a certificate from the county clerk to the effect that the subdivision plat has been correctly filed and is of record in his office."

"Mr. Ziskind, this land was platted in 1917. Every deed in the abstract, for the past fifty years, describes this lot by number. You aren't suggesting a defect in a subdivision plat filed fifty years ago?"

"Not at all. But the certificate is customary, and I'd like to have it."

"Well, are you suggesting I run down to the courthouse right now and get it?"

"To provide what's customary, Miss Brookover."

"Frankly, Mr. Ziskind, I don't give a damn what's customary. I have here what the law and our contract requires: a warranty deed and the lien affidavits. The contract gives you until noon today to pay my clients the balance of the purchase price: fifteen thousand, five hundred dollars. You have ten minutes to hand my clients a certified check. If you don't, I'm going to forfeit your two-thousand-dollar deposit and put the property back on the market."

Ziskind told a county-court judge the new woman lawyer with the flaming red hair was an abrasive smart aleck. A seventy-year-old trial lawyer who had overheard Ziskind met her by chance in a corridor in the courthouse and told her she might do well to try to avoid antagonizing established lawyers. She told him things she said that were taken as abrasive could be said by male lawyers and not be so taken. The old man scratched his head, grinned, and offered to buy her a drink and lunch. Over lunch he gave her some work to do: some commercial collections in small amounts and a couple of land titles to check.

She was making a start. Still, the fees she earned barely paid her office rent. So, she worked at night, still as a cocktail waitress, still as Tommy Jo. She had quit working topless. Even though it made more than twice as much money, it involved too much risk of lasting embarrassment now that she was practicing law and establishing an identity in the city. She took a job in the bar of a motel near the airport: a place called the DC-8 Lounge, in the Intercontinental Motel. She was supposed to look like an airline hostess in her costume: a waist-length dark blue jacket with brass buttons and gold stripes on the sleeves; a dark blue cap; and a few inches of dark blue skirt, showing her white panties that glowed in the black light and her legs in net stockings. She wore her hair combed out and a pair of tinted gold-rimmed glasses that resembled a pilot's sunglasses. She never saw anyone she recognized, and no one recognized her.

Kevin—still calling himself Jim Hedwig—had found the job at the DC-8 Lounge for her. He felt at home in Houston now and knew his way around. He had offered to support her until her law office did. When she refused to let him do that, he offered her a loan. She pressed him, but he would not tell her where he would get the money either to support her or to make her a loan. She saw him every ten days or so.

He would come in, sit at the bar and have two or three drinks, and talk with her. He took her out for steak and wine when she could find the free evening. Time had repaired most of the damage the penitentiary had done to Kevin. His hair was long again and curly. He had unlearned the prison jargon that had remained too long in his speech. He remembered the rules of simple grammar again. He had regained his charm.

XVIII

1971

"When are you going to start taking it a little easier with that stuff?"

Lois stopped her martini glass just short of her mouth and turned a lazy, heavy-lidded glance on Bart Josephson. She shrugged, took a sip, and put the glass down on the tray.

"I'm entitled to ask. I'm your doctor."

The martini he complained of was her third. She had been tired when she came aboard the plane, tired and tense, and the first two had relieved the tension. She relaxed now on a gentle surge of optimism: martini-induced but comfortable.

It was a coincidence that she and Bart were on the same flight. He was on his way to Washington for a medical conference; she was going for a women's meeting with the Texas congressional delegation, to press for an affirmative vote on the Equal Rights Amendment. They had met in the airport, and he had upgraded his ticket to first-class so he could sit with her.

She glanced out the window. That was probably Mississippi or Alabama below—depressing thought. "Are you my liver's keeper?" she asked Bart Josephson.

"I'm your doctor," he said again.

She smiled at him. "You're a doll," she said.

He swirled his plastic airline glass, rattling the ice cubes left from his single bloody mary. It was a gesture of impatience. He was an impatient man by reputation, a doctor who expected people to follow his medical advice and became annoyed with them, as well as concerned, when they didn't. She leaned back in the corner of her seat and cocked her head and smiled and looked at him. He was a big man, probably six-foot-four. His thick hair was white. His brown eyes were sharp, even behind the contact lenses she knew he wore because she had seen him take them out at the country club pool.

"I hope you get your amendment passed," he had said to her when their first drinks were served and he had wanted a topic for conversation. "I like the idea, philosophically. The notion of women as shrinking violets has never appealed to me."

"You'll generate a lecture from me if you're not careful," she had said.

"You've made it a cause?"

"Well—I'm not a fanatic. But, yes, it's a cause."

"Now that I think of it, you are the one who knocked down the Lawrenceburg ordinance, aren't you?"

"Yes."

"I've heard conflicting stories. Tell me about it."

Lois had smiled and had taken a sip from her martini before she told the story.

"The city of Lawrenceburg, Texas, had a city ordinance that prohibited a woman from entering an establishment where liquor was served at a bar unless she was escorted there by a man. There were all kinds of rationalizations: that a woman in a bar needed a man's protection, that a woman wouldn't go into a bar alone except to solicit—all the characteristic vicious ignorance a ministerial association can impose on a small southern city. Sarah Smith went into the hotel bar and ordered a beer. They asked her to leave. She wouldn't go. The hotel manager called the police. The police issued a summons. She appeared in court and was fined fifty dollars. I took the case up on appeal. I won, of course."

"I heard you compared it to black sit-ins at dime-store lunch counters."

"Tell me wherein it differs," she said.

Dr. Josephson had laughed. "You're my idea of a liberated woman," he had said.

The thunderheads standing twenty miles to the north of the airplane's course were beautiful and had occupied part of her attention while he talked of a golf tournament being organized at Bayou Oaks Country Club. She was not interested in golf; anyway, the lightning flashing red inside the towering dark gray clouds was too spectacular to be afforded anything less than most of her attention. She had ordered her second martini while he said something about how well Mac John played and how he might win the tournament.

They had talked a little about Daniel Ellsberg and the Pentagon papers, then returned to the subject of the country club; it was what they had in common, chiefly. He was soft-spoken, a quietly entertaining conversationalist. He had put his jacket overhead and sat in a seat half reclined, in a white, short-sleeved shirt. His arms were hairy and muscular. She was less comfortable. Skirts were short—you could hardly buy anything but a mini—and she had never learned to be at ease in a skirt that crept halfway to her hips when she sat. He had complimented her on the dress that now annoyed her. It was a knit, sunny yellow. He had tried to talk a little about her children, but she said something about President Nixon and changed the subject. When the hostess had offered her the third martini, she had taken it.

"Where are you staying, Bart?"

"At the Mayflower. The conference is there."

"I'm staying at the Madison. It's a lovely hotel. It's where my father stays in Washington. And you know Dan."

"Dan would take that third martini away from you."

"No, he wouldn't. Not anymore. Anyway, I've got one father. Don't you think that's enough?"

"And you've got a husband."

"I've got half a husband."

"Lois . . ."

"You want to deny it?"

"It's none of my business."

"But the martini is."

"All right. I'll quit playing doctor and mind my own business."

She put a friendly hand on his shoulder. "You're a fine, sweet, sincere, responsible man, Bart."

"I should crawl under the seat."

"With a sense of humor," she added. "I wish my father had ever had a sense of humor."

"Mac John has a sense of humor."

"Mac John is a philandering drunk. Of course, he *is* going to win the Bayou Oaks golf championship."

"*Lois* . . ." He reached for her drink, but she was too quick for him and jerked it away in her left hand.

"I'm not drunk. You've seen me drunk. You should know the difference."

"Why are you so anxious to swallow that?" he asked.

She put it to her lips and defiantly drank. "Doctor," she said, "if you want to treat me for what you see as a drinking problem, you will acknowledge, I believe, that there is more to it than just preaching and trying to steal people's drinks."

"Do you want to talk to me?" he asked. "This is as good a time and place as any."

She stared into her drink for a moment and, with a glance at him, took another sip. "I don't really give a damn if Mac John is sleeping around," she said. "I really don't, if he isn't public about it. Probably I should care, huh? But I don't."

Dr. Bart Josephson was distracted for a moment by the offer of another bloody mary. This time he told the hostess to bring it. He turned again to Lois. "Then what *do* you care about, Lois? I mean, what do you care about enough to try to drink the problem away?"

"How about eschewing your ready clichés, Bart? Don't give me any of the conventional wisdom about drinking. I am not a semiliterate, middle-class drunk. I am an effective person, who accomplishes a lot in this world and is going to accomplish more. If you are going to be my doctor, treat me with as much respect as you want me to have for you, or don't treat me at all, because I'm not going to sit here and listen to a lot of bullshit."

"Let's try my listening and you talking for a while," said Bart.

She nodded. "I started off on Mac John. I've had two important men in my life, and Mac John isn't one of them. My father is one. The other was a brilliant man who had a short affair with me and was intelligent enough to stop it there because he could foresee disaster. Let's talk about my father first.

"My father is basically a shallow man: a self-centered bully who has used a position he inherited as if he had created it himself. I didn't understand that for a long time. I understand it now, and it cuts a foundation out from under me.

"I married Mac John because he was rich and handsome, an ornament to the House of Farnham—as Lois Farnham was an ornament to the House of Hughes. Mac John is not important. I haven't learned anything from him. He hasn't learned anything from me, obviously. I don't respect his judgments. And that has nothing to do with how much he drinks. On his soberest days, when he is functioning at his very best, Mac John is a dummy."

"That's an exaggeration," Bart observed.

She shrugged. "*You* define him, then. The truth is, Mac John is an anachronism. He belongs in Edwardian times. His family then could have supported him as a wastrel—they have enough money for it—and he could have circulated from the club to the track to the whorehouse to the yacht to shooting in Scotland . . . and so forth, and nobody would have thought him odd. Today, he doesn't fit. He does his part in the family business, but he's not good at it. He doesn't care enough. He doesn't have to."

"Your brothers aren't like that."

"My brothers are nasty bastards. Either one of them would cut your throat, or mine, if it would increase the profits of the companies they run. I'm not like them. But I'm more like them than I am like Mac John."

"Your father. . . ?"

She sighed and snatched her drink off her tray for a last swallow. "It's a wise child that knows its own father," she muttered.

"What do you want from Mac John?" Bart asked.

"I want to be able to come home at the end of a day when I've done something tough and talk to him, to see what he thinks, to have an intelligent second opinion."

"Can you do as much for him?"

"I catch his mistakes, and he doesn't like it."

Bart accepted his second bloody mary from the hostess—who did not offer Lois a fourth martini. "Why did you marry him, anyway?" Bart asked.

Lois shrugged.

"Are you thinking of a divorce?"

She shrugged again. "He's no support, Bart. That's the trouble—he's no support. A man and wife are supposed to support each other, to stand behind each other—or however you want to say it—and I try to do it for Mac John, whether he appreciates it or not. But he doesn't do the same for me. He doesn't even try. He's incapable of it. Everything I do, I do alone. I'm the kind of person who needs support. I'm uncomfortable without it. It's not a man-woman kind of thing. Lots of people —men and women alike—need someone behind them, encouraging them, looking at what they're trying to do, thinking about it, talking with them. . . . I'm lonely, Bart. That's what it is. I'm lonely. Dammit. . . ."

Three martinis were not unusual for her. She could handle them. Occasionally, however, even one could make her sick. By the time they left the plane at Washington National, she was nauseous. Bart went with her to her hotel. He helped her register and went with her to her room. There he opened his bag and gave her two capsules from a bottle. She stretched out on the bed.

When she woke he was still there, sitting in a chair, reading a medical journal. She had been asleep two hours. It was eleven.

"Bart—my God!"

"Feel better?"

She sat up. She did feel better. Her mouth tasted bad. "You've missed your dinner."

"Not really," he said. He stood and laid aside his journal. "I've ordered dinner from room service and told them to hold it until I called. Are you ready for it?"

"I don't know."

He opened a bottle of ginger ale from the bar in the room and poured it over ice. He handed her the glass with a small pill. "Here. Wash that down. You'll feel better."

She took it. "What was that?" she asked.

"A little amphetamine. An upper," he said. "It'll help."

"The chemical life," she yawned. "Up and down with pharmaceuticals. And you chastised me for drinking martinis."

"You can't get these without a prescription," he said.

She used the bathrooom, brushed her teeth, combed her hair. The waiter brought what Bart had ordered: small sandwiches, fruit, cheese, coffee.

"You're staying," she said to him across the table shortly after they began to eat.

"I was hoping to be invited," he said.

"I suspected that pill was to wake me up. When I took it, that was your invitation. Did you take one, too?"

"I won't need it," he said.

She met the next day with the Texas congressional delegation—with the six members who took the time to see her group of women lobbying for congressional approval of the resolution for the Equal Rights Amendment. In the evening she attended a dinner of the National Organization for Women, where she was introduced and recognized as a woman who had used the power of her profession to make significant contributions to equality for women. She was pleased, but she had been distracted all day, and inattentive, and in the evening she could only think of how anxious she was to return to the Madison Hotel. In fact, if Bart had not had his meetings to attend all day, and his own dinner tonight, she would have thrown aside the original purpose of her trip and stayed with him all day, in the hotel, in bed. That was more important.

They had made love until morning, almost. She had not known a man and woman could sustain excitement as long as they had. Tonight they were going to do it again. She thrilled each time she thought of it.

It was all she wanted to think about. She had taken time off during the afternoon to visit a shop and buy herself a sheer short black nightgown, with a pair of tiny black panties; and during the dinner, when the topics for discussion were causes to which she had deeply committed herself, her attention wandered to delicious anticipation of showing herself to Bart in the black nightgown.

She had not known she wanted this . . . whatever it was she had started, whatever it would be called; but now that she had plunged into it, she wanted it intensely; it was so important to her that she was reckless about it. If there was risk, she would take it. Maybe it would only last a couple of days, but while it did last she meant to savor it. She had a strong sense of opportunity—that she had stumbled into something that potentially would enrich her life with color and feeling; and she had a sense that she should grasp it while she could, for God knew if she would ever have the chance again.

"*Lady* . . . Oh, lady, you are beautiful."

His reaction to the nightgown was all she had expected. For a second night he was meeting expectations.

She had put on the nightgown and brushed out her hair while she waited for him. As always, she was unable entirely to find confidence in herself displayed as flesh; but in the sheer black nightgown, with the wicked little panties that did not quite cover her pubic hair, she could feel that maybe, just maybe, the very sight of her could empty a man's mind of all the day's business and monopolize it for her.

Bart touched her nipples through the smooth sheer nylon.

"I bought it just for you, just for tonight," she told him. "I won't take it home."

She had champagne waiting in an ice bucket. He opened it and poured, and he toasted her: "To an exquisitely beautiful—infinitely desirable woman."

Lois smiled as she sipped her champagne. "I've wanted to tell you something," she said. "I was recognized at the dinner tonight, for my contributions to women's rights. But I treasure what you just said a lot more."

He took her hand and led her to sit down with him on the couch. "I wonder," he said, "if any of the other women from that dinner are dressed anything like you are now, or are doing anything like what you're doing."

"I hope you don't think it's inconsistent."

He blushed and chuckled nervously. "Old ideas leave a residue in the mind," he said. "For an older man, it's hard to overcome it."

He had referred to himself once last night as an older man, and she had ignored it. She ignored the comment now. She was not sure how

old he was—maybe fifty, maybe a year or two short of it. His hair was
white, but his complexion was taut, and his hairy body was hard. She
didn't want to think about how old he was.

What was important to her about Bart was that he was comfortably
confident of himself, poised, decisive, and even to a degree dominat-
ing. Maybe it was the lifetime habit of a physician who dealt with his
patients from a position of superior knowledge, often translated into
superior will, but in their lovemaking he had been the leader and she
the follower. He had dominated her—quite unconsciously, she thought
—naturally and inoffensively. She accepted it and took it for part of the
excitement she had savored. She had been surprised. It was the man.
It was Bart. She couldn't have accepted it from another man.

He undressed, and they lay on the bed and fondled each other and
talked while they finished their bottle of champagne. He told her a
little about his meetings. She told him a little about hers. When on
impulse he bent down and licked one of her nipples, she, on a similar
impulse, when he had sat up again, leaned down and kissed his penis,
with dry lips. He was startled a little, and he liked it; and after a minute or two he pressed her down to do it again. With his hand on the
back of her neck gently pressing her face down, she kissed his penis
again, but only for a moment; she turned her head away and would
not continue it. He nuzzled her neck for a while and again licked her
nipple; then again he pressed her down to kiss him. When she resisted,
he pressed harder, and only half voluntarily she rested her cheek on his
lower belly and in his pubic hair and kissed his rigid penis. He held
her there, and she nibbled the skin of his penis with her lips.

He did not force her further. He caressed her urgently: a suggestion
that for her to go on, to lick his penis, to take it in her mouth, would
be wonderfully loving. For herself, she was not sure it would be. She
decided no. Maybe later. She kissed his penis firmly, then kissed his
belly playfully, then lifted herself up and kissed him passionately on
the mouth. He took her in his arms and held her tightly and did not
try to press her head down again.

In a few minutes he pulled down her panties and rolled over her.
What they did was simple and strenuous and satisfying. When they
lay side by side after a few minutes, they were sweating and heaving,
and they grinned at each other with lazy grins of satiation. It was like
the first night.

Lois traced his initials on the damp skin of his thigh. "Barton M.
Josephson, M.D.," she said in a husky whisper. "What's the 'M' for,
Bart?"

"Myron," he said.

She spelled Myron on his belly. "Bart . . . What will we do when we get back to Houston?" she asked. "Can we go on with this?"

"Do you want to?"

She nodded. "Very much."

He looked into her eyes for a moment, then glanced away, down. "It won't be easy," he said.

It wasn't. To find time was not easy. To find a place was not easy. They lived busy lives, involved in too much to leave them time for hours of escape. When he had time, she made time. They met at the lunch hour, early in the morning, late at night, weekends.

Bart was a general practitioner, a family doctor, in Bayou Oaks. His office was in a medical center with suites arranged around a courtyard. He practiced with a partner. He was married. He had three grown children, the youngest a college senior. His wife looked older than he but probably was not; she was active in a music club, a garden club, and a bridge club; and she suffered migraines which caused her to withdraw, sometimes abruptly and dramatically, into darkened rooms to lie on a couch or bed and moan. He was a Jew. His wife was not. Lois had known all this about Bart before they met by chance at the airport and flew to Washington together. Now that she was his lover, she knew no more about him.

His wife was not demanding of his time. It was not clear that she cared where he was, and he could escape her whenever he wanted to. But his practice was demanding; his patients were demanding. His place in the community was demanding. More than that, his sense of duty and propriety was surprisingly demanding. It was that which was difficult for Lois to cope with: that he would commit himself to an hour with her only when his conscience was clear that duty had been done.

"Janice Theiss is in labor, Lois. I can't—"

"You're not her obstetrician."

"I'm her doctor. I have to be available."

Late one afternoon, in bed in a room at the Sheraton, he turned over and glanced at his watch. "I have one hour to make it to the Houston Club, dressed in a tux."

"To hell with it. You can't leave me now."

"I'm at the speakers' table. I'm on the program. I'm to introduce Dr. White."

"To hell with introducing Dr. White! Bart! We're in bed together. Is a goddamn introduction that important? Bart. . . ?"

She had herself appointed to the board of trustees for Milam Hospital so there would be occasion for her to be seen with Dr. Josephson at lunch or dinner. She became more involved in the business of the hos-

pital than she wanted to be, and actually found herself unable to take
advantage of a free evening of Bart's because she had to attend a meeting of the hospital board. He was not pleased to have her on the board.
He told her her appointment was a frightening manifestation of her
family's financial and political influence.

He came to her office—it was an evening in October—and they made
love hurriedly on her couch and then went to the country club for dinner. Their waiter said the fish was not good; they should have beef.

"I wonder," said Bart, "who eats the food the waiter thinks is not
good enough for a Farnham."

"Don't be sarcastic. Anyway, if you want to know, look around."

"*Si monumentum requiris, circumspice,*" he said, frowning and smiling. "Let's see . . . *Si alimentum malum requiris, circumspice.*"

She settled back comfortably in her chair and regarded Bart across
the white linen, the silver, a crystal vase with a yellow chrysanthemum,
with a friendly eye. He was unstylish, sometimes unkempt. His conversation was never sparkling, but it was pithy; she often recalled it
later and found depths in it that had passed by her at first. She admired
his unstructured, often surprising, essays into arcane knowledge. He
wasn't confident in some of these expeditions, but he was knowledge-
able enough to venture in. She was never bored with him.

But was she in love with him? Was he in love with her? Their second night together, in the Madison Hotel in Washington, she had told
him she loved him. She rationalized later that telling him she loved
him was not the same as telling him she was *in love* with him. The one
was a statement of fact; the other was a commitment. She knew she
loved him. The question was: How much was she committed? Then
the question came: How much was he?

"Bart," she said over their roast beef, "I need to talk to you."

"Sounds ominous," he said.

"I need to talk about Mac John."

"I'm not sure I should talk to you about Mac John."

"Then listen, anyway," she said. She put down her knife and fork.
"I—I have come to a conclusion about Mac John and me. I don't want
to be overdramatic. This is rational. I don't love him anymore. I don't
want him to touch my body anymore. I don't want to sleep with him.
He said something the other day about having another baby. I don't
want to have another child by him."

"You don't have to," Bart said. "You're on the Pill. You want your
tubes tied?"

"Don't be shallow," she protested. "Bart, for God's sake!"

"Sorry," he said.

"He's a drunk. He runs around. He's circumspect, but I know he's

been taking a waitress from the Hyatt to a room in the Holiday Inn.
I don't care. The more he humps her, the less he wants to hump me.
I haven't had relations with him for three months, and I don't think
I'm going to anymore. I don't have a real marriage now. It's been a long
time since I did, if I ever did. The question is, should I go on living
with him anyway? Do the kids need him? Is there any point in staying
married?"

Bart frowned deeply, his head down. "Lois . . ." he said painfully.
"How can I talk to you about your marriage? I, of all people? I can't."

"I *need* to talk with someone," she persisted. "Who better than you?
Who knows me better than you?"

He glanced around the dining room, concerned apparently that the
developing emotionalism in their talk might communicate itself to
others. "Is it because of—us?" he asked in a low voice. "Am I responsible for your deciding suddenly that you want a divorce?"

She smiled wryly and shook her head. "Cause and effect . . . might
be the other way around. And I don't have illusions. You needn't worry
about that. For a few days when we first came back from Washington
I played with the idea that I might divorce Mac John and you might
divorce Betty and . . ." She shrugged. "I'm not thinking of anything
like that, I assure you. All I want is advice."

"My advice would be very bad," he said. "It wouldn't be objective."

"Objective?"

"I would like you to be a single woman," he said quietly. "Of course
I would."

"*Why? Say it to me, Bart!*"

"Because I care for you very much."

She smiled, at first tentatively; then her smile widened until her
whole face was broadly smiling and flushed. "That's it, then," she said,
nodding enthusiastically. "So, tell me, Bart. Say it to me. Tell me you
want me to get a divorce. Tell me it's your advice."

"*Lois* . . ." he interrupted. "My responsibility . . . ? Do you want
your divorce to be my responsibility?"

"Why not? Why can't we share the responsibility?"

"Why do you need anyone to share it?" he asked. "You're a mature
woman—independent. You know what you want. You know how to get
it. To be blunt, I don't want the responsibility. I won't tell you to be
divorced. I won't advise you to. I care for you. It's not too much to say
I love you. But I won't tell you to break up your home, send away your
children's father, just to make it easier for you and me to meet and—"

"My decision, hmm?" she interrupted crisply.

"It has to be," he said.

"Thanks, Bart. Thanks a whole lot."

XIX

In jail it did not make much difference what day of the week it was, except that on Sundays any evangelist who applied was allowed to harangue and exhort to prayer through the cage bars. Some of the women sat on the floor outside the cells and watched these performances, for relief from boredom. A few prayed. Teejay lay on her bunk on Sunday mornings and read the Sunday morning paper.

This Sunday morning—it was in August—a woman stopped at the open door of Teejay's cell and spoke to her. Teejay did not hear what she said—couldn't hear over the singsong of the preacher—and only looked up over her newspaper, squinting, frowning. The woman stepped inside the cell.

"You're T. J. Brookover, I hear."

Teejay nodded.

"I'm Christine McElhay," the woman said. "We have a mutual friend."

Teejay put down her paper and sat up. She had read a story about Christine McElhay in the morning paper: that she was by reputation the boss woman of a string of teen-aged prostitutes, although she had never been arrested on any such charge and was in jail now on a charge of possession of two kilos of marijuana. She had been brought in Thursday or Friday.

"Who's our mutual friend?" Teejay asked. She was skeptical that she had any friend in common with this woman.

"Kevin," said Christine McElhay.

It was difficult to judge people in jail, where every woman was uniformly unkempt. Christine McElhay was a woman of maybe thirty-five, a little taller than average, a little heavier, with coarse features and coarse black hair tied with a rubber band to hang in a tail down her back. Her threadbare gray smock was tight and short, and she was barefoot. She leaned back against the bars of the open cell door and faced Teejay with a bland face that suggested nothing except that she had come to say what she had said: that she knew Kevin.

"How do you come to know Kevin?" Teejay asked.

"That's what I wanted to ask you," said Christine McElhay. "I thought I knew him pretty well, and he never mentioned you."

"He wouldn't have had occasion to," said Teejay.

The woman smiled. "I'm not a plant from the D.A.'s office," she said.

Teejay returned the smile. "Okay," she said. "I've known Kevin for a long time but never all that well."

"Not well enough to hire him to kill somebody for you," the woman said, still smiling.

"No, not that well," said Teejay.

"Kevin and I . . ." said Christine McElhay, and she grinned and nodded. "Some years ago. I can't picture him doing what they said he did."

Teejay shook her head. "Neither can I."

"I'll drop the subject of Kevin," said Christine McElhay. "He's too important to your case for you to talk about him."

"I can listen to you talk about him."

Christine McElhay shrugged. "What can I say? He was good in bed. He was a great guy. Sentimental . . ." She laughed. "You couldn't believe a word he said. He was always small-time. I can't believe he took a gun and shot a man." She shook her head. "I just can't believe it."

"Apparently he did it," said Teejay. "Otherwise I wouldn't be here."

"I can't believe you *are* here," said Christine McElhay. "That's something else I can't believe. If you weren't here, I'd probably want you for my lawyer. I've heard about you."

Teejay sighed. "Well, I can't spring myself, so I probably couldn't spring you."

"I'd bet on you," said Christine McElhay simply.

"Thanks."

"Come to think of it, though, you didn't get Perfecto Sanchez out. Did you?"

"You know about that case?" Teejay asked.

"I know Perfecto Sanchez is still doing time. I mean, I don't mean to put you down—but he is."

"Just remember," said Teejay, "that Perfecto Sanchez had pleaded guilty and was already in Huntsville before I got the case."

"When was that?"

"In 'seventy-one," said Teejay.

She had taken the Sanchez case, without fee, at the urgent request of Jaime Lujan, a man of undefined occupation and hazy reputation who was called by the newspapers "a spokesman for the Mexican-American community."

Sanchez had already been convicted. Lujan had asked her to get him out. She went to Huntsville and talked to Sanchez: a bewildered young man in white prison coveralls, with a bristly shaved head. He was a memorable, almost a haunting, figure; but conversation with him was not helpful. He said he had not committed the robbery, but he was not convincing.

The transcript was more helpful.

THE COURT: Do I understand now that you want to enter a plea of guilty to the charge of armed robbery?

THE DEFENDANT: Sí.

THE COURT: Now, Mr. Sanchez, I'm going to talk to you about your rights. Do you understand English? Do you understand what I'm saying to you?

THE DEFENDANT: Sí.

THE COURT: Can you answer me in English?

THE DEFENDANT: Yes.

THE COURT: You have a right to the advice of a lawyer.

THE DEFENDANT: Uh?

VOICE: Un abogado.

THE DEFENDANT: Sí.

THE COURT: Have you talked with a lawyer?

THE DEFENDANT: Yes.

MR. DOLBY: Your Honor, I have conferred with Mr. Sanchez in jail and here this morning, for a total of about thirty minutes. I have advised him of his rights.

THE COURT: You're the public defender.

MR. DOLBY: I'm sorry, Your Honor. My name is Fred Dolby. I'm with the Public Defender's Office.

THE COURT: Did he understand what you told him?

MR. DOLBY: He said he did.

THE COURT: Mr. Sanchez, has Mr. Dolby advised you of your rights?

THE DEFENDANT: Yes.

THE COURT: Do you understand that if you plead guilty you waive some important rights? The right to a trial, where evidence in your favor would be heard. The right to trial by a jury. The right to appeal. Has all that been explained to you?

THE DEFENDANT: Yes.

THE COURT: Do you understand that, if you plead guilty, that's the end of it, and the court will sentence you?

THE DEFENDANT: Yes.

THE COURT: With that advice, it is your decision to plead guilty?

THE DEFENDANT: Huh?

THE COURT: You have been advised of your rights and you understand them, but you want to plead guilty. Is that right?

THE DEFENDANT: I don't got *los testigos.*

THE COURT: What's he say?

MR. DOLBY: He says he has no witnesses, Your Honor.

THE COURT: You have no witnesses to testify in your defense?

THE DEFENDANT: (Shakes head no.)

THE COURT: Then you are ready to plead guilty.

THE DEFENDANT: Sí.

Teejay argued the case to the Texas Court of Criminal Appeals. "I respectfully ask the Court to take note that nowhere on the record is there any indication that Perfecto Sanchez was advised of his right to issue subpoenas and compel witnesses to testify in his behalf. He told Judge Holmes he had no witnesses. That was true; he didn't have, unless he could subpoena them, and he didn't know he could subpoena them. He—"

Judge Emilio Martin interrupted with a question from the bench. "But, Miss Brookover, Mr. Dolby says he advised the defendant fully of his rights. Is not the Court entitled to rely on the statement made by an attorney, in open court, that he advised the defendant of all his rights? And, in any event, didn't Mr. Dolby represent Mr. Sanchez as his counsel? And didn't Mr. Dolby's statement bind Mr. Sanchez?"

"That raises a number of questions, Your Honor. In the first place, Mr. Dolby was present as a representative of the Public Defender's Office, and he said he spent all of thirty minutes with this young man accused of a serious felony. It is not clear at all that Mr. Sanchez ever agreed that Mr. Dolby should represent him as his counsel. All he did was listen when Mr. Dolby gave him some advice."

"All right, then, Miss Brookover. The defendant was advised."

"Your Honor, it is established that a blanket statement by a defending counsel that he has advised a defendant of all his rights is insufficient to support a plea of guilty. It is the duty of the trial court to inquire of the defendant and be sure he knows his rights. Judge Holmes did not ask Mr. Sanchez if he knew he could subpoena witnesses. Even when Mr. Sanchez complained that he had no witnesses, no one told him he could subpoena witnesses."

Judge George Eckhardt commented: "That could be interpreted two ways, couldn't it, Miss Brookover? Maybe he *had* been told he could subpoena witnesses and was complaining there weren't any he wanted to subpoena."

"With all due respect, Your Honor, I think these things have to be interpreted in favor of criminal defendants and their rights. Courts should not entertain assumptions that procedures are correct when the record does not show that they are."

Judge Eckhardt: "Your application for a writ of habeas corpus is supported, I notice, by an affidavit by the public defender, Mr. Dolby, in which he says he doesn't remember if he advised Mr. Sanchez that he could subpoena witnesses. I'm looking for another affidavit, Miss Brookover. Couldn't the defendant, Mr. Sanchez, have supplied an affidavit naming the witnesses he wanted to call?"

"I am sorry, Your Honor. He does not have the names."

Christine McElhay laughed. "I never heard how it happened before."

"He couldn't name the witnesses because he didn't have any," Teejay explained. "He robbed the damn gas station. It's true. He did. Stuck it up with a gun."

"What'd he do, then—just put on an ignorant act in court?"

"No. He *was* ignorant. He didn't know his rights. He didn't understand half of what was said to him in English. They just rammed his case through, to get rid of him as fast as possible. That's what bothered Jaime Lujan. And, as a matter of fact, after we took this case up they changed their act. They were a lot more careful after that. That's what Jaime Lujan wanted."

The evangelist had left "B" Cage, and Teejay had walked out into the cellblock, where she and Christine McElhay could lean against the cage bars and smoke and talk. They sat down on the floor with their backs against the bars of Teejay's cell. They had more room, and more air circulated outside the cells.

"They'll bring up some bad things against Kevin," said Christine McElhay. "They may try to stick 'em on you, too."

"Like what?" Teejay asked. She tried to sound casual.

Christine McElhay ground out her cigarette butt on the concrete floor beside her. "When I was running around with Kevin, he was never a dealer," she said. "I've heard he was, but I don't believe that. If anything, he was straight about that kind of stuff. Also, I turned out when I was a kid. I was awful good-lookin' before I gained weight, and I turned out and made some real money at it for a while. When Kevin found out about that, he didn't like me so much anymore. He never had any girls on a string. That wasn't his game. Anybody says it was is not telling the truth, in my estimation."

"I always wondered what his game was," Teejay said.

"I once saw him sell twenty tons of peanuts that he not only didn't own but that didn't exist."

"He should have run for Congress," said Teejay.

Christine McElhay struck a paper match and lighted another cigarette. She worked the muscles in her shoulders. "Jesus," she said. "Somethin' else I never believed, I never believed I'd see the inside of this place. They stuck forty thousand dollars' bail on me. I don't think I can raise it. I'm gonna be here a while."

"I've been here a while," said Teejay. "Since April."

Christine McElhay stared disconsolately at her toes. "Jesus," she said again. "What I wouldn't give for a cold beer."

"What I wouldn't give for a lot of things," said Teejay bitterly. "A meal, just one decent meal, something that tasted good, and a table to sit down to, to eat it off dishes. Or how about a bath, a real bath?" She flipped her cigarette butt angrily through the cage bars. "*Shit!* I don't even want to think about it!"

XX

1972

"They call me Bart."

"They call me Teejay."

"Teejay . . ." he repeated. Then Dr. Barton M. Josephson grinned. "Sure. For T. J. Listen, I'm glad I ran into you. I appreciate your taking the time to sit down with me."

"People like you and me have to find the time to talk with each other," she said. "If we don't, we have big trouble."

"Let's make it all off the record," he said. "I mean, for me this is an attempt to learn something, and I'd like to speak entirely frankly."

"Fine," she said. "So would I."

He had encountered her in the parking garage. He had recognized her and said hello, and on their way down in the elevator he asked her if she had a few minutes to have a drink with him; he'd like to talk to her. It was Saturday afternoon. She had come downtown to shop at Foley's, and she was wearing a blue and green striped knit minidress, sandals, sunglasses. She felt underdressed for the bar at La Maison, where he took her for the drink; but she decided if he could be comfortable there in his golf shirt and slacks, she could be. He ordered a Heineken's, and she did the same.

"This could be a pretty heavy conversation for a Saturday afternoon," he cautioned.

"I knew you didn't want to discuss baseball scores," she said.

"You have a pretty good idea, I suppose, how I feel and what I want to say."

She nodded. She was lighting a cigarette.

"It's not personal," he said.

"I understand that."

"I've known Tom Kirkwood for many years, Teejay," said Dr. Josephson, frowning over his choice of words. "He's a damn fine man —and a damn fine doctor. His confidence is shaken. His reputation is ruined, he thinks. He may go so far as to give up the practice of medicine. Doesn't that trouble you?"

"I'm not so sure he shouldn't give up the practice," she said. "Three board-certified orthopedic surgeons from Dallas and Kansas City— brought in from Dallas and Kansas City, incidentally, because your colleagues refused to testify against Dr. Kirkwood—testified that Kirkwood's operation on Hugger was outside professional standards of care and competency. You should read the trial transcript."

"It's second-guessing," Dr. Josephson complained. "It's easy, after an operation has been performed and has not been successful, to go back and apply the wisdom of hindsight to the procedures that were performed."

"Bart," said Teejay, "you didn't hear the testimony. You haven't read the transcript. Trying to fuse two disks, Kirkwood damaged the man's spinal cord so badly that he's paralyzed for life. There's no second-guessing about it. It was butchery."

"That's what you told the jury," said Dr. Josephson.

"That's what the evidence told the jury."

Dr. Josephson shook his head and lifted his glass of beer. "So the jury awards Hugger five hundred and fifty thousand dollars and destroys Kirkwood's reputation."

"I don't think the money is enough to compensate Hugger for what he's suffered and is going to suffer," said Teejay firmly. "And so far as Kirkwood's reputation is concerned, why should a man who has carelessly paralyzed a patient for life continue to enjoy a reputation for being a good surgeon?"

"What concerns me most, I guess," said Dr. Josephson, "and what concerns my colleagues about this whole business of malpractice suits is: How can we practice medicine with a couple of lawyers and a jury looking over our shoulders?"

"Why not?" she asked. "I practice law with them looking over my shoulder. If I'm negligent and my negligence costs my client money,

I have to pay. I drive a car with a judge and jury looking over my shoulder. If I drive negligently and injure someone, a court will order me to pay damages. Why should it be any different if you practice medicine negligently and injure a patient?"

"Smart lawyers talk juries into huge verdicts," he said.

"Oh? You think jurors are idiots? Anyway, Dr. Kirkwood's insurance company provided him with a team of the most eminent defense lawyers in Houston. The jury heard both sides."

"Do you deny some lawyers take unfair advantage, for motives that won't stand examination?"

Teejay shrugged. "Do you deny some surgeons are butchers, some doctors are quacks? We can't base sound arguments on aberrations in our two professions."

The lawsuit they had been talking about had occupied most of her time for more than six months. It had been a risk for her to take it: a major gamble on her career. George Hugger was a twenty-three-year-old truck driver. As a result of the negligence of Dr. Kirkwood, he would never walk again. More than that, he would never have a normal bowel movement, would never urinate normally, and had been left impotent.

When Hugger's family came to her, the case had been rejected by four other Houston lawyers. Dr. Kirkwood had a high reputation, other Houston surgeons would not testify as expert witnesses against him, the hospital would not cooperate in making records available, and the family had no money for legal fees. What was more, the negligence of Dr. Kirkwood was not obvious; it would have to be established by thorough investigation and by marshaling convincing evidence. Building the case would require the investment of time she had and money she didn't have.

She warned the Hugger family that she was a young lawyer practicing alone, without the financial and investigative resources of a firm. They said the firms would not take their case. She took it, finally, on a contingency-fee basis: If she won the case, she would take thirty-three percent of the award; if she lost it, they would owe her nothing.

She sued for two million dollars. Dr. Kirkwood's insurance company retained Childreth, McLennon & Brady to defend. The firm assigned Byron Stryker, one of the most respected defense lawyers in Texas, to oppose the lawsuit. Stryker fought her every step of the way, from the filing of the suit until the jury returned its verdict. He was fair, but absolutely nothing in the protracted and complex procedure of the suit was unchallenged.

Almost a year passed between the filing of the suit and the date of the trial. It could have been longer, but it was in her interest and Stryker's as well to advance it as rapidly as possible—hers because she had to borrow money to pay for items like deposition transcripts and travel expenses for her expert witnesses; his because the faster a young solo lawyer had to work, the more likely she was to omit something that might reinforce her case.

Doctors, nurses, and hospital administrators would not talk to her; she had to obtain subpoenas to gain access to the most minor documents. The judge assigned to the case was hostile; she had to justify every subpoena she asked for. The insurance company offered Hugger a settlement of $25,000, and he almost took it.

That was a hard decision. If she advised him to refuse a $25,000 settlement and then the jury awarded him nothing, she would have to face George Hugger in his wheelchair and tell him she was sorry. But she was convinced his case was worth more and he should have more. He wavered. After all, he would have $25,000—less her one-third—and something in hand is better than the chance of ten times as much at the end of a hard-fought lawsuit that, with appeals, might go on for years. She argued with him. She talked him into going on. But she wondered how she would have faced him later if they had lost the case.

During the year the Hugger case was pending, her practice was growing slowly. In the last two or three months before trial, she had to turn down business; she did not have time to complete her trial preparation and take on time-consuming new business as well. It was another risk.

The case went to trial. At the end of the plaintiff's case, Stryker offered a settlement of $100,000. By now George Hugger had sat in the courtroom and listened to medical witnesses describe the negligence by which Kirkwood had crippled him, and he was angry and would not hear of a settlement. He thought he might even win the two million.

The jury returned a verdict of $550,000. Stryker notified Teejay that he would appeal, then offered another settlement—$200,000. They settled for $300,000. The appeal was dropped. Teejay deposited $201,000 to George Hugger's account and $99,000 to her own.

A week after she took her fee and deposited the balance of the settlement to the account of George Hugger, his sister came to her office. The family was not satisfied. They had thought, she said, George might get the two million, or at least one million; and anyway, if the jury awarded $550,000, why did Lawyer Brookover recommend George accept only $300,000? What was worse, the fee was far too much. Who

ever heard of a lawyer taking $99,000 out of a settlement of only
$300,000? The family had talked it over and decided $10,000 would
be generous. They wanted a refund of $89,000—less the expenses they
knew she had borrowed money and paid. They had been talking to
another lawyer about it, and they might just sue if she didn't agree
to $10,000.

"Well, I'll tell you what, Lavinia," she had said to the sister. "Maybe
you better just go ahead and sue me. But you better keep this in mind:
The lawyer you're suing is the same trial lawyer who squeezed three
hundred thousand dollars for you out of a case the other lawyers you
talked to wouldn't take. You got somebody that good to take the case
against me?"

Dr. Josephson had ordered them two more beers. He made conversation. It disturbed him deeply, he said, to see how little the world had
reacted to the murder of the Israeli athletes at the Olympic Games in
Munich in September. Houston particularly, he said, had paid the
tragedy too little attention. Mankind, he said, must find some way
to cope with international crimes.

"Ah. There's Lois. Lois! Here!"

The tall woman who walked toward their table obviously had come
to keep an appointment with Dr. Josephson. She did not successfully
cover her surprise—maybe dismay—at seeing Teejay with him. She was
wearing a pale yellow linen pullover dress, loose and cool for this hot
October Saturday but tailored and worn with a measured air of *hau-
teur*. She wore white gloves and carried a small soft-leather briefcase.

"Lois, I want you to meet someone. This is T. J. Brookover. Teejay,
this is Lois Hughes."

Lois Hughes, sure. Dan Farnham's daughter. Teejay had heard of
her since she was in law school. She had heard more of Farnham, but
she had heard of this daughter: the rich girl lawyering for the fun of
it. She was with Childreth, McLennon & Brady—which made her a
partner of Byron Stryker. She did a lot of *pro bono* work for her firm,
promoted a lot of causes, and they said she had political ambitions.
She was a tall one, with a long, somber face and a distant air.

"I'm pleased to meet you," said Lois Hughes. "Shall I join you?"

"What else?" asked Dr. Josephson. "Get all your work done?"

"Yes. God, get me a martini."

God, get her a martini! She relaxed quickly. She had analyzed the
situation and decided she had to accept it for the moment, apparently;
and she was tired and anxious to unwind.

"Let's see," said Lois Hughes to Teejay. "You're the one who just took By Stryker for three hundred thousand dollars."

"The nemesis of the Harris County Medical Association," said Dr. Josephson. "We passed a resolution the other night that if she gets sick, none of us will treat her."

"From what I hear of her courtroom performance, she won't need you," said Lois Hughes. "She'll command God to treat her, and He will."

"No, Satan," said Teejay. She nodded. "That's my ally."

"Ahh . . ." said Lois Hughes. "Come to think of it, that's what By Stryker said."

She said these things without smiling. There was a smile in her voice: subtle, ambiguous. She pulled off her white gloves. She wore a signet ring of yellow gold, with the initial "F" for Farnham, not "H" for Hughes. It looked old. She wore no other ring—no wedding ring. She had a strong jawline, strong mouth, strong nose, and heavy, un-plucked brows.

"We're using first names," said Dr. Josephson to Lois Hughes. "They call her Teejay."

"Teejay. And I'm of course Lois. Have you two just met?"

"By chance. I wanted to talk to her about the whole malpractice business, and she was good enough to interrupt her afternoon."

"And set you down firmly, I should imagine," said Lois Hughes.

"Yes, very firmly," the doctor said, grinning.

Lois Hughes wore her skirt one inch above her knee. The skirt was split four or five inches more, showing a little more of her stockinged leg. She looked as if she had never worn a mini, although she was obviously, within a year or two, the same age as Teejay herself. She had observed Teejay's upriding mini with one lofty glance.

Lois Hughes clasped her hands before her on the table. "By tells me," she said, "you had the Hugger case on a contingency fee. And I understand you settled this week."

Teejay nodded. "Right. Right on both counts."

Lois Hughes lowered her eyes and nodded. "Makes the practice of law a little more palatable, doesn't it?"

"A whole lot more," Teejay said.

"Well, congratulations," said Lois Hughes. "By Stryker was condescending toward you, I imagine, because you are a woman. You beat him. I like that, even if he is my partner."

Teejay was startled. And elated. "He was a gentleman," she said. "I'll say that for Mr. Stryker: He was a gentleman."

"I haven't heard anyone use the word 'gentleman'—except as a joke —for some time," said Dr. Josephson. "I like it."

"That's my west Texas background coming out, I guess," said Teejay. "We didn't know any gentlemen, but we thought we knew what one would be like."

Lois Hughes accepted her martini from the waiter and took a quarter of it in her first sip. "Teejay," she said, "are you a member of the Bar Association?"

"I'm a member, of course," said Teejay. "I'm not active."

"I'm chairman of a committee on women's rights," said Lois Hughes. "We have a lot of work to do. Do you do much *pro bono* work?"

"I'll be blunt about that," said Teejay. "I had to work my way through school, all the way from high school; and I had to open my own office and almost starve getting a practice started. I'm not ready to do any *pro bono* work. Maybe someday."

Lois Hughes gave most of her attention to her martini. "I won't lecture you, then, about its being a responsibility we all share," she said. "When you feel ready, let me know."

"I will," said Teejay.

In a few minutes Teejay took her leave. Lois watched her go. She had thanked Bart for the beer and conversation, said she was glad to have met Lois and hoped she would see her again, and left the table a little abruptly—moved maybe by a fine sense of social timing.

"That's a bit hard to believe, isn't it?" Bart said.

Lois nodded thoughtfully, watching her for another moment, then dropping her eyes to the martini between her hands on the table. T. J. Brookover was indeed a contradiction of what she'd heard of her, of every premature judgment she had made. Byron Stryker had described a hard, aggressive, beautiful, sensual young woman. The redhead was in fact delicate of build, graceful of carriage, slender and erect, with the body of a dancer. Her conversation was quick and sharp. She was defensive and intense.

Lois lifted her martini. "I'm glad you found someone to talk to while you waited. I didn't expect to be so late."

"It's all right. I saw Mac John on the golf course."

"Did you talk to him?"

"He was drunk."

"On the golf course?"

"On the golf course."

"His parents and mine had dinner together this week," she said. "They reached the conclusion, I am told, that the marriage must be saved at any cost."

"An admirable attitude," he said.

"Yes, but of course *I* am the one who is to pay the cost."

She had an appointment for dinner. She had to go home first. She had no time to go anywhere with Bart. All they could do was meet for a drink and talk. It had been more than two weeks since they had been able to coordinate their schedules and find two hours to be alone somewhere. It had been two weeks before that. Now all they could do was sit in the gloom of a bar, drink, talk aimlessly. They still met in a hotel room when they could, but sometimes she felt as if they did it more to conform to the roles they had chosen to play than because they really needed each other physically. (After all, what was an affair for if you did not fornicate?) They did not talk about love anymore. The words had only been a source of anxiety, and in time it had become apparent they were meaningless. Their urgent, energetic coupling was not always satisfying anymore, not for her anyway. She wondered if what they did had not simply become a habit, and, if that was all it was, why did they go on doing it?

Hal Spencer awkwardly lowered a tray to the patio table. The drinks sloshed precariously near the rims of their glasses, but he spilled nothing, and he grinned and handed Lois a martini. "Hope that's the way you like it," he said.

She sipped and nodded. "Very good," she said. She could have said nothing else. The big, ingenuous man was easily wounded. She could never be comfortable around him, for fear of saying something that would shatter his fragile comradely facade and leave him hurt and pondering over his shortfall.

"Thank you," he said. "Do you like the cheese?"

"It's quite good," she said.

"Hal is something of a connoisseur of cheese," said Norma Jean.

He grinned. "I've tried to learn something about it. I wish I knew something about wine, too."

It was a warm evening. Shortly he would switch on the lights over the patio, and they would have dinner outdoors, off the charcoal grill, which was smoking now. Grills smoked all across the neighborhood. The air was weighted with the pungent odors of burning charcoal and burning beef fat. Someone's radio was loud down the street and the rock-and-roll beat buzzed on the eardrums. People's children laughed and yelled.

Hal was a huge man to begin with, but in the past year or two Lois had noticed he was carrying more and more weight over his big bones and muscles. His hair had backed off to the middle of his head. Tonight he wore a pair of blue and white checked slacks, held up with a wide white belt, and a yellow golf shirt. Norma Jean wore shorts and a blouse. She was overweight, too, and with her spectacles prominently perched on her sunburned nose, she was not Bunny anymore. She had suggested Lois wear shorts tonight, as she was going to do; and Lois, conscious that both Spencers suspected she condescended to them, wore white shorts, a light blue knit shirt, and white tennis shoes.

The children were eating noisily in the kitchen. Norma Jean meant to put them to bed before Hal put the steaks on the grill.

"I'm sorry your husband couldn't come," said Hal. He sometimes called Mac John Mr. Hughes; he had never called him Mac John, to his face or otherwise, and lately he had settled on "your husband."

Lois held her martini up and turned the glass in her hand before her face. "What kind of gin do you use, Hal?" she asked.

"Beefeater," he said. "Isn't that the best?"

She nodded appreciatively. "Yes," she said. "It's the best."

He grinned. "I—wanted to have the best gin for you," he said with an excess of innocence.

He went inside to put the children to bed. Norma Jean listened to him talking to them in the kitchen, her eyes fastened on Lois, who glanced away self-consciously. His voice boomed as he romped with the children and hustled them away toward their bedrooms.

"He wants me to leave the firm and come practice law with him and his partner," said Norma Jean quietly.

"I don't see how you can do that," said Lois.

Norma Jean rubbed her bare leg. "I've been with Childreth, Mc-Lennon and Brady five years," she said. "I haven't made partner. I'm not going to. I think the time has come for me to start looking for an alternative."

"It isn't settled that you're not going to make partner."

"If I had any pride I'd have quit six months ago. In fact, I should have quit when Finley died. Your partners are waiting for me to quit. I would, but I can't afford it. Even as an associate at Childreth I make more money than Hal makes. Whatever you make, you spend it, you know. Or maybe you wouldn't know."

"You want to bring the matter to a head?"

Norma Jean shook her head. "I'd like to tell Childreth, McLennon and Brady to go to hell. But I can't afford the luxury."

Hearing Hal booming inside the house, Norma Jean looked away across the yards to a group of children playing on a swing. She ended the conversation.

It was a matter of style, partly. It was true that the senior partners at Childreth, McLennon & Brady were not going to make her a partner. She was intelligent. She worked hard. The resentment over her relationship with Finley had abated after his death, and she could have overcome it. But the partnership did not know quite what to do with her. As Bunny, she had been a little too flamboyant, and she had known it and had killed Bunny. Now, as Norma Jean, she was a little too nearly dowdy. She did not inspire confidence.

"Do you know what he does for a living?" Norma Jean asked suddenly, turning away from the children on the swing and snapping the question at Lois.

Caught off-balance by the quick change, Lois frowned and asked, "Who?"

"Hal. He's not a lawyer; he's a scrivener. He picks up the contemptible scraps of business that Childreth wouldn't touch. He does it like a goddamn insurance salesman: at church, at Civitan, at the lodge . . . I even had to join the goddamn Eastern Star. He glad-hands and picks up scraps. There's no goddamn dignity in it. I wouldn't practice law that way if my only alternative were to sell buttons and thread in a dime store. He has to scramble to make a living. He's got friends by the shitpotful, and they bring him their petty collections and their little wills and once in a while a divorce; and if they have something good, they take it to a better lawyer. He's always somewhere smiling. It makes me sick."

"Don't put him down that much, Bunny," Lois said. "He deserves better than that."

"He wouldn't play pro ball. He didn't think he was good enough to be a star, and he thought it was better to go to law school and learn a profession than to play football and not be a star. Now he's a lawyer, and he's sure no star. I wonder what he thinks, Lois. I don't know him well enough to know what's behind the grin and the handshake. I wonder what he thinks of himself."

"Would you rather have *my* husband?" Lois asked. Her voice was thin and hard. Her chin was up. "You have a pretty good idea, don't you, where Mac John is tonight and what he's doing?"

Norma Jean lowered her eyes. She nodded.

"Does Hal know?"

Norma Jean nodded.

Lois's voice broke. "Everybody knows," she whispered.

Mac John did not wear clip-on bow ties. Dressing for a dinner at Bayou Oaks Country Club, he stood at the mirror in the bathroom and knotted his tie. "No," he said to Lois. "I don't want to go. I think you should, but to me Thanksgiving is a family holiday, and I plan to eat my Thanksgiving dinner with my father and mother—or with yours."

"My father and mother will be in New York. They want to take Wendy and little Mac John."

"Then I will have dinner with my family," he said. "If you want to go to Mexico City, go ahead. Take a week off."

"That would be convenient for you, wouldn't it?" she said.

"I don't need convenience," he said. "I have all the convenience I can use."

"Yes. I know damn well you do."

"We'd make each other miserable," he said. "Why spoil a little vacation?"

She was sitting on the bed, in a half-slip and brassiere. "I don't want to go alone," she said quietly.

"Get Bart to go, then," he said.

"What?"

"Invite Bart," he said. He turned his back to the mirror and faced her through the bathroom door. He was heavy-lidded, a little drunk, and he was smiling. "He can tell his wife he has a medical convention or something. You two can have a whole week."

"What are you talking about?" she asked hoarsely.

He grinned, then turned back to the mirror and began to adjust his tie. "Don't be coy, for Christ's sake," he said.

"*What do you mean?*"

"Lois . . ." He glanced at her over his shoulder. "I may be a drunk. I may not, in your estimation, be very bright. But I am not entirely stupid. Bart has been fucking you for months. Did you suppose I didn't know?"

"*Mac—*"

"I do know. I have known for some time. What's more, his wife knows. I asked her, and she said she knew. She doesn't care. And neither do I. So there's no reason you and Bart shouldn't spend a week somewhere together and enjoy yourselves."

"*You bastard!*"

XXI

On Wednesday, August 30, Teejay was taken out of jail for an hour, to make her appearance before a federal magistrate, to plead not guilty to three federal indictments. They had to take her from jail to the Federal Building. They had to let her bathe and work on her hair, and put on a little makeup, and dress. She had looked forward to it.

She had given careful thought to what she would wear—something not somber, yet not flippant; something that would convey an image of who she was and what she was: T. J. Brookover, falsely accused and undefeated. She had chosen a cream-white suit—loose-legged pants, a long open-weave jacket worn over a pale green silk blouse—crepe-soled cream-white canvas shoes, a big green and blue silk scarf tied loosely at her throat. She had bathed and used talcum powder as well as deodorant. She wore a little lipstick. She had brushed her hair ten minutes, and it hung smoothly around her shoulders. The women in the jail, who had never seen her in anything but a gray jail smock, had stared at her with gaped mouths.

She felt good, even with the handcuffs locked tightly around her wrists, and she let her imprisoned hands hang loose; she did not clench her fists. She had thought about what was going to happen, and she expected to be photographed. She intended to smile. She had been photographed before, for the newspapers and for television, crying, jerking wildly at her handcuffs, stumbling into a police car. If they published pictures this time, she would not look like that.

The federal grand jury had indicted her on three counts of what the newspapers were calling stock fraud. If convicted, she could be sentenced to fifteen or twenty years in a federal reformatory. Realistically, a judge would sentence her to three to five years, and she would be released in twelve or fifteen months. Six months ago that prospect would have terrified her. It didn't now.

They were waiting outside the jail: the cameramen for the newspapers and for television. She was able to speak personally to two or three of the cameramen. She could speak to them by name, and they grinned at her and waved and called her Teejay.

In the car she asked the matron for a cigarette. The deputy had a pack of unfiltered Luckies and handed one back to her. The matron rolled the window halfway down to let the smoke out, and Teejay was able to smoke the whole cigarette on the way to the Federal Building. The deputy who drove the car turned to speak to her while he waited at a red traffic light. He said he wished her good luck.

Her moment before the magistrate was that: a moment. She pleaded not guilty to the three charges against her, and the magistrate fixed her bond on the three charges at $25,000. Since she was in jail on a state charge, she could not be released anyway, so she said she would not file the bond for now, and she was remanded to the Harris County jail where she would now be held, technically, as a federal and a state prisoner.

Lois, for some reason, failed to appear. Teejay waived her right to counsel and entered her pleas without her lawyer standing beside her. The magistrate and the United States district attorney were reluctant to accept the pleas, but Teejay reminded them that she was a lawyer herself and assured them that, anyway, she had been fully advised. Lois appeared only after Teejay had been handcuffed again for her return to jail.

"I'm sorry," Lois said. "I'm in contempt."

"I took care of it," Teejay said.

"There's a man in town wants to see you," Lois said. "I had dinner with him last night. I want you to talk to him this afternoon."

"Who?"

"Do you know an old country lawyer named Earl Lansing?" Lois asked.

"From back home," Teejay said.

"Yes. From Clayton County. It seems your mother has gotten up a little money and has retained Earl Lansing to defend you." Lois smiled broadly. "He's here. He wants to help as much as he can."

Teejay lowered her eyes to her handcuffs. "I'm sorry, Lois," she said. "They do things differently in Clayton County."

"No," said Lois. "I want him for associate counsel. He's a grand old man."

"He is the one who suggested I go to law school," Teejay said.

"He's a beautiful old man," said Lois. "He wants to help you. I think he can be a real help. When you see him, treat him like a wonderful friend."

"How else could I treat him?"

"He's coming to the jail this afternoon."

Teejay frowned. "Lois . . ." she said softly. "Is there any way I could see him— Could you arrange any way that I could see him out of jail, out of uniform, not—handcuffed or anything? He's someone I don't want to see me like this."

Lois shook her head. "I'll bring it up. I don't think they can do anything."

The matrons were sympathetic in their way. They allowed her to see Lansing in a small office outside the secure area of the jail. They issued her a new uniform, still crisp, of unfaded gray, with the words HARRIS COUNTY JAIL smartly stenciled across the back. They let her brush out her hair and put a little blush on her cheeks and a little lipstick.

Still, she flushed when she met the old lawyer, and her mouth was dry. "Mr. Lansing . . ." she whispered. "I never thought you'd see me like this."

He took her hand. "No," he said. "We neither of us expected anything like this. There are hazards in our profession." He held her hand, smiled with grim, stiff lips, and nodded. "I didn't know what had happened to you, or I'd have come and offered help before now."

Earl Lansing was grayer and balder and had become a little stooped since that day twelve years ago when she and Kevin had sat in his office in LaGrange and shared his whiskey and he had talked to her about becoming a lawyer. That was the only conversation she had ever had with him, before today, but he had remained in her consciousness as *the lawyer*, the archetypal lawyer; it was what she had seen of him —or thought she saw—that led her to enter the profession herself, and she had made him a standard against which she measured other lawyers and herself. She had envied him his independence. She had envied him the status his profession gave him: a little apart from and a little above the pinched community in which he lived; and she had envied his ability to live comfortably and confidently, untroubled by the resentment of a substantial number of the members of that community.

Sometimes over the years she had thought of inviting him to Houston, to sip whiskey in *her* office, to talk law—to see what she had become. She would have found more satisfaction in showing Earl Lansing she was a successful lawyer than she would have found showing it to anyone else she could think of—and now she felt more humiliation for him to see her a uniformed prisoner than she would have felt with anyone else.

"I'm 'bout half retired," he said. "I knew you'd become a lawyer. Your brother told me that. I didn't know you'd got in trouble. Nobody said anything about it before your mother came to the office last week and asked me to look into your case. Your family came up with some money."

"I don't need money from them," Teejay said. Her voice was small, her breath short. "I paid Lois a retainer. I can pay you."

Lansing glanced around the little office; then his eyes settled on her, conspicuously speculating, forming a judgment. His tongue pressed one cheek, then the other, and he sucked his teeth. "Lois tells me you did very well as a lawyer, until this trouble came up. I knew you'd gone to law school, got admitted. That's about all I knew, and I guess it's about all your family knew. You've played your game of independence mighty hard, Tommy Jo."

"I didn't have much choice in that, did I?"

He shook his head. "Very little," he agreed. "But they would have tried. Your mother, your brothers, even old Serena—they all would have done what they could to help you. Anytime. They are people of limited resources—in every sense. But they're good people in their way."

Teejay swelled with a deep breath. "I'd just about as soon be where I am as be where they are," she said grimly.

"Really?" Lansing asked. He smiled. "Well . . . Your mother wanted me to ask if you want her to come to see you. I suppose I tell her you don't."

"No. Tell her I'll write her. Tell her I'll come to see her when this is over and I'm out of here."

"You're confident that's the way it's going to turn out?" he asked.

Teejay closed her eyes and shook her head quickly. "If it doesn't," she whispered, "then she can come to Huntsville to see me."

"Smart lawyer, that woman you've got," said Lansing. "She wants me to help her. I'll do what I can."

"I'm grateful," she whispered.

He frowned. "I'm worried about the federal charges," he said. "You're guilty of those, aren't you, Tommy Jo?"

She nodded. "I suppose so. It's a complicated law."

"The securities law . . ." he said. "*Malum prohibitum.*"

She nodded. She had thought of the federal charges in exactly that phrase. In the law, the Latin phrase *malum in se* referred to an act that was wrong in itself and would be wrong whether the law prohibited it or not—like murder or rape. *Malum prohibitum* referred to an act that was wrong only because a law had been passed prohibiting it—like driving a car through a red traffic light. She could be punished for violations of the securities laws simply because she violated them, whether or not the violations involved any hurt to anyone or any breach of morals.

"They can disbar you on those charges," he said. "Even if the federal judge gives you probation."

"I know."

"What'll you do?"

She shook her head. "I don't know," she whispered.

He reached for her hand. "You have friends," he said. "Don't forget it. I'm not the only one that'd like to do somethin' for you. You have friends all over."

She wept. He held both her hands while she hung her head and sobbed.

On the Tuesday morning after Labor Day, Lois came to the jail in the morning. Teejay was sitting on the floor of "B" Cage, playing a game of double solitaire with Christine McElhay, and she was taken down to an interview cubicle.

"The news is not so good this morning," Lois said. "I've found out something that bothers me."

"Dump it on me," said Teejay.

Lois referred to a note on a yellow pad. "Did you ever hear the name James Hedwig?" she asked.

Teejay nodded.

"It's another name for Kevin Flint, isn't it?" said Lois. "He's used several aliases over the years. This is one of them."

"He's an Oklahoma parole violator," said Teejay.

"The Harris County District Attorney's Office has invited the FBI into the investigation of Kevin," said Lois. "The FBI is interested in Kevin. He's been involved in some odd business propositions. They came up with this name Hedwig. There's no question that Flint and Hedwig are the same person."

"So?"

"Well, it seems James O. Hedwig kept a safe-deposit box in a New Orleans bank. They opened that box on a court order and found some envelopes in there with Kevin's fingerprints on them. The envelopes were full of cash—eighty-three thousand, six hundred dollars. They suspect Kevin may have more somewhere."

"So?"

"Teejay," Lois cautioned, "don't play dumb. Kevin's story is that he killed Mudge while trying to rob him. That's our story, too. But why would a man with that much cash in a safe-deposit box do anything so stupid and risky as try a holdup in a parking lot?"

"Where'd he get the eighty-three thousand?" Teejay asked warily. "Maybe—"

"*Teejay!* You know damn well he didn't get it sticking up old men in parking lots. Their finding this money shoots a big hole in an important element of our defense."

Teejay trembled. "Lois, for God's sake! How do I know where he got it?"

Lois shook her head. "I don't think you've ever told me the truth about Kevin Flint."

Teejay clenched her fists on the table between them, hung her head and shook it, and whispered, "I've told you all you need to know."

"No! You can't hold back on me. You're a lawyer. You've defended people against criminal charges. I have to know *everything!* You understand that better than anyone else."

For a long moment Teejay sucked loud, shuddering breaths. Then she looked up into Lois's face. "Kevin may be the worst thing that ever happened to me," she whispered. She drew another breath and braced herself. "There's a woman in 'B' Cage who tells me Kevin once sold I-don't-know-how-many tons of peanuts that didn't even exist. I knew he was a con man, a flimflam artist. I thought he was small-time. He may have had more in common with Ben Mudge than I ever guessed. I believed he killed Mudge in a robbery. Why not? I supposed he needed money. But Jesus! If they've found out this, what else will they find out that will hurt me? Everything he's done is stuck on me. Why? *Why, goddammit!*"

She returned to the cellblock. She went into her cell and lay down on her bunk.

There was evidence she knew Kevin as James Hedwig. There was evidence if they could find it. Once—what year was it?—when she was working topless—it was her last year in law school—she wrote Kevin a small check when he broke his Oklahoma parole and needed money to buy some decent clothes. She wrote a check to James O. Hedwig—

for $200, she thought it was—on her account at the Bank of the Southwest. She had long ago destroyed all her canceled checks and bank statements from 1968 and 1969. The check could not be in her papers that the district attorney had seized. But did a bank keep microfilm that long? She tried to remember what she had heard about how long a bank kept checking-account records. Could the district attorney or the FBI find a microfilm of that old check? If they could, would they think of it? If they could and did, they would find the check: evidence that she had known Kevin by the name he had used in committing God-knew-what crimes somewhere.

Whatever Kevin had done, they would manage some way to tie it to her. She did not know all he had done. He had talked to her about some of the things. Sometimes she had not even paid him much attention; she had been bored by his overbright enthusiasm for some of his petty schemes. God, what had it all been? He had sworn to her he never dealt in narcotics. That would make a jury hate them both. But what else?

Kevin . . . That night, when she was locked in her cell and was alone, she sat cross-legged on her bunk and smoked and stared through her cell bars at nothing but more bars and a brick wall, and she thought about Kevin. She had loved him, really. How could she not? Right now he was sacrificing whatever remote chance he had to defend himself to try to defend her. Yet, as she had said to Lois, he was the worst thing that had ever happened to her.

And maybe she was the worst thing that had ever happened to him.

XXII

1973

Lois divorced Mac John. It became final in April. On impulse, late in the month, she flew to Paris, alone. It was one more thing someone had told her she couldn't do.

And maybe it was a mistake. A sullen rain was falling on Paris the morning she arrived. It was cold and gray. She checked in at the Windsor Reynolds: into one of those old French hotel rooms with the unique, unforgettable odor of must and dust and floor oil. She stood at the window and looked out on wet roofs and down on a narrow street where only an occasional pedestrian hurried for shelter. She stood there alone and faced the prospect of having to leave the room after a nap and find lunch, of having to arrange something for the evening, and having to arrange something for tomorrow—all alone. She undressed and slipped into bed, in midmorning.

"I am sorry," her mother had said. "I'm not sure it is appropriate to say this, but I can't help it; I have to tell you. No one in my family before was ever divorced. No one. I know it's done now. I know it's common. I guess I am old-fashioned, but I can't help feeling more than a little embarrassed facing my friends."

Mac John had been a gentleman about it. When she told him she had decided she wanted a divorce, he said he would go to a hotel that night, and tomorrow would move out of the house. She could have the house and custody of the children, of course. A few items in the house were Hughes family heirlooms, and he wanted those; otherwise everything was hers. He would pay support for the children and would pay for their education. He didn't really think alimony was appropriate in the circumstances. Did she?

One night after he had gone a few nights, she found herself rolling over in bed in the dark, reaching for him. She was cold and wanted his warmth. She had cried for him that night, and other nights, too. It had been entirely easy to decide, rationally, that she did not want him anymore, that she was not in love with him anymore, that she could not tolerate his faults. But when he was gone she missed him. She suffered from a sense of loss—something that was hers was gone. She recalled how she had once been proud of him.

The children blamed someone. She was not sure who. They were not open about it. But clearly they did not see the divorce as inevitable. They saw it as a failure by someone—maybe one of their parents, maybe both—to put *their* interests and needs first. Maybe it was something their grandparents had said.

Bart was bad. He was afraid it would be said *he* had broken up the Hughes marriage. (It was not said. Almost no one knew about him and Lois. Never had people been so discreet.) He was selfish. He did not help her.

She had asked him to come to Europe with her, knowing he wouldn't. "For a week or two, that's all. Or come over and join me after I've been there a week. Whatever . . ."

"Everyone will know I'm with you."

"So? I'm divorced."

"I'm not."

"Your wife? She couldn't care less."

"I practice a profession that is absolutely dependent on people's confidence in me."

"To hell with you."

So, on a rainy, chilly morning in Paris she lay alone in a hotel room and stared glumly through the tall windows opposite the bed, at dark rooftops and chimneys and low-flying gray clouds. She felt nothing much. She had no sense of relief. Distance did not expel from her head a thousand oppressive images. They had flown the Atlantic with her.

The next day she went to Flesselles et Frères. Was John Adams still an agent? Of course, *madame*, in the London office. If *madame* wished to see Monsieur Adams, he could be notified and— No. She had done business with him years ago and only wondered. No. She did not wish to see him.

She prowled through the galleries again. She sat in the cafés on the Champs-Elysées. She saw an opera. She ate well. She received indecent propositions, some of them persistent, from Frenchmen, Italians, a German, three Americans. She declined firmly. She remained alone. After a week she rented a car—a buzzing little red Alfa Romeo—and set out for the South. For another week she drove through France, avoiding anyplace where tourists congregated, exploring with no foreknowledge of what she saw, staying in tiny hotels in rooms with no water, sampling the local wine and food, keeping to herself among people who were entirely content to leave her alone.

One morning she visited the Abbey of Fontrevault—something she remembered John Adams saying she must see. It was cold and raining again that morning, and when she stood in the nave of the Romanesque abbey church, facing the recumbent stone tomb effigies of the Plantagenets, she shuddered and tugged her small jacket tighter around her. Here, in the cool, weak, gray light, lay the effigy of Eleanor of Aquitaine, and that of Henry II, and of John; and she was fascinated, even inspired, as Adams had promised. John Adams had shown her how to savor a place like this, how to allow it to inspire her imagination, how to let it move her, how later to recall and savor again the imaginings and the emotions the place inspired, and how to talk about it—all without restraint of rationalism and without embarrassment. She wished Adams were here. It would have been better.

Her impulse was to call him. Why not, after all? Probably he would come to France to see her—or she would go to England. What would John Adams think of her now, no longer the girl wearing too much underwear; instead a controversial lawyer, a mother, divorced, a calm, sober woman. She had changed. The trouble was, maybe he had, too. Everyone did. Everything had. Except memories of things that are finished. That was why she had not called him: for fear of risking the memory.

"*Madame? Vous êtes Américaine?*"

A soft voice. She turned and found a young priest standing beside her. She could not remember how to address a priest in French. "*Oui —monsieur.*"

"My English . . ." he said with a Gallic shrug and a smile. "If you might leave a small gift for the church. In the eleventh century already they have built it, and it wishes to fall down."

They talked. He refreshed her memory about Eleanor of Aquitaine and added much she had never learned. He showed her the octagonal tower which had once housed the kitchen for the monastery. As many as five thousand monks and nuns once lived here, he explained. When she suggested he let her drive him into the village of Montsoreau and buy him his lunch, to her surprise he accepted.

"I am traveling alone," she had explained. "Not once in two weeks have I spoken an entire minute to one person, until I met you just now."

He told her in the car his name was Father Henri Thiers. Except for his university years in Paris and six months spent studying in Rome, he had lived all his life within twenty kilometers of Montsoreau. He was five years younger than she: a slight, dark man, unmemorable in appearance. But he spoke with knowledge and charm. She wanted conversation.

"Over this land," he said, "they all rode. Those ones in the church. Later, the Black Prince. All of them, all those ancient ones." He was a provincial, proud of his corner of France. "I cannot think," he said later in response to something she said, "of any place where I would live happier."

Maybe because she was with Père Henri, they gave her a table at the window in the restaurant, where she could sit and watch the rain falling on the street. The sky lightened, but the rain kept falling. The paving stones glistened and reflected the facades of the houses. She and the priest ate sparingly of a dish of beef and noodles in a garlicky red sauce, but they drank thirstily of the rich red wine served in earthenware pitchers. They relaxed, and hours passed. The priest was not a memorable man, but he gave her a memorable afternoon.

He was a stranger and a listener; but he was also, eminently, a confessor, with no sense that his questions might be too intimate or his comments unwelcome. Unworldly in two senses, he was ingenuous and incapable of offense. He was intrigued that she should be traveling alone so far from home when she had both a husband (even if divorced from him) and a lover (even if the affair was over). "It is perhaps that these gentlemen have proved incapable of contenting you in—how is it said?—in that which is between your legs, madame. It is not uncommon, this problem, particularly for a woman your age."

"No, Father." She smiled at him. She could not snap back anything hard. He didn't deserve it. "That is not the problem."

He nodded, accepting her denial. "From what you say, I think you expect much of people. They disappoint you."

"Yes."

"I," he said slowly, "expect nothing except of Him who never disappoints."

"I can't accept that."

"Ah."

"I am not an atheist, Father. I rationalize perhaps, but I tell myself

I do work that is acceptable to God when I give my time and effort to doing things I believe are right."

"Like. . . . ?"

"I work for the poor. In my way. I prevented the government from taking away poor people's homes to build a highway."

"Ah."

"It was a mistake, Father. They didn't care about their homes. They didn't care if the highway was built. They wanted money. I fought their battle for them, and won, and afterward they hated me, because they got to keep their homes instead of getting money."

Father Henri listened and smiled. "You were to be paid in the coin of their gratitude," he suggested. "And of this you were cheated."

"You are too perceptive, Father."

"What is it you want?" he asked.

"Of people?"

"Yes."

"Help, I guess. Support . . . The feeling that—someone is behind me, to catch me if I fall back."

"Maybe it is you march too far ahead," he suggested.

"Maybe the people behind me are too weak, lack resolution," she argued.

"God is never too weak," he said.

When the rain stopped, people were soon busy on the street. She watched a woman arrive on a motor-powered bicycle at a shop next door and later pedal away, carrying an unwrapped loaf of bread in an armpit. She watched intently, her eyes fixed, her chin cupped in her hand, her face wistful; and the young priest studied her face and frowned and after two or three minutes he spoke softly.

"*Je crois que vous sentez très déprimé.*"

She glanced at him quizzically.

"De . . . depress-ed," he said. "Not happy."

She smiled and shrugged.

He began to talk about her depression, which he said he had seen in the church when he saw her looking at the tombs. He said she was a handsome woman. (She noticed he did not call her a young woman.) Many women, he said, at her time of life suffered depression. Often, he went on, it was from the same cause; and now, more emphatically, he began to talk about what he called the "*agité* between the legs"— until she understood he very much wanted to talk about her sex life, or, more correctly probably, to hear her talk about it. She understood that his motive was only faintly sacerdotal, and she was both amused and irritated.

"Do you want to hear my confession, Father?" she asked crisply.

"Eh . . . *Je me ne* . . ."

"You can't grant me absolution. I am not Catholic."

"No . . . But, if it would give you comfort to confess . . ."

Abruptly her irritation weakened and died, drowned in a flood of amusement. She laughed. "What would you like to hear me confess, Father?" she asked.

He was not a stupid man. He realized she understood him. He smiled. "Only your most interesting sins," he said blandly, open-faced, his smiling eyes held steadily on hers.

"I'm sorry," she said. "Mine are not very interesting."

"Ils ne sont jamais," he said. They never are.

"I suppose not," she said. "It's depressing to think of it."

"Non," he said quickly. "New sins"—he gestured, seeking a word— "make new sinners. Enough with the old sins."

Lois laughed heartily. "Father," she said, "you are a worthy man. God is lucky to have you. I wish I had just one worthwhile, colorful sin to confess to you, because I like you."

After a week back in her home and office, the memory of Père Henri evoked a twinge of regret and envy in her: for his simplicity. She retreated into a vivid recollection of him for a moment one afternoon a month later, as a relief from the tension of a meeting with two of her firm's senior partners.

"Well?" asked Ted McCadden, a sharp edge new on his voice. "Isn't it so?"

"To be altogether frank with you," she said wearily, "I really don't care."

"We have to care," he said. "We have to come to a decision, and it has to be the right decision."

In his corner office, McCadden kept the sills of four windows heaped with files and books, and layers of unfiled papers covered his desk. A large brass bowl in the middle of his desk served as the ashtray into which he cast each day as many as forty cigarettes—few of them smoked more than a puff or two before they were balanced on the edge of the bowl, forgotten, and allowed to go out. Sixty years old and gray, he sat in an oversize leather chair tipped back and rested his feet on his desk.

"It's not going to be my decision," Lois said.

"I'm not asking you to make the decision. I'm asking you to participate."

"It's difficult for me."

"Because Norma Spencer is your friend."

"Because she is my friend," Lois agreed.

The other partner, at ease in a deep leather armchair and sipping coffee, was Joseph Duncan. He was younger than McCadden; his hair was still dark; and his owly brown eyes were magnified by heavy, horn-rimmed spectacles that sat on his sharp beak of a nose. "Lois, are you prepared to recommend she be made a partner?" he asked.

"I am not, because she is my friend and everyone in the firm knows she is. My judgment should not carry much weight."

"In a week," said Duncan, "we will announce eight new partners. Some of them have been here only five or six years. She has been here seven and is not on the list. Will she quit?"

Lois shook her head. "I don't think so. She would like to, but she can't afford to."

"She's a good lawyer," said McCadden. "There are places where she could fit in."

"Why didn't she fit in here?" Lois asked abruptly. "Off the record, let's say it. Why not?"

"Have you looked through the Compton file I sent you?" Duncan asked.

Lois nodded. "What was I supposed to find in it?"

"Let me tell you," said Duncan. An aggressive, self-assured man, he had nervous hands nevertheless; and now, having stroked his long thin chin for a moment, he resumed finger-tapping on the arm of his chair. "You saw in the file, I hope, a memorandum from Norma to me, suggesting we attack the Compton problem on a theory of promissory estoppel."

"I saw that," said Lois. "I thought it was well reasoned."

"With the wisdom of hindsight, I think so, too," said Duncan. "I think we might have won the case if we had followed Norma's idea. So let me tell you why we didn't."

"This is very revealing," said McCadden.

"I didn't have much time for the Compton matter at first," said Duncan. "So I gave Norma the Compton file. She researched the law, came up with her idea of promissory estoppel, and wrote me the memo we're talking about. Her idea was contrary to mine, so when she came in to confer with me, I challenged her on it. I said something like, 'Norma, are you sure about this? Are you ready to bet the Compton case on this idea?' And you know what she did?"

Duncan paused to shake his finger in the air. "She backed down. Right now, she backed down. She said something like, 'Well, maybe you're right, Mr. Duncan. I'll work on it some more.' Just like that, she backed off her idea. She wouldn't defend it, even for a minute. Lois, I didn't ridicule her idea. I didn't even say it was wrong. I just asked her to defend it. And she wouldn't do it."

"That's the bigger problem," said McCadden. "What would you call it, a question of character?"

"I'm not going to argue for a partnership for Norma," Lois said. "I said I wouldn't, and I won't. Let's acknowledge something though. She's not just a good lawyer. She's a brilliant lawyer. But she has lacked confidence in herself as long as I've known her—and, let's face it, we haven't done anything to build confidence for her."

"We're running a law firm here, not a psychiatric clinic," said McCadden.

"Talent is rare and expensive, Ted," said Lois. She sighed. "Norma is the daughter of a service-station operator. He's a fine old man but barely literate. She's his daughter. She never forgets that. She suffers from what you might call a Cinderella psychosis—she has a sense of having climbed above her origins, and she's afraid every minute she might fall back. I think she comes into this office every morning bearing some kind of fear somebody's going to hand her a broom and tell her to sweep out."

"Relate that to the Compton file. Relate it to promissory estoppel," said Duncan.

Lois smiled. "She desperately wants to please, Joe. She thinks her place here depends on it. When you challenged her idea, she took that as a rejection, and she hurried to tell you she'd work the file up in a way you'd like better."

McCadden stubbed his half-smoked cigarette in his brass bowl. "So what do we do about her, Lois? Are you suggesting she'd overcome all this if she had the status of partner?"

"No. She wouldn't. She'd still defer to Joe because he would still be more senior. She'd defer to me because I have more money than she does. She might defer to a young partner like Oakes because he has a Harvard degree. It's a fatal defect."

"We can't give her entire responsibility for anything," said Duncan. "She might defer to a client. She might defer to opposing counsel."

"I will not argue for a partnership for her," said Lois. "I will argue against asking her to leave."

"We have never," said McCadden, "kept anyone on in the firm once it had been finally decided he was not to have a partnership."

Lois nodded. "I would like to find an alternative solution."

"You want us to help her find something else?" Duncan asked.

"Yes. I feel an obligation."

McCadden reached for his cigarette pack. He frowned over it for

a moment, then tossed it back down on his desk. "It's not *our* obligation," he said.

"Whether it is or not," said Lois.

A smile developed on the face of Joseph Duncan. "Lois," he said,
"why can't one of the Farnham companies put her on its staff as house
counsel?"

Lois shook her head firmly. "I will not make Norma a Farnham
family servant."

"How about the government?" asked Duncan. "Could we have her
appointed an assistant United States attorney?"

"What are her political credentials?" McCadden asked.

"She's a registered Democrat," said Lois.

"Well . . ."

Duncan grinned. "Why not a judgeship?" he asked.

McCadden laughed. "Why not?"

"Yes, why not?" Lois demanded sharply. "She's as capable as most
judges. Besides, if you two gentlemen will use your heads about this,
you'll see it's a perfect solution. It's good for everybody, including the
firm. 'Childreth, McLennon and Brady is pleased to announce that Mr.
So-and-so, Mr. So-and-so, and Mr. So-and-so have been made partners
in the firm, and that Mrs. Norma Tyler Spencer, formerly an associate
with the firm, has been appointed judge of the District Court of Harris County.' Perfect!"

"Can we get her appointed?" Duncan asked, frowning deeply.

"If this firm and my family cannot between us make one district-
court judge, we had better take a hard, painful look at our standing in
this community," said Lois.

Judge Tom McDade of the First District Court of Civil Appeals
was old and ill and hospitalized. He was urged to take his retirement.
Judge Martin Weller of the Criminal District Court of Harris County
was appointed to take his place. Mrs. Norma Tyler Spencer was appointed to fill the vacancy in the Criminal District Court. The Democratic Executive Committee of Harris County endorsed her. The Harris
County Bar Association endorsed her. The *Post* editorially welcomed
her appointment, saying it was about time an intelligent young
woman gained a place on the local judicial bench. Good things were
expected of her, it said.

On the day she was sworn in, the firm held a luncheon for her at the
Hyatt. Her husband was there, and her two children. Her father had
come to the swearing-in, tearful with pride, but awed and timid; he

had declined to come to the luncheon, saying he had to keep his station open. Her husband, Hal, bustled around the luncheon, beaming, shaking hands, thanking everyone for coming and for their congratulations. Norma Jean wore a pink suit and a white corsage Hal had bought for her. After the luncheon, she made a little speech, saying how grateful she was for her appointment, promising to be a good judge.

She watched for an opportunity to speak to Lois alone. She had tried twice during the morning to take Lois aside to say something private, and each time she had been interrupted. Now, at the window, while the last of the luncheon guests were shaking hands with Hal at the door and taking their leave, Norma Jean stopped Lois.

"I want you to know I'm grateful," she said quietly to Lois. "I know how this happened. I understand what you've done for me. I'll never stop being thankful, and I'll never be able to repay you."

"It's something you deserve, Bunny," Lois said. "A lot of people wanted you to have it."

"Maybe. But I know you're the one who arranged it, and I'll never get over being thankful to you. It's the greatest thing anybody ever did for anybody."

Norma Jean's eyes filled with tears, and she blinked them out. Lois put her hand on her arm. Norma Jean smiled and wept.

XXIII

1974

Teejay stared at her bare feet. She sat on a straight, uncomfortable kitchen chair, wearing a pair of soft, faded, ragged blue-denim shorts and a white T-shirt, and she yawned and stared at her bare feet. She had to keep an eye on the red light on the oven. As soon as it went off, the oven would be hot enough for the TV dinner that lay ready on the counter. She was tired. It was nine o'clock and she had only been home ten minutes. She had drunk a couple of Scotches too many downtown, and though she felt tamely euphoric, she also felt a little heavy. She needed to eat something, and the Mexican TV dinner would be ready fast, with no trouble. Jim Rush would call, probably, before the TV dinner was ready.

She glanced at the *Chronicle* she had tossed on the table after a hurried scan of the headlines. Nixon had tax trouble now. Christ! He was promising to pay four-hundred-and-some thousand dollars in back taxes, plus interest and penalties. There was no end to him, no end to his death wish, no end to the unrelieved ugliness of the man and his presidency.

They had talked about him over the drinks at happy hour. About 5:30 she had checked the bar at the Pound Sterling. Jim was there and she had joined him and two other young lawyers, whose names she had missed, at a table. She had stayed an hour more than usual, absorbed in entertaining conversation, and she had drunk two or three more Scotches than usual. She had left her car downtown and come home in a cab.

Jim Rush was her own age—thirty-two—and was an associate of Vinson, Elkins, Connally & Smith, largest law firm in Houston. He was a Rhode Islander transplanted to Houston and was what they called H-squared—Harvard undergraduate, Harvard Law. He wore round, horn-rimmed glasses and dark gray three-piece suits. He played a role of intensely sober young lawyer, but showed her a sharp wit he was willing to use to prick his own balloon as readily as anyone else's. She liked him. They had become friends very quickly, over early-evening drinks at the Pound Sterling.

Ten days ago, when they were left alone at their table after the others left, he had put his hand abruptly on hers and said, "Teejay, I'm sorry if what I'm going to say here is out of line, and I certainly don't mean to offend you, but I just can't sit here with you and not tell you I would—I would very much like to go to bed with you."

She had looked for a moment into his steady, intent blue eyes, judging him critically, with a skepticism long hardened against statements like this. She had looked for condescension. She had heard too many condescending propositions (maybe they were by definition condescending). She did not find it in him. He was honest. "Jim," she had said quietly. "Raise the subject again sometime when you haven't had anything to drink—after you've had a day or two to think it over and be sure it's really what you want to do—and I just might agree to it."

Three days later he had called her at her office late in the day and said he had thought about it and was dead sober and wanted to see her. She had told him she would go home; he could come to her apartment.

They had sat together in the living room for half an hour before they went into the bedroom. She enjoyed that first half-hour more than the second. She had poured Scotch for them and put out a bag of potato chips. They sat together on the couch. She let him undress her. He was genuinely awed by her; he could not have feigned the loving admiration in his staring eyes. She had enjoyed being naked while he only cast off his gray jacket and loosened his tie and sat in his vest and white shirt, stiffly erect, stiffly self-conscious. He had told her she was a goddess. He touched her breasts only with his fingertips at first; then he fondled and kissed them. He whispered that she was the quintessential female. He said he had never known a woman like her before.

In bed he became hurried. She knew what he had done—he had called his wife and told her he was working late. He had told her he would be home by 7:30—or whatever he had told her—and he was watching the time. He was a competent lover. He actually managed to give her satisfaction. But he did not want to talk, and when both of them had climaxed he was ready to go. After he was gone, she had walked about the apartment naked, smoking, annoyed. She had called Kevin, told him to pick up two of the biggest steaks he could find and a bottle of red wine and come by for a late dinner.

Jim called evenings. She saw him at the Pound Sterling almost every afternoon, and later he would call. She had not agreed to another date with him. He told her on the telephone that he thought about her all the time. He told her he was almost ready to say he was in love with her. She told him he had better apply some cold logic to that.

When the telephone rang, she expected it would be Jim. She checked the oven timer. She could talk for ten minutes before her TV dinner would be ready to eat.

"Miz Brookover?" It was not Jim Rush. It was a deep male voice, southwest-accented. She stopped the languid "Hello" she was about to use and said curtly, "Yes." "Miz Brookover, you don't know me, but my name's Reno Parrish. The cops've picked up my son-in-law and have got him on some kind of charge down t' police headquarters, and my daughter's awful upset, and we guess we need some lawyer help. I guess we need it pretty bad and right now."

The son-in-law's name was Gary Lethbridge. He was charged with the armed robbery of a beer dock, where he and two companions had allegedly held up the night man with a pistol and stolen $451.66 and two cases of Budweiser. Reno Parrish paid the bondsman, and the tall blond boy was released into the arms of his tearful, chubby young wife at five minutes before midnight. Teejay, whose head was by now throbbing, firmly told the family to take Gary home and keep him there until they could bring him to her office in the morning. No, she would *not* talk to him tonight.

"Hey, Teejay, you don't look so happy!" The man who spoke laughed as he stopped before the bench where she had sat down to cram papers into the vinyl folder she had carried with her from her apartment; but when he saw she actually was pale and nauseous, he knelt solicitously in front of her. "Hey you *don't* feel good. Whatsa matter, honey?"

"Hi, Hardison," she said weakly.

"Hey." He put his hand on her arm. "You sick?"

"It started off a good night, with a little happy hour, and then I got a call to come down here and get that innocent kid out of jail, and I haven't had anything to eat."

"I'm off. Twelve o'clock. C'mon and have a hamburger with me."

Tom Hardison was a Houston detective. A month ago she had cross-examined him roughly in the trial of two young women charged with burglary, and after the trial she had seen him in the hall outside the courtroom and stepped up to him to tell him she was sorry to have had to give him such a hard time. He'd said it was okay, and they had had a couple of drinks at the Lamar Hotel.

Tonight they had their hamburgers at a McDonald's. He brought them, with Cokes, out to her car.

"Teejay, this kid you got out of jail tonight is guilty," Hardison said unemotionally, chewing vigorously. "Thought you'd like to know. They's no question about this one."

"What happened, can you tell me?"

Hardison shrugged. "Nothin' much. The Lethbridge boy was drivin'. They were drunked-up on beer, he and his two buddies. They got to cruisin' around, see what they could find. I 'spect what they'd liked to find was some—you know."

"Pussy," said Teejay.

Hardison nodded. "Pussy. They'd run out of beer and out of money to get any more, so they drove up to this beer dock, and they waited till they were the only car in there, and then they held the old man up. The gun belonged to the Morley boy. He's only seventeen."

"Where'd he get the gun?" Teejay asked.

"He'd been carryin' it in his jeans all evening. We don't know where he got it."

"What about the B-and-E Lethbridge was arrested on last year?"

"Same thing. Ran out of beer and money, so he broke a back window, climbed in, tossed a bunch of six-packs out to his buddies, and climbed back out. One of the buddies gave some of the beer to a fourteen-year-old girl before the night was over, and when she got home drunk her old lady called in, and we had to find out where the beer came from. Judge suspended a thirty-day sentence on Lethbridge. He copped a plea."

In the office the next morning Teejay met with Gary Lethbridge and his mother, Amelia Carmen. The boy sat with one leg propped over the arm of his chair and slouched deep. He smoked and watched Teejay with narrow, hostile eyes. His mother spoke for him.

It was a long recitation. Gary, his mother said, had gone to school regularly and minded his business until he became involved with the Parrish girl. The Parrish girl insisted Gary was the father of her child, though she, Mrs. Carmen, still doubted it. ("Baby never did look like Gary, never did.") Being a father, being married, when he was only seventeen had been hard for Gary.

Teejay studied her client coldly while his mother talked. She did not like his boots, did not like the tarnished brass buckles on the straps over the insteps. She saw arrogance in those boots—arrogance and the empty threat of a bully.

His mother went on. The old man and the little bitch, she said, would call the police when Gary did not come home on time—when all he was doing was having a little fun with his friends—and that got the police down on him, so every time anything happened they suspected Gary.

"What about the robbery of the beer dock?" Teejay asked.

"Gary was only drivin' the car," said Mrs. Carmen with a lofty air of justification. "That's all he was doin', was drivin' the car, and Tommy Morley pulled the gun and pointed it at the old man."

"Then what happened, Gary?" Teejay asked.

Gary shrugged. "Jis drove off," he said.

"You drink any of the beer?"

He nodded.

"Take any of the money?"

He nodded. "Some of it."

Teejay tipped back her big leather chair. "You're guilty of armed robbery," she said. "Maybe I can do something for you, but chances are you're going to the state penitentiary, and chances are you're going to do three or four or five years."

The boy's jaw dropped. He turned pale. His mother shook her head violently. "All Gary done was drive the car!" she shrilled.

Teejay shrugged. "You're lucky the Morley boy wasn't nervous with the pistol. If he'd shot that old man, and he died, the charge would be felony murder and Gary could go to the chair—and 'all Gary done was drive the car,' " she said with cold sarcasm.

"That ain't the law!"

"If you know more about the law than I do, then you don't need me, do you?"

"I need somebody!" The boy was frightened. "I—Jesus Christ!"

"Put your feet on the floor and sit up straight in that chair," said Teejay. "We'll start with that. Mrs. Carmen, you wait outside. I want to talk with Gary alone."

Every Sunday Billy Tyler went to church. On alternate Sundays he stopped by his service station and selected six bottles of cold soda pop, in assorted flavors, from the cooler; and he took the six bottles of pop to Norma Jean's house, to put in her refrigerator until after lunch as his family treat. He came in the blue suit he wore to church— he never stopped at Norma Jean's house without his suit, a white shirt, and a necktie—and besides the soda pop he brought the Bible tract from Sunday school for Norma Jean's kids.

He was broad-shouldered, muscular, white-haired. His hands were gnarled and scarred. His maroon satin necktie—with white and yellow flowers—had been knotted just once; after that, he loosened the knot and slipped it on and off over his head. He wore white socks. He smiled a broad, patriarchal smile on Norma Jean and her husband and children, and he was proud.

"Dad," she said to him, "you have to face it. I do have to run for a full term. I might not be elected. I will have opposition."

His smile only broadened. It was not conceivable to him that she would lose the election.

"We have to think about the way things are," she said. They were sitting on the patio behind the house. The children were romping on the grass, and their grandfather's attention was focused more on them than on what his daughter was saying. "My judgeship was handed to me, dad. It was a gift. It was given to me by—certain people."

"Because you deserved it," he said innocently.

"Because they wanted me to have it," she said.

He shifted his attention to her. "Nobody expected you to do nothing you shouldn't for it, did they?" he asked soberly.

She shook her head. "No. Nothing like that."

"Well, then . . ."

"They watch me," she said. "I'm being watched."

"Why?"

"To see if I'm a good judge," she said.

He grinned. "Ahh, then . . ."

Norma Jean glanced at her husband. "Not everybody agrees as to what's a good judge," she said.

The old man was distracted for a moment by one of the children, who turned a somersault and expected him to notice and laugh. He did, and when he turned again to Norma Jean he shook his head and asked, "Well, who decides what's a good judge? What do they expect? The papers say you're a good judge. I've seen it said on television that you're a good judge."

"I've got a reputation for being tough on crime," she said grimly.

"That's right," her father said, nodding. "It's the only way to ever stop it—get tough on it."

"I've been criticized for it, too," she said.

Her father frowned. "I guess that goes with the job, don't it? What do they expect, anyway?"

"That's the problem," she said unhappily. "I don't know what they expect."

"I don't understand, I guess."

Hal Spencer tried to explain. "Norma Jean's worried about a case that's in her court, dad," he said. "She doesn't know what to do about it."

"Is it so important?"

"They're all important," said Norma Jean. "This one—it could be more important than most."

"Why?"

"Because of the young man's lawyer, mostly," she said. "He's got a lady lawyer, a tough redhead by the name of Brookover, and she's trying to make it out that this young man shouldn't be sent away. He robbed a beer dock, and the jury found him guilty; but she's got a lot of people believing he shouldn't be sentenced. She's going to argue tomorrow that I ought to put him on probation. She's got the whole town watching."

"Well, what are you gonna do, Norma Jean?"

She shook her head. "I don't know." She smoothed her skirt and reached for her bottle and the last sip of orange pop. "I don't know. I've built a reputation for being tough on crime. It's what I'm known for as a judge, if I'm known for anything. I haven't had time to build a reputation for anything more. This Brookover woman has stirred up so much fuss over this case that I may wind up in the public mind as the judge who sentenced, or didn't sentence, Gary Lethbridge."

"The woman's a shyster, dad," said Hal Spencer resentfully. "She doesn't care anything about the ethics of a lawyer. She's tried this case before the newspaper and television reporters more than before Norma Jean."

"Why? Why would she do that?"

"I suppose she thinks," Spencer went on, "that if the case just came up quietly in the ordinary course of things, Norma Jean would just sentence him to the penitentiary and be done with it. She thinks the publicity will put pressure on Norma Jean to give him probation."

"Which is wrong," said Norma Jean. "I have some sympathy for the kid. The publicity makes it harder, not easier, for me to give him probation."

Her father frowned thoughtfully. "Well . . . is there a right and a wrong about it, Norma Jean?" he asked.

"No, dad. I wish it were that simple."

Her father's frown hardened. "Must be, seems to me. Either this boy is bad enough to be sent away, or he isn't. Ain't that what you've got to decide?"

Teejay saw Judge Spencer glance at the clock, and she raised her voice to be sure of the judge's attention. "I am well aware, Your Honor, that only a year ago the defendant Gary Lethbridge was arrested on a charge of breaking and entering, and that he was allowed to plead to a lesser charge; that he was given, in effect, leniency on that occasion. I am fully aware that he has been arrested a number of times on charges of being drunk and disorderly.

"I am well aware of all that, and I am going to reveal to this Court now something more about Gary Lethbridge, something that the prosecution was not permitted to reveal. With the consent of my client, I advise Your Honor that Gary Lethbridge, when he was fifteen years old, was adjudicated an incorrigible juvenile and was sent to the state training school. I want the Court to know that. Gary wants the Court to know that. We want to place all there is to know about Gary Lethbridge before this Court for consideration—and then we can talk to the Court about his future, about what this Court is going to do with Gary Lethbridge."

She stood at the defense table, above Lethbridge, who sat stiff and frightened and stared at her. All the seats in the courtroom were filled. The courthouse reporters sat in their usual places, and other reporters, from the radio and television stations, filled the front row of the ordinary seats. Two judges sat in the jury box; they'd come in from their chambers to hear T. J. Brookover argue the Lethbridge case. Judge Norma Spencer, in her black robe, held her face rigidly without expression.

"I place Gary Lethbridge's juvenile record before this Court, Your Honor, because it reveals something this Court should know about Gary Lethbridge. The facts are on the record of the juvenile court. More facts are on the records of the Houston public schools.

"Gary was adjudged incorrigible late in 1970, Your Honor. Through the 1968–1969 school year he had a good record. He was not an 'A' student by any means, but he kept a 'C' average. He had a good record of attendance. He played football and basketball. He was no disciplinary problem. Then in 1970 he began to be absent from school. Indeed, he simply refused to go to school. He was consistently a truant. When school opened for the fall term in 1970, he did not appear at all. It was for his truancy—and for noncooperation with the school officers trying to stop his truancy—that Gary Lethbridge was ultimately adjudicated incorrigible and sent to the state training school."

Teejay paused and stepped around the table to stand in front of it, her bottom touching the table lightly. She wore a cream-white skirt and jacket and a lime-green blouse. Her red hair lay smoothly over her shoulders. "Why, Your Honor?" she asked dramatically. "Why do you suppose Gary Lethbridge suddenly refused to come to school? The answer, I submit, is found in yet other public records. It is in police records, in the files of the police prosecutor, and in the files of the criminal courts. It is found in the record of one James Lethbridge— Gary's father. *Nine times,* Your Honor, over a period of ten months in 1969 and 1970, James Lethbridge was arrested. Assault: fine and costs. Assault: no prosecution. Assault: ten days suspended. Assault: thirty days served. Assault: fine and ten days. And so on. Nine arrests for assault, Your Honor—and who knows how many more assaults were committed without arrests?

"Assault. Assault. And always the same victims. There were just two victims, Your Honor. Mrs. James Lethbridge—now Mrs. Immaculato Carmen—Gary's mother. And Gary. It is a matter of public record, Your Honor, that in August of 1970 Gary Lethbridge was admitted to a hospital through the emergency room—his teeth broken in a vicious assault by his father. Criminal nonsupport charges were filed against James Lethbridge about the same time, I might add."

Teejay stopped. She reached behind her, picked up a yellow legal pad, and took a long moment to frown over her notes.

"One more thing, Your Honor," she said. "Mrs. James Lethbridge— Mrs. Immaculato Carmen—has herself been arrested four times since 1970 on charges of public intoxication."

Teejay put the note pad down on the table. She spoke with a lowered voice. "After Gary Lethbridge had been at the state training school four months, he was offered a leave, to go home, to try living at home again, maybe never to come back to the state school. He refused to go home. His grades in his classroom work at the state training school were better than the best grades he had ever made before."

She talked about what happened to the young man after he came home. His mother had divorced Lethbridge while Gary was away. He lived with her in a small apartment. Lethbridge paid support irregularly. Gary worked in a gas station and went to school. His mother drank heavily, and Immaculato Carmen began to sleep in the apartment, often drunk too. Then his mother married Carmen, and Carmen moved in.

Patty Parrish was pretty and quiet. Gary married her in 1972, and their daughter was born four months later. They rented a stranded house trailer sitting on a lot behind a tavern and tried to make a home there. Gary worked hard, but he had only a tenth-grade education. He never owned a car. His clothes were shabby. Their meals were drab. Patty loved Gary and never thought of leaving him, but she whined. Their baby was sick often, maybe from the way they lived and what they fed it, and the doctor bills kept Gary constantly broke. Patty's father gave her money. That shamed Gary. Patty whined that she had to have what her father gave her.

"I am talking to you, Your Honor, about a young man whose character was formed in a home that fell violently apart around him. I am talking about a young man who told the authorities at the state training school that he would rather stay there than go home. I am talking about a young man whose drunken father beat his mother as Gary watched, helpless to stop it—and when Gary did try to stop it, he was beaten, too. I am talking about a young man who might have turned to his mother for love and emotional support—but his mother was, and is, a drunk. I submit to you, Your Honor, that Gary Lethbridge deserves much credit for being the young man he is.

"And what kind of young man is that? He has supported his wife and child, Your Honor, to the best of his ability. He has kept his jobs. He has found better jobs. He works hard. Each of his employers interviewed by the Probation Department reported that Gary came to work every day. He drank, but he did not miss work. He paid his rent. He paid his bills. He met his responsibilities.

"The files of law-enforcement agencies and social agencies are filled —stuffed—with the records of men who walked away from their responsibilities when life got drab and tough. Nonsupport. Abandonment. Abuse. But Gary Lethbridge, for two years, has struggled to make a living for himself and his family. . . ."

Teejay had walked to the corner of the empty jury box and stood looking at Gary Lethbridge as she spoke. She had told him to fold his hands on the table before him and keep them there. She had told him to stare at his hands when she talked about his life. He was wearing an ill-fitting blue and white checkered sport jacket and dark blue slacks. He wore brown, laced-up shoes. He did not know how to tie a necktie, so his shirt was open, and the collar wings lay on the lapels of his jacket.

"So why is Gary here today? What does Gary do? Gary drinks,

Your Honor. When life bears down so hard he thinks he can't stand it, he drinks beer. Too much beer. He's a Saturday-night drunk, Your Honor. He goes out Saturday night, Your Honor, and he meets the boys he thinks are his friends, and they drink and cruise, and sometimes they stay out all night. In the joints where they go for their beer, fistfights are nothing unusual. Gary has been in some. He gets drunk and his good judgment abandons him, and Gary does stupid things.

"Gary climbed in the back window of a store last year and stole some six-packs of beer. That's a crime, Your Honor, and I'm not suggesting it's anything but. Gary drove Tommy Morley's car into a beer dock—drove it because Tommy Morley was too drunk to drive—and Tommy Morley used a pistol and held up the old man working there. And that's a crime. And Gary was part of it. There's no question about that. But—"

"You argued to the jury, Miss Brookover, that your client was not guilty," said Judge Spencer in a cool, measured voice.

"Another jury might have found him not guilty, Your Honor—on the ground he was too drunk to form an intent to commit a robbery, that he didn't know his friend was going to commit a robbery, and so on. This jury found him guilty, and it is on the assumption of guilt that I now proceed."

Judge Spencer nodded. "Proceed."

Teejay walked across the front of the courtroom and placed herself against the prosecutor's table, her hip touching it. "This court can send Gary Lethbridge to the penitentiary," she said. "Up at Huntsville they'll shave his head, put a pair of white coveralls on him, and set him to work at some menial job. They'll keep him there for three years, or four, or five—whatever—and then someday he'll come home. Can anyone say he'll come home any better? Will he come home any less likely to drink too much beer again some night and stumble through some senseless crime? Indeed, will he come home still the young man who goes to work every day to earn money to support his family? Or will he have learned different habits?

"What good will it do, Your Honor? What possible good will it do to send this young man to prison? What good for society? Will his imprisonment deter others like him from doing what he did? Not by the remotest stretch of the imagination. Informed people don't even argue deterrence anymore—not, at least, in cases of petty crime like this. So what good will it do? What good? What possible good?"

She returned to her own table and stood beside Gary Lethbridge. "This crime has a victim, Your Honor. Tommy Morley pointed his pistol at Robert James and took his money and some beer—and frightened him very badly. He is a victim, and he has our sympathy. But if this court sends Gary Lethbridge to prison, then this crime has four victims. It has four. Besides Robert James, it has Gary Lethbridge, Patty Lethbridge, and Kathy Lethbridge, their little girl. I might say that in a real sense it already has four. Gary Lethbridge is as frightened as Robert James ever was—and he has been frightened for six months. Patty Lethbridge is frightened and worried. Little Kathy doesn't know what's going on, but she knows her daddy and mommy are scared of something, and so she's scared, too.

"Whatever the system of criminal justice is to accomplish, it has accomplished already in this case. Gary Lethbridge will never commit another crime. If there is deterrence, he has been deterred now. What is more, he has been punished. He has been punished severely. Free under the supervision of the Department of Probation, he will continue to work and support his family. The interests of society will be furthered. Putting this young man in prison serves no legitimate interest, Your Honor—not society's, not his own, no one's. I respectfully urge the Court to admit the defendant to probation."

Teejay sat down beside Gary Lethbridge. She looked behind him. His wife was weeping softly. Reno Parrish held her hand. Gary was pale, rigid, trembling.

"The defendant will rise and face the Court."

Teejay rose to stand beside her client.

Judge Spencer wiped her upper lip with her right index finger. "It is the sentence of this court"—her shrill voice betrayed the strain of emotion—"that the defendant be committed to the custody of the Texas State Department of Corrections, to be imprisoned for a term of . . ."

Teejay did not hear the judge's last words. Patty Lethbridge shrieked, and Gary began to sob.

XXIV

Over the years, many thick layers of paint had been slapped over the steel walls and bars of the jail. Some places it was chipped away, down to bare brown steel, and you could see the colors of the layers—under the gray, beige; and under the beige, off-white; and under the off-white, institutional green. Graffiti were scratched so deep into the layered paint that old names and words, scratched into earlier layers, remained entirely visible under the coat of gray. Beside Teejay's face where she lay on the upper bunk, crudely lettered was the name LINDA. Above that, JESUS. On the wall opposite, FUCK. Below that, BRENDA—1954. It was depressing to think that a woman had been imprisoned in this same cell almost twenty-five years ago. She did not wonder who BRENDA was, or LINDA, or BARB or TERRY. All she wondered was how long some of them had been here.

For herself, shortly she would have completed six months in jail. It was longer than most women stayed. She had had two more cellmates: a young Mexican girl held for immigration authorities, who spoke no English and had been locked in with her for three days; and a fat teen-aged West Virginia girl, who had spent most of eleven days lying on the lower bunk crying. Teejay had resented the teen-ager's awed

judgment that she, Teejay, was a veteran prisoner, an old jailbird
who knew how to cope with the place.

This was a Friday evening. She knew it was Friday because Lois
had come this morning. Lois came every Tuesday and Friday, whether
or not there was anything in particular to talk about. She brought
cartons of cigarettes, and fruit and candy, and books. Last week she
had brought a letter. It was a letter from her mother, sent by Earl
Lansing. It said nothing much, except that Tommy Jo would always
be welcome to come home, once her trouble was over. Teejay had
written a letter in return, telling her mother not to worry, that she
was all right. (What else could you say?) She had to write the letter
on the jail letter paper and write her prisoner number after her name.
It was the only letter she had written from the jail, and she was determined to write no more.

She had received another letter—a note, actually. It was a tiny slip
of paper, rolled. A black woman whose name she did not know had
pressed it into her hand just before they had to go into their cells
for lockup—with the whisper, "Don't ask me where this comes from
or how I got it. Don't look at it now." Teejay, lying on her back in
her panties, smoked a cigarette and slowly, carefully burned the little
slip of paper with the fire at the tip of the cigarette. In penciled letters
so small and faint as to be barely legible, the message on the paper
had been—

IT WILL BE OK TRUST ME K

She could not trust him, and it frightened her. If his judgment was
so bad as to risk sending a note from one part of the jail to another,
using God-knew-who as his messenger, she could not trust him at all.
She shuddered to think what the prosecution could do with a note like
that, intercepted as it was being smuggled through the jail. Worse,
if he had done this, what other romantic notion would move him to
take what other foolish risk?

It was still hot in the jail the first week in October and she sweated
as she lay there and burned Kevin's note. She picked up the book she
was reading—*The Final Days* by Woodward and Bernstein. She could
not read. She was compelled to wonder whom Kevin had taken into
his confidence. What had he told whomever carried the note? Whom
had he trusted? Goddamn Kevin!

She remembered the day in 1975 when she met him at the airport
in Acapulco. She had not recognized him at first. He had stood there

grinning at her, half hidden behind oversize sunglasses and carelessly disguised in shaggy straw hat, open-necked Mexican white shirt, ragged gray shorts, sandals, a deep suntan. He had a jeep outside, an outlandish vehicle painted in pink and white stripes. He heaved her bag into the back and helped her into her seat. "I was afraid you'd back out," he said. "I've been dreading the telegram or the call— 'Kevin, I really haven't got the time.' Lady, you look like death. I think I got you out of Houston in the nick of time."

She had felt like death. There was nothing wrong with her at all, except that was the year she overworked. She knew how she looked. She looked pale. She looked drawn. Her eyes were hollow. It was how she looked in the mirror, more than anything Kevin had said, that had made her surrender at last and agree to meet him in Acapulco. He had come down ten days earlier. She had promised to join him. But he was right to have suspected she would change her mind and not come.

She had bought the building on South Louisiana Street, had remodeled it and expanded her offices to fill all of it, and the mortgage payments on it were a demanding new obligation. She had had calls this week from two prospective new clients, each worth a retainer of $2000 or more, and she had been reluctant to tell either of them she was about to leave for a vacation and would have to postpone her first conference with him for two weeks. Each had accepted the delay without demurrer, but on the plane flying to Acapulco she had brooded over the possibility of losing either as a client, and she had tentatively plotted calls she might make to them from Mexico.

Maturing had been kind to Kevin. He looked good. He had a capacity she envied sometimes, and other times condemned, for looking foolish, for *being* foolish, putting everything out of mind. In his grotesque Mexican resort clothes, he had that endearing ingenuousness he had shown when she first saw him hustling pool in El Paso. She doubted he could afford this trip. She wondered if he would not haul back a few kilos of marijuana—though he denied sharply that he ever dealt in anything of the kind. She wondered what con had been so successful as to allow him to fly to Mexico and rent a suite in an Acapulco hotel. She wondered if he would not slip out of town later, leaving the hotel stuck for the bill. Driving this silly-looking pink and white jeep, smiling and humming, he was the picture of innocent American—and he was capable of taking a profit off anyone who came near him.

Teejay was not a sunbather. Her light complexion burned before it tanned, and then tanned little. She wore the bathing suit Kevin had bought her at the hotel—an abbreviated light blue bikini (the style they called "the string" that year)—and she enjoyed the appreciative glances she inspired (she enjoyed the hostile stares just as much); but she could not spend many hours in the sun and spent more hours lying on a shaded lounge chair near the pool, sipping gin and tonic. Kevin forced her to relax. He would not let her talk about Houston; he interrupted her whenever she tried, with some inane comment about the ugly bodies of some of the Americans lying around the pool, or about the funny syntax of some Mexican's English; and when he observed her withdrawn into her thoughts, he interrupted those, too, with the suggestion they go for a walk on the beach or a drive in the jeep.

They shared a suite. But it had two bedrooms, and they did not sleep together. She offered to sleep with him, but he did not accept the offer.

"I'm not pressing it," she said to him over dinner. "But I've done it with men who meant less to me."

"I've never done it with a woman who meant much to me," said Kevin.

"That's an odd statement," said Teejay. "Do you think it's inconsistent with—"

"Ah don' know," he said. "I grew up to believe that a man doesn't do that with a woman he's not married to, unless it's a woman he doesn't much care about."

"I was brought up to believe that, too," she said.

Kevin shrugged. "Well, you've had a lot of education, so you can throw off anything that was taught you as a kid that you don't think is right anymore. I haven't got much education. I have to stick with the notions I was given."

"You're a wonderful friend, Kevin."

"If I hadn't known that marrying me would have spoiled your whole life, I'd never have let you get away from me."

Teejay picked up *The Final Days* again and this time became absorbed in it. Woodward and Bernstein described the July 11, 1974, cruise on the Potomac aboard the *Sequoia*—the Nixons, Eisenhowers, Coxes, and friends named Harrington. Teejay had had to force herself into some of the books she had read in jail, but this one held her attention, filled her mind with imaginings, and relieved the oppression of confinement. Lois brought the books, mostly paperbacks, and in the six months Teejay had read more than a hundred. She favored books like *The Final Days*, but she would read anything.

The lights went out. The jail was never dark, and she could read on—often she did—but tonight she closed the book and lay on her back and thought about those summer days in 1974 when the Nixon presidency finally collapsed. She had been elated. She had developed an absolute hatred for Richard Nixon. She had hated Ford, too, for putting a period on the cover-up with his unconscionable pardon.

She thought about the day when Kennedy was murdered. She remembered how she went home to her room that night and wept. Looking back later, she knew she had not simply succumbed to the emotion of the moment. Something had gone out of the whole world that day. The murder of Kennedy represented the end of optimism for America. That was how she saw it. A people with any optimism, with any confidence for its future, could never have elected a man like Richard Nixon to be a national leader. The politics of pessimism. The country had been in its grip ever since. That was her analysis.

She rolled off the bunk and dropped to the floor. She lit a cigarette and took her habitual late-night stand at the bars of her cell. Half consciously she gripped the bars hard in both hands and gave them an angry jerk. The heavy cell door moved slightly in its track and thumped loudly. Teejay put her forehead against the steel and sighed.

Frank Agnelli had sent word that he could not continue to meet the mortgage payments on the building and the other expenses out of the fees he could collect from her clients and his, so he proposed to rent half the office space to a partnership between two black lawyers. She had to consent. What else could she do? Frank was a good young man. He had managed to hold some of her clients for a while; but now the newspapers had said she would almost certainly be disbarred, even if she were acquitted of murder, and he could hold only the ones who wanted him for their lawyer. He was a good lawyer, but he lacked her flair, and certainly he lacked her reputation for establishment-baiting aggressiveness.

She sent back word with Lois that he should do what he thought best. Her office furniture would go in storage in the cellar of the building. They would take down the pictures and certificates from her walls. Someone else would occupy her office. Her apartment had been disassembled, and now her office. This cell was where she lived. Existed. When she got out, she would have no place to go. She had cried about that last night. She shrugged away the thought tonight. Crying was painful. It drained your strength. She gripped the bars and drew a deep breath and fought it back.

"What you gonna buy next, Tommy Jo? A big house in Bayou Oaks?"

In Acapulco, Kevin had listened to her talk about the debts she had acquired and the money she had to make to meet the payments, and he was scornful. He was scornful of her silver-gray Mercedes, even though she owed nothing on it but had bought it out of the fee she earned for winning a $113,000 judgment against the state of Texas for taxes unlawfully collected from a group of Mexican-American businessmen who had developed a shopping center in Brazoria County. It was his own philosophy, Kevin said, that the less you owned, the faster you could move.

"Well, I'm not going anywhere, Kevin. In my line of business, you don't have to be ready to pack your tent and run any minute."

Kevin laughed. They were lying on lounge chairs beside the pool, he in the sun, she just out of it in the shade of some great-leaved tropical shrub. Her skin glowed pink from the sun she had taken before she moved out of it. He was wet. She was dry. Teejay had never learned to swim. She wore her light blue string bikini and sunglasses, and her red hair hung loose around her shoulders. They had been nibbling on some mysterious Mexican hors d'oeuvres the waiter had brought with their drinks.

"You're a big lawyer, Tommy Jo, for a young woman just six years out of law school. It hasn't been so long since you were tendin' bar with your tits hangin' out. What you have in mind for yourself?"

She glanced at him, then relaxed again in her chair and spoke toward the sky. "Someday," she said quietly, "I'm going to retire, full of honors as they say—full of money, anyway—and go someplace a long way from Houston, a longer way from west Texas, and live a different kind of life."

"I don't believe it. You've absolutely thrown yourself into what you do."

"When I worked topless," she said, "people stared at me. I was a phenomenon. And I'm still a phenomenon. Lawyers stare at me, and I know what they say—'How could a redheaded girl with big boobs get to be a lawyer and compete with us? My God, she doesn't chew cigars! She's cute, but she'll get pregnant and have to pull out of the practice of law.' Kevin, I—"

"You're exaggeratin', honey."

"I bought and remodeled the building because I want an office that looks like an office. Someday I'm going to have a whole floor at 1100 Milam or somewhere. Until then . . . I bought the Mercedes to intimidate some smart-aleck little punks in a couple of big firms, to show them my practice can buy me something their association with big firms won't buy them for another ten years."

"You'd better think about this, Tommy Jo. Is this how you want to live?"

"No," she said irritably. "But I have to compete some way. I'll compete whatever way I have to, till I've made enough money to quit."

In the morning she asked for special permission to make a telephone call to her lawyer. She called Lois at home and told her she had to come to the jail; what she had to tell her could not be said on the phone. Lois came Saturday afternoon. No one was on duty to take Teejay down to the visiting area, and since Lois insisted on her right as Teejay's attorney to see her client whenever she needed to, they let Lois come up and talk to Teejay through the bars of "B" Cage.

"You've got to talk to Ron Steen," Teejay told Lois. She stood pressed to the bars, speaking only in a hoarse whisper. "Kevin can ruin everything."

"What'd the note say?" Lois asked.

"Nothing. 'It will be okay, trust me.' That's all. But he had to pass it through somebody's hands to get it to me, and whoever had it could have turned it over."

"In fact, we don't know it wasn't shown and copied before it was passed on," Lois suggested.

Teejay nodded. "Tell Ron to come and see Kevin today."

Lois shook her head unhappily. "I'm not sure he listens much to Ron. Ron's only his lawyer."

"Have Ron tell him I sent the word."

"All right. I'll call Ron as soon as I leave here."

Teejay sighed. She put her cigarette to her lips and drew. "Kevin's dangerous," she said.

"I've told you that all along."

"Yeah. . . ." She had noticed Lois glancing guardedly around the cellblock. Half a smile came to her face. "Say, you've never been up here before, have you?"

"No," Lois said. She glanced uncomfortably at the knot of uniformed women standing halfway up the block, staring at her. She looked away, self-conscious, and with a finger she traced an invisible line down a bar and across one of the horizontal braces to the next bar. "It's pretty damned gruesome," she said to Teejay.

"My world and welcome to it," said Teejay.

Lois stood, feet apart, firm, and looked around the cellblock. The prisoners stared with unguarded animosity at the tall, coiffed, and polished woman standing outside the jail bars. The contrast between her and them—and between her and Teejay, imprisoned behind the heavy steel bars—was painful to the ones inside, Teejay included.

"I had another call about you," Lois said to Teejay. "I would have left it for Tuesday, but since I'm here . . . Do you know a man named Calvin Fitzgerald?"

Teejay, standing with a hip nudged into the bars and one hand loosely draped around a bar, nodded. "He owned the place where I worked topless."

Lois smiled. "He called and asked me to tell you that you have a job whenever you want it. With maybe a share of the business."

Teejay frowned and shook her head. "Cal . . ." she whispered. "Cal, for God's sake . . . Hey, call him Lois. Tell him I thank him." She smiled nervously. "Hey, can you imagine? Goin' back, working topless for Cal? I'm thirty-six years old! Jesus! Lois, you gotta get me out of this goddamn place!"

XXV

1976

"It's nice to see you here."

"Thank you, judge."

Judge Norma Spencer brushed past Teejay with that greeting and hurried on toward the far end of the room. Teejay was reminded of the pious "nice to see you here" of church ushers back home—an unsubtle, supercilious comment on one's past absences. The judge, in a blue and white checked polyester pantsuit, took a carefully selected seat, one chair from the end of the left-hand table—one chair removed from the table where the chairwoman of the committee and the secretary and treasurer were shuffling their papers.

The chairwoman tapped an empty water glass with a pencil. "Ladies. Ladies. The meeting of the Women's Committee of the Harris County Bar Association will come to order. The secretary will read the minutes of the last meeting."

The secretary opened a notebook on the green cloth of the table. Teejay, sitting toward the rear of the room, poured herself a glass of water. It might be true, she speculated as she looked around the room, that the meeting was packed and that the right-to-life crowd was going to try to pass an antiabortion resolution. Doris Schmidt had said that was what was happening, and she had called Teejay and asked her to make a point of attending this meeting. It might be true, since twenty-five women at least sat around the tables, and the most Teejay had ever seen before at one of these meetings was six or eight. The right-to-lifers had offered their resolution to the Executive Committee of the association a month ago, and the Executive Committee had sidestepped it by passing it along to the Women's Committee. The resolution demanded the state legislature call for a constitutional convention to amend the Constitution of the United States to forbid abortions. The right-to-lifers were a shrill crowd who had given the Executive Committee an uncomfortable hour.

It was a Friday evening, and the various committees of the association were meeting at the Hyatt Regency Hotel. Jim Rush was in another room, sitting in a meeting of the Antitrust Law Committee, of which he was an active member. He and Teejay had spent two hours at the Pound Sterling and had had dinner as well as their usual late-afternoon drinks before they walked to the Hyatt. They had agreed to meet in the bar in the lobby at 10:30, whether their committee meetings were over or not.

They would not have time after their meetings to go to her apartment. In the two years she had known him, they had gone there, and to bed, only six times. Neither of them felt strongly compelled to it. Yet they were intensely drawn to each other and sought every hour they could, to sit together somewhere and touch each other and talk. Almost always they sat in a bar. They liked places where they could sit side by side, with their backs to a wall, and hold hands under the table. He would caress her legs if he could. She liked that. She enjoyed the quiet hours of talk with him; she respected his ideas and was stimulated by his crisp, logical radicalism. His conversation was a challenge if he trusted you and thought you would not call him a radical around town. There were no verities for Jim Rush. There were few for Teejay, but he challenged even those. When they went to bed, what they did was usually uncomfortably short of gratifying. She was not sure why. Her disappointment in that did not diminish her emotional attachment to him. She wanted to be with him. She missed him when she did not see him. He said he felt the same for her.

The preliminaries—minutes of the last meeting, subcommittee reports—took half an hour. Under the heading of new business, the chairwoman recognized the woman with the right-to-life resolution. Her name was Constance Flaherty and she said she was a lawyer with Gringham & Gringham. She had a high, thin voice, and after she had thinly thanked the committee for giving her a place on its agenda, she raised her voice and began a strident tirade about "the mass murders sanctioned by the immoral old men" of the Supreme Court.

Teejay studied the faces of the women listening. Many were scornful. Patricia King smiled at her and winked. It was plain, though, that
others were anything but scornful. Some did not find the rhetoric exaggerated. They sat and listened grimly, two or three nodding.

Mary De Shettler, a specialist in domestic relations whom Teejay had
occasionally encountered in the courtroom, was the first speaker against
the resolution. Teejay was disappointed. She had seen Mary DeShettler
perform effectively in the courtroom. She did not argue effectively now.
She was as strident as Constance Flaherty, and her argument was a
catalog of the stock phrases of this debate, just as Flaherty's had been.
Teejay leaned toward the woman at her left—she was not sure who she
was—and whispered, "These people deserve each other." The woman
arched an eyebrow and looked away.

Teejay would say later, when she told Jim about the meeting, that
the resolution had not inspired a debate, it had generated a squabble.
If the nervous young women taking notes wrote down all the phrases
that were used, they noted "immoral atheists," "semiliterate Bible
bangers," "pot-smoking apologists for promiscuity," and "remorseless
brat-breeders."

"If a man can plant a fetus in my body," one woman said, "and compel me to carry it for nine months whether I want to or not, then he can
also hang a chain around my neck and force me to carry that."

"Does *anybody*, I mean *anybody*," one young woman pleaded tearfully, "care what *God* wants?"

Constance Flaherty was recognized a second time. She stood. "We
have here . . ." She paused. She had not spoken since she was the
first speaker, but in the emotional intensity of the argument, she was
breathless. "We have here in our meeting one of the judges of the
criminal district court. I think we ought to know what the judges here
in Houston think—at least what the one judge who has come tonight
thinks."

The chairwoman tapped her glass with her pencil. "I believe," she
said, "we have no right to put Judge Spencer on the spot that way."

"We have every right," said Constance Flaherty. "We have elected
judges to enforce the law for us. We expect them to act morally, ethi-
cally. A judge's position on this issue is a test—"

"It is not!" a woman shouted. "Your damned insistence that you have
a monopoly on good morals and that anyone who disagrees with your
damned irrational voodoo is immoral is the most arrogant thing I've
ever heard. If I were Judge Spencer I'd tell you to go to hell, and I
hope she does."

"*Please* . . ."

Judge Spencer stood. She looked at the woman who suggested she tell Constance Flaherty to go to hell, and she smiled. "Madam Chairwoman," she said evenly. "I'm not going to tell anyone to go to hell—although I appreciate the lady's effort to get me off the hook. Actually, I don't think I'm on a hook. Or a spot." She paused to adjust her glasses. "The question before the committee will not come before my court, really. As some of you know, I am one who believes judges should enforce law, not make it. If a case comes before me, I will apply the law as it stands. I have no other choice. So, if a woman or her doctor were before my court, charged with criminal abortion, and the evidence was that the abortion was performed in the first trimester, I would have to dismiss the charge. I would have no option. That is the law, as the Supreme Court of the United States has pronounced it."

Constance Flaherty interrupted. "Judge Spencer," she said, tapping the table firmly with her right index finger, "do you favor the right-to-life amendment? Yes or no?"

"Tell her to go to hell," said the woman in the back of the room.

Judge Spencer smiled again and shook her head. "I think I favor the amendment," she said. She stopped while half a dozen women clapped their hands. "I think the moral judgment of most people in our community is that abortion is wrong. I've heard the matter discussed a great deal at my church, among the mothers who work with Little League and the Girl Scouts, and in many kinds of meetings that I attend around Houston, and it is my observation that people are deeply troubled by this thing. Generally, people I talk to feel abortion is immoral. It's a violation of some of the principles set forth in the Bible. I know, for myself, I could not face the prospect. I know I would feel endless guilt and shame if I let a living fetus be removed from me. I think abortion is wrong." She sat down, and more women applauded.

The argument went on. The chairwoman suggested a vote, but women wanted to talk. She suggested a fifteen-minute limit on further discussion. A woman rose to speak, and the suggestion was ignored. Doris Schmidt came around the table and asked Teejay if she wanted to say anything. Teejay shook her head. She knew how she would vote, but she doubted anything she could say would change anyone's mind. "I'm pretty confident we're going to vote it down," Doris whispered in her ear. "We have the votes."

The door at the back of the room opened. Lois Hughes held it open for a moment while she nodded and said something to Judge Leonard Kinney in the hall; then she came in and looked around for a chair. She saw one along the wall, not at the table, and she sat down. She was chairwoman of the Committee on Unauthorized Practice of Law, which apparently had now adjourned. She looked troubled and distracted, and she ignored the noisy argument around the table and studied some papers out of her suede briefcase. She glanced toward the table from time to time, nodding greeting to women whose eyes she caught, and when she glanced at Teejay and saw Teejay was looking at her, she nodded at her. They had been acquainted since the day Bart Josephson had introduced them, and they saw each other from time to time and usually stopped to exchange a few words. Teejay had helped Lois establish a case of unauthorized practice against a notary public who was writing wills, and she had sat beside her at a Bar Association luncheon one day.

Lois Hughes, as Teejay saw her, accepted a certain degree of deference as her due. She seemed comfortable with a reputation for money, position, and some political influence. She was younger than most of the women in this room; yet she entered the meeting late and was greeted and accepted as if she were one of the seniors of the Harris County bar. She sat there now with her back to the wall, a little too tall for her chair, wearing a light yellow shirt dress so loose and voluminous that she might have been pregnant under it, her legs crossed, studying the papers on her lap and apparently ignoring the shrill dispute going on around the table.

The chairwoman tapped her glass again. "I notice Lois Hughes has come in," she said. "Lois presided over another committee tonight and has come on to our meeting. Lois, would you like to speak to the motion before the committee?"

Lois Hughes shook her head. "I don't think I have anything special to contribute. I'll just vote," she said.

"Will you tell us how you're going to vote?" asked Constance Flaherty.

Lois Hughes glanced at her. "I'm going to vote no," she said.

"May we know why?" Constance Flaherty asked.

"Because I don't think some people have the right to tell other people how to live their lives."

A woman on the far side of the table stood and pointed a finger at Lois Hughes. "It's pretty easy for you, I gather," she said, "to come in here and vote for murder, without listening to the arguments against it." The woman—plump, gray, angry—flushed red, then added: "That's what makes the murder of unborn babies so easy—people who don't care enough to hear the case."

"*Please* . . ." said the chairwoman.

Lois Hughes looked up at the woman for a moment, as the meeting became silent. "Are you a lawyer?" she asked the woman.

"I most certainly am."

Lois Hughes lifted her eyebrows. "Curious . . ." she muttered, and she looked down again at her papers.

The chairwoman tapped her glass again. "We will vote on the resolution," she said irritably. She ignored two or three women demanding to
be recognized. "Those in favor of the resolution, please signify by raising your right hand." It was immediately apparent that the resolution
had failed. Of the twenty-five women in the room, eight or nine voted
yes.

The woman at Teejay's right nudged her and nodded toward Judge
Norma Spencer. The judge sat with her eyes down, staring grimly at
her hands folded on the table before her. When the chairwoman called
for the votes against the resolution, the judge still stared down but
raised her right hand.

"Well, if you really want to know, here's somebody maybe can tell
you," Jim Rush laughed, and he pointed at a tall, dark-haired man who
stood in the doorway to the bar and looked around. He was a thin,
long-jawed man with little round gold-rimmed spectacles, and he was
peering into the dim light of the crowded, noisy bar, looking for someone. Jim got up and went to the man in the doorway, and after a
moment's conversation he led him back toward the table where Teejay
sat with a Scotch and water before her. Jim was laughing as he pointed
toward the table, and when he reached it he leaned down over Teejay
so he could hear and said, "Honey, this is Bob Peavy—Robert T. Peavy
—of Stimson and Guthrie. He can tell you what influence Lois Hughes
has over Judge Spencer."

The tall man, Peavy, sat down opposite Teejay, across the small
table, and laid appraising eyes on her for a long moment. "It's a pleasure to meet you," he said. "I've heard your name often."

"Bob's a securities man," said Jim. "Talk is, he may get an appointment to the SEC. Tell him about the judge's performance."

Peavy looked around, whether for a waitress or for the person he had
been looking for earlier, Teejay could not tell. She waited until she had
his attention before she said anything. "I was just curious," she told
him. "Judge Spencer was upstairs in the Women's Committee meeting.
We had the right-to-lifers on our backs tonight—"

"I heard you did," Peavy interrupted. "You beat them down?"

"Fourteen to nine. But Judge Spencer was there and spoke in favor
of the resolution, and when the vote was taken she voted no."

"She's a dummy," said Peavy. "She probably forgot what she was
voting about."

"I had the impression Lois Hughes changed her mind for her," Teejay said. "I've heard she's Lois's creature, so to speak."

"That's an exaggeration," said Peavy. He glanced around the room again.

"Hell, Bob," said Jim. "That story's around."

"She make an ass of herself?" Peavy asked.

"I wouldn't go that far," said Teejay. "But she jumped from one side to another pretty conspicuously. It was not what you'd call a smooth performance."

"Did Lois come down when the meeting broke up?" Peavy asked.

"She was talking to somebody when I left."

Peavy ordered two martinis from the waitress who stopped at the table. Conversation in the bar was not easy. The amplifiers were set loud on the guitars and bass being played by a group of black musicians on the platform behind the bar. Under the red and yellow lights, the lawyers coming down from their meetings were drinking, joking, laughing. Teejay smoked, but the oppressive atmosphere of tobacco smoke stung her eyes. Jim squeezed her hand on the seat between them, out of Bob Peavy's sight. The waitress brought two martinis. Peavy put one aside, sipped from the other. After another few minutes, Lois Hughes came in and sat down beside him and picked up the other martini.

She nodded, she acknowledged she knew Teejay Brookover and Jim Rush, and she lifted her drink to them before she took her first sip. She looked around at the room. It was plain this was not her choice of bars. Conversation was all but impossible. Lois Hughes said something to Peavy that was manifestly meant to be heard by Jim and Teejay, but neither of them heard a word. Teejay rubbed Jim's leg, idly, and he showed her an overbroad, tolerant smile.

"Teejay," said Peavy forcefully after a while. He leaned toward her and spoke up so his voice would come through. "Tell Lois about Judge Spencer."

Teejay had decided to drop the subject, but Lois Hughes leaned forward, frowning curiously to hear her amplify something Peavy had obviously said to her about the judge. "Well, tell me," Teejay said, "when you file your income tax, do you claim depreciation on Norma Spencer?"

Lois Hughes laughed. She shook her head. "I haven't figured out how long she's likely to last."

Peavy drove her car—her BMW—and Lois relaxed and explored her consciousness for any effect from the two martinis she had drunk. Nothing. She yawned. "Tell me," she said to Peavy, "what was that about Norma Spencer? What was Teejay talking about?"

His attention was fixed on the traffic, and he peered intently at the cars changing lanes ahead of him in the eerie orange glow of the street-lights. "I'm not sure," he said. "It was about the right-to-life vote in the Women's Committee. Apparently Judge Spencer spoke in favor of the resolution and then voted against it. Teejay has the idea the judge changed her mind when she heard you say something against the reso-lution."

Lois grinned, but she wrinkled her nose and shook her head. "Norma . . . Jesus!"

"It was Teejay's opinion the judge made an ass of herself."

"God . . ." said Lois.

"Forget it," said Peavy. He stopped for a traffic light just turned red, and he leaned across the gearshift to kiss Lois. "Hey . . ." he whis-pered.

She put her arms around the back of his neck and kissed him eagerly and hard. She clung to him until the light changed again and he had to pull abruptly away and grab the gearshift; then she settled back in her seat, turned toward him, and watched him with a lazy, happy smile as he frowned and concentrated again on the traffic. Everything between him and her was fresh and uncomplicated. He was a new interest, and she was enthusiastic.

On the Allen Parkway, traffic was light and there were few street-lights. Peavy relaxed. "I don't see any big trucks," he said with a grin.

"Pee-vee!" she laughed. It was a joke between them. One night two weeks ago, when they were driving home from a ball game at the Astrodome, he had playfully pulled up her skirt, saying he really did enjoy the sight of a nice pair of legs; and when, a little later, a truck in the lane to the right of them kept their speed and cruised alongside them for several blocks, she told him the driver was looking down into the car and obviously was another man who enjoyed a nice pair of legs. She pulled her skirt back now, as far as it would go. She was wearing stockings and a white, lace-trimmed garter belt. Peavy glanced down repeatedly, and she saw him fill himself with breath. It excited her to know she was exciting him, and she turned her hips and tugged the skirt back even more, so he could see her panties.

"Boss-lady of the Committee on Unauthorized Practice of Law," he said deep in his throat, "you got all it takes, all that good stuff."

She was comfortable and did not respond. She watched his eyes shift from the road to her legs and back.

It was true he might be appointed to the Securities and Exchange Commission—depending on the outcome of the presidential election in the fall. It would have to be a Democratic appointment. Ford would never appoint him. Carter might. She had thought actually—already, even though they had been lovers only a few weeks—of marrying Peavy and going to Washington with him if he were appointed. He was divorced. She was divorced. They had a lot in common, and they liked each other. She respected him. He was a sound, responsible man. Still, he was impulsive sometimes, and fun. It was easy to think of being married to him. It was appealing.

"Anywhere you want to go besides home?" he asked.

"No," she said. "Just home. I've had a long day."

"Aside from the foofaraw in the Women's Committee, did anything interesting happen in your meetings?"

"No," she said. "How much of that talk about Norma had I missed when I came in?"

"Only a little."

"I'm thinking of a comment someone else made in the elevator. I didn't understand it at the time."

"I'm afraid the bar doesn't think much of your friend Norma Spencer as a judge," he said.

"Bob, she's a brilliant woman," Lois said earnestly. "She was a first-rate law student, and she was a good lawyer in our firm."

"So you kicked her up to a judgeship," he said dryly.

"It's the end of her professional career," Lois said. "We're rid of her at Childreth. We won't take her back. If she isn't reelected and re-elected again, she'll be out in the cold. Consequently, she'll do any-thing she thinks will please the people who arranged her judgeship— for fear that those who gave it can take it away."

"Which they can," said Peavy. "The Democratic Committee—"

"No. It's more than that. The committee helped her, sure. *I* helped her. The firm helped her. The newspapers helped her."

"So, she's beholden to all of you."

"Well . . . We don't ask much of her—just to be a competent judge."

"*In your estimation,*" he said firmly. "That's what she's afraid of: that you'll decide she's not a competent judge."

"I've never suggested she's beholden to me, that she be anything but independent."

"I don't know," he said. "I'm glad *I* don't practice in her court."

"Do you think it's really widely supposed that—"

"I don't know," he interrupted. "Tell you what, though. There are *really* no trucks around."

XXVI

1976

Teejay smoked a second cigarette, not entirely able to conceal her impatience. It was almost nine, and it was a Friday evening. She worked long hours and did not count them; still, it was presumptuous of a prospective client to expect her to be available at this hour, and rude of him to talk on the telephone for thirty minutes while she sat and waited. What was more, Benjamin Mudge was apparently oblivious of the presumption and rudeness. He sat behind his desk and talked expansively, without so much as an apologetic glance toward her. She had drunk the whiskey and soda he had poured for her when she first arrived, and she had smoked, and she had walked around his office, looking at his plats and certificates and photographs. She had considered leaving.

Mudge was an ugly man. He was nearer seventy than sixty and showed his age by his liver spots, his baldness and wispy gray fringe of hair, his bad teeth, his trembling hands; yet, he was vigorous, hard and incisive of speech, a conspicuously active businessman with a wide reputation. He smoked a cigar as he talked on the telephone. He talked from one corner of his mouth most of the time, distorting his face to do it. His pale blue eyes bulged from his head like the eyes of a bullfrog. His head was massive, oversize for his diminutive body. He wore an exquisitely tailored dark blue suit, a white silk shirt, gold cuff links, highly polished shoes. He smiled and laughed as he talked and seemed genuinely to enjoy his conversation.

"By God, Joe, I am indebted to you for bringing that to my attention. You are a *friend* to tell me. . . . Of *course* I will. . . . Of *course* I will. Please give my very best to your lovely family. And call me again. Call me often."

He hung up the telephone, and, turning to Teejay, he picked up the conversation interrupted half an hour before, without losing a breath. "Your name, Miss Brookover, was recalled to me by a mutual friend. Charlie Donaldson. In a lifetime one is privileged to form a few treasured and enduring friendships, and mine with Charlie Donaldson has been a genuine boon to me. A genuine boon . . ." He repeated the phrase in a voice that trailed off, and he frowned as if what he had said reminded him of something else, that he had forgotten. He opened a drawer of his desk, took out a small package, and handed it across the desk to her. "There," he said. "Open that."

She opened the package. In a box inside the paper was a Cross pen-and-pencil set, of gold, with her name engraved. "Mr. Mudge . . ." she said.

"I've changed a long-standing habit, Miss Brookover. I used to give people a case of liquor—or half a case. Now I give pen-and-pencil sets. I decided the people who got the liquor often forgot who gave it to them by the time they drank it up. Anyway, I hope you enjoy those."

Unprepared, Teejay smiled nervously. "I—Thank you. It's very kind of you."

"I had heard your name often before Charlie Donaldson recalled it to me one day last week. You have established a fine reputation as an aggressive young attorney." He nodded. "A fine reputation. Over the years I have employed many attorneys. Some of the more prominent attorneys in Texas have represented me in my various interests over the years. I have paid them some handsome fees for their advice. I am a strong believer in having the finest professional assistance before I embark on any enterprise. My principal counsel today is the Houston firm of Todd and Graybar. I have begun to feel, however, that I should have more personal counsel with respect to some of my interests, and of course I am thinking you might qualify to fill that position for me."

"I would be pleased to," Teejay said quickly.

He pinched between a thumb and index finger the loose pale flesh under his chin. "I pride myself, Miss Brookover, on knowing something of the law that relates to my lines of business. I am not, of course, an attorney, but I do read as much as I can, and I have learned a great deal, I think. I fancy myself something of a lay expert on the law of land investments. I know something about oil and gas law, as well. Not every lawyer is comfortable with the idea that the client knows something about the law."

"It wouldn't trouble me, Mr. Mudge."

"Ah. Well, then . . . I have a small matter I would like to entrust to you." The file was at his hand, and he took from it a paper. "I have been working to establish a small shopping center in Fort Bend County. It is nothing very big, but I believe it is a sound investment and will earn a reasonable return. I have options on all the necessary land. A woman named Gimbel owns a small piece of it, and she has refused to honor the option she signed. I have tendered the money, but she will not accept it. She is influenced by her son, a veterinarian. I believe he has influenced her to think she can hold me up for a lot of money, since I must exercise all the options and acquire all the land if I am to develop the shopping center. I entrust this matter to you. It may be necessary to sue."

Dr. Albert Gimbel, the veterinarian, was fifty-five years old; his mother was eighty-one. "When they first approached her about this, I called Benjamin Mudge and told him not to trouble my mother with any business," he told Teejay a few days later. "She's too old, her health is bad, she is easily excited. I told Mudge if he wanted to discuss buying that piece of land, he would have to deal with me. If it was a fair deal, I told him, I would recommend my mother sign his option, and I would get her signature on the paper. In spite of that, he sent his option agent to see her at home, and he got her to sign something he now calls an option; but it is not a valid option, and I don't propose to honor it."

Teejay had a Xerox copy of the option in her briefcase. She took it out. "In what respect is it not a valid option, Dr. Gimbel?" she asked.

She had come to his office. He sat in a squeaking aluminum-and-vinyl swivel chair, at a gray steel desk, in his white coat. Dogs barked incessantly in the kennels outside his office window. "I have a copy of this, too," he said as he scanned the document.

"It's an option, Dr. Gimbel," she said. "What's wrong with it? I've checked the sale prices of similar pieces of land in the vicinity, and I don't think you can argue your mother was influenced to give up her land for too little money."

The veterinarian shoved a finger of heavy black hair back off his forehead. "It's not that," he said. "It's the way Mudge does business. I told him to stay away from my mother."

"Unless you want to argue she's incompetent, what's that have to do with the validity of the option?" Teejay asked.

The veterinarian sighed impatiently. "Look at the signatures," he said, tapping his finger irritably on the paper. "'Emma D. Gimbel'— that's my mother's signature. First witness: 'Harry Gottschalk'—and he was Mudge's agent who came to the house. Second witness: 'Robert Milligan.' Notary public: 'Ernest Gabriel.' My mother swears to me— and I believe her—that neither Milligan nor Gabriel was with Gotts- chalk or that she ever saw them. The paper says she signed in the pres- ence of Gottschalk, Milligan, and Gabriel. This paper is a fraud."

The veterinarian was annoyed and in a mood to do something irra- tionally defiant. Teejay pitched her voice low. "Dr. Gimbel," she said, "let me make two or three points to you. In the first place, your mother inherited this piece of land from your father, who bought it in 1941 for three thousand dollars. Mr. Mudge is offering you twenty-eight thou- sand for it, so your mother is not being taken unfair advantage of. The other owners in the area have sold to Mr. Mudge for the same price per acre."

"But this paper is a lie," the veterinarian insisted.

"Mr. Milligan and Mr. Gabriel will testify to the contrary, if it comes to a suit. So will Mr. Gottschalk. All three of them are prepared to tes- tify they went to your mother's house together and she signed the option in their presence."

"You would sue," said the veterinarian. "You'd put my mother through a lawsuit."

"There's another point, Dr. Gimbel," said Teejay. "If Mr. Milligan and Mr. Gabriel were not present—even if I were to grant you that— then what your mother signed, although not a valid option, is still a valid contract to sell the property."

"What do you mean by that?"

"Check with your own lawyer, Dr. Gimbel. To be valid as an option, a paper must be signed before two witnesses and acknowledged before a notary. Without the witnesses and the acknowledgment, it is still a contract to sell. It is enforceable, and we will definitely go to court to enforce it."

"So you think you've got me by the short hairs."

Teejay shook her head. "I have here a deed form and Mr. Mudge's certified check. Your mother accepted two thousand dollars when she signed the option, so the check is for twenty-six thousand. I'm leaving the deed with you, so your mother doesn't have to be troubled with the matter—as you have asked. But I would like to have the executed deed —signed by your mother in the presence of two witnesses and a notary public—within seventy-two hours. If I don't have it, Dr. Gimbel, I'm going to file a suit."

"I've heard of you," the veterinarian muttered between clenched teeth. "You and Mudge make a fine pair."

"This is well done, Miss Brookover," said Benjamin Mudge when he saw the deed signed by Emma Gimbel. "This makes it possible for us to advance the development of this little shopping center, which I believe will prove to be a profitable venture." He ran the tips of his fingers over the deed, as if it had sensual significance to him; then he handed it to the option agent, Harry Gottschalk, who stood by his desk. This was Sunday afternoon, in Mudge's office. "I might suggest to you, Miss Brookover, that you accept stock in the shopping center corporation in lieu of a cash fee. I will of course gladly pay your fee by check, but I do suggest a few shares of this stock as an attractive investment. I am holding a majority of the shares and will continue to do so, but I can transfer to you, say, five of my shares as your fee for your excellent services in this transaction."

"I'd be pleased to have those shares, Mr. Mudge," she said. She had no idea what they were worth, if anything, but it was her sense that accepting them instead of money would improve her chances of doing more and bigger business with Benjamin Mudge. He spoke of them as an investment. They would be an investment for her, but in a sense in addition to the one he had in mind.

For a moment Mudge watched Gottschalk unlock and open a filing cabinet and insert the Gimbel deed in a folder. Gottschalk was a small, thin man with a flushed face, and even though it was a Sunday afternoon he was dressed in a gray-checked, double-breasted suit. Mudge was dressed in blue suit, white silk shirt, cuff links, as he had been the night she met him. Gottschalk was deferential to Mudge: conspicuously, ceremonially deferential.

"Pour Miss Brookover a whiskey, Harry," said Mudge.

"Aren't you having one?" Teejay asked as Gottschalk hurried to the cabinet to pour her drink.

"I have a sip of wine now and again," said Mudge. "I will light a cigar. That is my vice. That and good cheese, Miss Brookover. Do you enjoy good cheese? I will make a point of having a wedge of a special Camembert I have imported delivered to you. I believe you will find it delicious."

She watched Gottschalk pouring her a Scotch from a bottle of Chivas. "I wanted to ask a question, Mr. Mudge," she said. "Since Mr. Gottschalk is here . . . Tell me, just who did witness the Gimbel option?"

Mudge's face darkened. The red spread over his huge bald forehead. He frowned. He kneaded the fluid folds of his chin with one hand as for a moment he pondered. "Well," he said. "As you know, Miss Brookover, I have been in business for many years. I told you I take some pride in understanding the law as it pertains to my endeavors. I wanted an option on that property, but I knew, of course, an option signed without a second witness and a notary would be a valid contract of sale. Dr. Gimbel had made a point of his mother's being a dear, fragile old lady, so I decided we would not trouble her by sending a host of witnesses and notaries into her home. I sent Harry. He obtained her signature. We added the second witness and the notarization later. That is not uncommon as a business practice, Miss Brookover, as I suppose you know. If the doctor had not decided to attempt to hold us up, it would have made no difference at all."

Teejay accepted the whiskey from Gottschalk. "May I assume, then, that Messieurs Gottschalk, Milligan, and Gabriel would not, if it had come to it, have testified—"

"No, of course not," said Mudge quickly. "I would not permit anyone in my employ to testify falsely."

Teejay smiled at him across her glass, but if he saw the smile he did not return it. He lit his cigar. He was comfortable with what he had said. He was not embarrassed. He was not embarrassed that the witness Milligan had signed a false statement or that the notary Gabriel had misused his office. It had come out all right in the end—with her help—and he was satisfied. He was secure. She had heard that he did business this way. He had a reputation for it.

"It has long been my judgment, Miss Brookover," Mudge said pontifically, "that if a man will but invest his capital in some of the fine land of this wonderful country of ours, and if he will hold that investment patiently and give it time to mature, he will be richly rewarded. That is my advice to young people."

"I suppose it depends on what land we are talking about," Teejay said, again with a smile that invited a smile, to probe behind the speech that rolled so easily from him.

This time Mudge returned her smile. "Precisely," he said with a chuckle. "I, of course, have a particular piece of land in mind. Tell me, Miss Brookover, what do you know about corporation law and securities?"

"I can't tell you I'm a specialist," she said. "I'm competent. I can handle corporation problems. I know when I'm in over my head and need help."

Mudge put his burning cigar aside in a heavy glass ashtray and he pushed his loose lips around with his tongue, whether to savor the smoke in his mouth or to dislodge a morsel of tobacco, she could not tell.

"I am in the process of acquiring some land in Calhoun County," he said. "I want to form a new corporation to take title to that land and raise the money to develop it. I am thinking, too, of acquiring some shares in a small corporation here in Houston and asking the stockholders of that corporation to invest in the enterprise. I think this venture has great promise, Miss Brookover. It is a far larger venture than the small shopping center we have just worked together to rescue from the misguided avarice of Dr. Gimbel. Would you like to represent me in the matter?"

"I would indeed, Mr. Mudge."

"It will be a residential subdivision," said Mudge. "The lots will have access to the seashore. It will be what is called a second-home subdivision, a subdivision of weekend homes, vacation homes. We will attempt to acquire options on perhaps two thousand acres. I am thinking in terms of five thousand lots, to sell for an average of eight thousand dollars apiece. It will be, I think, a substantial enterprise."

"Forty million dollars," said Teejay softly.

Mudge nodded. He drew a delicately measured puff of smoke from his cigar, rolled it around in his mouth, and blew it out. He studied her face and—as she guessed—judged her sufficiently impressed and adequately greedy for a part in what he was planning. She hoped he judged her that way. She did not mean to be subtle about it. A forty-million-dollar proposition! It was a breakthrough for her.

"I have certain—associates," said Mudge, "who are prepared to participate in this venture to the extent of about two million dollars. It will be necessary to find the balance of the funds that will be required. I want to do this, Miss Brookover, on the basis of my own name being subdued in the matter. I am involved in a number of other enterprises at the moment, and it is better that my name be used with respect to this one as little as possible. Do you understand?"

She nodded. "I believe so."

"I want you to form a corporation," he said. "Let us call it Lago Aguila, Incorporated. The three incorporators will be Mr. Roberto Luiz, who is an associate of mine, Mr. Gerald Skelton, and perhaps yourself as the third. Set it up with ten thousand shares of no-par common stock. I should appreciate it if you had the corporation formed this week. Mr. Luiz will transfer to its ownership some options he has already acquired, which will be the corporation's initial assets, and we will issue him a few shares as compensation. I suggest you take a similar number of shares as your fee for handling the incorporation. Is that all right with you?"

Teejay nodded, but she frowned too. "I assume there will be some fees in cash," she said.

"I have here a check made out to you in the amount of five thousand dollars, Miss Brookover. That is meant to be your retainer."

Jim Rush sent his wife and children home to Rhode Island for Thanksgiving. It was only in part untrue that he was so hard pressed by a piece of business he was trying to complete for his firm that he could not get away. He did in fact work until late Wednesday evening, and only then did he come to Teejay's apartment—where they had planned he would stay until Friday morning. He bought a bottle of Dom Perignon, "because I have something to celebrate." He had been told during the afternoon that he was about to be made a partner.

"You *have* called Rhode Island, haven't you? Listen, you really must."

He grinned. "Sure. I called from the office."

"Oh, Jim!" She seized him around the shoulders and kissed him. "I'm so glad for you."

He opened his bottle of champagne and they toasted his good fortune. It was, she told him, his reward for being so well organized—so well organized that tonight he had brought his kit: his shaver, toothbrush, deodorant, comb and brush, clean socks, clean underwear. She laughed. She sipped his champagne and told him she would make him sleep on the couch if he persisted in sitting there "like a hoot owl, in that silly three-piece lawyer suit." Tugging and teasing, she got him to shed his jacket and vest, then his necktie, then his shirt, then his shoes. In his skivvy shirt with the tail pulled out of his pants, he looked almost comfortable, she told him: almost as comfortable as she was in her blue jeans and white T-shirt. They drank the champagne. She sat close to him and kissed him, and they talked.

A little of their talk was serious. He had made a point, he said, of talking to a friend of his at Todd & Graybar, and his friend had told him the firm often had to haul Benjamin Mudge up short, to counsel him firmly against some of his propositions. He was not an easy man to rein in, the friend had said.

"He's a tough old son of a bitch," said Teejay.

"The town is full of stories about him," said Rush. He was standing in front of one of the prints on her wall, peering over his glasses at the signature and the number. "I hadn't noticed this before," he said.

"What kind of stories, Jim?"

"All kinds. Some pretty funny. At Todd and Graybar they have a story about one of the younger partners commenting on Mudge's wardrobe. He remarked to Mudge that he had never known anyone who had so many beautifully tailored suits. He said, 'Mr. Mudge, you must spend a small fortune on your clothes.' Mudge is supposed to have said, 'Young man, if you were as ugly as I am, you'd spend as much as I do.' "

"I've seen no sign of a sense of humor," said Teejay.

"They don't think he meant to be humorous," said Rush. "That's the point. Where'd you get the print?"

"I stole it, for Christ's sake. You've seen it there before. What'd you think I did, clip it from a calendar? You ought to see my office sometime. I've got a couple of nice prints there, too. I'd like to collect things like that."

He stood peering at the print, openly appraising it. "Four hundred dollars at least," he said.

"Five-fifty—and you can go to the devil."

"Jesus, Teejay—honey," he whispered. He lifted his glass to her. "You are one hell of a woman. Every day I see something more to like about you. God, I wish I could tell everyone I'm spending Thanksgiving with you."

Her face flushed deep red. "Well, I wish you could, too, Jim," she whispered thinly.

"Oh, Teejay, *I'm sorry!*" he protested. He hurried to sit down beside her and to put an arm around her. "I am sorry, really."

Stiffened against him, she rose from the couch. "There may be one more glass of champagne in the bottle," she said.

"Please—"

"Even if you weren't married to Mousy-Jane, you couldn't tell people how close you are to me. In fact, we shouldn't be seen together so often at the Pound Sterling. It will damage your reputation as a sober, conservative young lawyer."

He sighed. "To hell with being a sober, conservative young lawyer."

"Brave talk," she said.

"Really—"

"You'll have to excuse me a minute," she said.

She went through her bedroom to her bathroom, closing both doors behind her. She stood at the basin, facing the mirror, and she gripped the edges of the basin and did not cry. After a moment she splashed cold water on her face, smoothed her hair with a comb, and opened the bathroom door. He had come into her bedroom.

"What can I say?" he asked her quietly, standing just inside the door.

"I'd just as soon you said nothing," she said. "I have a couple of steaks and a bottle of Châteauneuf-du-Pape. Will you open the wine? It needs to breathe."

"Teejay . . . I love you."

She braced her back against one of the tall bookcases in her bedroom and she stood with one bare foot drawn up, looking at him, smiling wanly. "There's a man," she said very quietly, "who loves me. He's loved me for a long time. I wanted to be what I am: a lawyer, independent, prosperous maybe. I wouldn't drop out of school to marry him. I wouldn't give up my career now to marry him. But he loves me very much. He still does. I love him, too—but not enough to give up everything for him. I love you, Jim, maybe right now more than I do him. But I wouldn't ask you to be anything but the sober, conservative young lawyer. You've got too much invested in it."

"I want you to know," he said, "it's tempting to think about: just to throw away every damn demanding thing in this world and come to you."

Her smile broadened and warmed. "Don't think of me as an escape, my love. I might be the most demanding person you ever knew. Are you going to open that bottle of wine for me?"

XXVII

1977

"Uhh—you'll expense that, I assume," he would murmur, and he would push the luncheon check across the table. Teejay would take it reluctantly, and she would, as he suggested, charge it as a business expense to Benjamin Mudge. Thomas Glencoe, the president of Futures Dynamic, would not come to her office. He resisted receiving her at his. He liked to do business over protracted lunches, preceded by drinks—usually at the Houston Oaks Hotel. Over the lunch table, spreading the papers across the silverware, Teejay and Glencoe planned the Mudge acquisition of control of Futures Dynamic.

"Did Ben explain the history of Futures?" Glencoe asked. "You ought to know, it all started with a grand old man, Teejay. Bunker Harvey. The corporation was formed to own and exploit Mr. Harvey's patents."

"When was the corporation formed?" Teejay asked.

"In 1948. Mr. Harvey believed he could make more money from his patents if he manufactured and sold some of his inventions himself, instead of just taking a royalty on others' use of his ideas. He wanted investors. Some of us formed the corporation."

Glencoe talked readily enough about the business during their first luncheon, but she would learn subsequently that it was difficult to hold his attention on any one subject for very long. He liked to talk about golf and his friends at the country club. He was a social man; his friends and acquaintances stopped at their table often, and he invariably offered drinks and sometimes interrupted the business talk for half an hour while he and a friend explored the odds on the week's basketball games or discussed the condition of several area golf courses. He drank two Beefeater martinis before lunch and a stinger after—ritually; he never varied. He was some fifty-five years old, a generally loose and overfleshed man, ruddy of complexion, with little left of his sandy-gray hair. He told Teejay during their third lunch that he would like to sleep with her, hoped she would not be offended by his suggesting it, and assured her he would not be offended if she declined. She said she was not offended but did decline, and he seemed not to be offended either, as he had promised.

He and others had organized Futures Dynamic in 1958. Bunker Harvey had transferred ownership of certain patents from himself to the corporation in return for 50,000 shares of stock. Another 50,000 were sold to investors. With these patents and this capital, the corporation had established a small manufacturing plant in Houston, where it began to make the essential components of the Harvey Laser Micrometer. Other Harvey patents were licensed to outside companies, and Futures Dynamic collected the royalties.

"Mr. Harvey was entirely pleased with the arrangements," Glencoe said. "He was president of the corporation. I was vice-president. I handled all the administrative work, so Mr. Harvey would be free to spend his days in his lab. He came up with some improvements on the micrometer. He was a grand old man."

"But he died," she said.

Glencoe nodded. "In 'sixty-five."

"And then the corporation stopped making money," she suggested.

"No. The corporation has always made money. The problem is, the corporation has no future. It continues to manufacture and sell the micrometer, on which it makes a respectable profit. We have to expect, though, that someday someone will develop something better—it's an advanced technology, after all—and the market for it will disappear. That's what's happened to a couple of the other Harvey patents—people just quit using the Harvey idea and moved on to something else."

"What you need is another Harvey," she said.

Glencoe shook his head. "What we need is a major new injection of capital," he said. "The corporation needs to diversify and expand. But to do that, you need money; and the stockholders won't put in any more money. Of course, if the stockholders won't, nobody else will either."

"Who are the stockholders?" Teejay asked.

Glencoe was nibbling on a breadstick. "Mrs. Harvey died three years after Mr. Harvey," he said, cleaning his teeth with his tongue. "They left most of their stock to their son and two daughters, but some to a niece and nephew. None of them have the least interest in the corporation and they've sold off some of their shares, but among them they still have about thirty-eight percent of the stock. Other than Mr. Harvey, no one else has ever owned more than two percent of the stock. There are some six hundred stockholders."

The stock had sold for $100 a share when it was first offered in 1958, and because of the reputation of Bunker Harvey the original offering had been taken up within two months. Glencoe himself invested $40,000 and bought four hundred shares. The stock traded desultorily over the counter, declining on the death of Harvey to a low of $12 per share, then recovering gradually to a post-Harvey high of $34. In the fall of 1976 the stock had sold for $27. So far in 1977 it had been traded only once. The estate of one of the original investors sold two hundred shares for $26.50.

Glencoe gave about half his time to the corporation and drew a salary of $45,000. At the small plant, twenty-two employees manufactured the micrometer components. The number of units sold had declined by four percent in 1976. Royalties from the Harvey patents owned by the corporation had declined nine percent. The corporation would pay a dividend of ten cents a share.

Futures Dynamic was what Mudge had said it was, and it was what he wanted: a shell.

Teejay had to stay in the kitchen while the steaks broiled, and Jim stayed with her. She sat at the vinyl-and-chrome kitchen table, with a glass of red wine before her, and Jim stood beside her. His hip was pressed to the back of her chair. She held him, and he could not step back without wrenching loose from her. Her left hand was cupped over his taut, hairy buttock, pulling him. With her right index finger she gently stroked the underside of his penis, and she watched it intently as it pulsed and swelled. His glass of wine was in his left hand. His right kneaded her breast.

They had been in bed—had, in fact, come from the bedroom to the kitchen—and she was surprised to see him rise so soon again. He did not usually do it. She nuzzled his belly. "In about a minute I'm going to forget the whole conversation," she said huskily. "I might even forget the steaks and let them burn."

"Uhm-hmm," he said. "Me too."

She looked up at his face and laughed. "I thought there had to be some way to take your mind off business," she said.

They had been talking as they left the bedroom and came to the kitchen, as she put the steaks in the broiler and he opened the wine, about Benjamin Mudge and Tom Glencoe. She had explained how Benjamin Mudge planned to take control of Futures Dynamic, and why.

Mudge and his investors (whose names Teejay did not know) had $2 million available in an investment trust called Twelve-Twenty. Twelve-Twenty would invest the $2 million in Futures Dynamic. The trust would buy 67,000 Futures shares at $29.85 a share, provided Futures had contracted to invest the $2 million in the shares of Lago Aguila. Glencoe, as president of Futures Dynamic, was prepared to execute a contract committing Futures to the purchase of the Lago Aguila shares, but the stockholders would have to meet and ratify such a contract. Also, the Futures stockholders would have to authorize the issuance of the 67,000 new shares.

Owning 67,000 of the 167,000 shares Futures would then have outstanding, Mudge's Twelve-Twenty would have effective control of Futures Dynamic. If there were any problem, Glencoe customarily had proxies for ten or fifteen thousand shares at a stockholders' meeting, and those proxy votes added to Mudge's would easily control the corporation. Futures Dynamic would then borrow to the limit of its credit and invest whatever it could raise in Lago Aguila. Using its plant and machinery for security, Futures might be able to borrow as much as $4 million. Certainly it could borrow $3 million. So, with the cash from Twelve-Twenty and the loans from banks, the total investment by Futures in Lago Aguila could be as much as $6 million. That was money enough to promote the $40-million Lago Aguila subdivision Mudge had planned.

Their steaks were done—hers rare, his medium—and they carried them, with the bottle of St.-Émilion and tossed salads, into the living room, where they would eat off the long coffee table before her couch. She lit candles on the table.

"Do you think the Futures Dynamic stockholders will agree to all this?" Jim asked.

Teejay shrugged. "Most of them would like to see the company diversify and expand, Glencoe thinks. Anyway, he will write a letter to the stockholders, recommending the deal. He'll ask for proxies. We'll have to wait and see."

"Who's writing the letter?"

"I am."

"Who's your client?"

"Mudge."

"Well, then, what's the relationship between Mudge and Glencoe?"

"Glencoe works for Mudge. I'm not sure what the arrangement is, but I'm sure Glencoe is being paid something right now and expects to be paid more if the deal goes through."

"Do the Futures stockholders know that?"

"No."

"Teejay . . ." Rush warned. "Jesus Christ!"

"I suggest you do a little calculating, Miss Brookover," said Benjamin Mudge. He tucked his chin against one shoulder and smiled. "You own one hundred fifty shares of Lago Aguila. I suppose they did not seem like much when you took them as your fee for forming the corporation; but consider: If we sell five thousand lots for an average price of eight thousand, the gross return from Lago Aguila will be forty million dollars. We will not spend more than fifteen million to establish the subdivision and sell the lots. If our profit is twenty-five million, your shares will be worth three hundred and seventy-five thousand dollars."

Teejay nodded. "I had already calculated that," she said.

"Yes . . ." said Mudge, glancing around his office as if distracted by some small noise he was not sure he heard. It was a Saturday evening, just after ten. She had, at his request, picked him up at the airport and brought him to his office. As had become customary, he had offered her a whiskey, although this time she had had to pour it for herself, since they were alone. "I cannot help but feel, Miss Brookover, that any legal difficulties, such as those you foresee, are simply problems to be solved, obstacles to be overcome. We are too committed to this venture to contemplate abandoning it."

"I'm worried about criminal liability," she said. "People go to jail for violations of the securities laws."

"Then do not violate them. Is not that, after all, your function as attorney: to be certain we do not expose ourselves to such liabilities?"

"Mr. Mudge," said Teejay, "Mr. Glencoe is going to send a letter to his stockholders recommending that they accept the Twelve-Twenty proposal and, in effect, turn over control of Futures Dynamic to new management. I am writing that letter for Mr. Glencoe. What he does not propose to tell his stockholders is that he is receiving money from you already and expects to receive a good deal more."

Mudge shook his head. "Mr. Glencoe receives nothing from me."

"Directly or indirectly, Mr. Glencoe is being compensated, Mr. Mudge," she said firmly. "He has told me so himself. He is a little vague about how and how much, but he has told me so."

Mudge interlaced his fingers and laid his hands comfortably on his belly. "Mr. Glencoe," he said grandly, "has performed some independent services in connection with an entirely separate enterprise in which I have some interest, and my associates there have seen fit to reward him—rather generously, I might say—for his services. It is entirely independent of this enterprise, and you need not worry about it."

"Has it been agreed that he will remain president of Futures after Twelve-Twenty acquires control?" Teejay asked.

"I see no reason to throw him out," said Mudge. "The board of directors will change. That is what is important."

"What will his compensation be?"

"It hasn't been agreed upon."

"But it will be two or three times what it is now."

"Futures Dynamic will be two or three times as big a business, Miss Brookover."

"That's another point, Mr. Mudge. Lago Aguila is to a degree speculative. If something goes wrong—if for any reason the lots don't sell—Futures Dynamic will probably be bankrupt, because it's going to pledge its patents and everything else it owns as security for the loans necessary to open Lago Aguila. Is the letter to the stockholders going to say it is a speculative venture?"

"Miss Brookover," said Benjamin Mudge with a pedagogical mien, a condescending smile. "I have put money in this venture. My associates have put in money. Each Futures stockholder is putting in a little. That is the way venture capital is raised, is it not, by many people risking a little?"

"Yes," Teejay conceded. She sighed loudly. "But they take their risk *knowledgeably*, Mr. Mudge. That's the point. The federal securities laws require full disclosure to the Futures stockholders so they can make an informed, intelligent judgment about the risk."

"Well, what then do you propose Mr. Glencoe's letter should say, Miss Brookover?" Mudge asked. He was angry now and spoke with his teeth clenched, his loose lips forming the words he growled forth from one side of his mouth, jutting his face forward, nodding in arrhythmic jerks. "Should the letter warn the Futures stockholders that Benjamin Mudge is involved in the proposition—'So, look out, dear stockholders; clutch your wallets'—hey? Should the letter tell them this Lago Aguila place is nothing right now but a mudhole with little apparent promise of becoming a beautiful subdivision? Should Glencoe tell his stockholders to discount anything he tells them—since I have bribed him? Is that the kind of thing you propose to tell them? Would that satisfy you, Miss Brookover?"

He leaned back in his chair and contemplated her with abated anger but with sustained impatience and scorn, his bulbous eyes still glowering, his face hot pink.

Teejay frowned, shook her head, and slackened. "I started this conversation by telling you I am worried," she said quietly. "I believe the Federal Securities Act definitely requires Glencoe to disclose to the Futures stockholders any compensation he has received or expects to receive from you, directly or indirectly, no matter how remote the connection. And I think the Act requires Glencoe to tell them that Lago Aguila is to some degree a speculative venture." She shrugged and sighed. "If we tell them that, they may not ratify the contract for Futures to buy the Lago Aguila stock."

"Precisely," muttered Mudge. His lower lip was thrust out and his chin was wrinkled. "So . . . You're the lawyer. What do you counsel?"

Teejay turned her head to one side and drew the back of her hand across her mouth. "Of course . . ." she mused softly, ". . . if it all works out, it will be a good deal for everybody."

The stockholders of Futures Dynamic accepted the recommendation of their president, Thomas Glencoe, and voted to authorize the issuance of 67,000 new shares of stock. Within a week, Twelve-Twenty Investment Trust purchased the 67,000 newly issued shares. Effective control of the corporation passed to Mudge.

A new board of directors was elected. The old directors were retained—including Bunker Harvey's son and son-in-law—but the board was expanded by four seats, and four new directors were elected: T. J. Brookover, Roberto Luiz, Dale Kirkbriar, and Xeno Demaret. The four new directors, plus Glencoe, controlled the board. A new general counsel and corporation secretary was elected: T. J. Brookover.

Futures Dynamic duly bought 9700 shares of Lago Aguila. That corporation was reorganized. President: Thomas Glencoe. General counsel and secretary: T. J. Brookover.

Nowhere in the organization of either corporation did the name Benjamin Mudge appear.

XXVIII

"Y' know, you're going to plug up the toilet," Teejay said.

Her new cellmate sat on the lower bunk. With a knife she had somehow acquired during her first day in jail, she sat and hacked off her hair. It was long, to her waist; and with the knife she was cutting it off, as close to her scalp as she could, and flushing it down the toilet. She called herself Amy. She had confided to Teejay tonight that she was only fifteen years old. She had told everyone she was eighteen, so she would be put in jail and not locked up in the juvenile detention center "with a lot of crazy brats"; and she pretended at least (it was as likely to be true as anything else she said) that she was pleased and proud to be in jail—"doing my first time," she called it.

Teejay had seen little of her during the day. Amy had pressed herself on some of the younger women in "B" Cage, trying to ingratiate herself with them. In the cell, after they were locked in, she had stalked back and forth and spent a lot of time hanging on the bars, gripping them in her fists—apparently playing a dramatic role of angry prisoner—and savoring with irrational fascination her confinement inside a barred cell. She had sat down a few minutes ago and begun to carve off her hair. Teejay had ignored her until this began, but she was uneasy to see that Amy had a knife.

"Mah mama wouldn' nevah lemme cut it off," Amy drawled. "Amy hasta have her bee-ootiful long hayer."

Teejay, sitting cross-legged in panties and brassiere on her upper bunk, was reading again the story in the *Chronicle* of the sentencing of Thomas Glencoe and Roberto Luiz. Both men had been sentenced in federal court this morning: four years in prison, $10,000 fine. They had pleaded guilty: Glencoe to three counts of an indictment charging violation of the Securities and Exchange Act of 1934, by fraudulent solicitation of proxies, deception, and withholding of material information in the manipulation of the stock of Futures Dynamic, Incorporated; Luiz to twenty-two counts of an indictment charging violation of the Federal Land Sales Full Disclosure Act, by fraudulent misrepresentations in the sale of lots in the Lago Aguila Subdivision. In return for these pleas, the remaining federal charges against the two men had been dropped. Also, the state would drop charges under the Texas Securities Act.

It was the same deal, essentially, that Lois had made for Teejay. She would plead guilty to the indictment charging her with fraud in the manipulation of Futures Dynamic stock, and the indictments charging fraud in the sale of Lago Aguila lots would be dropped. In her case the deal had two more provisos: She would surrender her license to practice law; and if she were convicted in the murder of Benjamin Mudge and sent to a state prison for a term of five years or more, all federal charges would be dropped.

Glencoe and Harris were in this same jail tonight, on another floor—federal prisoners awaiting transport to a federal institution. Glencoe, interviewed briefly outside the Federal Building, complained that he had put too much trust in "Ben Mudge's lawyer." "She kept telling me," he said, "that everything was okay, everything was legal. I believed her, and that's where I made my mistake." The *Chronicle* reporter explained to his readers that "the lawyer Thomas Glencoe referred to is Houston attorney T. J. Brookover. She remains in the Harris County Jail, awaiting trial on the charge she conspired in the murder of Houston real-estate developer Benjamin Mudge."

Since the newspaper came she had sat here and read the story a dozen times. A little while ago the cell door had closed, locking her in for another night, and she had been startled—stricken in fact—by a sudden thought: that if she had not already been here because she was accused of murder, tonight she would be in jail anyway, a federal prisoner to be held here until she could be moved to a federal reformatory.

It was painful to think that she could be condemned to this, to the hell of confinement, for nothing more than she had done.

For, after all, what had she done? She had written a couple of letters for Glencoe and Twelve-Twenty to send to the Futures stockholders, and she had drafted the prospectus for the Lago Aguila subdivision.

True, she had not told the Futures stockholders that Lago Aguila was a highly speculative business proposition that could bankrupt their company; she had not told them that Glencoe was already on the payroll of Mudge and expected to profit richly from Mudge's takeover of Futures; and she had not told them that it was Benjamin Mudge who was really taking over Futures Dynamic. She had written a prospectus for Lago Aguila that did not tell the buyers of lots that many of the lots would not naturally drain and would become mudholes after a rain unless a lot of expensive bulldozing were done. She had not told prospective buyers of lots that septic tanks could not be installed on some of the lots.

She had not lied. She had just not told the whole truth. For that—if they didn't send her to Goree for life for murder—they would hustle her out of here one day soon in handcuffs, to a reformatory, and God knew when she'd get a parole. There was something drastically unfair about a law that sent some people to prison just because some other people's greedy expectations had been disappointed. Because that was how it was—if everything had worked out all right, everybody would have been happy. If no one had lost any money, no one would have asked how many lies had been told.

Her back touched the steel wall. She reached for a bar and pulled herself to the edge of her bunk. Amy was still hacking away at her hair, insanely grim.

You had to be realistic. And she had been. She had read the securities acts to find out what the maximum penalties were if everything fell apart. She had taken her risk, realistically. If it had all come out the other way . . .

Lois said she would be granted a parole in about one year. The *Chronicle* said the same about Glencoe and Luiz. Lois guessed she would be sent to the federal women's reformatory in Alderson, West Virginia.

Teejay sighed and folded the newspaper. "You really are going to plug up that goddamn toilet," she told Amy.

Amy looked at her. She had at first ignored Teejay, even though Bess had told her Teejay would be her cellmate; but this evening, shortly before lockup, someone had told her Teejay was in jail on a charge of murder, and the girl now regarded her with a certain guarded awe. "Well . . . Want me to throw it on the floor?"

"Yes. Outside," said Teejay, pointing out through the bars.

The girl nodded. She gathered a double handful of her long hair and tossed it disdainfully out of the cell. She had cut off so much that her scalp showed white between the weedy-looking tufts that were left. "They tell me y' killed somebuddy," she said.

"I didn't," said Teejay.

Amy nodded with a distorted little smile, as if she had just been made a party to a sly secret, "Y' done much tam?" she asked.

"I've been here since April."

"Hey-ey!" exclaimed Amy with a grin. "Y' done other tam? Like in other jails?"

"No."

Amy shrugged. "Ah got a sister's been in a lot, different places."

"Too bad," said Teejay.

"Mebbe," said the girl. She turned down the corners of her mouth and began to saw with the knife on a surviving strand of her hair. "Ah don' mand it," she said. "Ah guess evvybuddy does some tam, sometam. Part of laf, ain't it?"

Teejay shook her head. "No."

The girl shrugged again. "Well . . . Ah'm heah. Yore heah. 'Pears lak it's part of *ahr* lafs."

"Well, good! I was beginning to wonder if you were coming down. Beer?"

Norma nodded as she dropped heavily onto the couch in Hal's basement den. As he passed by the television set on his way to the refrigerator, he turned down the sound and silenced a commercial portraying a husband who was ecstatic about a wife who had found a product that washed the yellow stains out of his undershirt armpits. The couple continued its antic message, now in involuntary mime.

She turned her eyes emphatically away from Hal after a glance at the stained seat of his jockey briefs, hoisted for her view as he bent over the little refrigerator to take a can of beer. Here, in his den, as he watched TV, he did his calisthenics—sit-ups, push-ups, sprints on his exercise bicycle—and he did his exercises in his underwear so his clothes would not stink with his sweat. It had been a domestic ritual for years now: for Norma to come down late in the evening, to find him sprawled on the couch in front of the TV, or maybe still pumping his bicycle, damp with sweat, sipping his third or fourth beer of the evening, wiping his forehead with the tail of his skivvy shirt, absorbed in whatever the television networks had to offer. He had a bar. Sometimes he brought his friends down. Trophies and plaques from his football days sat on the shelves behind his bar. A sign in orange Day-Glo letters above the bar said NAME YER PIZEN. It hung beside his certificates of merit from the Boy Scouts. The framed certificates and his sign were fastened to the wall with tape; he did not like to drive nails into the knotty pine he had put up himself.

She curled her nose over the odor he left in the couch.

"Hey!" he said, handing her a Budweiser. It was difficult to nag a man like Hal, any more about the stench he left in his den couch or about lounging every evening in his jockey shorts and undershirt than about his haphazard practice of the law and his ingenuously enthusiastic boosterism. He settled on the couch beside her and was for a moment distracted by the capering figures on the silent television set. "Pooped?" he asked.

She nodded.

She had spent two hours at her desk in their bedroom, studying the memoranda supporting and opposing motions made by a dozen lawyers in half a dozen cases—motions to suppress confessions, to grant new trials, to put offenders on probation, to reconsider sentences. Prolix lawyers: no end of them. Malefactors: every one with rights to be meticulously respected. Society had no idea what it took to stand between it and its chronic losers. "The time is out of joint; O cursed spite/That ever I was born to set it right!" It was a wearying business.

Hal put his arm over her shoulders. He tipped his beer can. She tipped hers. He slipped his hand between the folds of her housecoat and touched her breast, but she shrugged and grunted a protest, and he withdrew it.

"Lois Hughes," she said quietly, "wants to keep out of the Brookover trial all mention of Teejay's being under indictment for securities fraud." She kicked at the evening's *Chronicle* lying on his hassock. "She called this afternoon."

"Called? Does she argue her motions on the telephone?"

Norma glanced at him and took a sip of beer. "I can't refuse to talk to Lois Hughes, Hal."

"You'd refuse to talk to any other lawyer. It's improper. She shouldn't call you and try to discuss a pending case."

"Don't be naïve."

"Norma—"

"You know what's about to happen? Her boy friend—Bob Peavy—is about to be appointed to the Securities and Exchange Commission. Lois and her father have got a lot to do with that."

"That story's been hangin' around for two years."

"You watch and see it happen. This is the woman you want me to give a lecture to on judicial proprieties when she calls and wants to talk about a case she has before me. Grow up, Hal."

"I—I think we better pray for guidance, honey," Hal said with a decisive nod. "You're gonna be faced next month with somethin' where

you're gonna need help. I think we better pray right now and every
night till that trial is over, for the Lord's guidance."

"All right," she said. "When we go upstairs . . ."

Bob Peavy, at the wheel of Lois's BMW, turned into the driveway at
her house in Bayou Oaks. Lois was in front with him, and her two children were in the back seat. They had been to dinner with Daniel
Farnham at the country club. He pulled the car up beside his Jaguar,
which he had left in the driveway.

"Coming in?" Mac John, Jr., asked Peavy as they got out of the car.

"He's coming in, and he'll be staying," Lois said to Mac John, Jr.

The boy smirked and nodded. (He called Peavy "mother's live-in
lover," according to Wendy.) "We'll be going to bed early," he said.

"So will we," Lois said to him.

Mac John, Jr., laughed and ran up the walk toward the door.

During the summer, Lois and Peavy had talked about marrying.
They had agreed they would not marry until the Brookover trial was
over—because, in the first place, Lois felt she could not take the wedding trip she wanted to take until the trial was over; but also because,
cynically and realistically viewed, they had to face the fact that marriage to Lois, in the midst of the publicity the Brookover trial would
generate, could damage Peavy's chances of appointment to the Securities and Exchange Commission. Her father and brothers had taken up
their political cudgels for Peavy—it was a family matter, almost—and
they had some assurances from Washington that he was more seriously
under consideration than ever before. Dan Farnham's dream now was
for Lois to go to Washington as the wife of an SEC commissioner—and
as congresswoman after the 1980 election—and he had complained
irritably over dinner that the Brookover case stood in the way of more
important things.

In the bedroom, Lois sipped coffee into which Peavy had poured a
generous measure of Kahlúa. She was relaxed. She arched her back and
stretched. "My father is right, you know," she said. "Teejay's trial does
stand between us and everything. I'm sorry it does. I didn't plan that it
should."

"Couple of months it will be over and we can go on with things. We
can wait that long. Anyway, it's something worth doing, Lois. It really
is. I think that woman is innocent, and I think someday you'll look
back on your defense of her as one of the best things you ever did in
your professional life."

"Seriously?"

"Seriously. I'm not the only one who thinks so. I know a number of fellows downtown who do nothing year in and year out but tax work, or securities, or whatever, who can't understand exactly why you'd take a case like this but are willing to acknowledge, just the same, that they're more than a little envious of you. It's a real piece of lawyering —the kind of thing most of us thought we'd do, at least once in our lives, when we chose this profession. I have to admit to you, I couldn't do it. I've worked securities law so long, I couldn't try a case if my life depended on it."

"I've appreciated your advice on some of it. I'll be asking you for more."

"All I'm worried about, Lois, is that you protect your professional reputation very carefully in this trial. Look out for it."

"What makes you say that, Bob?"

"I said I think Teejay is innocent—but I mean innocent of the murder of Ben Mudge; I don't mean innocent generally. She was in that Lago Aguila fraud up to her neck, and she helped those bandits to rape that little corporation. She had to lie to do that. She'll lie now, to defend herself. Be careful about her."

"I know what you mean."

"Be careful she doesn't talk you into tearing up any more evidence and flushing it down the toilet."

"Pour me some more of that. There's an inconsistency in your telling me I'll be proud of my defense of Teejay Brookover and then telling me I've destroyed evidence."

"What I'm telling you is, don't forget to defend yourself while you're defending her. Don't forget you're involved in something potentially damaging."

"I want you to be proud of me, Bob. It's important to me."

"I am proud of you. The fellows downtown who are envious of you are even more envious of me. You may be the lawyer defending Teejay Brookover, but I'm the lawyer who sleeps with the lawyer who's defending Teejay Brookover."

"Do they know I'm a good lay?"

"I'm very circumspect. But I imagine they have the idea."

"I like that. I'd like that to be part of my reputation."

"I'm not sure it ought to be part of your *reputation*."

"I've liked myself better since I've learned to be a good lay."

"You were always good, Lois—since I've known anything about it, anyway."

"Haven't you seen me struggling? Don't tell me I'm not better than I was two years ago."

"Well . . . Sure. You're better."

"I've had to work at it. It's not something that came naturally to me.

I wasn't educated for it. I guess I was more than adequate for Mac John, and I know I was more than adequate with Bart. But it's only with you that—"

"Hey. You never shaved it for either of them, did you?"

"No. I never shaved it in my life before you asked me."

"It looks good. I've never seen anything quite so naked. Spread your legs a little."

"I thought I was beyond your making me blush."

"It's smooth. Have you shaved it again?"

"This morning. I'll have to do it every couple of days if it's not going to be bristly. How long do you want me to keep it this way?"

"For a while. Till we get some Polaroids taken, anyway."

"I really feel funny. It's like you can sort of hide behind your pubic hair. Without it . . ."

"What you're showing is beautiful, Lois. You're a handsome woman. You have everything it takes."

"My legs are good. My tits aren't. I guess my belly and butt are okay: flat and smooth. Pussy . . . Well, I don't know. What are the aesthetic standards for pussies, shaved and unshaved?"

"I haven't the faintest idea. What are the aesthetic standards for cocks? Is mine good?"

"I never thought of it as beautiful. Formidable maybe . . ."

"It's functional."

"Okay. Form follows function. By that standard it's beautiful. And I guess pussy form follows pussy function, too. There's your aesthetics of genitalia."

"Spread a little more, Lois. C'mon, spread. That's it. That's good."

"This has always been one of the hardest things for me: just to give you a show when you're sitting apart from me. And it's one of the things you like most. You love it, don't you? It gives you some kind of sense of power over me."

"No. Sense of power . . . ? No. But—to see polished, self-assured Lois Farnham Hughes sitting like that . . . Jesus! I like that. I like that very much."

"It makes me something other than the polished, self-assured lady lawyer, doesn't it? *I* like that. I like to escape my definition."

"I'm going to watch some of that trial. The most erotic woman in the courtroom will be the one stalking up and down in front of the jury, telling them what's what, not the one on trial. I like that."

"So do I."

"I love you very much, Lois."

"I love you, Bob. You're the best thing that's ever happened to me. You and I. We're going to put it all together, aren't we?"

"We're all going to have what we want. All of us."

XXIX

1977

Lying facedown on her bed, Teejay heard the key turn in the lock. She heard the apartment door open. She heard the rattle of the paper bags in Kevin's arms. He opened the refrigerator. She could hear him unloading his bags, popping jars or cans down on the countertop, putting his steaks (she was sure he had bought steaks) in the refrigerator—moving around the kitchen with a happy enthusiasm she could hear in the quickness of his steps. He had brought a bottle of wine, too, she could be sure. He was back in her apartment, where he had not been for months, and they were going to have dinner together, and he was happy.

"You know," she said to him in the doorway to the kitchen, "you really should have told me to go to hell."

He glanced shortly at her from the sink where he was washing a head of lettuce. "Not much chance of that, was there?" he said.

She came in the kitchen and opened a cabinet for a bottle of Scotch. "Want a drink? I had no right to call you."

"You always have the right to call me, Tommy Jo. Don't we have that understood yet?"

She splashed Scotch into two glasses and opened the refrigerator for ice cubes. "You're the best friend I ever had," she told him.

"Sure," he said.

He was taller than Jim Rush. His shoulders were broader, his arms were more muscular, and he was tanned. He wore a golf shirt and a pair of slacks, and he looked in fact as if she had called him in from a golf course. He wrinkled his nose over the Scotch. It was not his choice of whiskey, but it was what she had.

She sat on one of her kitchen chairs and guarded her glass in both hands wrapped around it. She was wearing shorts—cut-off blue jeans— and a white T-shirt, and she had tied her hair back. Her eyes were swollen. She had been crying. "I want you to stay with me," she said to Kevin. "All night. I want you to sleep with me."

He shook his head.

"Well, you can sleep in the same bed with me, dammit. If you don't want anything, you don't have to take it."

"I'm not sure I could manage that," he said.

"Anything you want, Kevin," she said. "Anytime. Don't we have that understood yet?"

"Maybe someday," he said. "I'm beginning to think somethin' might work out for us yet."

"It's the one thing I'm not very smart about, isn't it?"

He looked up from his head of lettuce, which he was now cutting into wooden bowls. "You said it, I didn't."

She had called. Jim's wife had actually called, hysterical, and shrieked across the telephone line that she, Teejay, was destroying Jim's career, spoiling his marriage, ruining his life. He came to the apartment a little while later and said his wife had told him to come, to talk it out with Teejay, to settle things one way or another. He had alternatives, he admitted. He could have a divorce. It was not out of the question.

"It's such a cliché," Teejay had said to him. "There is nothing different or original two people—three people—can say or do in a situation like this. We're trapped in a cliché."

He had sat in her kitchen, on one of her chrome-and-vinyl chairs, in one of his dark blue, pinstriped, three-piece suits, with vest unbuttoned and collar and tie loose, his shoulders slack, his face stricken with tension and defeat. He said his wife would sue for divorce on grounds of adultery and would name Teejay.

"I'm not particularly vulnerable, Jim," she had said. "And maybe you're not as vulnerable as you think."

"I'm not sure my firm would let me stay. . . ."

"It all depends on what you want and how much you want it, Jim," she had said to him quietly. "I love you. If you want to, you can move in here with me tonight, and I'll help you all I can with whatever happens. If you want me, I'll make you the best wife any man ever had. . . ."

"Is that the right kind of wine?" Kevin asked. She was turning the bottle in her hand. "You've got so you know a lot about wine."

Teejay nodded. "I've had a good teacher lately."

Kevin glanced at her scornfully, then looked back to the salad he was tossing.

"Where've you been?" she asked him. "I hadn't heard from you for a long time."

"You knew where to find me."

"You know where to find me, too."

"I knew what you were doin'," he said. "I kept an eye on you, all the time. I've been around. New York . . . Chicago."

"You doing okay?"

He nodded. "You know me. I'm small-time. But I'm doing all right. I've even been to Africa since you saw me. James O. Hedwig even has a passport."

"What in the world were you doing in Africa? Anyway, where in Africa?"

Kevin put their two bowls of tossed salad on the table and he pulled out a chair and sat across the table from her. "You know what a Schmeisser is?" he asked. He folded his arms on the tabletop and leaned over them toward her. "It's a mean, ugly machine pistol the Germans used in World War Two. In Africa there's a mean, ugly man who'll pay a thousand dollars apiece for them—Generalissimo President Kwumbwabwe. All his police carry them.

"I knew where one could be had—from a gun dealer here in Houston. It's strictly illegal to own one in this country and he was anxious to be rid of it. I bought this one for five hundred dollars and took it to Abidjan. The generalissimo's agent, fellow named Natubi, met me there, and I made him believe I knew where a thousand Schmeissers could be had. The generalissimo's short of hard cash, so he wanted to work out some kind of deal so he could pay for the thousand Schmeissers—a million dollars' worth—with peanuts and cotton. I said I thought somethin' like that could maybe be arranged. Anyway, he paid me ten thousand dollars for the one Schmeisser I could deliver. He didn't know that was what he was doin', but that's how it worked out."

"You're lucky you brought your head home," said Teejay grimly.

Kevin smiled. "Natubi was a smart and careful fellow. He was bein' so careful to make sure Generalissimo President Kwumbwabwe didn't get ripped off for his million dollars that he let the ten thousand slip out of his hands like a wet wiggly worm. He almost begged me to take it. He probably hasn't figured it out yet."

"That's not small-time stuff, Kevin," she said. "That's strictly big-time—and dangerous."

He shook his head. "I'm small-time, and that's where my advantage was, what made it a sure thing. It never crossed Natubi's mind that I'd come to Abidjan to take him for ten thousand dollars. He wasn't on guard against that."

"I'll say one thing for you: You've always had guts. You've never been afraid to take a chance."

"Neither have you," he said. "But this Rush guy you were mixed up with was. Wasn't he?"

She nodded. "Part of his problem was he's afraid I'm in trouble."

"What kind of trouble, Tommy Jo?"

Teejay focused on nothing in the center of the table between them. "I'm involved in a very big deal," she said dully. "As a lawyer. If it works out, I'm going to make a lot of money. Big-time money. If it doesn't . . . I could actually wind up in jail. I mean—I'm talking about a quarter of a million dollars or more, if the deal works out; and, on the other side, I could find myself serving a year in a federal reformatory."

Kevin shook his head. "I don't believe it," he said.

She had taken an instant dislike to the man who'd faced her across her desk three weeks ago. She did not like his light green leisure suit. She did not like the pink tint in his large silver-framed eyeglasses. He was bald, fifty years old, ruddy, and winded. His name was Saunders, and he held title to a hundred and fifty acres squarely in the center of the Lago Aguila subdivision—land he had acquired virtually by theft.

To open the subdivision required some two thousand acres. The two thousand acres were in thirty-one separate tracts, ranging in size from a six-hundred-fifty-acre farm to a string of lots along a highway, one-half acre each. The method of acquiring this land was to obtain options first; then, if—and only if—enough of the land could be brought under option to make the subdivision feasible, the options would be exercised and the land actually purchased. If any significant number of the land-owners held out, the project could be dropped, and all the promoters would lose was the money paid for the options—typically less than one percent of the agreed purchase price.

The option agents acquired the options in their own names, to defer as long as possible the day when the landowners would realize that a major subdivision was being developed on their land. Roberto Luiz obtained from Dorothea Pear the option on her six-hundred-fifty-acre farm for $1000—telling her he was acting for a Houston automobile dealer who was thinking of buying a country home and raising horses. Harry Gottschalk took the options on two adjoining farms of sixty-five and eighty-five acres each, telling the owners that as a real-estate agent —which he in fact was—he wanted to open a small subdivision, of a few lots, for homes for retired people. Teejay herself took the option on a house and lot. She told the man and wife who owned it that she was an attorney acting for a client who wanted to buy the place, who had forbidden her to say who he was. She had to agree to pay almost twice the market value of the house and lot, but she did agree; it was a piece of land important to the subdivision.

Of the twenty-nine options obtained, Luiz got sixteen, Gottschalk got four, Teejay got one, and the remaining eight were obtained by John Saunders.

By the first of May it was apparent that enough options had been obtained to make the subdivision feasible. By May 15, Lago Aguila, Incorporated, had enough capital to buy the land—$2 million invested in its stock by Futures Dynamic, Incorporated, plus $3 million more which Futures had borrowed on the security of its patents and other assets and passed on to Lago Aguila as a loan. The option agents assigned to the Lago Aguila corporation the options they had taken in their own names, and Lago Aguila began to exercise the options. By the end of May, Lago Aguila, Incorporated, owned almost eighteen hundred acres.

But John Saunders had exercised one of his options himself. It was squarely in the middle of the subdivision: a farm of approximately one hundred fifty acres. He had taken the option to purchase the tract, called the Rummy farm, for $215,000; and instead of assigning the option to Lago Aguila, he had borrowed the money and bought the land himself.

"There's a word for this," Teejay told him sharply in her office. "The word is embezzlement."

Saunders shook his head jerkily. "No. You aren't going to pressure me with talk like that. I'm not scared in the least. You think you want to charge me with embezzlement? Go ahead. Try it. I'm betting you won't. I'm betting I'll make you wish you hadn't if you do."

"Look," she said impatiently. "When you took the option to the Rummy farm, who were you working for?"

Saunders grinned. "That's a good question, isn't it? So far as I'm concerned, I was working for Ben Mudge. Who's he want to say I was working for?"

"What'd you pay for the option?"

"Ummm . . . Two thousand, I believe."

"Whose two thousand?"

Saunders grinned again. "Look, we don't have to play games. Ben Mudge saw to it I had money to pay for the options. Lago Aguila, Incorporated, provided the money."

"Then Lago Aguila owned the option."

Saunders shook his head. "No."

"Why not?"

"Because when I went to work for Ben, to get him some of these options he wanted, he told me I could do exactly what I did: I could hold out one option, exercise it myself, sell the land to Lago Aguila for a profit, and so be paid for my work. You don't think I was working this game of yours for ten dollars an hour, do you?"

"Is that what you were paid for your time as an option agent?"

"That's right, and I put in a bill for fifty-five hours—five hundred and fifty dollars. What are you billing for, lawyer lady? Don't tell me you're mixed up in this game for a hundred an hour or whatever you bill. You got a piece somehow. Bobo Luiz has got a piece some way. Harry Gottschalk has got a piece. And I've got mine. I've got the Rummy farm, which I expect your little company to buy for three hundred thousand. That's my piece—eighty-five thousand. You better get Ben to explain it all to you."

"He *has* explained it all—and not in this way, either."

"What's he want?" Saunders asked suspiciously.

"He wants his land."

"For how much?"

"For what the option said. For what you paid for it."

"Bullshit."

"He told me to sue you."

Saunders shook his head so jerkily it set his jowls flapping. "He'll never sue me. You tell him for me that he has forty-eight hours to buy the Rummy farm for three hundred thousand. After that it's three hundred fifteen. And you take a lesson from me, young lady. If you're going to deal with Ben Mudge, deal the way I do. Remember, you can't believe a word he says. Get yours and make him pay for it. Otherwise you'll wind up on the short end of the stick."

A few days later, Mudge paid. "There is, of course, not a single word of truth in what he says; but one cannot, in the midst of an enterprise of this magnitude, allow oneself to be frustrated by eighty-five thousand dollars. I would rather pay him."

Glencoe was in Mudge's office that Sunday morning. "Dammit, Ben," he complained. "We're being held up, that's all."

"Held up is what I do not wish to be," said Mudge. "I do not wish to be held up in platting the subdivision."

"We can sue, even after we pay what Saunders demands."

Mudge shook his head. "No. Miss Brookover will advise you, as any lawyer will, that the lawsuit would degenerate into a courtroom charade in which John Saunders would testify one way and I would testify another, about a conversation to which supposedly only the two of us were witnesses; and in the end, after days of anguish, a jury would be left with the question of which of us to believe—which would depend on which of us, forensically, was the better witness. I do not choose to take part in that."

"As soon as the suit was filed," Glencoe mused, "the word would be about that you're behind Lago Aguila."

"Precisely," said Mudge.

Jim Rush had been frightened by this story, which she told him over late-afternoon drinks at the Pound Sterling. "He let Saunders take him for eighty-five thousand, Teejay, rather than face him in court. Saunders knew he could do that to him."

"Saunders is a creep," she said.

"Who picked him? Anyway, you know something else? It's not Mudge's money Saunders got away with; it's the stockholders', plus maybe the investors in Twelve-Twenty. Honey, you're mixed up with some evil people."

Mudge explained it differently, over coffee served in his office at 3:00 A.M. the following Saturday morning. "We are the victims of a theft. We must not allow that to divert us from our purpose."

They were reviewing her draft of the prospectus for lots at Lago Aguila. She had explained to Mudge and Luiz that the Federal Land Sales Full Disclosure Act required exact statements of all the pertinent facts about the lots in the subdivision.

"Yes, of course," Mudge said. "You may not have heard this, Miss Brookover, but I was in Washington when this legislation was being drafted, and I conferred repeatedly with several congressmen, advising them on various aspects of the Act. I am very familiar with its requirements."

Mudge, at three in the morning, was still crisply dressed, still alert, comfortable with the hour and unconscious that anyone else was tired and impatient to break off the meeting. Luiz, always a taciturn man, had long since shed his coat, had drunk several shots of Mudge's whiskey, and now sipped hungrily of the hot black coffee Gottschalk had brewed somewhere in the offices. Luiz was thin and beak-nosed, dark, straight, hard. His intense dark eyes spoke for him sometimes, and now they expressed scornful tolerance and complete skepticism of Mudge's statement about his part in the drafting of the federal act.

Teejay was concerned about certain statements that were being put into the prospectus for the lots:

> The topography of the land at Lago Aguila—sloping, lightly wooded for the most part—assures adequate natural drainage. Each lot is suitable for building without the necessity of any grading or the laying of any tile to facilitate the runoff of surface water.
>
> Percolation tests on each lot have demonstrated that the soil is suitable for septic tanks with leaching beds. The necessary permits from the local health authorities will be readily obtained.
>
> By the end of 1977 construction will be well under way on the Olympic-size heated swimming pool that will be accessible to all lot owners, their families, and guests. The pool will be adjacent to a bathhouse, with saunas, which will be under construction by the end of 1977. These facilities, which will be the focus of recreational activity for many residents of Lago Aguila, will be ready for use by the beginning of the second quarter of 1978.

"I've seen water standing in low places on some of the acreage," she said. She was tired. Her skirt was wrinkled under her and felt as though she were sitting on three or four electric cords. Her back hurt. She sounded more petulant than she had intended. "How can we say no grading or tile will be necessary to make each lot suitable for building?"

"What we are saying in the prospectus and property report will be true when we have finished grading the roads and streets through the subdivision, Miss Brookover," said Mudge.

"Then shouldn't we say in the prospectus and property report that the land will be drained when the roads and streets are graded?" Teejay asked.

"That would impede the sale of the lots," said Mudge firmly. "You cannot sell lots to people if you admit in advance that water stands on them when it rains."

"But if that's the fact—"

"It will not be the fact when the roads and streets are graded. We are entitled, in our statements, to describe things as they will be when the subdivision opens. We do not have to describe them as they are now, before the work is done."

"I'm sorry, Mr. Mudge, but that isn't the law. The facts must be stated as they are, not as they will be. If the facts disclose a defect in the property, you can promise to correct it; but the fact of the defect must be stated."

"I worked on the drafting of this law, Miss Brookover."

Teejay sighed and rubbed her eyes. "Even so . . ."

"What difference does it make?" Luiz asked. His speech was faintly accented. His R's rolled up from his throat. "By the time the people see the lots, the grading will have been done, the water will be draining away nicely, and nobody will know it used to stand in the low places. Isn't that what counts?"

"In other words, if everything works out . . ."

"People want to know what they are buying," said Luiz. "They don't need to know what it once was."

Teejay tapped the typed paper on her lap with an impatient finger. "What about these percolation tests? I didn't know we'd run one on every lot."

"We've run them on a hundred lots," said Gottschalk.

"A hundred isn't five thousand," said Teejay. "Our property report says we've run the test on 'each lot.'"

"It is possible, Miss Brookover," said Mudge, "to conduct careful engineering studies, identify the types of soils that exist over the entire acreage of the subdivision, and then run percolation tests on one hundred lots that will accurately measure the suitability for private sewage-disposal systems of all the lots in the subdivision."

"Why doesn't the prospectus say that, then?"

"We can tie ourselves up in legalisms, Miss Brookover, and seriously impede the sale of lots. You are a very careful lawyer, and I appreciate that. But you lack experience in organizing and promoting real-estate enterprises."

Teejay stared dully at the documents in her lap. The papers had been typed in her office the preceding afternoon, from specifications provided by Luiz. Mudge had arrived at the airport at eleven and had come to his office. Teejay and Luiz had been waiting for him.

She wondered when Benjamin Mudge slept, when he took recreation, and what he did to relax—if anything. She had met with him at night, on Saturdays, on Sundays—rarely, in fact, during what might be called regular business hours. He telephoned at any hour. She took off, she knew, on planes that left Houston at four or five in the morning, and he seemed regularly to arrive on flights that came in at midnight or after. She could find no reason in his work hours and certainly no break in them. Yet he was always fresh and energetic. His shirts were never wilted. His neckties were never loose. His trousers were always creased. He never removed his jacket.

He had an awesome memory for the facts and figures of his business. ("I am distressed by the price we have had to pay for the Nathansen lot. There are only 5.6 acres there, and we paid $24,500; that is $4375 per acre; and we purchased the O'Donnell land for the Galena center last year for $24,000, which was 6.2 acres, and that is about $3870 per acre.") His memory extended to the smallest details. ("I am curious, Roberto, as to why we are paying $1121 for this sign we erected on the highway at Lago Aguila. The one we erected for the Chambers County project last year was a lovely sign—in fact, I think handsomer than this one—and we paid only $850 for it.")

Glencoe, who had not worked this closely with him before, ventured to contradict him a few times. ("I think your figure is off a little, Ben. As I recall, we laid about eight hundred linear feet of that pipe." "Tom, the figure is seven hundred and forty-two linear feet. If you will check, you will find so; and you will find, too, we were given an excellent price.")

He let no detail go past unnoticed. ("These maps you are framing for the sales offices should have glass over them; otherwise people will make pencil marks on the maps.") He studied every word of every document Teejay prepared. ("Are you quite certain, Miss Brookover, that 'T' was the middle initial of Mrs. Pear's late husband? It is my impression it was 'D'—for David.") He marked every draft extensively, with tiny, neat pencil marks—inserting and deleting commas, making two sentences one by deleting a period and inserting a semicolon, changing the syllable at which a word was broken at the end of a typed line. Nothing was insufficiently important to be discussed. ("How do you divide the word 'corporation'? 'Corpor-ation' or 'corpo-ration'? I think the latter is correct, but it looks odd, does it not? When this is printed, we want the word divided the better way. Which is better, do you think?")

Teejay was concerned about Section 1703, Title 15, United States Code. Mudge one day recited it to her:

" 'It shall be unlawful for any developer or agent, directly or indirectly, to make use of any means or instruments of transportation or communication in interstate commerce, or of the mails—

" '(1) To sell or lease any lot in any subdivision unless a statement of record with respect to such lot is in effect in accordance with Section 1706 of this Title and a printed property report, meeting the requirements of Section 1707 of this Title, is furnished to the purchaser in advance of the signing of any contract or agreement for sale or lease by the purchaser; and

" '(2) In selling or leasing, or offering to sell or lease, any lot in a subdivision—

" '(A) To employ any device, scheme, or artifice to defraud, or

" '(B) To obtain money or property by means of a material misrepresentation with respect to any information included in the statement of record or the property report or with respect to any other information pertinent to the lot or the subdivision and upon which the purchaser relies, or

" '(C) To engage in any transaction, practice, or course of business which operates or would operate as a fraud or deceit upon a purchaser.'

"All right, Miss Brookover? You see, I do know something about the law."

There would have been no point in telling him that memorizing a section of statute and understanding the law were entirely different things.

Anyway, he used the section as a weapon against her. "The law talks about 'fraud' and 'deceit' and 'misrepresentation,' Miss Brookover. Now, just where in what we are doing are we perpetrating a fraud, do you think?"

When she left that meeting, at 4:00 A.M., she found in the back seat of her car a case of Glenlivet and two cases of Beaujolais Villages, 1976.

"I don't think I can put up with the idea of you goin' to jail. Ah don't think I can stand it," Kevin said angrily.

She had helped him with the steaks, which were on plates before them in the kitchen. The wine was open. He was banging the bottom of a salad-dressing bottle over his salad.

"I mean, as far as I'm concerned it's just out of the question. It's a stupid law anyway, but the idea of you doin' time is more than I can handle. Ah can get you out of the country, Tommy Jo. Mexico . . . Maybe someplace else. . . . It can be done. I won't see you put away. I just won't stand for that. I know what it is; you don't. You're not goin' to any reformatory."

"Maybe I've exaggerated," Teejay said. "Maybe I'm just nervous about it. The whole deal is beginning to come unstuck, and I'm worried."

"It didn't help to have this Rush fellow chicken out on you right now."

"I had no right to call you."

"You had no right not to."

As always when he was disturbed, Kevin ate his meal hungrily, hurriedly. For herself, when she was upset she usually could not eat. For Kevin, anxiety offered an impetus to eat more. It was from his origins, where not eating was vaguely immoral. For her it had been the same, but somehow over the years she had changed; more than he, she had dropped the detritus of her origins.

"I'm afraid you've made a mistake, Tommy Jo," he said soberly. "I suppose everybody does, sooner or later. Ah sure did. Maybe you let this idea you could get rich all of a sudden get the better of your good judgment."

"You put it too simply," she said blankly.

"On the other hand, there's nothin' good that's accomplished without pain and worry. Maybe it's not so bad."

"All I've done is fudged a little," she said.

Kevin chuckled. "That's all I've ever done," he said.

They took their coffee to the living room and put the cups on TV trays. He had distracted her by telling her about Abidjan and his meetings there to sell the Schmeisser machine pistol. She was not sure he was telling the truth entirely. It made no difference. He had tried to give her some ease, and if he had lied to do it, anyway his motive had been good. She lay back in the corner of the couch, with her coffee cup resting on her chest, and looked at Kevin sitting stiff-backed, rigid with thoughts he wanted to express and was withholding.

"Will you stay?" she asked quietly.

"You let that Rush fellow in your pants, didn't you?" he asked. He did not look at her. "Didn't you?"

"Yes."

"And some others, I expect," he said.

"Remember the man I lived with when I was in law school? He was the only other one."

Kevin glanced at her. "Is that the truth?"

"I swear it."

Kevin slumped, and he fixed his eyes on the coffee in his cup. "If it had been me," he said, "I'd never have let you get in this trouble."

"You couldn't have stopped me."

He shot her another glance, scornful. "Ah'd 've tried."

Teejay smiled warmly. "You're an old-fashioned man, Kevin. You'd take care of your woman."

"What can I do for you, Tommy Jo?" he demanded abruptly, in a shrill, urgent voice.

"Nothing, I'm afraid," she said. "It will probably work out."

"I'm not gonna stay here tonight," he said through clenched teeth. "I'm not gonna sleep in your bed and not touch you, and I'm not gonna touch you. Not now, anyway. I could've, times past, before it got to you didn't need any part of me. But now . . . Not now. That part of life is not that big a deal. I want something more from you. I want you to get something more from me. *Has it ever made any sense, Tommy Jo?*"

"It always has, and it makes more all the time," she whispered.

XXX

1977

Tom Glencoe slapped a paper on Teejay's desk. "Look at that," he said. He was short of breath, and for a moment he stood facing her, his mouth open, his body heaving; then he strode to the window, parted the curtains, and stood staring nervously down on Louisiana Street, with his back to her. "I just scribbled that out. As a summary. Some of the figures aren't exact. But look at it!"

She looked. The paper was covered with his handwriting and figures.

"You see?" he said. "We're half a million dollars short right now. In another two months . . ." He shrugged.

"Have you talked to Mudge?" she asked.

"He just smiles."

"The banks, then," she suggested.

Glencoe shook his head as he turned away from the window and returned to the chair facing her desk. He sat down. "We've gone about as far as we can with banks."

"The land is worth almost eight million dollars," Teejay said.

"It's not worth that. That's what we paid for it. We've borrowed as much on the land as the banks are willing to lend. I'm sure of it. They went four million on the acreage. I was surprised they went that far.

LAGO AGUILA, INC.

Condition December 20, 1977

To acquisition of 1838 acres	$ 7,747,170
To surveying and engineering	411,000
To grading and paving (so far)	1,348,718
To water lines and hydrants	544,988
To advertising and promotion	78,210
To miscellaneous	82,421
Total outlay	$10,212,507
From capital (Futures stock purchase)	2,000,000
From Futures loan, secured by debentures	3,000,000
From bank borrowing (secured by mortgages)	4,000,000
From sale of lots	1,328,000
	$10,328,000
On hand	$115,493
Interest due banks December 31	$180,000
Interest due Futures Dynamic on debentures	155,000
Additional paving cost to be incurred (est.)	318,000
Known immediate obligations	$653,000

Anyway, we're going to owe a hundred and eighty thousand dollars interest on December thirty-first, and if we default on that—"

"Not to mention the interest on the Futures debentures," she said.

He sighed loudly. "Yes. If Lago Aguila doesn't pay the hundred and fifty-five thousand it will owe Futures Dynamic on December thirty-first, then I'm not sure how Futures can pay the bank the interest on the three-million-dollar loan that's secured by the Harvey patents."

"In other words, we're facing insolvency in both corporations."

"Exactly."

Teejay pressed her temples and closed her eyes. "There is only one answer to it," she said. "We have to sell some lots. We've sold a hundred sixty-some; we've got to sell another two or three hundred. Just that many—even if we have to sell some of them below the listed price—will get us over the hump. Then in the spring—"

"Then in the spring the subdivision will begin to sell out," said Glencoe. "So I hear."

"Well? Isn't that the answer? If we can move a few lots—"

"How can you sell lots with the goddamn water standing out there?" Glencoe asked. "You know what that goddamn Luiz did last week? He took a couple around the subdivision, and by driving just the right roads he kept them away from the water. They bought a lot.

They found out about the water, called a lawyer, and exercised their right to rescind. We had to refund every damn dime they paid us, and then Luiz had the gall to argue he ought to have his commission on the sale of a lot—because he did, after all, sell one. If those people talk much . . . If word gets around that we pull stunts like that, we won't sell ten more lots."

"We've got to talk to Mudge," said Teejay.

"He's in New York. I don't know when he'll be back."

Mudge returned Sunday, December 24. Glencoe picked him up at the airport and brought him to Teejay's office, late in the afternoon, Christmas Eve.

"I am pleased to be able to say," Mudge pronounced—he was seated comfortably in the leather chair facing Teejay's desk, looking around the office, appraising her furnishings—"that I have an abiding faith in God. My mother—may the Lord bless her soul—taught me that from my very earliest years, and I have had many occasions in life, many, to be grateful to her for it. At this season of the year, I recall her memory. I recall those Christmases when I was a child. It brings tears to my eyes."

"Ben, I . . ." Glencoe faltered. "Are you aware of how deeply we're in trouble with Lago?"

"No. I have been gradually withdrawing from that," Mudge said. "I put the series of transactions together, but I have intended all along to withdraw from the enterprise once it is well established and leave it to you to sell the lots and accumulate the revenues."

"We've sold one hundred and sixty-six lots, Ben. We haven't sold one in a week. We're a half-million dollars short of the cash necessary to meet interest and other obligations that are coming due as of the end of the year. If we default on the interest we owe the banks . . ."

"You won't default. How could you default?"

Glencoe's mouth stood open. "Ben . . ." He was short of breath again. "When you don't have the cash to meet an obligation, you default."

"Tom . . ." said Mudge, lowering his chin, burying it in the layers of fat shoved up when they met his chest. He shook his head. "How could you be cash-poor? You are president of a corporation that has opened one of the most attractive and potentially profitable subdivisions that has been developed in this country in many years. I am satisfied in my mind that it will reap a handsome profit for everyone concerned."

"Look at this," said Glencoe. He handed Mudge the same paper he had shown Teejay four days before.

Mudge, with his chin down and the corners of his mouth turning down, studied the figures Glencoe had written with a ballpoint pen. He shook his head. "I don't understand why grading and paving is costing one and two-thirds million," he said. "It was my distinct impression that work could be completed for under a million and a half."

"We have to pay it whether you understand it or not," said Glencoe. "Anyway, if it cost two hundred thousand less than it did, we'd still be short of the money we need to meet our interest payments. Goddammit, we're gonna *default*, Ben—unless we come up with some money within the next week."

Mudge continued to stare at the figures on Glencoe's sheet. He took a mechanical pencil from his inside jacket pocket and began to write figures and notes. "Do you have any idea," he asked, "why you are unable to sell lots any more readily than appears to have been the case?"

Glencoe, gasping silently, looked weakly to Teejay.

"It would help," she said, "if we didn't have two hundred lots under water."

Mudge frowned. "If this grading had been done properly," he said, tapping his pencil on Glencoe's paper, "we wouldn't have two hundred lots under water."

Glencoe closed his eyes and shook his head. "That's not so, Ben. Look at the topographical map."

Mudge looked up from the paper and smiled. "Tom," he said, "if there is one thing I know, it is land development. When all the roads in the subdivision are graded according to the plan I approved, all surface water will flow along the edges of the road embankments and drain into Murphy Creek."

Glencoe sighed and continued to shake his head. "Even if that's true—and I don't think it is—the remaining grading can't be done until we come up with the money to pay for it."

Mudge leaned back comfortably in his chair and clasped his hands over his belly, allowing Glencoe's paper to slip to the floor. "We have raised more than ten million dollars to finance this enterprise," he said. "I am sure we can raise half a million more—or whatever it takes to see us through the brief period before the lots begin to sell very readily."

"Where?" Glencoe asked. "Where's it going to come from?"

Mudge shrugged condescendingly. "Banks," he said.

"No," said Glencoe. "I've talked to them already. We paid too much for the land. We've borrowed as much on it as we can."

"You should have let me talk to the banks."

"You were in New York. Anyway, I did talk to them, and we can't get the money from them. Lago Aguila has no more credit."

"More could be arranged if we had time," said Mudge calmly. He took out a cigar and lowered his big heavy-lidded eyes to the unwrapping, the cutting, the lighting. "I am sure we can raise the half-million through Futures Dynamic, Incorporated. It can borrow what is necessary on a short-term basis and purchase some more Lago Aguila debentures."

"No," said Glencoe. "The banks won't do it. I'm telling you, Ben, both corporations are on the verge of insolvency."

Pursing his huge lips around the cigar, Mudge worked his cheeks and tongue and pulled flame into the tobacco. "No . . ." he said. "No. . . . A company that owns almost two thousand acres of the finest second-home subdivision in Texas is not on the verge of insolvency."

"Well, where is the money going to come from?" Glencoe asked weakly.

"We will simply sell some lots," said Mudge.

"Fifty or sixty lots between Christmas and New Year's?"

"I am thinking of two hundred lots, maybe two hundred fifty," said Mudge, puffing intently. "I believe I can obtain the cooperation of my associates in Twelve-Twenty."

"You mean your investors would put in another two million?" Glencoe asked. Teejay could hear in his voice that he was anxious to believe his problem had just been solved; yet, he was skeptical. For herself, she was more skeptical than optimistic.

"No," said Mudge. "Very obviously I can't ask my associates to put another two million dollars where the banks won't put it. On the other hand, I could probably convince them that they should buy two hundred fifty lots at, say, three thousand dollars apiece. That will provide you with seven hundred fifty thousand dollars, which will pay the obligations now coming due and leave you with some funds on hand to tide you over until the lots begin to sell rapidly."

Glencoe sat heavy and silent for a moment, looking at Mudge with stricken eyes. "Ben," he said thinly, "we've been able to get an average of eight thousand apiece for lots. The asking price really isn't out of line. I . . ."

Mudge blew a thin, solid stream of cigar smoke toward the floor. "You have a little more than ten million dollars invested in five thousand lots," he said. "They have cost the corporation a little more than two thousand dollars apiece. My associates will pay one hundred fifty percent. That will provide the cash to get you over a cash-flow crisis. It is generous, Tom."

"I understand it now," Teejay said to Kevin that evening. He was with her in her apartment, where he had agreed to stay through Christmas Day because she had protested she could not endure the holiday alone. "He may not even have any associates. Twelve-Twenty may be Mudge and no one else. Anyway, he's taking two hundred fifty lots. If he sells them for eight thousand apiece, he has a profit of one million, two hundred fifty thousand. If he unloads them for as little as six thousand apiece, he'll make seven hundred fifty thousand.

"And it's going to happen again. Lago Aguila will be short of cash again in a month, and again the month after that. If Mudge and his so-called associates pick up a thousand of the lots at three thousand apiece and sell them for, say, seventy-five hundred each, their profit on the sales could be four and a half million. After you take away the two million they invested, they still have a two-point-five-million-dollar profit. If they pick up more than a thousand of the lots, they'll make even more. It's a scam like you never heard of."

Kevin, relaxed and sleepy on her couch, shook his head. "Maybe the lots won't sell. After all, part of the land is under water."

"I think Mudge is right. It can be drained. He doesn't want it to be drained too fast. As long as the company is short of cash, he can keep on picking up lots for less than half-price. He's going to *keep* it short, intentionally."

"The lots will get harder and harder to sell, the longer the water lies there," Kevin said.

"He picked his lots; that's another thing," she said. "He picked choice lots. He stayed in the office with me after Glencoe left and showed me on the map which lots to make him deeds for. I tell you, Kevin, that was his plan from the start. If Lago Aguila goes broke, and if Futures does too, the subdivision will still be there: more than four thousand lots that are not under water, with streets and pipes in place. Mudge is going to wring the two companies out and pick up the better part of the subdivision cheap."

Kevin grinned. "You gotta give the man a certain amount of credit," he said lazily.

"Look. If he picked up two thousand lots at three thousand dollars . . ." She was standing, holding a glass of Scotch, wearing white ski pants and a white cashmere sweater. She was high atop her subject. "He'd have six million in the lots, plus his two-million original investment. That's eight. If he sold two thousand lots for as little as sixty-five hundred apiece, he'd walk away with five million profit. We've sold a lot of them for eight thousand apiece. If he could sell his for that, he'd make eight million. He talked about a forty-million-dollar subdivision, with a profit on the deal of maybe twenty-five million. That was his come-on. What he really had in mind was to pick up five to eight million—and maybe more—by investing and risking other people's money."

"Wait a minute, wait a minute," Kevin protested, twisting himself up out of the corner of the couch. "You told me Mudge and his associates own about a third of Futures Dynamic—"

"They own forty percent of it."

"All right. It's more to Mudge's advantage to have the subdivision a success, to make the twenty-five million. Assuming Lago Aguila pays its profit over one hundred percent to its parent corporation, Futures, and assuming Futures pays out the profit as dividends, Mudge and his friends pick up ten million."

"Not after the corporations pay corporate income tax," said Teejay. "I tell you, Kevin, he wants it to fail. He can make more that way. And it's surer."

Kevin shook his head. "I just think he's fixing it so he comes out with a profit either way. If it succeeds, he makes a profit; if it fails, he makes a profit. Smart man."

"Not so smart," said Teejay. "If Futures Dynamic is driven into bankruptcy, the stockholders will go to the SEC. Not only will they sue; they'll file criminal charges."

"Still smart," said Kevin. "It looks to me like he's set it up so *you* get sued, *you* get criminal charges filed against you—not him."

She shook her head vehemently. "Not with this little girl. If I'm sued, I'll bring him in. If I'm charged, I'll tell the United States district attorney exactly what Mudge's part in the game has been. He's not going to hide behind me."

Kevin still smiled. It was one of the very few times in all the years she had known him that she saw him drink enough to be loose and euphoric. He had brought his own whiskey—bourbon—and had been sipping at it all evening. "Maybe he thinks you're gonna let him," he said. "He gave you a nice present."

That was true. At the office that afternoon, after Glencoe left, Mudge had crushed his cigar carefully, until it ceased to smolder, and had sat in his chair, contemplating Teejay sitting behind her desk. He rolled his tongue around inside his cheek. "If it has seemed to you, Miss Brookover, that I have been insufficiently aware that you are a singularly attractive woman, let me assure you that I have always been aware of it."

"Thank you, Mr. Mudge," she had said quietly. She was full of thought—so full it drew her inward, so she was not fully aware of what he had said. He had paid her a compliment; that was as much as she had noticed.

"You're from Clayton County, I believe," he said.

"Originally," she said.

"I have been there several times."

"It's not a very attractive place," she said. "I don't recommend it."

"You are not going home for Christmas, then?"

She shook her head. Obviously she wasn't.

He was a heavy, pompous old man, dumped into her leather chair, from which he would rise only with strain; he sat there, decayed and ugly, making inconsequential conversation. She had begun to understand now that he meant to make his profit from the failure of Lago Aguila. That she and Glencoe and Luiz—not to mention the stockholders of Futures Dynamic—were bound to suffer did not trouble him. He rationalized it some way, obviously. He was insensitive. He was ego-centered. Yet there was about him, as he sat there, undeniably a decadent sort of charm: what had made it possible for him to do what he was doing, what had made it possible for him before, as she had heard. For all his aggressive amorality, he appealed in some clever, contrived way, and it was difficult not to be taken with him.

With his big, bulging blue eyes he looked down at his hands, and he nodded as if conceding something. "I had the good fortune," he said, "to be married to a woman who was unparalleled among the creatures of this earth—a jewel, a saint. She died the same week President Kennedy was assassinated. My two sons are successful men, but they live far from here, with their families. I was invited to both their homes for Christmas, but I did not feel I should go. Tonight I shall attend midnight services at one of the churches. I have done so every year for more than sixty-five years, without missing a year. I go to one church and another, sometimes with friends. I suppose you are dining with friends?"

Teejay nodded. "Yes," she said.

"Of course," he said. "Of course. If, however, you had been alone, I should have suggested you dine with me and accompany me to church."

"I appreciate the suggestion," she said dully.

For a moment once again he had sat motionless and looked at her. She was tired. She was impatient for him to leave. She was conscious that her tied-back red hair had escaped and that strands were loose over her ears and around her forehead. She was wearing a white blouse and a black skirt, with only a gold chain looped around her neck, hanging no pendant. The effect was severe, she knew. She had felt severe when she dressed to come to the office this afternoon, on this Sunday before Christmas.

They were alone in the office. It was quiet—as it never was in her offices during the week. The telephones were strangely dead; no lights blinked on any of the buttons. The street was quiet outside. There was a faint odor on the air: of an oil the cleaning woman had used to polish the wood of Teejay's desk, not anticipating she would be in the office again before Tuesday or Wednesday. The faintly sweet odor penetrated the sharp stench of the cigar Mudge had smoked. She could still see wisps of his smoke, hanging in the beam of light that rose from the shade over her desk lamp.

"A few men, in their lives," Mudge mumbled slowly, again nodding, "are privileged to be married to women who are almost perfect. My wife—her name was Carrie—was almost perfect. She was beautiful, intelligent, loving. . . . She was an innocent, Miss Brookover. If she had possessed your shrewdness, she would have been the perfect woman. In some ways you remind me of her."

It was not the truth. She knew it was not the truth. He glanced around hurriedly, as if moved by an abrupt thought; and he reached to the floor and found leaning against the chair a soft leather briefcase he had been carrying when he came in. "I have something for you, for Christmas," he said. He took a small package from the case. "I should appreciate it if you would open this here, before we leave. Then you can drop me at the Hyatt Regency, if you will, and I shall catch a cab from there."

Kevin reached for her hand. He held her hand and wrist close and squinted over the watch Mudge had given her. "That's worth five thousand if it's worth a nickel, Tommy Jo," he said.

It was a Piaget, set on a gold bracelet studded with diamonds. Mudge had stunned her with it. From the moment in the office when she tore open the paper and saw the Cartier box, she had been stricken fumbling and dumb. His motive mystified her. It frightened her.

"What do you think he wants?" Kevin asked now. He had not asked when he first saw it. "What's next?"

Teejay shook her head. She looked into her glass of Scotch, now almost empty, and a frown flickered over her face. "Nothing carnal, I assure you," she said. "Maybe it eases his conscience about what's going to happen to me."

"You're sure it's going to happen?"

"It is, for sure, unless the sale of lots at Lago Aguila takes off like a rocket. If everything works out—if the lots sell and we can pay all our obligations, including the debenture loans from Futures Dynamic, and if Futures makes a good profit too, so the stockholders will be happy with their deal—then I'll be off the hook and richer by a quarter of a million or so. If anything goes wrong, I'm going to lose everything I own, plus my license to practice law, and I may go to jail."

"I'm not gonna stand by and watch that happen," said Kevin.

XXXI

Another day out of jail. She had chosen to wear the tan, suedelike vest and pants, with the warm-colors print shirt, that she had been wearing the day she was arrested. They had been in a box in the jail property room for several months, but with her trial date coming she had sent them out to be cleaned and pressed, in the thought they might be appropriate for one of the days in the courtroom. She had combed out her hair. It always looked best lying around her shoulders with this outfit. She had put on a little pink lipstick. She even had time to brush some blush on her cheeks and darken her eyebrows slightly. Now, with her lips tight and grim, she watched the deputy loop a chain around her waist. One link went through another to close the loop; then he forced one handcuff through that oversize link. The handcuffs hung at her waist. The deputy seized one wrist and locked a cuff on it. She seized the other, firmly, and locked the other cuff more tightly. Teejay's hands were chained to her waist. She could raise them a few inches, no more.

"You think I'm safe?" she asked the deputy sarcastically.

"Okay, missy," the deputy said. She was a black woman: a sheriff's deputy, not a jail matron.

She led Teejay to the main gate out of the women's jail, then down the jail elevator to the basement garage. A car was waiting. A tall, pimply young deputy was waiting to drive. They put Teejay in the back seat, behind the screen, and both of them rode in front.

"I been a deputy six years," said the black woman, "and this is the *first* time I ever saw anybody get to go visit their lawyer in their lawyer's office. You got some clout with that judge, missy."

Dispirited by the shackles, Teejay slumped in the back seat, hardly heard what the woman said, and did not respond.

"Judge Spencer's order," the woman said to the driver, "is for me to stay there as long as it takes, all day like, maybe."

Judge Spencer had ordered the district attorney's office to provide defense counsel with, alternatively, an inspection of all documents taken from the home and offices of Benjamin Mudge, in the presence of the defendant, or copies of all such documents, made at the expense of the defendant, delivered to the office of defense counsel. Lois Hughes had asked for the copies. Then she had obtained from Judge Spencer an order requiring the sheriff to bring the defendant from the county jail to the office of defense counsel, on one or more days as might be required to enable the defendant as well as her counsel to examine the Mudge papers. It was an unusual order, which had been criticized around the courthouse. Teejay had taken some satisfaction in it. It was the first evidence that perhaps she had made a shrewd tactical decision in insisting that Norma Jean Spencer be her trial judge.

It was a short drive to the 1100 Milam Building, but the lights were against them in the heavy traffic of morning rush hour, and Teejay had time to look at the wet streets, a cool, misty morning. She would go on trial in only two weeks—on the Monday after Thanksgiving. She stared dully at the people hurrying along the streets. It had been eight months since she'd been on the streets, eight months since she had been able to walk anywhere. If she were convicted, it might be twenty years, maybe more. She had hurried in these streets on mornings like this for years, feeling harassed, feeling poor, often finding the streets ugly. They looked good now.

"Say, missy, you mind if I smoke one of your cigarettes?" the deputy asked. She was carrying two packs of Teejay's cigarettes. "Fact, I can light one for you if you want."

"Don't see how I can," Teejay mumbled.

"Girls do all the time," the deputy said cheerfully. "We know how. Put y' face up heah."

Teejay leaned forward until her face almost touched the heavy steel mesh that separated prisoners in the back from drivers in the front of the car. The woman pushed a cigarette through and between her lips, and she lighted it for her while Teejay held her face to the screen. Leaning back, Teejay found that if she hunched over her hands, she could pull the chain up just far enough so she could reach her cigarette. She could smoke, and that eased her a little.

"If you didn't kill that old fella, you been in jail a long time for nothin', haven't ya?"

Teejay nodded. "A long time."

"That always bothers me," said the deputy. "Y' evah think on it? There oughta be some way people wouldn't have to sit in jail. . . ." She shook her head. "Some different way of doin'."

At 1100 Milam the driver stopped at the curb, and the deputy unlocked and opened the back door. She beckoned Teejay out, and, taking her firmly by the arm, she led her across the sidewalk and into the building, through the unyielding stares of the startled rush-hour crowd. She took her up the escalator and then into an elevator. Teejay was faint. Her legs were weak. Her humiliation was total and painful.

Lois spared her, at least, the reception room and a walk through the corridors at Childreth, McLennon & Brady. She was waiting when the elevator stopped, and she led them down an outside corridor and in through a back door, to a conference room. There Earl Lansing was waiting, and there the conference table was piled with boxes of files. Lois explained to the deputy that she could sit in a chair just outside the conference room, from which she could see both doors. The deputy assented to that arrangement. She took out her key and unlocked Teejay's handcuffs. She left the handcuffs and the waist chain conspicuously on the credenza beside the coffee urn.

Teejay sank into a chair at the conference table, put her elbows on the table and her face down in her clasped hands, and held her breath for a moment. Earl Lansing stepped behind her and put a hand gently on her shoulder. "It's the trappings, Tommy Jo," he said. "Just the trappings. Mustn't let the trappings get you down. It's like at funerals. I think people sometimes cry more for the gruesome funeral trappings of our so-called Christian society than they do for the loss of the deceased."

"Would you like some coffee and a roll?" Lois asked. "I'll tell you now, I've got a real meal coming up for lunch, complete with something to drink. It seemed an opportunity like this shouldn't be wasted."

Teejay nodded and sighed and took control of herself.

They began to go through the files of Mudge's documents and correspondence. Lois and Lansing had worked in these files for a day already, and they had set aside in one group all the letters to Mudge from Teejay. Some of them would probably be used against her, they warned her.

December 29, 1977

Dear Mr. Mudge:

Enclosed in this package are the deeds for 250 lots at Lago Aguila, the ones you chose December 24. Twelve-Twenty's check for $750,000 has been deposited.

Thank you once again, most sincerely, for the beautiful watch. I know I was not able to thank you adequately on Sunday, so let this note add to what I said then.

Sincerely yours,
T. J. Brookover

January 12, 1978

Dear Mr. Mudge:

Having been unable to reach you today by telephone, I am sending this letter by messenger to tell you that we are threatened with suit by four lot owners at Lago Aguila. The county health department has refused to grant permits for the installation of septic tanks and leaching beds on Lots #453, #454, #455, and #786. The county says the percolation tests on those lots are not within the limits for the installation of private sewage disposal systems on one-third-acre lots.

If any significant additional number of lots fail these tests, we are faced with an absolute debacle at Lago Aguila, unless we install a central sewage disposal system for the entire subdivision. Since such an installation is wholly beyond the company's ability to fund, we can be in desperate trouble in a very short period of time. Please give this problem your immediate attention.

Sincerely yours,
T. J. Brookover

February 2, 1978

Dear Mr. Mudge,

Enclosed is a copy of a letter I have this morning received from Brenda Harvey Rose. You will notice she asks a number of questions about the status of Lago Aguila, Incorporated—its financial condition, the validity of the rumors apparently in circulation about Lago Aguila, etc. You will recall she is one of the heirs of the late Bunker Harvey and stands to lose the value of her Futures Dynamic stock if the current difficulties at Lago Aguila damage that company too. For that reason I am more concerned about the questions in the second paragraph of her letter, about the relationship between yourself and Tom Glencoe. It seems to me we are overdue for a long hard meeting. The questions she is raising can constitute a personal threat to both of us.

Sincerely yours,
T. J. Brookover

March 9, 1978

Dear Mr. Mudge,

Enclosed are copies of letters I have this morning sent to Tom Glencoe in his capacity as president of Lago Aguila, Incorporated, and Futures Dynamic, Incorporated, in which I am resigning as an officer and director of both corporations.

I have been unable to reach you by telephone, but I want to make it a matter plainly of record that I refuse to be a party to any further transfers of lots at Lago Aguila to you or to Twelve-Twenty for prices distinctly below, not just the listed prices for those lots, but indeed distinctly below their reasonable value. Such transfers are nothing short of embezzlement from Futures Dynamic, and I am now quite certain that the complaints of Futures stockholders are under investigation by the SEC and the United States district attorney.

Furthermore, I will decline in future to handle any further legal affairs for you or for your trusts and companies. It is my wish to disassociate myself, as much as I can, from the disaster that has been brought upon Futures Dynamic and its stockholders, and I want nothing to do with any other such manipulations.

Sincerely yours,
T. J. Brookover

"You were only a little short of hysterical at about this point, weren't you, Tommy Jo?" asked Earl Lansing.

Teejay nodded. "It was a disaster. It was an absolute disaster."

She had entertained hope for a long time. With the $750,000 paid by Twelve-Twenty for the lots transferred to it on December 29, 1977, Glencoe had paid the current obligations of Lago Aguila, Incorporated; and during the first week in January, fifty lots were sold. When the bulldozers resumed the grading of the remaining lots in the subdivision, the embankments formed did in fact channel the runoff, which no longer ran into the low places to stand; and in the sunlight the wet land began to dry up.

Percolation tests had been run in December, when fourteen lot owners applied for permits to install septic tanks. A percolation test involved punching a small, standard-size hole in the soil, pouring it full of water, and then watching and recording the time it took for the water to disappear from the hole—to percolate, in other words, into the soil. If the soil was not sufficiently porous to allow water to percolate rapidly, the effluent from a septic tank would not seep into the soil but would stand on the surface, a threat to health. The alternative to rapid percolation was a larger leaching bed, to spread the effluent over a wider land area. The health authorities had published standards; on a one-third-acre lot—which was what the average lot was at Lago Aguila—the percolation test would determine if a septic tank could be installed.

Four lots failed. The landowners were notified around January 10. When they received no sympathy from Roberto Luiz, immediately they threatened to sue.

Lago Aguila, Incorporated, repurchased two of the four lots. The other two owners accepted an exchange of lots, taking lots that had passed percolation tests, and shortly one of them began to build a house. Lago Aguila paid all attorney fees.

Glencoe hired a firm of engineers in Dallas to come to Lago Aguila and run percolation tests on all the lots, secretly. The tests showed there were almost twelve hundred lots on which houses could not be built because septic tanks could not be installed. Lago Aguila, Incorporated, paid a premium price to repurchase six more lots, where the owners were planning to build immediately—in an effort to prevent the owners from learning they could not obtain Health Department permits.

None of the two hundred fifty lots Mudge had bought on December 29 were in the area where septic tanks could not be installed.

The engineers from Dallas submitted a design and cost estimate for building a central sewage-disposal system and laying sewer lines to the lots that required it. The estimate: $2,325,000. Lago Aguila, Incorporated, could not finance it. Twelve-Twenty bought seven hundred fifty more lots at $3000 apiece.

Still, it had not become impossible that Lago Aguila would prove an immensely profitable enterprise. After the sales to Twelve-Twenty, almost four thousand lots remained with the corporation. Lots that did sell brought between $7500 and $8000. The twelve hundred lots that would be attached to sewer lines would bring maybe as much as $10,000 apiece, since their owners would be spared the cost of installing and maintaining septic tanks. The cost of opening the sub-division was far higher than had been anticipated, and the profit would be far less. Even so, the remaining lots might bring as much as $33 million, and the corporation might profit by as much as $15 million.

The first week in February, Teejay had learned that the two hundred and fifty lots sold to Twelve-Twenty on December 29 had been transferred in a block to a Memphis corporation.

"Explain that part," said Earl Lansing in the Childreth conference room.

Teejay was nibbling on her second Danish, visibly savoring it and the hot black coffee. Unconsciously she rubbed her left wrist: a small developing bruise from the handcuff.

"It turned out that my suspicions about Twelve-Twenty were wrong," she said. "Mudge did have associates. He wasn't Twelve-Twenty all by himself. In fact, his own investment in Lago Aguila had been $250,000—his share of the original two million Twelve-Twenty invested in Futures Dynamic stock.

"On the other hand, when we had to sell two hundred and fifty lots on December twenty-ninth, he bought those himself. He put in $750,000 of his own money. I found out that he went to his associates in Twelve-Twenty and told them he had put up three-quarters of a million of his own money to boost the company over a little cash-flow problem, and he asked them to let him sell the two hundred and fifty lots he had bought, to get his money back.

"They agreed. He peddled his two hundred and fifty lots to a real-estate investment trust in Memphis for $5250 each. He got $1,312,500 —personally, to his own account. With that, he was home free."

"One way or the other, he made out," said Earl Lansing.

Teejay nodded. "He had one million invested—his original $250,000, plus the $750,000 he paid for the lots. Now he had $312,500 profit, and whatever happened to the rest of the business, he was okay."

"Even his associates in Twelve-Twenty weren't safe from him," said Lois.

"Well, he took care of them in time," said Teejay. "But he took care of himself first."

Lago Aguila, Incorporated, had borrowed $4 million from Houston banks—part of the cost of acquiring land for the subdivision. The loans were secured by mortgages on the subdivision land. Each time a lot was sold, Lago Aguila, Incorporated, had to pay one or the other of the banks $800—representing that lot's share of the four million. When Mudge bought two hundred and fifty lots on December 29, Lago Aguila had to pay $200,000 against the loans. When seven hundred and fifty additional lots were sold to Twelve-Twenty, Lago Aguila had to pay $600,000. Again the corporation was cash-poor.

Also, Roberto Luiz and two of the salesmen had begun to sell the seven hundred and fifty lots owned by Twelve-Twenty at $6500 apiece. They sold them from the Lago Aguila sales office, to prospects attracted to the subdivision by the advertising paid for by Lago Aguila, Incorporated. ("My associates, after all," Mudge had said blandly, "have twice bailed this enterprise out. They are entitled to their return.") If they had sold all seven hundred fifty of their lots for $6500 apiece, their return would have been $4,875,000—on the $2-million investment. Mudge's personal share of that would have been $609,375.

"It troubled him not at all," said Teejay to Lois and Earl Lansing, "that Lago Aguila, Incorporated, could not sell lots for full price when Luiz was selling Twelve-Twenty lots for sixty-five hundred. Of course, none of their lots required sewer lines. All the ones Twelve-Twenty took had passed percolation tests."

"I gathered that," said Earl Lansing. He had been unable to suppress a few wry smiles at the story of Lago Aguila. He shook his head. "You were working with a real operator, Tommy Jo."

"I guess it was about the first of March that I gave up," said Teejay. "Glencoe was trying to contract for the building of the sewage-disposal plant. In spite of the money we'd gotten from Twelve-Twenty, there wasn't enough in the corporation to build it. We were not selling lots. Then, just as I had expected, Mudge suggested his friends in Twelve-Twenty might buy another five hundred or a thousand lots. It was a *goddamn debacle!*"

They went through the boxes of files on the conference-room table. Mudge had paid Glencoe $35,000 for his "consulting services" in 1977. He had paid him $15,000 in 1976. Glencoe had also received $17,000 in 1976 from the Memphis group that bought Mudge's two hundred and fifty lots. Even after Lago Aguila was on the verge of collapse, in March of 1978, Glencoe received a payment of $23,000 from the Memphis group. A letter referred to his "compensation for his excellent advisory services." The federal grand jury had seen these records of Mudge's before it indicted Glencoe.

Lois and Lansing had set aside a group of letters from Mudge to Teejay. (Copies were in the Mudge files; the originals were in Teejay's office files seized by the district attorney.)

"Allow me, Miss Brookover, to summarize your advice, as given me during our meeting Saturday afternoon. As I understand, you advise it will be lawful for us to . . ."

"I am pleased, Miss Brookover, that your investigation of the law demonstrates that we may properly and lawfully . . ."

"On the basis of your assurance that our prior relationship with Thomas Glencoe does not involve us in any question of illegality or impropriety with respect to prospective dealings with the corporation of which he is president, it is my intention to offer . . ."

"I am pleased to approve the text of the report, conditioned of course on your assurance that it complies fully with the applicable federal law. . . ."

"Tommy Jo," said Earl Lansing with quiet sadness. "Couldn't you see, honey, that he was suckering you something awful?"

Teejay nodded. "I knew it. I could see it. But I didn't understand that he could make more money if Lago Aguila failed as a business than he could make if it succeeded, so I assumed he was as much interested as I was in making it succeed. I kept telling myself I was dealing with a confidence man. I just couldn't believe he was suckering *me.*"

"There were angry scenes," said Lois.

Teejay nodded. "When they proposed to transfer another thousand lots to Twelve-Twenty, I refused to have anything to do with it. I told Mudge to his face he had raped Futures Dynamic. He told me— oh, he was calm and smooth!—I was a naïve young woman, and ungrateful; he said he had tried to help me become a prominent lawyer but he knew now I would always remain a scrivener."

On March 9, Teejay resigned as an officer and counsel to Lago Aguila, Incorporated, and Futures Dynamic. On March 13, Brenda Harvey Rose filed suit for $1,300,000 against Thomas Glencoe, T. J. Brookover, Roberto Luiz, and Benjamin Mudge, charging fraud in the acquisition of Futures Dynamic stock by Twelve-Twenty. The following day, March 14, all the Harvey heirs and fourteen other Futures stockholders brought a shareholders' derivative suit against Thomas

Glencoe, T. J. Brookover, Roberto Luiz, Benjamin Mudge, and Twelve-Twenty, charging a conspiracy to defraud the stockholders and to loot Futures Dynamic; asking an injunction against any further transfers of property from Lago Aguila, Incorporated, except for the full value of such property; asking for an accounting and for the impoundment of the assets of Lago Aguila, Incorporated, Futures Dynamic, and Twelve-Twenty; and asking, finally, for damages of $55 million.

March 14, 1978, was one week before the death of Benjamin Mudge.

"You got a drink of whiskey, didn't ya?" the deputy asked Teejay as they waited to be picked up by the driver for the ride back to jail. Lois had arranged for them to leave the building by a freight elevator and the loading dock, and they stood and waited for the driver to bring the car around. Teejay was shackled, but she was not distressed. She had been spared the ordeal of stares she had undergone in the morning. The deputy had lighted a cigarette for her, and she hunched forward and tugged up her chained hands to take a puff. "I noticed they brought you a real nice dinner, with a drink or two and all. They brought me a nice dinner, too."

"It's the first taste of anything but jail food I've had since April," Teejay said.

"You'll get turkey and all for Thanksgiving," said the deputy. "Get it again on Christmas if you're still in."

"God forbid," said Teejay.

"I understand your boy friend goes on trial Monday."

"He's not my boy friend," said Teejay.

The deputy grinned. "Wish he was mine. I've seen him around the jail, and he's a good-lookin' fella."

Teejay nodded. "He's a handsome man," she said thoughtfully.

Kevin Flint went on trial on Monday, November 13, before Judge Bernard Newcastle of the Criminal District Court. District Attorney John William Hornwood handled the prosecution personally. A jury was seated Monday afternoon, and in his opening statement the district attorney said the state would prove that Kevin Flint had murdered Benjamin Mudge with deliberate and premeditated malice and that the state of Texas would therefore demand the death penalty.

Rumors came up to the jail. Teejay sat alone in her cell and tried to distract herself by reading; but whenever a rumor came, Christine McElhay would bring it to her.

"Hornwood's got nobody but the cops. It's just the cops testifying against Kevin. That's good for you, huh?"

Lois Hughes sat in the courtroom and watched the trial, and at the end of each day she came to see Teejay. Once again she came to the jail itself and spoke to her through the bars of "B" Cage. "They're not even mentioning your name," she said. "It's a straight-down-the-line prosecution, point by point, simple."

"If he can prove Kevin killed Mudge, he doesn't have to prove I hired him to do it," Teejay said. "That's what he has to prove against *me*."

"He can prove that," said Lois. "He can prove premeditation, too. He doesn't have to bring you into it to prove Kevin killed Mudge and did it with premeditation."

"It would give us a couple of weeks to look at what evidence he's got," Teejay suggested.

Lois nodded. "I'd hoped he'd show us something."

Kevin Flint did not testify in his own defense. His attorney had little to offer. The case was clear. Late Wednesday afternoon the jury returned a verdict finding Kevin Flint guilty of the premeditated murder of Benjamin Mudge.

The judge did not pass sentence. Under Texas law a second trial would be held, at which the jury would hear evidence as to whether or not the death penalty should be imposed. The district attorney suggested to the Court that it would require thirty days for a thorough presentencing investigation to be conducted. The judge ruled that the second stage of the trial would begin on Tuesday, December 12.

"He's a clever son of a bitch," Teejay whispered through clenched teeth. She clung to the bars of "B" Cage and shook her head. Her face was flushed. Her eyes were full of tears. "He's going to hold that over Kevin's head until my trial is over. Kevin won't know if he gets a death sentence or not, until after the middle of December. If he testifies for me . . . He *can't* testify for me, Lois!"

"I'm not so sure he'd do us any good," Lois said in a quiet, low voice. She stood close to the bars, close to Teejay, talking so the women in "B" Cage could not hear. "I've never been sure we should risk him."

"Hornwood means to put a limit on what we can use to defend me," Teejay whispered shrilly. "If we lay it too heavy on Kevin, they'll use it against him at the penalty trial."

"It's a shrewd tactic," Lois admitted.

"It's a dirty goddamn trick!" Teejay hissed.

XXXII

March, 1978

Kevin nibbled on a potato chip. He had a bourbon and soda in hand, and he had brought a bag of chips from her kitchen. "Do you have any cash laid aside, Tommy Jo?" he asked grimly.

"Not much," she said.

"Where the ones that are suin' you can't get it?"

She shrugged. "I've got eighteen thousand or so in cash, stuck away where they won't find it. But that's all."

"Smart girl," said Kevin. "I've got some here and there, too. You see what I've got in mind."

Teejay shook her head and sighed. "I can't. I've got to sit still and face it."

"Up to a point, maybe," he said. "Up to a point. But you've talked about goin' to a federal jail over this deal. I don't know if that's real or if you're just nervous and—"

"It's real," she said firmly. "I'm not exaggerating. I've got something to be afraid of. The federal securities law and the federal land sales full disclosure law both have stiff criminal penalties. People do go to jail. It happens all the time."

"Well, not to you, Tommy Jo," he said angrily. "They're not going to lock you up in some filthy hole somewhere and treat you like an animal. We can scram somewhere. Ah think maybe it's time you started listenin' a little more to Kevin. I know something about this kind of thing."

Teejay drained her Scotch. "There's time, Kevin," she said as she swallowed. "If I'm indicted, and if I can't swing a deal, maybe I will run away. I don't know what I will do if I'm really facing time in a federal reformatory."

"The idea . . ." he said. He shook his head. His face was dark. "The idea of *you* locked in a slammer somewhere. That's more than I can handle."

"Pour me another drink while I change clothes, will you?" she asked. "I guess I'll take a quick shower. I've sweated today."

She made the shower hot. She stood in the scalding flow, in steam that took her breath, and flexed the muscles in her back and shoulders. She was tired. She was worried and afraid. She was at the end of her strength and her resources.

The federal investigation had begun. This afternoon she had signed a consent for SEC investigators to examine her bank records. Glencoe and Luiz had done the same. If they hadn't, the investigators would have obtained court orders allowing them to examine the accounts. Only Mudge was holding out. He'd been quoted in this morning's *Post:*

"I am at a loss to understand why I should be sued or why my associates in Twelve-Twenty should be. We are only investors. We put some of our money in these two companies, and we put our confidence in their management. Frankly, I very much doubt there is any substance to any of the allegations against them, but if there has been any wrongdoing, it has been theirs, not mine and not that of my associates."

He had sued Teejay for malpractice. She had been served with the papers the day before. She had assured him, he charged, that there was no unlawful misrepresentation in the proceedings by which he and his associates acquired their sixty-seven thousand shares of Futures Dynamic and that the transaction was in full compliance with every applicable state and federal statute and regulation. He swore she had advised him his acquisition of lots at Lago Aguila was, similarly, lawful and proper. She was guilty of negligence in her advice to him, he charged; and, besides, she was guilty of conflict of interest in advising both him and the officers of Futures and Lago Aguila. Her misconduct as attorney had involved him in two lawsuits, he said, and he asked that she be required to pay his counsel fees in defending himself, plus any judgment a court might return against him. The suit was for $60 million.

He did not, of course, suppose she had $60 million—or even one percent of it. He did not expect to collect anything from her. All he wanted from his lawsuit was a prop for his own defense against securities-law charges and in the suits pending against him. He would insist he acted only as his lawyer advised him; learning now that her advice had not always been correct, he had sued her for malpractice. The juries before whom he would be tried might be impressed.

"Scotch," said Kevin when she returned to the living room. She took the glass from his hand and sat down again. He had poured the chips into a bowl and scraped some dip from a can into another bowl; and he had brought from the kitchen a package of Swiss cheese and some crackers. She had wet her hair in the shower, and she rubbed it now with a towel. She wore a short white terry-cloth robe. Her skin was pink from the hot water. Kevin regarded her critically. "Scotch . . ." he repeated quietly.

"Is there anything on TV?" she asked. It would be well to be distracted.

" 'MASH,' " he said. "But it's over." He sighed. "Listen, Tommy Jo. What about your license to practice law?"

"I haven't been exaggerating about that either. I'm going to lose it," she whispered hoarsely.

"What'll you *do?*"

She shrugged. "What every disbarred lawyer and law-school flunk-out does," she said. "Sell insurance."

"Shit, Tommy Jo, I'm serious."

"So am I."

Kevin faced her across the couch. His face twitched. His eyes filled with tears. "Tommy Jo, honey," he whispered. "You mean you're gonna lose everything you worked for all these years? Are you really?"

She threw herself across the couch and into his arms, and she allowed herself to cry. At first she kept some measure of her restraint, but in a moment she let herself fall. She sobbed deeply. She pressed her face to Kevin's shoulder and shook. For half an hour, maybe, she clung to him, crying, loudly, then softly, and after a while only in shuddering breaths. He held her, frowning grimly. He finished his glass of bourbon while he held her.

"Tommy Jo," he said calmly when she had stopped crying, when she reached for the Scotch sitting on the TV tray. "There's somethin' I was gonna bring up . . . later. But now . . . Hold on a minute."

He went into the kitchen. He came back carrying a brown paper bag she had noticed on the table and had supposed contained something he had brought for dinner. He put it down on the floor and pulled out of it a ragged white shirt wrapped around a heavy object.

He unwrapped a .38 Smith & Wesson revolver.

"*Kevin . . .*" she whispered. Her mouth open, she shook her head. "*No . . .*"

He hefted the pistol, then sighted along it. "Mudge," he said.

"No," she whispered again. "*No.*"

"Why not? He's ruined everything, maybe your whole life. Why not, Tommy Jo? It'll be easy."

She nodded. "Yes. I could—be for it. But what good would it do me, Kevin? It won't help. Besides, I'd be the first person the cops would come looking for. I've got too much motive."

"A thousand people want him dead," Kevin argued. "Anyway, you're not going to do it; I am. All you have to do is make a point of being in a crowd somewhere when I do it. I've got *no* motive anybody knows about, so nobody's gonna look for me. It'll work out perfect."

"It won't help me," she protested. "It might even make it worse."

He laid the pistol on the TV tray, beside the bowl of chips. "Listen to me," he said. "I've been thinkin' about this a long time. If they put you on trial, Mudge is gonna be a witness against you. He's gonna lie against you, to make him look better by makin' you look worse. The more blame he can lay on you, the less there is for him; and the more he manages to lay on you, the harder it's gonna go for you. Ah don't know what kind of sentence you can get, but, whatever it is, Mudge is gonna try to get you the maximum, so he gets the minimum or maybe none. I mean, Tommy Jo, there's a man in this town tonight, alive, that *wants* you to go in the slammer, that *wants* you to get hurt. As far as I'm concerned, what he's done already is enough for me to kill him, but what he's gonna do if I don't stop him is the clincher."

"Kevin—"

"I don't have to have your permission, you know," he said darkly.

"It's a terrible risk," she whispered.

He turned down the corners of his mouth and shook his head. "Not unless I do somethin' dumb."

"Kevin . . ." she said. She took a drink of her Scotch and rose and began to pace slowly. "I'm facing something. I've got myself under control about it. Anyway, I think I have. I'm going to be indicted. I can probably arrange some kind of plea. I may have to do six months or a year, or maybe even a couple of years. If I'm damn lucky, I might get probation. Either way, I'm going to be disbarred. And I'm going to lose everything I have. So—"

"*You're not thinkin',*" Kevin snapped impatiently. "You say a judge could let you go on probation, or give you six months, or maybe give you two years. Maybe he can give you more. And what's it gonna depend on? A lot of it, I'm tellin' you, will depend on what Mudge says against you. If he makes a judge believe you led him along—"

Teejay interrupted, shaking her head. "He could never make a judge believe that. Mudge has a reputation—"

"He had it before," Kevin insisted, "and *you* believed him. You believed a lot of what he told you, when he was suckerin' you into God knows what. He's a devil, Tommy Jo. He can still hurt you."

"Then it's obvious I'm the one who wants him dead," she said. "And that makes me a prime suspect." She grabbed her Scotch and took another big swallow. "If anybody kills him, I'm a suspect."

"Right. But you didn't kill him, and you can prove you didn't. There are plenty of suspects. What about those people who bought lots they can't build houses on? What about the people who lost a hell of a lot in the stock in Futures Dynamic? Sure, you'll be a suspect. But so will plenty of other people. Only you'll have an alibi."

Teejay sat down. "How would you do it?" she asked.

"I've thought about that. The best way is the simplest way."

"So what's the simplest way?"

"We've got to set him up," Kevin said. "Where does he go? When? I want to make it look like a robbery."

Teejay was disturbed by how Kevin warmed to his idea. She grabbed her glass again and stood. "Jesus, I—I can't believe I'm talking to you, seriously, about how we might kill a man."

Kevin smiled. "You read history," he said. "I've been lookin' at the books in your bedroom. You know somethin' about history. How many people, when the situation came up that really required it, got rid of somebody that was the key to their troubles? What's so wrong about it? We're all entitled to defend ourselves."

He followed her into the kitchen, where she went to pour more Scotch over her ice cubes. "I'm gonna do it, Tommy Jo," he said. "For me and for you."

Teejay, who had meant to put another ice cube in her Scotch, stood with her back pressed to the refrigerator. "Kevin . . . I haven't been that good to you."

"Better than you know," he said. He reached for his bottle of bourbon and poured over his own almost-melted ice.

"Why bother?" she asked. "I've got some money. You've got some. Why not just *go?* You've talked about it. You know how to change your name and hide. I'll go with you now. Tonight if you want to. We can just walk out of here and leave the doors open."

Kevin shook his head. "Maybe they won't look for you long, or far, if Mudge doesn't get the chance to tell what a rotten crook you are. If he does, they may put you on a wanted list like I never was on."

"He doesn't count, Kevin! Not like you think."

"The son of a bitch does, honey. He's hurt you so bad—"

"*The future, Kevin!*"

He nodded. "Yeah. Some kind of future. We're gonna leave some for ourselves. We've got to leave ourselves some room."

Teejay sighed. "Jesus," she muttered. "God, it all goes back—*so far*. When I met you, all I had to do was show my legs and carry trays of drinks. That's all. I wanted something more. And what'd it all come to? You remember the house I showed you, outside LaGrange, out on the highway? I used to sit on the porch and count the cars that went by. They knew me: the redhead that sat on the porch and waved at the cars that went by. I never saw a Mercedes like I've got. But, Jesus Christ, Kevin, what've I paid for it?"

He stood and took a step toward the refrigerator, to face her. "What you paid for, somebody's stolen from you," he growled, nodding hard. "You paid a lot. You paid a Christ lot." He shook his head. "I'm not gonna stand back and watch it happen and nobody pay for what they took away from you. I'm not! I won't! I'm gonna put a bullet in—"

"*Kevin!*" she cried. "Kevin . . . Okay. All right." She sighed and took a swallow of Scotch. It had begun to reach her head, and she stopped her words, to reassemble them. "On a condition . . . I'll even help you. But it's on a condition."

He nodded.

"We've played a silly game too many years," she whispered deep in her throat. "The fact is, Kevin, you love me. You say you do. And I love you. We make a pair, you and I: a better pair than we ever let ourselves admit. So this is it. We do what we have to do. Not what you have to do—what *we* have to do. And when it's all over, no more shit. It's going to be you and me. We're going to start sleeping together. Regularly. Man and woman, you and me. I've been wrong about that, and you have, too. But that's over now. We're going to do something rotten. But together. *Together*, Kevin. Okay? I'm willing that way. But only that way."

Kevin only nodded—regarding her intently across his glass of bourbon, his eyes fixed and narrow, his face brooding, rigid.

Over dinner they did not talk. They sat at the kitchen table, looking at each other, not saying what they thought—each of them stunned by what they had agreed to do. After dinner they talked about it. She knew little of Mudge's habits: where he might be found alone, where Kevin might confront him. She had heard him say that he often ate at a place on the west side of Houston called the London Broil. As a widower, he ate alone most of the time, and he had said the beef

was good at the London Broil. Kevin knew the place. It had a parking
lot, he said, that would be a perfect place to meet Mudge. If Mudge
ate there often, all he, Kevin, had to do was wait for Mudge there,
until he came out alone and walked to his car in the lot. Then, if there
were not too many people around . . .

Mudge kept irregular hours, she pointed out. Not that irregular,
Kevin said. If he ate at the London Broil and liked roast beef, he ate
when the place was open and before the best of the roast was gone.
The only question was, would he eat there tomorrow night, or any
time this week, or any time this month? Teejay guessed he ate there
two or three times a week.

An alternative would be to wait for him outside his garage, behind
his house. Kevin did not like that idea, although it would remain a
possibility. "In the parking lot at the London Broil, he's just a man
shot by a mugger. At home he's specifically Mudge: got by somebody
that specifically wanted Mudge."

His office? The escape was too complicated, too risky.

Kevin liked the London Broil.

This night they slept together, both of them in her bed, naked—as
she insisted. She wanted his penis in her. She had thought about it
during their silent moments over dinner; and she told him she would
not have him go out to kill a man for her when he had never mated
with her. But when she went to the bathroom she found her period
had begun, suddenly and with a strong flow. She had to put in a tam-
pon, and in bed she could not let him enter her. She offered him her
breasts to be fondled and kissed; and she kissed and licked his penis
and then massaged it with her fingertips until he had an orgasm in her
hands. It was the most they had ever experienced together.

In the morning he left before she was entirely awake, and under her
shower she remembered what they had said and agreed to the night
before—with a shock, as if it were something she had forgotten and
only remembered after a long time. It did seem distant, that conversation: distant and unreal, impossible. She reconstructed what they had
said, every word. They had plotted murder.

She could stop him. She could telephone him. She could go to the
London Broil, find him in the parking lot, and stop him. (She wondered for a moment if he would really be there. She knew he would.)
All day she knew she could stop him. All day in her office, as she took
calls, fended off the angry complaints of Lago Aguila lot owners and
Futures stockholders, and tried to do some law business, she knew she
could stop him. The idea would recede and then return to her with

the shock of recall, as it had done in the shower. It distracted her. She decided to go, to stop him. She decided not to. She reconstructed the conversation repeatedly. Emotion had overcome reason; that was clear. She had known she was letting emotion overrule reason, had known it and let it happen, intentionally, for once.

She was not afraid. She was confident Kevin could kill Mudge and escape. She knew she would be suspected, but they had worked out the elements of an alibi—that tonight she would sit in the Pound Sterling until ten o'clock (which was not unusual), tomorrow she would attend a bar meeting that would last until ten at least, Thursday night she would find some pretext for keeping two of her office staff late and would then insist on buying them dinner or drinks. Kevin would kill Mudge before ten o'clock or not at all. He would stalk him each night until he caught him. If he did not catch him by Thursday night, they would meet and plan something different.

Conscience was no part of what she thought and felt. Kevin was right about Mudge—for what he had done to her he deserved anything she could do to him. The world would be better off without him, and no one would care that he had died. It was a strange judgment to make of a human being, but she was convinced it was a correct judgment and a reflection of what he had made of himself. He was a despicable man.

She went to the Pound Sterling. Jim Rush was there. It was the first time she had sat down with him and talked since he had stopped visiting her apartment. He told her how very sorry he was that she was in danger of indictment and disbarment. He talked with her for an hour.

After he left, she stayed, talking with two of his friends. She drank. She made a point of not glancing conspicuously at her watch. She tried to conceal the emotion that hung in her gut like a hot stone. It was not easy. Once in the women's room she almost vomited. She lost the thread of conversation and had to smile vapidly at the two chatting young lawyers. She ordered dinner. That was a mistake—having ordered it, she was compelled to eat.

Ten o'clock. It was too long to have to stay there. The two lawyers left. She moved to the bar. She was propositioned. She hardly heard it. The man became more aggressive. She rid herself of him. By nine there was no one she knew left in the Pound Sterling. She engaged the barmaid in rambling conversation, as if she were drunk. At 9:50 she paid her bill and left.

She drove with methodical, exaggerated caution. She was sick with apprehension. Kevin had said he would not call her. She would have to depend on news reports to learn if he had found Mudge. If he killed him, he would not see her for maybe two months. He would wait until the investigation had cooled. He himself would not be a suspect and could only become one if he were identified with her. He would not leave town. He would be around. He would know what she was doing. She heard no news on the car radio. She fought off an impulse to drive past the London Broil. Kevin would have been contemptuous of that idea. She drove home.

She turned on the television as soon as she was in her apartment. Nothing. She thought of going to Kevin's apartment. (She had never been there, but thought she knew where he lived.) She would tell him not to do it. She could not endure another evening like this; and if he killed Mudge, every day and every night would be like it, until she could know for certain the investigation did not focus on her. It would go on for weeks. Anyway, she had another idea: If she abruptly associated herself with an ex-convict with no visible means of support, anytime within a year or more after Mudge was murdered, the investigation, wherever it then was, would return to her. And she had not asked Kevin how he would dispose of the gun. He did know enough to get rid of it immediately—

The telephone rang. It was Tom Glencoe. "Teejay? Listen, I— Listen, Ben Mudge was killed tonight. Shot! Gottschalk called. They'll ask you and me questions. And Luiz. I know you didn't do it. And I sure as hell didn't. But—Jesus Christ! Jesus Christ, who'd do a thing like that? It's the worst thing that could possibly happen, the way things are."

What Glencoe meant was that the murder of Mudge would generate an explosion of newspaper and television stories about Lago Aguila and Futures Dynamic. It did. Lago Aguila and Futures Dynamic moved to the front pages, to the first, featured stories on television news programs. Facts that had been overlooked, elements of the Mudge manipulations that had until now remained obscure, became topics for breathless reporting, complete with speculation.

Teejay did not much care. She read about the shooting itself, and about the investigation.

Police arrived no more than five minutes after the fatal shots were fired, according to Lieutenant Harold Dye of the homicide investigation unit. They found Mudge lying facedown beside his car in a pool of his own blood.

There were no less than five eyewitnesses to the crime, although none of them witnessed it from closer than fifty yards, apparently. Waiting at a traffic light on Alabama Street, Walter Baxter, 54, an automobile mechanic, heard the two shots and turned to see Mudge fall and his killer, a white man of medium height and build, walk quickly away and out of the restaurant parking lot on the side opposite Alabama Street. Baxter left his car and ran to the dying man. The killer had disappeared from sight, he says, having walked out of the lighted parking lot and into the darkness. Mudge was dead or at least unconscious when Baxter reached him.

Wanda Ballinger, 23, a model, was closer than Baxter, but several rows of parked cars intervened between her and the shooting. She was entering her car when the shots were fired. She heard Mudge scream, she says, and she dropped to her knees on the pavement, to shield herself from other shots she feared might be fired. When she stood up again, she saw Baxter running toward the place where the shots had been fired, and she saw the killer momentarily, as he rushed from the parking lot.

Other witnesses were farther away, in the parking lot. Their accounts substantially agree with the statements of Baxter and Miss Ballinger.

The killer is described by all witnesses as a young man, perhaps six feet tall, with light brown hair. He was wearing a light tan jacket and dark-colored trousers.

The first news stories inspired in Teejay a tenuous confidence that Kevin had in fact killed Mudge and walked away. Two days later she read the first story that suggested a problem.

YOUTHS PLAYING BALL
MAY HAVE SEEN KILLER

A group of black youths playing a game of softball in Leech Street, four blocks from the scene of Tuesday night's shooting in the parking lot at the London Broil restaurant, may have seen the killer of Benjamin Mudge enter his car and drive away.

According to their account, the youths, 14 through 17 years of age, were playing softball in the street and around a dark blue late-model Ford parked at the curb. The car was not familiar to them. It had not been parked on their street before, they said. They heard the shots that killed Benjamin Mudge at about 9:15, but took the reports as the sound of a backfiring car. A few minutes later a man they describe as of middle age, about six feet tall, having light hair, wearing a khaki jacket and dark pants, walked up the street, entered the blue Ford, and drove away. He was, they said, nervous and hurried.

None of them attached any importance to the appearance of the man, and they did not take the license number of his car. All the youths, who remain unidentified, spent an hour today repeating their story to homicide investigators and answering questions. Police believe the man they saw was in fact the man who shot and killed Houston real-estate developer Benjamin Mudge.

She read everything that was written, listened to every account she could—comparing, searching the words for some nuance of meaning, some suggestion a reporter had picked up from an interview, that would tell her more than the bare words told. At first, the police said they had little to work on. Then they fell silent. Were they covering their want of leads, the failure so far of their investigation? Or had they fallen silent to protect a promising line of inquiry? She lived miserable days, unable to sleep, unable to fix her mind on anything but the inexorable process of the police investigation.

When by Saturday they had not named a suspect, she began to relax a little, to feel that maybe the worst danger was over. Sunday she thought maybe Kevin would call. He had said he wouldn't, and she regretted now they had not agreed on some telephone contact, through public telephones at appointed hours, so she could at least have a few words from him, some reassurance. She told herself on Sunday that maybe his own feeling for what had happened would suggest to him he could call without risk. He did not call. Sunday night she dropped into depression and again could not sleep.

Then, Monday morning—

ARREST, CHARGE SUSPECT IN MUDGE KILLING

Kevin Flint, 38, an Oklahoma ex-convict described by police as a drifter, gambler, and small-time swindler, was arrested by Houston detectives Sunday evening and charged in the Tuesday murder of real-estate developer Benjamin Mudge.

Flint, found by police in a two-room apartment on the south side of Houston, was unarmed and surrendered meekly to officers who surrounded the apartment building Sunday about 6:00 P.M. Police found $10,000 in cash in a dresser drawer in his apartment.

Detective Bradley Goshen described how Flint was identified as the alleged killer. He referred to the black youths who saw

Flint enter his car on Leech Street within minutes after the murder. All of them were emphatic in asserting that Flint was not then carrying a gun, which they insisted would have been visible under his tight-fitting khaki jacket. Detectives reasoned that if the man the youths saw was indeed the killer and if he was not carrying the murder weapon, then he must have gotten rid of it somewhere between the parking lot where Mudge was shot and Leech Street where he had left his car.

"If he'd stashed it somewhere, either he'd come back for it or it was still there," said Detective Goshen.

Police searched the area with metal detectors during the night of Wednesday, March 22, without results. On Thursday they entered the storm sewers on the streets between the parking lot and Leech Street. There, thrown far back out of sight in a storm sewer, they found the .38-caliber Smith & Wesson revolver used to kill Mudge.

Ballistics tests established that the pistol was in fact the murder weapon.

"He'd wiped it pretty clean for fingerprints," said Detective Goshen, "but he hadn't wiped off the shells in the chambers. There were prints on them."

A quick check with the FBI showed the prints matched those of Kevin Flint, who has a criminal record that includes a term in an Oklahoma prison for larceny by trick. Flint was known to be in Houston. He has been involved in a number of gambling schemes and other manipulations that have resulted in complaints to police.

Although it has been assumed that the motive for the murder was probably robbery, police said, the investigation has not overlooked the possibility that the murder is in some way involved in the huge Lago Aguila land fraud. Finding $10,000 in cash in Flint's room suggests, a spokesman said, that Flint may have been hired by someone to kill Mudge.

It was a matter of a very short time, Teejay assumed, before she would be arrested. She knew Kevin would never tell the police she had plotted with him to kill Mudge, but she could not believe her long-standing relationship with Kevin had been so secret they would not discover it.

She did not panic. She was surprised with herself for the calm with which she waited. The days were not as tense as the ones between the killing and Kevin's arrest. She knew what would happen. The uncertainty was resolved.

She prepared. She went through her office files. She found twenty documents she felt she should destroy—none of them relating to Mudge or Lago Aguila, actually; they were letters about other clients, other matters, that could embarrass her if her files were seized and read by investigators. She burned these letters and flushed the ashes down the toilet. She had at home two letters from Kevin. She could not bear to destroy those. She did not have even a picture of him, and those letters might someday be all she had from him. She hid them.

She considered running away. You could do it, maybe, on fraud charges. You could not do it when the charge was murder. They would find you and extradite you from anywhere if the charge was murder.

Two weeks passed. They were slow. The federal investigators came. She spent hours with them, going over the Futures Dynamic acquisition, then over the Lago Aguila fraud. It became apparent she would need another lawyer to represent her and defend her against the federal charges. She thought of Lois Hughes.

She expected to plead guilty to federal charges. The point would be to negotiate a plea, to cooperate in return for a light sentence. As Glencoe had suggested, the murder of Mudge not only inspired publicity for the federal investigation, it toughened it; it told the federal investigators how much was at stake. She talked to Jim Rush on the telephone. He suggested Lois Hughes. She had, he said, important political influence, and that would help in a plea-bargaining situation. Teejay decided to call her.

They indicted her before they arrested her. She had not expected that. The grand jury returned a secret indictment on Wednesday, April 5. She learned of it late the next afternoon, Thursday, April 6.

She had expected a call. She had expected to go to the sheriff's office in a cab and surrender herself. They didn't let her do that. They came to her office late in the afternoon. They took her to jail in handcuffs, in the back of a police car.

XXXIII

Monday, November 27, 1978

At the end of the tunnel between the basement of the jail and the basement of the courthouse, Teejay confronted the cameras. In the glare of the television lights and in the clamor of jostling cameramen and reporters, she was led toward the elevator that would take her up to the courtroom. Two deputies led her: a woman to her left, a man to her right. She was loosely handcuffed and her clenched hands hung before her as she walked. She wore a cream-colored linen blouson and a matching flared skirt with pockets. Her hair was brushed out and hung smoothly around her shoulders. In the moment she was under the lights and before the cameras, she turned and said something over her shoulder. She was followed by her two attorneys—Lois Hughes and Earl Lansing; and—strangely—walking between them and chatting amiably with them was the six-foot-five district attorney, John William Hornwood.

From a distance Hornwood looked handsome and distinguished. His hair was iron-gray. His face was tanned. He smiled warmly at Earl Lansing as he said something to him. He walked with easy confidence. Closer, an observer would notice that his face was coarse: His nose was big, and burst red veins marked it; his complexion was pitted with old acne scars; his broad smile uncovered big teeth, widely separated and stained; his lips were full and protruding. His hair was coarse and unruly; it fell across his forehead, and stiff strands stood straight up at the back of his head. He smiled. He seemed always to smile. One of the newspapers had called his personality "sunny."

When she was brought out of jail, he had been standing there, between her two lawyers. "I stopped over here to have a word with you before the trial starts," he had said to her. "Since I can't properly talk to you outside the presence of your counsel, I asked Lois and Earl to walk over with me."

His smile broadened. It looked honest, sincere. She knew he would be a formidable prosecutor.

"All I wanted to say is, I'm sorry to find myself prosecuting you. I hate to prosecute a fellow lawyer, but, more than that, I hate to prosecute *you*. I've watched your career. You've given some of my boys a hard time. I was shocked when the Police Department told me they believed you were the one who hired Flint to kill Mudge. I'd rather it were somebody else. I won't kid you. I think you did it, and I'm going to prosecute hard. But I don't like it much, and some way or other and off the record, I wish you good luck, just the same."

Teejay had not been able to answer him. She had just stood, stunned, and stared at him, until he nodded to the two deputies and with a toss of his head told them to move their prisoner to the courthouse.

Lois had stopped Teejay for a moment and told her quietly, "Some news. They're not going to ask for the death penalty. He told Earl and me on the way through the tunnel."

Once again Teejay had said nothing. The deputies took her by the arms and led her, and until she turned to Lois as the camera lights made her grimace, she had said nothing since she was brought out of the jail.

They were all crammed in the elevator, going down from the jail, and now going up to the courtroom. Hornwood studied Teejay thoughtfully in both elevators. He had not seen her since she was arrested. Maybe he was studying the way her ordeal—seven months in jail—had damaged her. She had thickened from want of exercise and from eating jail food. She had developed lines at the corners of her eyes and mouth. She was pallid (prison pallor was no myth). Her lips trembled. She held her hands clenched in fists so tight the knuckles fairly gleamed white.

The elevator—it was a private elevator, used only by officials of the courts—opened on a corridor that ran behind the criminal courtrooms. With a final smile and nod, Hornwood left Teejay and her lawyers and walked toward the clerk's office. The deputies took Teejay to the holding pen for Judge Spencer's courtroom. They put her in the pen, locked it with the padlock, and left her alone with her lawyers for their final fifteen minutes before the trial.

The pen was tiny: no more than four feet square. It was made of chain link stretched over an angle-iron frame. It was furnished with a flat bench—a wooden shelf on brackets on the rear wall. Teejay sat.

Lois stood beside Earl Lansing outside the chain link, awkwardly facing Teejay in the pen. There was no chair or any other furniture in the little room. "Did you hear what I told you over there?" Lois asked. "They're not going to ask for the death penalty."

Teejay looked up. "Thank them for nothing."

Lois frowned. "It's a concession," she said.

"It's a tactic," said Teejay. Unconsciously she rubbed her wrists where the handcuffs had been—even though this time they had been on so loose she could probably have slipped them off at the cost of a couple of abrasions. "It makes it easier for him to get a conviction. Eases the jury's conscience."

"You have time for a cigarette before we go in," Lois said.

"Thanks."

Lois handed her a cigarette through the chain link—the pack would not have gone through—and Teejay held her face up to the barrier so Lois could touch the cigarette with the lighter flame.

"You look good," said Earl Lansing. "I think that's a good dress for going before a jury."

"We thought about it a lot," said Teejay. "Lois and I. Thought I ought to look like a woman, not like the tough-bitch lady lawyer."

"You look like a woman," said Earl Lansing. "Like an *innocent* woman."

"A rumor came round in the jail last night," Teejay said. "The word is that Glencoe and Luiz were brought back to the jail yesterday."

"I'm sure they were," Lois said. "You can be sure they'll be witnesses against you."

Teejay sighed. She sat again on the shelf. With her foot she reached forward. She could lay the sole of her shoe flat against the chain link. "When I was lawyering," she said, "I used to stand where you are and talk to people who were where I am. This is bad. It makes me feel like an animal. And I'm scared, Lois—Earl. I'm *scared!*"

"All rise! The Criminal District Court for Harris County is now in session, the Honorable Norma Spencer presiding."

Judge Spencer swept across the front of the courtroom, her black robe billowing. For a dramatic moment before she sat she glanced tensely around her crowded courtroom: at the smooth, undeniably beautiful defendant standing between her two lawyers; at Lois Hughes, whose calm, penetrating eyes met hers almost defiantly; at the six-foot-five district attorney standing beside his assistant and smiling comfortably; at the reporters filling the front rows; at the dense crowd behind, filling every seat. The judge was—and looked —anything but happy. She sighed to herself as she sat down. She did not see how anything good could come of what was about to begin.

"Case Number 78-5403, the state of Texas versus Tommy Jo Brook-over," she announced in a flat voice. "The charge is premeditated murder. Is the state ready to proceed?"

"The State of Texas is ready, Your Honor," said Hornwood with a nod and a smile.

"Is the defendant ready to proceed?"

"The defendant is ready, Your Honor," said Lois.

"Let the record show," said Judge Spencer, "that the State of Texas is represented by the District Attorney of Harris County, John William Hornwood, and that the defendant is present in the courtroom with her counsel of record, Lois Farnham Hughes."

"If the Court please," said Hornwood, rising. "I should like to present to the Court a new member of my staff, Mr. Kenneth King, who will assist me. I have had the pleasure also this morning of meeting Mr. Earl Lansing, an attorney from Clayton County, Texas, who is seated beside Mrs. Huges and will be co-counsel for the defense."

Judge Spencer kicked off her shoes and stretched her legs under her desk. She settled herself for what she supposed would be a long process: the choosing of a jury.

It was apparent to Judge Spencer after only a few minutes that Hornwood would be what he always was in the courtroom—comfortable, affable, graceful, a vivid picture of reason and sincerity. *He* did not want a conviction: no, not he; he would be pleased with an acquittal if only it were the acquittal of an innocent person; all he wanted was justice. Justice, he would tell the jury sooner or later, did not consist only in freeing the innocent; it consisted also of convicting the guilty—for society, too, was entitled to justice. Sincerity was his game, and he was good at it. When she ruled from the bench, he would stand nodding, thoughtfully smiling, often bowing slightly from the waist, showing the jury how pleased he was to hear the ruling of so reasonable and learned a judge. He rarely frowned in the courtroom. When he did, it was always a puzzled frown, suggesting he did not quite understand how a witness could have answered as he just had, or how a judge could have ruled as she just did.

Lois was uneasy. She was wearing a jacket and skirt of maroon silk with a printed pattern of white leaves. She fiddled with a yellow pencil and whispered often to Earl Lansing. She had some trouble with prospective jurors.

"Mrs. Cobb, do you know anything about this case?"

"I know all about it."

"You've read about it in the newspapers? Heard about it on television?"

"My husband and I've got some friends that got stuck with one of them lots at Lago Aguila."

"Would that influence your verdict in this case?"

"Might. I don't think much of any of that whole bunch."

"If the Court please, the defense moves that Mrs. Cobb be excused for cause."

Hornwood rose, smiling. "Really, Your Honor, I have heard nothing that so much suggests a reason, under the rules, to excuse Mrs. Cobb for cause. If the defense wishes to exercise a peremptory challenge . . ."

The problem for Lois was that she had only a limited number of peremptory challenges. If she used one on every panelist who knew anything about the Lago Aguila land fraud, she would soon run out. She had discussed the problem with Norma on the telephone, Saturday afternoon. She wanted to excuse for cause every panelist who had any personal contact with a loss in Lago Aguila land or in Futures Dynamic stock. Jurors with any direct, personal knowledge of those losses would talk about it in the jury room, she insisted, and inspire in the jury a passion to hang Teejay Brookover.

Judge Spencer sighed loudly, puffing out her cheeks. "Mrs. Cobb," she said, "the Court will excuse you from serving on this jury."

Hornwood bowed toward her, nodding and smiling. His eyes, looking up into her face from beneath his shaggy gray brows, were in contempt of court.

The judge pushed herself back in her chair, took off her glasses, and watched only blurred images as the questioning of prospective jurors resumed.

As far as she was concerned, Teejay Brookover was guilty. She had no doubt the woman had sent Flint to kill Mudge, and she had been disturbed to hear how vehemently sincere Lois was in arguing otherwise. Lois had not lied to her. She believed Teejay Brookover was innocent. She believed it on a personal and emotional level, so intensely that she had broken all the rules of propriety and ethics in a foolish, unguarded effort to win her client's acquittal before the case even came to trial. She had argued her case to Norma, on the telephone. She had discussed issues that were likely to arise and had asked for rulings in advance. It had been—and it continued to be—the most direct and distressing pressure ever brought on her, Norma, as a judge. Lois could be disbarred for it, if it should become known; and she, Norma, could be removed from office for failing to report it.

Lois was flawed. She was cynical and ruthless enough to bring personal and political pressure on a judge, but she was not shrewd enough to see through her client's lie. She was polished, she was intelligent, she was capable; but she had been shielded from people whose cynicism went further than her own. She would believe a lie she could not herself tell.

"If the Court please, the state moves that Mr. Walsh be excused for cause."

Walsh's cousin had been represented by T. J. Brookover in a small suit to collect overdue rent. She excused him.

Personally, she hoped the jury would convict the redhead. The emotional issue of capital punishment was out of the case, at her insistence; she had called Hornwood and told him she did not want to have to contend with it in this case. If she bent everything to the side of the defense—which was as much, after all, as Lois could ask of her —she would have satisfied Lois; and if Teejay Brookover were convicted anyway, she, Norma, would escape the criticism the bending was bound to engender. Conviction would be a tidy resolution for a nasty case. Acquittal would be decidedly untidy.

They were quick about selecting their jury. She was surprised. They might get through opening statements before noon.

Hornwood made his opening statement. He stood at his table, with the backs of his legs touching it, bent forward slightly toward the jury, and nodded and smiled at them as he spoke. He spoke quietly. He was persuasive, as Teejay judged him. He was frighteningly persuasive.

He accused her of murder, and her twelve jurors stared at her. They did not look at him so much as they looked at her. She tried to face them. She tried to make eye contact with each juror.

Twelve of them. Two were blacks: a housewife, the mother of six grown children; and a slender, coffee-with-cream-colored young woman who had told the court she was unemployed. In fact, six of the jurors were unemployed in one way or another—the young woman drawing unemployment compensation, a younger white woman who

said she was a waitress but had not been able to find work lately and
lived with her parents, and four retired men. One of the retired men
was a former mail carrier. One had been an insurance agent; he was
eighty years old, but alert and attentive. His age would have excused
him from jury duty, but he had said he wanted to serve. Besides the
woman with six children, there were two other housewives on the
jury. One was the wife of a truck driver; the other was newly married
to a medical student. One juror was the manager of the meat-cutting
department at an A&P supermarket. One was head groundskeeper at
a country club. One was a professor of economics at Rice Institute.

If one, just one, held out for acquittal, she would not be convicted.
She had tried enough criminal cases to have learned something of the
psychology of juries, and what she most feared was a rush for a verdict. Coming into the jury room, tired, often disgusted with what they
had heard in the courtroom, and impatient to be finished and go
home, a jury could rush to a verdict. The rush usually led to a verdict
of guilty. If only one held out and would not join the rush, then the
case would have to be discussed, and then the doubts would come.
She needed one who would not be rushed.

The old man, the retired insurance agent, could be the one. She had
been glad to see him seated on her jury. He would be in no hurry. At
his age he had seen a lot of life, and he was likely to have developed
a practiced tolerance. The young judged more quickly than the old. It
was easier for them. Life was more simply defined. They had not seen
enough of it to learn its subtleties.

The old man stared at her. He was curious, obviously. He was
thinking. He was comparing her to what he knew of people. He was
skeptical of the district attorney's smooth accusations.

The young wife, the one married to the medical student, stared
impassively, her eyes distorted by the rings of reflection in her black-
framed, teardrop spectacles. She sucked her cheeks in between her
teeth. It was easy to imagine that she had already reached a decision
and was only waiting to vote. It was easy for Teejay to imagine that
the young woman resented her for being a more beautiful woman.
Many women had.

How could you tell? What could you tell? These were the people
who would decide if she was to spend the rest of her life in prison—
twelve mysterious strangers. Was there among them a fanatic of
some kind who would judge her against some obscure private standard no one could guess? Did any of them harbor an angry resentment
of lawyers? Would one of them remember during the trial that she had
once served him a drink? Had she been working bare-breasted at the
time? Might one of them remember having seen her with Kevin

somewhere? What would the two black women think of her? What would they think of her clothes? What would the unemployed waitress think? The wife of the truck driver? Had she dressed too well? Was she too cool and poised? What did they want?

The black woman, the one who was mother of six children, nodded at her! It was an almost imperceptible nod, maybe unconscious—but it might be an expression of sympathy. She nodded back, a cautious, measured nod, also barely perceptible, not enough to suggest she presumed an understanding. She pondered. What did it mean?

Earl Lansing made the opening statement for the defense. It was short. All he said was, "Ladies and gentlemen, this is the time in a trial when lawyers get up and tell you what they're going to prove. Mr. Hornwood says he's going to prove a lot of things. For our side— the defense for Miss Brookover—we're not going to prove anything. We don't have to. As I'm sure you know, and as the judge will charge you later, it's the state that has to prove its case. That's the American system. So Mr. Hornwood says he's going to prove all these things. And what we say is, he's not going to prove them. He says he is, but he isn't—because Miss Brookover didn't kill that man, nor have anything to do with killing him, and Mr. Hornwood can't prove she did. It's as simple as that, and that's all there is to it. I thank you."

Dr. William English, chief pathologist for the Harris County Coroner's Office, had performed an autopsy on the body of Benjamin Mudge. He was the first witness for the state, called to the stand immediately after the noon recess.

"The subject was a male, Caucasian, 168 centimeters tall, weight 83.9 kilograms, age 69 years," the doctor recited in monotone from a sheet of notes in his hand. "The autopsy was begun at 11:06 P.M., March 21, 1978, and was concluded at 1:24 A.M., March 22, 1978. . . ."

The doctor was a slight, bespectacled young man with a somber, owlish look. His tone never changed. The flat, sober set of his face never changed.

". . . the bullet had shattered the upper medial surface of the spleen . . . path through the inferior vena cava, then through the superior pole of the right kidney. . . . The bullet had ruptured the superior mesenteric artery less than one centimeter from its junction with the aorta . . . massive loss of blood . . ."

"Dr. English," said Hornwood when the doctor finally looked up from his notes and stopped his recitation, "will you now state to the jury, in laymen's terms, the cause of the death of Benjamin Mudge?"

"Two gunshot wounds—one in the chest, one in the upper abdomen. Destruction of vital organs. Loss of blood."

"Dr. English, I now hand you a photograph and ask you to identify it."

The doctor squinted at the photograph handed him by Hornwood. "During an autopsy, photographs are taken of the body, to create a visual record. A set of photographs was taken during this autopsy, at my direction and according to my instructions. This was taken before the autopsy began. It is probably the first one taken."

"The state asks that the clerk mark this photograph as State's Exhibit One, and the state moves that it be received in evidence."

The clerk stamped the photograph on the back, then marked it, and Hornwood carried it to the defense table for the required examination by defense counsel. He handed it to Lois with a slight bow and his faint smile; then he stood back while Lois and Teejay and Lansing huddled over it.

It was a glossy 11 x 14 color print, showing Mudge lying naked on the autopsy table. His eyes were open. His lips were parted. The body glistened with drops of water; probably it had been hosed down to wash off blood and urine and feces before the autopsy began. The wound in the abdomen was only a hole, which the pathologist had described as one centimeter in diameter; the wound in the chest had shattered and collapsed a rib, and the hole seemed to lie in the bottom of a fist-size crater.

Lois had seen the picture before—this one and all the rest of the set. She glanced up from it, into the face of Teejay, which was immobile and pale.

"Your Honor," Lois said, rising, "we will object to the introduction of this photograph, or any others of the body. The question before this Court is not whether Benjamin Mudge died of gunshot wounds inflicted by Kevin Flint; the question is whether or not this defendant conspired with Flint and procured him to fire those shots, and gruesome photographs of the corpse have nothing to do with that question."

"If the Court please," said Hornwood softly, deferentially. "The question before the Court is whether or not the defendant committed murder. What murder does to a human being is always relevant."

"The objection is sustained," said Judge Spencer.

Hornwood inclined his head toward the judge, then toward Lois; and he picked up his picture and carried it back to his table, where he laid it facedown. Lois looked at Earl Lansing, who was smiling faintly. It had been a petty trick by the district attorney—and one of his favorites. Prosecutors liked to show juries the autopsy pictures. The pictures made them sick and angry. They made them hunger for vengeance. Or such was the theory. Usually Judge Spencer let the pictures in. Lois wondered when Hornwood would begin to keep score on Norma's rulings.

"I have no further questions of Dr. English," said Hornwood.

"Defense may examine," said the judge.

Lois said she had no questions of the pathologist.

The district attorney then called Detective Bradley Goshen, who described how he was dispatched by a radio call to the parking lot at the London Broil and how he found Benjamin Mudge lying facedown on the pavement. He told how he and other detectives reached the conclusion that the killer must have dropped the gun somewhere between the lot and his parked car. He described the search for the weapon. He told how, in a storm sewer, they found the .38-caliber Smith & Wesson revolver.

Hornwood introduced the pistol in evidence.

"Did you find any fingerprints on this pistol?"

"No, sir. It had been pretty cleanly wiped off. We found some pieces of prints and some smudges—nothing you could base an identification on. But on the cartridges in the chamber . . ."

Hornwood introduced four .38-caliber cartridges and two empty shell cases in evidence. The detective testified that fingerprints had been found on all of them, sufficient for a positive identification. The lifted prints, checked with the FBI, turned out to be those of Kevin Flint.

"You interrogated the suspect Kevin Flint, did you not?"

The detective was a young man: still in his twenties probably. He ran his hand nervously over his bristly, crew-cut sandy hair. "Yes, sir. I did."

"During the course of the interrogation, did the name of the present defendant, Teejay Brookover, arise?"

"Yes, sir. It did."

"How?"

"We thought it was possible Mr. Mudge had been killed by somebody who had—business connections with him. We asked Flint about several people we thought might have some connection with the murder."

"And one of those people was Miss Brookover?"

"Yes, sir."

"How did Flint respond when you asked him about Teejay Brookover?"

"Objection," said Lois. "The answer will be hearsay."

"I will rephrase the question," said Hornwood quickly, with a nod and smile for Lois. "Sergeant Goshen, did Flint say he was acquainted with Miss Brookover?"

"Yes."

"How did he describe his relationship with Miss Brookover?"

"He said he'd known her for a long time."

When Lois cross-examined, she returned immediately to his answer to that question. "Sergeant Goshen, do you remember exactly how Flint answered you when you asked if he knew Teejay Brookover?"

"His exact words, ma'am?"

"Yes. Do you recall them?"

The detective nodded. "He said he'd known her on and off for a long time."

"He'd known her 'on and off' for a long time," Lois repeated. She stood behind the defense table, leaning over the table, bracing herself with both hands flat on the tabletop. Her yellow note pad was between her hands. "What does 'on and off' mean to you, Sergeant Goshen?"

"I will object, Your Honor," said Hornwood quietly. "Sergeant Goshen is not a recognized expert on the meanings of words."

"We will hear his answer for what it's worth," said Judge Spencer.

"'On and off,'" mused the detective, frowning. "Well, I guess it means he knew her sort of, from time to time, now and again. Like that."

"All right. Now, sergeant, can you tell me how you asked the question? In what words?"

"As best I recall, I asked him if he knew a lawyer by the name of T. J. Brookover."

"And how did he answer—in his words?"

"He said he knew a woman lawyer named Tommy Jo Brookover."

"Tommy Jo. Did he refer to her any other way?"

"No, ma'am."

"Did you ask him if she had anything to do with the murder of Benjamin Mudge?"

"No. He denied he had anything to do with it himself, so there wasn't any point in asking him who else had to do with it."

XXXIV

Tuesday, November 28, 1978

The deputies brought the prisoners over from the jail at their own convenience, and this morning they locked Teejay in the holding pen forty minutes before the court would be in session, half an hour before Lois Hughes and Earl Lansing arrived. The door to the hallway remained open, and courthouse functionaries, bustling about the morning's business, peered in at her as they passed. Two of them stopped in for a moment to speak with her. One of them offered her coffee and went off to find a deputy to open the pen for a moment, since the paper cup could not be passed in through the chain link. He stood and talked with her—a gray, bald man who told her he was retiring soon after the first of the year. He told her in confidence the word was around in the courthouse that the case against her was weak and there wasn't a chance she would be convicted. He was one of the shirtsleeve clerks whose name she had taken the trouble to learn over the years, who had been a help to her from time to time in the practice of law.

The flat shelf on which she could sit was painfully uncomfortable, so she stood most of the time in the pen. In her cell in the jail, whatever else she had suffered, she had never felt the incipient panic of claustrophobia; but in this tiny cage of chain-link fencing, locked in with a small laminated padlock, she felt physical oppression. She had worn today the light tan, suedelike pants and vest and the warm-colored print shirt; and they reminded her, this time, of the fear she had felt—the panic, in fact—when she realized she would not be allowed to walk into the sheriff's office and surrender but was being arrested, to be taken in in handcuffs. Later they had taken her finger-prints and mug shots, which for some reason she had not anticipated: a process that had, even more than the handcuffs, fixed in her mind that she was a prisoner and an accused criminal and was going to jail and was going to stay there for a long time. The pen was the same: a harsh reminder of what she was and what she faced.

Under the present law, she was entitled to see the police record they made of her. She had insisted that Lois bring a copy of her card to one of their interviews. In the set of photographs—one front-on, one left profile, one right—her grim face was swollen from crying. The board that hung around her neck in the front-on shot carried the record of the mug shots—HOUSTON PD 4-6-78—0143215. The finger-prints were on the back of the card. On the front—Name: BROOK-OVER, TOMMY JO. Aliases: T. J. BROOKOVER, TEEJAY BROOK-OVER. Ht.: 67″ Wt.: 131 W/F Identifying scars, marks: NONE Age: 36. Arrested: HOUSTON PD 4/6/78 Charge: PREMEDI-TATED MURDER (INDICTED) Disposition: HARRIS CO. JAIL. The card would be on file forever, even if she were acquitted in Houston, in Austin, and in Washington.

The reporters had been given little to work with on the first day of the trial. They had heard almost all of it before—during Kevin's trial. They had seized on the mention of Jim Rush. He was described in both Houston newspapers as a young attorney, partner in a prominent firm, who had spent nights, even weekends, living in her apartment. She was sorry. In another sense, she was not sorry. If her neighbors had told the police about Jim Rush and had not told them about Kevin coming to her apartment, they didn't know about Kevin; and that was important. His ludicrous, even offensive, sneaking in and out had been good judgment after all.

Maybe, too, Lois would have to use Jim Rush's name. Depending on what evidence Hornwood had of the relationship between her and Kevin, Lois might want to offer evidence that James Rush, not Kevin Flint, had been the defendant's lover and slept in her apartment. It would be better if nothing had to be said about it at all; but if it did, the accidental introduction of Jim's name into the trial would be an advantage.

When Lois and Earl came, they were apologetic. "Never mind," she said to them. "There's no reason you should have to sit in here, too. Just ask them to take me to the bathroom before we have to go in."

The morning's first witness for the prosecution was Thomas Glencoe. He looked haggard and thin—maybe the consequences of total abstinence from alcohol since he went to a federal prison. His clothes hung loose on him. His wrinkled throat did not fill his shirt collar. He stared at Teejay for a thoughtful moment when he first sat down in the witness chair; then he did not look at her again.

Hornwood, looking refreshed and renewed in confidence, sat at his table and led his witness through the story of Mudge's acquisition of Futures Dynamic.

"At the time, Mr. Glencoe, when you were encouraging your stockholders—that is, the stockholders of Futures Dynamic, of which you were president—to accept a deal which diluted their interest in the corporation and would give control of it to Mr. Mudge and his associates, you were in fact already on the Mudge payroll. Is that correct?"

"That is correct," said Glencoe somberly.

"Did you tell your stockholders, or any of them, of this relationship between you and Mudge?"

"No, sir."

Hornwood had popped a small mint into his mouth and was letting it dissolve. He worked his tongue languidly as he spoke and as he listened to the answers from Glencoe.

"Were you obligated to tell them?"

"I was."

"Legally obligated."

"Yes. I was legally obligated."

"Morally obligated."

"Yes, sir."

Hornwood paused for a moment, staring at his witness and working his mint. "There is a word for that kind of conduct, is there not, Mr. Glencoe?"

Glencoe nodded. "Fraud," he said uncomfortably.

Hornwood pushed back his chair and rose, and he walked around to the front of his table. "How did the stockholders of Futures Dynamic receive the proposition to issue sixty-seven thousand additional shares of stock and sell those shares to the Mudge group?"

"They were given a written proposition."

"Who prepared that written proposition?"

"It was prepared by Mudge's lawyer, T. J. Brookover."

"The defendant sitting there?"

"Yes."

"Did that written proposition reveal to the stockholders that you were paid by Mudge, or that they would lose control of their corporation, or that its assets would be committed to a land-development proposition that entailed substantial risk?"

"No."

"Were essential facts omitted from that written proposition?"

"Yes."

"Did Miss Brookover *know* those facts?"

"Yes."

Hornwood then led Glencoe through a description of the stockholders' meeting and of what she said to the Futures Dynamic stockholders. After that he turned to Lago Aguila and the misrepresentations of the lots. Glencoe's testimony, consistently, was that Teejay had known every fact and had chosen, with Mudge, to withhold certain facts and even to misrepresent facts, to facilitate the quick sale of lots.

"Were you not aware, Mr. Glencoe," asked the district attorney, "that you were risking prosecution and prison terms?"

"I knew it. I didn't know it very well," said Glencoe in a low voice.

"Explain that."

Glencoe lifted his chin, pulling his thin neck up out of his collar. "I —In the first place, we all relied on our lawyer. I mean, Miss Brookover. I don't feel I was ever adequately warned of the risk we took. Anyway, we were sure that the propositions would make money and everybody would be happy. It was like any other risk you take in business. If things had worked out, nobody would have lost anything, everybody would have been happy, and nobody would have been prosecuted for anything. Fraud doesn't matter if everybody comes out all right."

"But it didn't come out all right," said Hornwood. He walked to the rail of the jury box. "How badly have you been hurt, Mr. Glencoe?"

Glencoe dropped his eyes and mumbled. "I'm in prison," he said. "I'm bankrupt. I've lost everything I ever had, including friends."

Hornwood walked back to his table, giving Glencoe time to recover. Glencoe sat with his head down. He clutched his chin in one hand and squeezed.

"Now, Mr. Glencoe," said Hornwood. He sat down again. "I would like to invite your attention to a meeting held on Sunday afternoon, March 5, 1978. Do you remember that meeting?"

"Yes."

"In fact, you and I have talked about it, and your memory was refreshed by the discussion. Isn't that correct?"

"Yes."

"Tell us about that meeting."

"It was on a Sunday afternoon at Mudge's office. He had a way of holding meetings at times when it was inconvenient for other people—weekends, the middle of the night . . . He had called. I came. Teejay Brookover was there when I arrived. Harry Gottschalk was there. The talk was about selling some more lots to Mudge. She didn't want to do it. Then she got off on how we were all going to be prosecuted."

"Be specific about that, please," said Hornwood firmly.

Glencoe glanced at Teejay—only the second time he had looked at her since he came into the courtroom. "She told Mudge we were all going to go to jail. She said it was because he had raped the corporation, meaning Futures Dynamic. That's the term she used: 'raped' the corporation. She said we would all be prosecuted. She said there wasn't any getting out of it; we'd all be convicted. She said she'd lose her license to practice law and she'd go bankrupt. She told Mudge he had caused her to lose everything she had worked for all her life."

"Was she emotional?"

Glencoe nodded. "Very emotional. She cried."

"Did she see any way out of it all?"

"Yes, maybe. She told Mudge he had enough money to bail out Lago Aguila. She told him if we could keep the land company solvent and keep the work going on the sewage-disposal system, we still might be able to earn a profit on the subdivision and prevent Futures Dynamic from going under. That way the lot buyers would have lots they could build on, the Futures stockholders would not lose the value of their stock, and the prosecutions wouldn't happen. She begged him to put enough money into Lago Aguila, Incorporated, to bail it out."

"And what did he say?"

"He refused. He preached to her about lending money to borrowers whose credit was not good at banks."

"Then what happened?"

"She got very angry. She told him if he thought he was going to get out of it free while she went to jail, he was crazy. She said he had suckered us all, but if he thought he was going to get away with it and let everybody else take the rap for him, he didn't know her very well. She said she would testify against him."

"What did Mudge say to that?"

"He laughed at her. He said she was the lawyer and all he had done was follow her advice. He said if he'd done anything illegal, it was only what she had advised him to do."

"Did he call her names?" Hornwood prompted his witness.

"He called her a little bitch. He said she was nothing but a petty shyster that he'd tried to help work her way into the big time but she'd failed him as a lawyer and turned against him. He told her she blamed him for her own carelessness and stupidity. He said he was wrong ever to have trusted her."

"What happened then?"

"She left."

"Angrily?"

"She was crying. She screamed at him on the way out the door that she'd see him in hell. Oh—and she threw something at him. It was a watch. A wristwatch. She snatched it off her arm and threw it at him."

Lois cross-examined. She was wearing that day a rose-colored knit suit. She did not rise. "Mr. Glencoe," she said, "did Miss Brookover ever, in your hearing, threaten violence against Mr. Mudge?"

Glencoe shook his head. "No," he said.

"Did you yourself ever threaten him with violence?"

"No."

"Did you threaten to testify against him, as Miss Brookover did?"

"Yes. I told him I'd give evidence against him if we were prosecuted. And he said it would go worse for me if I did. He said the federal government didn't know everything I'd done, and if I weren't careful he'd see they found out, and there'd be other charges against me."

"What charges?"

"I don't know."

"Did anyone else ever threaten to kill him?"

"Well, he told me one of the stockholders of Futures Dynamic called him and threatened to kill him."

"I'll have to object to the hearsay, Your Honor," said Hornwood quietly.

"Sustained," said the judge. "The jury is instructed to disregard Mr. Glencoe's statement as to what he says Mr. Mudge told him."

After Glencoe, Hornwood called Roberto Luiz. The testimony was much the same. Luiz said all of them—himself, Mudge, Glencoe, Teejay—had realized they were violating the federal laws about stock and land frauds, but that they had thought of it as a minimal risk, not out of the ordinary in business. Teejay, he testified, had been a party to all discussions, had known all the facts, had participated in decisions to withhold some facts and to misrepresent others. He had relied on her counsel to the effect that the risk was minimal.

"When we were making up the property report that the federal law requires, she didn't like some parts of it. We said we had run percolation tests on all the lots, when in fact we'd run them on a few only.

She didn't like that. She said we shouldn't say we'd run tests on all the lots when we hadn't. She said that was against the law. She and Mudge argued about it."

"What happened then?"

"The report went out saying we'd run percolation tests on all the lots."

"Who put the report out?"

"She did. She took the draft back to her office and had it typed up for the printer."

"In other words, she went along."

Luiz nodded.

He testified, as Glencoe had, about how Lago Aguila, Incorporated, became insolvent in December 1977; about how it was insolvent again in January and February, even though Mudge was buying lots for himself and his associates; and about how Teejay became desperate and ultimately hysterical. She'd said she was going to lose everything she owned, her license to practice law—everything she had worked for all her life. He testified that she told Benjamin Mudge she hated him.

The court recessed for lunch before Lois had the opportunity to cross-examine Roberto Luiz.

All morning Lois had listened with grim concentration to the testimony of the witnesses. It was wearying to listen to every word. She had fastened on words here and there and had made notes: "G—afraid —or beaten?" "LA 'insolvent'—means?" "What did M know?" "Did L consult other atty.?" She noticed with moments of annoyance that Lansing sat easily, heavy-lidded, listening with no apparent strain of concentration. Early in the session he made a few doodles on his yellow legal pad, but most of the time he only sat slouched, looking bored.

Teejay was worse. All morning she had seemed distracted, as if the testimony of these witnesses against her did not engage her attention and did not bother her. She turned a pencil in her hand, but she did not make a note; and when Lois asked her a question about something Glencoe had said, she could not answer; she had lost the thread of his testimony and did not know what he had said. She sat with her eyes fixed on the yellow legal pad in front of her, hardly even glancing at the jury. Lois was accustomed to Teejay's moods—anyone living through what she was living through was entitled to them—but this abrupt withdrawal into introspection was new, confusing, alarming.

Even now, in the holding pen, she sat squirming on the hard shelf and ate listlessly, conceding short answers to Lois's questions about things that had been said by the witnesses, not allowing herself to be led into a conversation. There was no point in telling her she was backing away from her own trial, or of demanding she discipline herself to pay attention. It was unlikely she realized she wasn't. Lois tried instead to suggest the return of her attention, by questions.

"Was Gottschalk there when you were discussing the property report?"

"He was in and out. Mudge used him for an errand boy."

Her responses were like that: short, responsive, but volunteering nothing. Lois pulled apart the hamburger the boy from the office had brought. She ate the slice of tomato and the lettuce and left the bread and meat. She felt thirsty, unusually so; she drank her Coke and wanted another one. She asked Lansing and Teejay if they wanted more drinks from the machine. They didn't, so she went herself.

When she returned, Lansing and Teejay were talking urgently: he standing with his shoulder touching the pen, she pressing the chain link, her fingers curled in it. (The galvanizing had been corroded and the chain link was rusty in the door, from waist to shoulder-high, where prisoners had clutched it with sweaty hands.) She was nodding. He was frowning.

"Lois, listen," Teejay said. "C'mere. Something to think about."

Lois popped the ring on her can of Coke and stood near the door to the pen.

"I want to call Kevin as a witness," Teejay said.

Lois shook her head. "How many times have we discussed it?" she asked.

"I let you talk me out of it," said Teejay quickly. She spoke breathlessly, with a thin voice, as if her mouth were dry. "I've been thinking. It's really all that counts—whether he and I were . . . sleeping together, or whatever. All this bullshit from Glencoe and Luiz means nothing unless Hornwood can make the jury believe Kevin and I were . . . Look. They're not going to believe Kevin killed Mudge for the money when they hear about all the cash he had stashed in deposit boxes. They're going to *wonder* why we don't call him. They're going to wonder why we don't bring in his testimony."

"I'll tell you why we don't," Lois said in a hard voice. "Because we don't know what he'll say."

"We *will* know," Teejay insisted emotionally.

"*How?*"

Teejay glanced at Earl Lansing. "You've got to get Judge Spencer to order the sheriff to let us meet with Kevin," she said in a low, half-whispered voice. "The four of us. You, me, Earl, Kevin. We're entitled to a session with our witness."

Lois shook her head. "I've met with him. I can again. So can Earl. But not you. Not you, Teejay."

"*Get your judge to order it,*" Teejay demanded in a shrill whisper.

The cross-examination of Roberto Luiz was short and dull. Lois questioned him. She elicited nothing new. His testimony, for whatever it was worth, stood as he had given it. He was followed to the witness stand by Harry Gottschalk, who testified about angry scenes between Mudge and Teejay, during which, he testified, she had threatened unspecified revenge on Mudge. Earl Lansing cross-examined him. He elicited an admission from Gottschalk that Teejay's threats had never been couched in terms of violence and might have referred to her repeated statement that she would testify against him. Gottschalk was conspicuously hostile on the witness stand, and Lois thought the jury would discount anything he said.

Hornwood was building his case element by element. An essential element was motive: to establish that Teejay had motive to hire Kevin Flint to murder Benjamin Mudge. His emphasis in his questioning of these witnesses was on what Teejay stood to lose from the failure of Lago Aguila, and on her anger at Mudge for causing that loss. It was important testimony, but it included nothing they had not expected to hear, nothing for which they were not prepared.

The last witness of the afternoon was an assistant superintendent of the Oklahoma Penitentiary, who testified that when Kevin Flint was a prisoner there in 1966 he applied for permission to write letters to one Tommy Jo Brookover in El Paso, Texas, and to receive letters from her.

"Did he make this application in writing, Mr. Crum?"

"He did, sir."

"And does that application remain in his file?"

"Yes, sir."

"Have you brought that record with you, Mr. Crum?"

"Yes, sir."

"Is the document you have in your hand the application made by Kevin Flint to the warden of the Oklahoma Penitentiary to place Tommy Jo Brookover on his list of approved correspondents?"

"Yes, sir."

"It is a printed form?"

"Yes, sir. A form we use. He filled it out with a ballpoint pen."

"Will you read the form to us, Mr. Crum?"

" 'Kevin W. Flint, number 15451786, applies for permission to add the person listed below to his list of approved correspondents. Name of person: Tommy Jo Brookover. Address: 85 Wilson Street, Apartment B-5, El Paso, Texas. Relationship: girl friend.' "

Lois's motion for an order permitting a meeting between Teejay and Kevin Flint caused the first show of emotion by District Attorney Hornwood. Lois had made her motion out of the presence of the jury, after they had been led from the courtroom by the bailiff.

"There can be only one reason for such a motion," Hornwood said in a hard, angry voice. "Flint is going to take the stand and lie. Miss Brookover is going to take the stand and lie. They want to coordinate their lies."

Lois argued that a criminal defendant, free on bail, and a defense witness have every opportunity to meet and discuss their testimony, and no one suggests it is improper. Why, then, should this defendant not have that opportunity, just because she is imprisoned and her witness is too?

The judge, reluctantly and quietly and without comment, granted the motion. She ordered the sheriff to arrange a meeting between the two prisoners.

The sheriff was reluctant. Lois once had to threaten to call the judge and appeal from limitations his office tried to put on the meeting. She refused to tolerate any limit on time. She refused to allow a jailer and a jail matron to be present in the room. The meeting was arranged, finally, for seven o'clock, in the matrons' lounge in the women's jail—a room inside the main gate of the jail, yet outside the cellblocks.

Flint was brought in before Teejay was. Once again, he impressed Lois as a personable, handsome man, continuing fully in possession of his personality: in short, intact in spite of what was happening. He wore his faded jail coveralls with the sleeves cut off at his shoulders and frayed, unbuttoned to show the curly hair on his chest. He carried a pack of cigarettes in the breast pocket and was smoking when he was led in. He spoke to Lois with a tolerant smile that suggested she amused him, and he shook Lansing's hand firmly and said he looked younger than he had when they met thirteen years ago.

The room was furnished with varicolored fiber-glass chairs arranged around two tables. Some ragged magazines—*Outdoor Life, Cosmopolitan*—were scattered on the tables. The tabletops were marked with the dried rings of cups and glasses. Flint looked around scornfully. He knocked an empty potato-chip bag off the table. "Don't look like there's much to choose between the ones that guard and the ones that's guarded," he said.

Teejay was brought in. She was wearing a short, threadbare, gray uniform dress and a pair of brown penny loafers. She took Flint's outstretched hand in both of hers, and for a moment they stood looking at each other silently, both of them rigidly controlled. They sat together, facing Lois and Earl Lansing across the square, Formica-topped table.

"Somethin' I want to say to Tommy Jo," Flint said immediately. "Before we talk about anything else." He turned toward her. "I'm sorry I got you in this mess. I'm really sorry."

Teejay shook her head. "It's not your fault. I'll never think of it as your fault."

Flint nodded solemnly. "Even so . . ." he concluded softly.

Maybe she touched his hand; Lois could not see under the table.

"You want to testify for me, Kevin?" Teejay asked. "It'll be a risk for you, you know."

"I've always said I'll testify," he said. "I'll say anything you want."

"There are two risks in it," Lois interjected crisply. She was troubled by the visible communion between these two and felt excluded. "One, if they trip you up in any kind of lie, you'll do us more harm than good. Two, if you do testify for her, Hornwood will probably be inspired to fight very hard for a death sentence against you. You have to think about it."

"Ah have thought about it," said Flint. He flipped the butt of his cigarette on the floor and ignored it burning another scar into the linoleum. "I've had a long time to think about what I'll say. Tommy Jo has too. As far as the death sentence goes, I'm not worried about that. They'll never do it. They haven't got the guts anymore. And if they do—well, a man'd be better off that way than livin' all his life in Huntsville."

"I don't know how I'd live, thinking you'd put yourself in the electric chair to help me," said Teejay. "Let me have a smoke."

He lit a cigarette for her. And he shrugged. "Aside from that idiot Gilmore . . ." he said, and he shrugged again. "Anyway, the appeals will run on for five or six years. In that time I might die of a bad heart. Or they might drop the bomb. Who knows? I never in my life worried about things that far off. I don't care. If it will help, I want to testify. I was about to give up on the idea. Ah hadn't heard from you all in so long, I was beginnin' to think you'd give up on me."

Teejay, with her hands clasped tightly on the table before her—on a shiny brown coffee ring, Lois had noticed—stared blankly in front of her and only glanced up skeptically at Flint when he said he suspected they had forgotten him. She held the cigarette in her mouth (an ugly way to smoke) and now reached for it and said to Flint,

"We can't deny we've been friends. They know it. They have evidence of it."

"I never said I wasn't a friend of yours," said Flint. "I won't say it. I'll say I killed Mudge for my own reasons, and they can't shake me on that, no matter what they've got."

"Boy," said Earl Lansing. He was sitting with an arm looped over the back of his chair, listening to Flint and regarding him with one slightly lifted eyebrow. "What about that paper you filled out at McAlester, saying she was your girl friend?"

"Ask me about that when I'm on the stand," said Flint. "The rules were that you couldn't write to anybody except your lawyers, your family, or maybe, if they wanted to give you a special favor, a girl friend. I needed a little money and didn't have anybody to ask but Tommy Jo. I called her my girl friend to get permission to write her."

"Easy story," said Lansing with a little smile.

"You got a better one?" Flint asked.

"Well, is it the truth, or not?" Lois asked.

"Sure it's the truth," said Flint. "Let 'em prove it isn't."

"Let me tell you what I'm afraid of," said Lois. "You'll testify you and she were only casual friends, only saw each other occasionally. She'll testify the same way. Then Hornwood will come up with rebuttal witnesses who'll testify they saw you together . . ." Lois turned up her palms. "Where? Who knows what he can come up with? He might hold back some of his evidence about your relationship, to use after you testify. The best use he could make of it would be to prove you lied on the stand."

"I'm not afraid of that," said Earl Lansing. "Tomorrow your prosecutor has got to put on evidence that these two know each other very well. If he doesn't have something pretty good, his case lacks an essential element. If he doesn't put on something pretty strong, I'd move for a directed verdict."

"That's what I've been thinking," said Teejay. She, too, tossed her cigarette butt on the floor. "If he didn't have something, he would never have indicted me. He hasn't let me sit in jail since April on a case that lacks an essential element. He has a witness that saw you at my apartment, Kevin. Or something like that. And *that*, Lois, is why we have to have Kevin as a witness: to explain away whatever Hornwood's got."

"Wait till we *hear* what he has," Lois argued. "Then we'll decide whether to call Kevin as a witness. Maybe we won't need him."

"We'll need him," Teejay said grimly.

The conversation ran down after that. Teejay and Flint sat and stared at each other, smoking fresh cigarettes, talking disjointedly about nothing important. She asked him how he felt. He said he could live with what he had to live with. He asked her if she could do the same. She shook her head and said she was trying.

"If it hadn't been for me doin' somethin' stupid, you wouldn't be here," he said to her.

She frowned and shook her head. "Don't talk that way. Don't *think* that way," she whispered.

It was Lansing who suggested the meeting was over.

"How about letting us have a minute, you two?" Teejay said.

Lansing nodded to Lois and took her arm as they stepped into the corridor outside the room. The matron on duty at the end of that corridor saw that they had come out and picked up her telephone to call men to come for Kevin.

"What do you think? Two more days?" Lois asked Lansing. It was only to make conversation. Lansing understood that, apparently, and only nodded.

Lois turned her head and looked back through the open door, into the harsh-lighted, smoky matrons' lounge. Teejay and Flint had stood. They were in each other's arms. She clung to him, hauling herself up on him with her arms crossed behind his shoulders, and they kissed fervently, noisily, their mouths locked together as they twisted their heads and bruised their lips. Lois could hear Teejay moan.

"*Oh, my God!*" Lois cried at Lansing. Her eyes wide, her mouth hanging open, she stared in shock at the clutching couple. "*Oh, my God!* Earl. . . ! I—*oh, my GOD!*"

Lansing frowned quizzically. "What'd you think?" he asked.

XXXV

Wednesday, November 29, 1978

"Thank you, Mrs. Drake," said Hornwood, bowing, smiling. "You signed a lease. So you have lived in that apartment complex since—since when?"

The witness nodded and grinned. She was momentarily amused that the district attorney was asking her to repeat something to which she had already testified. "Well, it was April of 'seventy-five," she said. "I moved in there in April of 1975; about the first of April, it was. Lived there since."

"Are you then acquainted with the defendant, Miss Brookover?"

The witness nodded again. "We've met. Talked together once in a while. We were neighbors."

"Yes. Describe for the jury, please, the relative locations of your apartments. . . ."

Her name was Alice Drake. She had lived across the courtyard from Teejay. Her door had faced Teejay's. She was forty-five maybe, an unstylish but personable woman who had testified she sold real estate. She described how her front door faced Teejay's, across a courtyard some thirty feet wide. Each apartment, she explained, had a front door and a back door. Tenants parked their cars around the periphery of the building and carried in their groceries through the back door.

They received guests, she said, through the doors facing on the court-yard.

"Mrs. Drake, do you know the man convicted of murdering Benja-min Mudge—Kevin Flint?"

"I don't know him, no. I've seen him."

"When was the last time you saw him?"

"The last time I saw him was in a police lineup, when I was asked to pick him out of a group."

"Were you able to pick him out?"

"Yes."

"What were you asked to do at that lineup?"

"I was asked if I could pick out anyone I had seen go in and out of Miss Brookover's apartment."

"And you identified Flint?"

"I picked out a man, and they told me he was Kevin Flint."

Hornwood pushed back his chair and crossed his legs. "How many times had you seen that man before?"

"Once for sure. Twice, I think."

"Tell us about the 'for sure' time. When was that?"

"As best I can remember, it was about a year ago. It was between Thanksgiving and Christmas. I couldn't tell you what day."

The woman looked constantly at Teejay. It was plain she was un-comfortable testifying against her former neighbor; and she meant, probably, for Teejay to understand she would testify only to facts she knew for a certainty, not to anything more. She would do her duty as a citizen. She would do no more.

"Describe what you saw."

"I saw the man I picked out of the lineup, Kevin Flint, come to the door of her apartment, and ring the bell, and go in."

"What time of day was this?"

"It was in the evening."

"After dark?"

The witness nodded. "It was dark, but there were always lights on in the courtyard."

"Did you get a good look at the man?"

"Yes. It was Flint."

"What about the other time, the one you are not so sure about?"

The witness wiped her upper lip with the back of her hand, then she ran the back of her hand across the lapel of her pink polyester pantsuit. "Well . . . I thought I saw the same man go in another time about a week later. But that time I wasn't really looking and didn't get so good a look."

"Between Thanksgiving and Christmas last year, you saw Kevin

Flint enter the apartment of the defendant, Miss Tommy Jo Brookover, at least one time, maybe twice. Is that correct?"

"That's right."

Lois was leaning toward Teejay, listening to Teejay whisper; and Lansing leaned more, to hear what Teejay was saying. Lois looked up at the judge. "If Your Honor please, we need a moment." The judge nodded, and the conference at the defense table continued for another half-minute.

Earl Lansing cross-examined. "Mrs. Drake, on this first night when you think you saw Kevin Flint, how did you come to be looking so close?"

Alice Drake was distracted by the whispering still going on between Teejay and Lois. She frowned. "Well, I happened to be looking out the window—checking the weather or something."

"Did you see Miss Brookover come to the door and let this man in?"

"Yes."

Lansing sat with his arms folded, confronting the witness with both a posture and an expression that bespoke tolerant skepticism. By the tone of his questions he did not accuse the witness of lying, or even of being mistaken; all he was doing was exploring the facts in more detail. "How did she welcome her visitor? Could you tell?"

"No. She just let him in."

"Did you see him leave later?"

"No."

"Were you watching for him to leave?"

"No. I closed the drapes a little while later, so I could undress."

"And the other time, when you think you might have seen him. Was that the same?"

The witness nodded. "I didn't spend my time staring out the window to see who came to my neighbors' doors."

Earl Lansing smiled. "Fine. I—" He stopped to take a note handed him by Teejay. He glanced at her. He nodded to her. "Mrs. Drake," he said, "were you aware of Miss Brookover's marital status when you were her neighbor?"

"I knew she was not married."

"Did she, so far as you were able to observe, receive many men as visitors to her apartment?"

"Not that I noticed. Only the one, really."

"By 'only the one' do you mean Kevin Flint?"

The witness shook her head. "No. I mean somebody else. I don't know who he was, but he came more often."

"This other man you refer to—did he—is it your impression he stayed overnight?"

"I think he did. I saw him leave one morning."

"What did he look like?"

"Dark hair. Wore glasses. Always dressed in a suit. I knew she was a lawyer. He looked like one, too."

"When did you see him?"

The witness frowned. "What do you mean, 'when?' "

"At the time you saw Flint, did you see this man, too?"

"I guess so. Yes. They were both coming to see her at the same time."

"But Flint came once, you think—possibly twice—and this other man came often and stayed overnight. Is that correct?"

The witness thought about it for a moment. "Yes. Yes, that's correct."

"Thank you, Mrs. Drake."

Lois looked at Teejay. "It still proves he came to see you," she whispered. Teejay shrugged, and Lois looked away. It made no difference to Lois that the woman had not seen Flint leaving the apartment in the morning; she knew he did. He was Teejay's lover, and he had killed Mudge. He had killed Mudge in a vain, mad attempt to save Teejay from federal prosecution, or he had killed him at her insistence, with her help. Teejay had lied to her, as much as Flint. God knew what more she had lied about. It was difficult now to go on with her defense.

Bob Peavy last night had congratulated her on her argument in favor of the motion to let Teejay meet with Flint. Her argument that due process and equal protection required it had been inspired, he said. She had not told him she had seen the pair clutching, kissing hungrily. She had not told him she was now satisfied that Teejay had done just what he had cynically suggested: employed her as counsel so she could exert her personal and political influence on Norma Spencer.

Bunny, hiding in a black judicial robe, presided over the trial as if she did not see it: placid, corruptible, contemptible. Booster, pounder of sand down a hundred bottomless ratholes, she had betrayed her education and her promise. The cynicism of making her a judge now earned its reward, *quid pro quo*, exactly as expected; and it was nothing to be proud of.

Lois was discouraged, disillusioned, to the point of illness.

The next witness was Roosevelt Starr, a black man about forty years old, who testified that he was a high-school teacher and had become acquainted with Kevin Flint because he enjoyed playing pool and had played Flint many times over the past five years.

Hornwood was at ease, enjoying himself with this witness.

"Are you any good as a pool player, Mr. Starr?" he asked.

The witness smiled. "I think I shoot a pretty good stick," he said.

"Stroke, don't poke," Hornwood suggested.

"Yes, sir."

"And Mr. Flint. Is he pretty good, too?"

"Better than I am," said Starr. "I used to make him spot me a few balls."

"Did Mr. Flint usually play for money?"

Earl Lansing, who had been listening with his chin cupped in his hand, abruptly raised a finger. "Your Honor," he said, "if the district attorney proposes to explore irrelevant subjects such as how well a witness plays pool, or how well Mr. Flint plays, and whether they bet on their games, this trial is going to go on for a month, and personally I'd hoped to be home for Christmas. Unless Mr. Hornwood can establish some special relevance for this line of questioning, I'm going to object for relevancy and ask the Court to order him to get on with it.

"If the Court please, we'll go on to something else."

Teejay glanced at Lansing with a small smile. Of course he had been bound to object. He could not let Hornwood put in evidence that Kevin was a hustler, a gambler. But he had stated his objection in a way that had surely won a point or two with the jurors—none of whom were happy sitting here day after day in the holiday season, spending their nights in grim hotel rooms, out of touch with their families. He had drawled his objection in his best country-lawyer style, and two or three of the jurors had smiled.

She glanced at Lois. Lois was not smiling. Lois was sullen. To hell with her. She, Teejay, had no attention to spare for Lois's mood. At this point it would almost be as well if Lois withdrew. Lansing could carry it from here—probably better than Lois could.

". . . the place is called Le Steak," the witness was testifying. "I take my wife there one night every couple weeks. You can have a drink there and a steak or roast beef for a reasonable price. The place isn't fancy, but the food is good."

"Did you ever encounter Kevin Flint there?" Hornwood asked.

"Yes, one time."

"And when was that?"

"I can tell you exactly," said Starr. "It was the week after Thanksgiving last year. It was a weeknight, maybe seven or eight o'clock."

"Was Flint alone?"

"No, sir. He was in the company of a young lady."

"Did you recognize the young lady?"

"I didn't at the time."

"Is the young lady present in this courtroom?"

"Yes. It was the defendant, T. J. Brookover."

Lansing did not cross-examine Starr. He was a credible witness, and to cross-examine him would only serve to emphasize his testimony. Lansing pretended he was busy scribbling a note, and when the judge asked him if he wanted to cross-examine, he looked up as if momentarily confused and said no, he had no questions. It was an old-time courtroom trick, to suggest the testimony of this witness was not important enough to have his full attention. Teejay doubted little tricks like that worked anymore.

"The state calls Ivor Zubanski."

She nudged Lois and Lansing. This one was a surprise.

"I am manager of zee Intercontinental Motel, on Highvay Seventy-fife, nort' off zee city."

"And how long, Mr. Zubanski, have you been manager there?"

"Since nineteen hundred sixty-six. I am also half-owner."

"Do you know the defendant, Miss Brookover?"

"Yes. She vorked for me one time, for about six months."

"What did she do for you?"

"Vee had at dat time in de motel a cocktail lounge vee called zee DC-8 Lounge. She vorked for me as a cocktail vaitress."

"Under what name?"

"Tommy Zho Brookover."

"Were you aware at the time when Miss Brookover worked for you that she was an attorney at law, practicing law in Houston?"

"No. She did not tell me dat."

"When did you find out she was an attorney?"

"Only after she quit. I saw her name in zee newspaper. I called her. I sought it vass nice."

Hornwood picked up a pencil by its eraser and idly tapped the point on the table, taking a pause for dramatic effect. "Mr. Zubanski," he said, "how did you come to hire Miss Brookover?"

"Her boy friend asked me to hire her."

"And who was her boy friend?"

"He vass a young man I knew as Jim Hedvig."

"Jim Hedwig," said Hornwood firmly, correcting the witness's pronunciation. "When did you last see Jim Hedwig?"

"In a police lineup," said the witness.

"By what name was he called in that police lineup?"

"He vass called Flint—Kevin Flint."

It was damaging. Judge Spencer, watching the case for the prosecution slowly unfold, had begun to wonder if Hornwood could make any case at all. But this hurt. She could see on the face of the defendant that it hurt, and she wondered if the jury saw it. Probably not. She suspected the jury had developed a sympathy for Teejay Brookover. Two or three of them had, anyway; you could see it. Two of the older men, the retired men, would be unwilling to believe, no matter what Hornwood presented, that a young woman as pretty and appealing as the defendant could have committed a crime of violence. Hornwood would have to win them over when he cross-examined her, after she testified for herself. With the others, this Hedwig business was going to hurt.

"In what connection did you know Hedwig?"

"He met a lot of people in my bar. Seemed to transact business."

"Did he ever transact any business with you?"

The witness paused, frowned, sighed. "Yes. He sold me liquor."

"What kind of liquor?"

"All kinds. Wizout zee tex."

"Untaxed liquor," said Hornwood. "How much did he sell you?"

The witness shrugged. "Fifty cases over a period of a month, I guess. It vass zee only untexed liquor I effer bought."

"Where did he get it?"

"He neffer said."

"Where did you think he got it?"

"Objection."

"Strike the question. Who delivered it?"

"He did."

It was surprising that Lois Hughes or Earl Lansing did not object to some of this. Since the defense had not called Flint as a witness, his character was not an issue, and testimony about illegal transactions in untaxed liquor was irrelevant. She, Judge Spencer, would have excluded it on motion. There were three lawyers at the defense table, including the defendant herself—all three of them trial lawyers with experience and enviable records of success. If they did not object to this line of questioning, they had a reason. She guessed it was that they had decided to let Kevin Flint appear to be an habitual criminal —to make it more readily believable that he had killed Mudge in an armed robbery. Hornwood, in fact, was visibly uneasy at how they were letting him proceed. He dropped the questioning abruptly and turned Zubanski over for cross-examination.

"Mr. Zubanski," said Earl Lansing slowly, "do you happen to recall just what Hedwig, or Flint, said to you when he asked you to hire Tommy Jo Brookover to work as a cocktail waitress in your bar?"

"He said she vass a nice, expee-rienced girl vot needed a job."

"You testified he said she was his girl friend. Is that what he said?"

Judge Spencer watched the witness scratch his head and ponder over his answer. She almost held her breath. The jury didn't know it, and spectators in the courtroom didn't know it, but Lansing was taking a very dangerous line in this cross-examination, and tension was high at the district attorney's table as well as at the defense table. What was dangerous was that Lansing did not know the answers to his questions. It is a fundamental rule of cross-examination that you never ask a question if you do not know the answer. If Zubanski now answered that Flint had indeed told him Teejay was his "girl friend" in 1969—or if he testified that Flint told him he slept with her—it would be the most damaging testimony the prosecution had yet obtained; and it would have obtained it from a question asked by the defense.

"He said . . ." the witness ventured hesitantly, ". . . he said the young woman vass his friend."

Lansing ran his hand over the top of his head. "Mr. Zubanski," he said cautiously, "are you aware of the difference between the terms 'friend' and 'girl friend'? Do you know that the term 'girl friend' means a special, intimate relationship between a man and a woman? I would really like to know if Hedwig, or Flint, told you Miss Brookover was his 'friend' or his 'girl friend.'"

Again. It was a risk. Teejay Brookover was pale as she waited for the witness again to ponder.

Zubanski was a bulky man, blond, florid—and a conspicuously reluctant witness, here under subpoena. "He did not . . ." he said slowly, ". . . say he slept viss her, if dot's vat you mean."

"Did he use the term 'girl friend'? Do you recall?"

Zubanski shook his head. "I don't sink so. I sought he brought me a girl vot vass his friend. She needed a job." Suddenly Zubanski grinned. "Zee girl friend of Jim Hedvig vould not haff needed a job."

Teejay's face turned pink. The tension was off. Even Lois, who for some reason this morning had sat rigid and silent at the table, as if she were nauseous, looked to Teejay and smiled.

Lansing bore in. He asked if Zubanski had ever seen Hedwig/Flint in the company of other girls. He had. Had Hedwig/Flint asked him for jobs for other girls? He had not. Had he ever brought Teejay to the DC-8 Lounge as a date? He had not. Had he brought other girls as dates? He had. Had he ever bought Teejay a drink or a meal? No. But he had bought drinks and meals for others? Yes. Had he ever kissed or fondled other girls in the DC-8 Lounge? Yes. Had he done the same with Teejay? No. Thank you.

When the court recessed an hour and a half for lunch, Lois told the deputies that she would not need to confer with her client during the break; and Teejay was handcuffed and returned to the jail. She was put in a cell outside the cellblocks, where there was a bunk and a basin and toilet, and she was able to sit on the bunk, eat her lunch from a tin box, and afterward lie on the bunk and close her eyes.

Lois hurried out of the courthouse. She met Bob Peavy and her father for lunch at the Houston Club.

"Where's your co-counsel?" her father asked.

"Meeting with our witness," Lois said. "Kevin Flint."

"Why aren't you meeting with him?" her father asked.

"Lansing volunteered. He can handle that. I need my hour away from it."

Daniel Farnham smiled wryly at her over his glass of sherry. "Do I detect that you have concluded your famous client killed her man, after all?"

Lois was looking around for their waiter. She wanted a martini. "She killed him," she said quietly.

"Good," said her father, lifting his glass to her. "Then you'll have achieved something when you win her acquittal. It's nothing to congratulate yourself on, after all, when you've won acquittal for an innocent person."

Earl Lansing, having met with Kevin Flint one last time before calling him as a witness, stopped at the women's jail to speak with Teejay before the afternoon session began. She stood at the bars of the cell and talked to him in a low voice, so the matron on duty would not hear. She rested one elbow on the cross brace and wrapped her hand loosely around a bar. (She was wearing that day her off-white linen skirt and jacket, with the lime-green blouse.)

She had not realized that Lansing was not as tall as she was. He was fragile. She had not thought of him that way, all the times she had thought of him over the years after the day she had sat in his office, sipped his whiskey, and listened to him tell her to become a lawyer. She had never seen him lawyering before, although she had thought of him as the archetypal lawyer. In the courtroom these past two days she had seen him inspired and vital, conscious obviously that this was *lawyering*, real lawyering, practicing an honorable pro-

fession, with pride. He was not as gray. He had colored in the courtroom.

Somewhere, out of his briefcase probably, he had taken a drink. She
could smell it.

"It's not so bad," Lansing said. "I thought Hornwood would have
more."

"What would happen if we went to the jury now, with no witnesses?" Teejay asked.

"My dear, that's what we are doing," said Lansing. "You have to
testify. If you didn't, the jury would wonder why you didn't. But they
won't believe anything you say; you're the defendant, after all. We
have to put you on the stand, simply to give Hornwood the chance
to trip you up. If he doesn't, you've won a major point. His case is
weak. The only way he can win it now is by catching you by the
short hairs when you testify. You've got to be careful."

"It comes down to a confrontation, then," Teejay suggested.

Lansing nodded.

"Then, Kevin. . . ?"

"The jury is so curious about him now, we have to let them see he
doesn't have two heads. I think he'll do all right. He's clever, and he's
tough."

"He's more than that," said Teejay solemnly.

"I need hardly tell you, he has the capacity for the stupid mistake
sometimes," Lansing said quietly. "If he had used his head about the
pistol . . ."

"I've sat in here and thought about that for eight months."

"Lois has no idea, has she?"

Teejay shook her head. "Apparently not. I would have supposed
she understood."

"She won't walk out on you. It's a matter of pride."

"I could stand it if she did. You could do better for me now."

"She's shaken. Be careful with her. Don't tell her anything more."

Teejay reached between the bars and took his hand. "I'm grateful
to you," she said. "You're the key to it now."

When the court was again in session, the district attorney stood,
bowed and smiled to the judge, then to the defense table, and said,
"The state calls Christine McElhay."

The bailiff hurried to the door beside the jury box to tell the deputy
outside to bring in the witness.

Teejay whispered to her lawyers. "*Anything she says is a lie. She
knows nothing about the case.*"

Christine McElhay, escorted by a matron, crossed the front of the courtroom and took her place on the witness stand. She wore black pants and a white blouse, and her hair, pulled loosely around and fastened with a rubber band, hung down her back to her waist. She glanced briefly at Teejay, then licked her lips and fixed her eyes steadily on the district attorney.

"State your name."

"Christine McElhay."

"Where do you live, Christine?"

"Omega Street."

"You are a prisoner in the county jail, are you not?"

She nodded. "Yes."

"How long have you been there?"

"About three months."

"Are you acquainted with the defendant, T. J. Brookover?"

"Yes."

"Is she held in the same part of the jail as you are?"

The witness nodded. "In the same place. I see her every day. I can hardly get away from her."

"Does she talk to you?"

"Yes."

"About what?"

"Well, we've talked about a lot of things. Mostly we talk about Kevin Flint."

"Do you know Kevin Flint?"

"Yes."

"When and where have you known Kevin Flint?"

"He's been around Houston on and off. I've known him for years. In fact, I used to go with him, as you might say."

"Did you have a romantic relationship with him?"

"Yes, sir."

"A sexual relationship?"

"Yes, sir."

"What did he do for a living?"

"Anything that would make money."

"Work?"

Christine McElhay laughed. "No. Anything but work."

"Did he—"

"If the Court please," Lois interrupted. "I fail to see the relevance of the employment record of Kevin Flint."

Judge Spencer took off her eyeglasses and looked blankly at the district attorney. She tapped a pencil. "Mr. Hornwood—"

"The charge in this case, Your Honor, is that the defendant procured
Kevin Flint to kill Benjamin Mudge. The character of the man she
procured is definitely an issue."

"It is not an issue," Lois argued sharply.

The judge sighed. "Counsel," she said, beckoning the attorneys to
come to the bench. They clustered before her: Hornwood, towering
over them all; his small, owlish assistant who had not as yet spoken
a word in the trial; Lois; and Lansing. "Just where is this going?" the
judge asked Hornwood quietly, out of the hearing of the courtroom
and the jury.

"Flint was a pimp and a pusher," said Hornwood quietly.

"Which is irrelevant to this trial," Lois whispered angrily. She looked
up at Hornwood. "What are you trying to do?"

"If you put him on as a witness, it will be relevant," warned the
judge.

"Well, I haven't put him on yet."

The judge sighed again and shook her head. "All right. I'm going
to rule it out. But if you call him as a witness, I'll allow it." She spoke
up, for the jury and the record. "The Court sustains the objection.
Proceed to another subject, Mr. Hornwood."

Hornwood, looking grim, walked back to his table. He stood in front
of it with his arms folded. "Miss McElhay," he said crisply. He paused.
"Did Kevin Flint ever say anything to you about T. J. Brookover?"

"*Objection!*" snapped Lois. "He's asking for hearsay."

Hornwood glanced irritably at Lois. "All right, Mrs. Hughes," he
said, nodding. "I'll ask the question differently. Miss McElhay, did
Kevin Flint ever say anything to you about his feelings toward
T. J. Brookover?"

"Yes. He said he loved her."

Hornwood stood rigidly erect, still, grim—looking, apparently, at
his shoes as he waited for the judge to silence the sudden excited
clatter of talk in the courtroom. "Now. Miss McElhay. Did the defendant, T. J. Brookover, ever say anything to you about her feelings
toward Kevin Flint?"

"Yes. She said she loved him."

The judge banged her gavel. Even the jurors, some of them, had
turned to each other and begun to talk. Teejay, her face flushed with
anger, whispered furiously to Lois.

"Thank you, Miss McElhay," said Hornwood. He walked around
his table and sat down.

Lois rose. She stood at her place, staring for a long moment at
Christine McElhay. Her face was long and somber. Her eyes were sad.

She had her own forensic tricks. "I noticed, Miss McElhay, that when the district attorney first questioned you he called you Christine. Do you mind if I call you that?"

The witness shrugged. "Whatever you want," she said.

Lois rubbed her fingertips together, frowning. "Why are you in jail, Christine?"

The witness sneered. "No reason," she said.

"Ah. But you can't leave, I take it. I mean, the door is locked, is it not?"

"You better believe it."

"Then there must be some reason. Are you charged with something?"

"I'm not guilty."

"Even so, what do they *say* you did? What's the charge?"

"Possession of marijuana."

"I see. How much marijuana?"

"Two kilos."

"Possession for sale, in other words."

"I never sold any."

"Two kilos. That's four and a half pounds, roughly, isn't it? That's a bit more than you'd keep on hand for personal use, isn't it?"

"If I'd had it, it would be. But I didn't."

Lois glanced all around the courtroom as if looking for some clue to this puzzling dialogue. "Were you indicted by the grand jury, Christine?" she asked.

Hornwood spoke. "If the Court please, the state will concede that the witness is under indictment on a charge of possession for sale, two kilograms of marijuana."

"Is that right, Christine?" Lois asked.

"That is right," said the witness impatiently.

"Why aren't you out on bail?"

"It's too much. I can't make it."

"Now, Your Honor," Hornwood interjected, "that *is* irrelevant."

"If the Court please, it is *not* irrelevant," Lois argued. "In a moment I am going to ask this witness if she has entered into any kind of deal with the district attorney for leniency in return for her testimony. I think the jury should know she is in jail on a serious charge, has been there a long time, and would probably like to get out."

"Well, there is no objection before the Court, really," said the judge. "Nothing to rule on. Go ahead, Mrs. Hughes."

"How does it happen you are a witness in this case, Christine?"

The witness glared at Lois. "I volunteered," she said.

"When?"

"A long time ago."

"Tell us about it. How did you volunteer? To whom?"

Christine McElhay, prodded for every answer, testified grudgingly that she made Teejay's acquaintance shortly after she was put in the county jail and that within the first month she was there she volunteered to engage her in conversation if she could and to report to the district attorney anything Teejay said to her. Yes, she did hope he would let her plead to a reduced charge in return for her cooperation. No, she had no specific deal. Yes, she had tried to cultivate Teejay's friendship and had encouraged her to talk.

"Lois," Teejay said quietly. Lois bent down, and Teejay whispered to her for a full minute.

"Christine," said Lois briskly. "Tell us. Are you a prostitute?"

"No. And if she just whispered to you that I am, she's lying."

"Were you ever a prostitute?"

"No!"

"Have you ever recruited girls to be prostitutes?"

"Objection," said Hornwood calmly. "This is going pretty far afield, Your Honor."

"The credibility of the witness is at issue," said the judge. "We'll hear her answer."

"The question," said Lois—standing now before her table, leaning back against it, her hands resting on it—"is whether you ever recruited girls to work for you as prostitutes."

"The answer is no," growled the witness through clenched teeth.

"Then newspaper stories saying you did are lies, hmm?"

"Objection!"

"The objection is sustained."

"I have no further questions for the witness," said Lois, turning her back on Christine McElhay and walking around her table to her chair.

Hornwood rose and stood watching as Christine McElhay was taken into custody by the bailiff and led from the courtroom. He nodded and smiled at the judge, then at Lois. "The state rests, Your Honor," he said.

Lois rose again. "The defense moves for a directed verdict of acquittal," she said.

Judge Norma Spencer had no intention of granting a directed verdict. If Teejay Brookover was acquitted, it was going to be by the jury, not by her. She supposed Lois made the motion only *pro forma,* for the record, and was surprised when Lois argued vigorously for it. With the jury out of the courtroom, Lois demanded a verdict, arguing that the prosecution's case was flimsy.

Hornwood sat at his table and smiled tolerantly. He allowed his assistant to argue against the motion. The young man spoke softly, deferentially, and said the state had proved motive, threat, and opportunity—a case of circumstantial evidence that was complete with all elements. "I'm afraid Mrs. Hughes is asking us to produce the proverbial smoking gun, Your Honor. But the smoking gun is just that—proverbial—and the law does not require us to produce it."

It did not, indeed. Judge Spencer denied the motion.

She was intensely curious as to whether or not Lois would call Flint to the stand. She was curious in the first place to see Flint—as of course the jury was. She was curious, too, as to Lois's strategy. It was a risk to call Flint. It was probably a risk not to. From the look of the tight little conference going on at the defense table, maybe they had not yet decided. It had been apparent all during the trial that there was some disagreement among Lois and Teejay and Lansing. She was curious about that, too.

Lois stood. "If the Court please," she said, "for its first witness the defense calls Kevin Flint."

They had to recess briefly while Flint was brought over from the jail. The judge went to her office. The *Chronicle* was out. The reporter covering the trial was critical of her order of yesterday afternoon, allowing Teejay Brookover to meet with Kevin Flint. It was unprecedented, the story said, and gave the two "alleged murderers" the opportunity to match their stories. *Damn!* Damn Lois for demanding such an order!

The word came in: Flint was in the clerk's office. She put on her robe and returned to the bench.

"Do you, Kevin Flint, solemnly swear that the testimony you are about to give will be the truth, the whole truth, and nothing but the truth, as you shall answer to God?"

"I do," he said brusquely, as though impatient with the little formality; and he sat down and crossed his legs.

He glanced up at the judge for an instant, his eyes meeting hers; and maybe he saw the small, inward smile on her face—she supposed he did and hoped he did not read the thought behind it: that if this man had been Teejay Brookover's friend and lover, then Teejay Brookover had been a lucky woman. She liked him, instantly. She didn't want to, but couldn't help it. He was aggressively comfortable: comfortable, that is, in the face of scores of people staring intently at him, some of them hostile. He glanced around the courtroom, returning their curiosity.

"Will you state your name, please?"

Lois began her examination. He testified confidently, concisely. He was not embarrassed to say he was a prisoner in the Harris County Jail or that he stood convicted of the murder of Benjamin Mudge. He did not look like a prisoner, as he unquestionably knew. He wore a navy blue blazer, gray slacks pressed sharply, a white shirt, a blue and red striped tie, black shoes and socks. His face was pink, as if he had been out in the sun somewhere. With his elbows resting on the arms of the witness chair, he clasped his hands loosely before him, and he hunched his shoulders a little and leaned forward slightly. He spoke conversationally and with some animation.

Lois, quite obviously, was uneasy with him. She was tense. She held a yellow pencil tightly between her hands.

"Mr. Flint, I'm sorry to have to ask this question, but I hope you will understand I have no alternative. You understand, too, that you have a right to refuse to answer. You have been convicted of the murder of Benjamin Mudge. Did you, in fact, kill him?"

Flint nodded. "Yes."

The judge rapped her gavel to silence the buzzing and shuffling in the courtroom.

"Why?" Lois asked. "Why did you kill him?"

"Well, of course, Ah didn't intend to," said Flint. "I intended to rob him. I thought he'd have a lot of money on him. Ah'd read about him in the papers. He was a wheeler-dealer, the kind that carries a lot of cash, and I thought he'd have several thousand dollars on him. I was robbin' him and shot him. In a sense it was accidental."

"How did you happen to shoot him?"

"I was nervous. Ah don't know—I think he must have made some kind of quick movement. I'm not sure. Anyway, I shot him."

Lois looked unhappily at Teejay and at Lansing. "Was he in fact carrying a lot of money?"

"I don't know. I was scared and ran away."

"When you were arrested and your room was searched, you had ten thousand dollars in cash. Where did you get that money?"

"It was mine, from deals, gamblin' . . . It wasn't Mudge's."

Judge Spencer watched the jurors listening to Flint. They never glanced away from him, not even to Lois as she asked her questions. They would decide this case on the basis of what he said and how much of it they believed. Her own thought was that he was lying, but he was good at it, and Hornwood would have no easy time tripping him up.

"Now, Mr. Flint, I want you to tell us about your relationship with the defendant, Miss Brookover. How long have you known her? How well? Tell us about it."

Flint drew a deep breath. He looked at Teejay Brookover for a moment, and she looked up at him. "I've known her about thirteen years," he said. "I wish I knew her better. I met her in El Paso. She was workin' as a waitress, workin' her way through school. I thought she was the most beautiful girl I'd ever seen—and probably the smartest. Ah took her out to dinner a few times. I'd have liked to take her more, but she worked and studied, and she didn't have much time.

"Then I got in trouble and had to do some time in the Oklahoma Penitentiary, and I didn't see her for a long time. I wrote her one letter and got one back from her. When I got back to El Paso I asked for her, and somebody told me she'd moved to Houston. When I got to Houston I looked her up. She was goin' to law school. She had a boy friend at the time and was pretty close to him, so I couldn't take her out on dates or anything like that. I did see her a couple of times, where she was workin'. She was still a waitress.

"Over the years I sort of settled here in Houston, and I knew she became a lawyer. I'd see her once in a while, just to have dinner and talk about old times. I've always liked her. I've always thought she's an amazing person. I always wished I could be closer to her than I ever was. But—we're not the same kind of people. To put it sort of a tough way, the fact is I've never been good enough for her. I mean, that's my own judgment."

"Were you ever in love with her?"

Flint smiled for the first time. "Well, sort of, sure. But I never told her so. I never expected anything could come of it."

"Did you ever tell Christine McElhay you were in love with Teejay Brookover?"

Flint nodded. "Probably. I probably said somethin' like that to Christine some time."

"What was your relationship with Christine McElhay?"

Flint smiled again and shook his head. "I slept with her sometimes. She and I *are* the same kind of people."

"Were you ever physically intimate with the defendant, Miss Brookover?"

"No."

Lois pushed her chair back from the defense table and crossed her legs. She pondered for a moment. "Referring to the last six months before you killed Mudge, how often did you see the defendant during that time?"

Flint rubbed his chin with one finger. "Twice, I think. Maybe three times."

"Where?"

"We always went out to dinner, whenever I saw her. We went different places."

"Did you ever go to her apartment?"

"I've been in her apartment maybe three or four times over the years. Ah picked her up there to take her to dinner. We had a drink there before we went out."

"Did you ever spend the night there?"

"No."

Lois looked again at Teejay and Lansing. They returned her look, blandly. They had no questions to suggest.

"All right, Mr. Flint," Lois said. She drew her chair close to her table again. "Tell us now what the defendant, Miss Brookover, had to do with the killing of Benjamin Mudge."

Flint lifted his chin high. "Absolutely nothin'," he said firmly.

"Did she ask you to kill him?"

"No."

"Did she know you were going to kill him?"

"I didn't know that myself."

"Did she know you were going to rob him?"

"No."

"Did she know you had done it? That is, before you were arrested and she read it in the newspapers, did she know you were the one who killed Benjamin Mudge?"

"No."

"Did you see her or talk to her between the time you killed Mudge and the time you were arrested?"

"No."

"Did she ever talk to you about Benjamin Mudge?"

"No."

"Did she ever talk to you about Lago Aguila and the problems she had with it?"

"No."

"Did you know about that?"

"I read some about it in the paper."

"Did you know that because of the conduct of Benjamin Mudge she might lose a lot of money and maybe lose her license to practice law?"

"No."

"Did you, in fact, know she was in trouble of any kind?"

"No. I didn't understand that from what I saw in the papers."

Lois glanced once again at Teejay and Lansing. For a moment she drummed the table nervously. "The charge against Miss Brookover," she said, "is that she hired you, or procured you, to murder Benjamin Mudge. Is it your testimony that the charge is false?"

"It is false," said Flint emphatically. "She had nothin' to do with it."
Lois nodded at the district attorney. "Mr. Hornwood," she said.

As Hornwood rose to begin his cross-examination, Lois interlaced
her fingers on the table and fixed on them a blank, unseeing stare. She
was miserable. Bob Peavy and her father had come back to the courtroom with her and were sitting in the back of the room. Bob Peavy
understood a little of what her father entirely failed to understand:
that she had no control, in fact little influence, over this trial. Her questions had been no more than the cues for Flint's lies; and tomorrow,
when Teejay testified, it would be the same.

Teejay was guilty. She had conspired with Flint to kill Mudge, probably to prevent his testifying against her in federal court. They had
botched it somehow—probably because Flint panicked. Teejay, fighting
for her freedom, had put everything together: a naïve lawyer who
could be deceived into destroying evidence, corrupting a judge, and
playing her role, obedient and docile; and a corrupt judge who would
slant the trial as far as she could without open scandal, to accommodate the naïve lawyer. Lois glanced at Teejay sitting beside her. The
woman was shrewd. She was ruthless. In the circumstances it was
difficult to blame her, but she was a little frightening.

"Mr. Flint," said District Attorney Hornwood—he was sucking on a
mint again today. "You have quite a criminal record, haven't you?"

"Yes, sir," said Flint.

"You were in the penitentiary in Oklahoma. Why? What was the
crime?"

"Larceny by trick," said Flint.

"In other words, you took someone's money or property by deceiving them, lying to them. Right?"

"That's right."

"And you had been put on probation on a similar charge before."

"That's right."

"Have you been arrested since you left the Oklahoma Penitentiary?"

"No, sir."

"But you were—are—a parole violator, aren't you?"

"Yes, sir."

"Who is James O. Hedwig?"

"I am."

"That's a false name you've used. Why?"

"To keep from being picked up as a parole violator."

"How did you make your living?"

Flint crossed his legs again. "Different ways. Confidence games. I sold things I didn't own, sometimes things that didn't even exist."

"Did you ever kill anyone before?"

"No, sir."

"Did you ever commit an armed robbery before?"

"Yes, sir."

"Where and when?"

"Over the years, when things were really tough and I needed a little money for a stake, I robbed people. But I never shot anybody before."

"Would it be wrong to say you've made your living generally by being a small-time trickster and liar?"

"Would it be wrong to say that?" Flint asked, frowning.

"Yes. Would it be wrong to say that?" Hornwood persisted.

Flint shook his head. "No. Ah wouldn't argue with that."

Hornwood looked at the jury and smiled toothily. "Well, why, Mr. Flint, should anyone believe anything you say as a witness in this case, if you're a professional liar?"

"If I wanted to lie here today, Mr. Hornwood," said Flint smoothly, "I'd have started by denyin' all these things you've just been askin' me about."

The judge did not try to stop the laughter in the courtroom. Hornwood had been bested, and she had to hold down her own laugh.

Hornwood smiled grimly at the jury and shook his head. "You hope the jury will believe you, don't you?" he asked Flint.

"Yes, sir."

"Why?"

"I want to help Tommy Jo. I think it would be a terrible shame if she had to go to prison for life for killin' Mudge, when she didn't have anything to do with it."

Hornwood ceased to smile. This straightforward openness by Flint was impossible to cope with. The purpose of these initial questions was to force Flint into evasions, to make him look slippery. But obviously that was not going to work. Hornwood picked up his pad and looked at his notes.

"Mr. Flint, you have admitted you shot Benjamin Mudge. When you went to the parking lot at the London Broil on the evening of March 21, 1978, did you go there to rob Benjamin Mudge specifically, or just to rob whomever happened to be available?"

"I went there to rob Mudge."

"Why Mudge?"

"I'd been readin' about him in the paper. He was a bigger con man than I ever dreamed of bein', and it looked to me like he'd carry a lot of cash."

"How did you know where to find him?"

"I'd been watchin' him a couple of days."

"No one told you where he ate his dinners?"

Flint shook his head. "I followed him."

"Had you ever seen him before? I mean before you began to stalk him?"

"No."

"So you just picked him out, from reading a newspaper story or two, and decided he was the man you wanted to rob?"

"Yes."

"Had you ever done that before? I mean, had you ever before identified a prospective robbery victim that way?"

"Yes."

"When and where?"

"Dallas. I don't know exactly when it was, but it was shortly after I got out of the Oklahoma Penitentiary."

"What was the person's name?"

"I don't remember now."

"Did you get a lot of money?"

"More than two thousand dollars."

Hornwood sighed audibly. He picked up his note pad again. "Were you in need of money?"

Flint smiled. "I always needed money. Doesn't everybody?"

"Well, were you broke? Were you desperate for money?"

"No, sir. I had about ten thousand dollars in my room."

"You had more than that, didn't you?"

"Not in my room. But I had other money in a safe-deposit box. I think it was something like eighty thousand dollars."

"In whose name did you have that box?"

"Hedwig."

"All right. So you had eighty—ninety thousand dollars. Why did you want to commit a robbery?"

Flint clasped his hands comfortably together. "To begin with, Mr. Hornwood, I never touched the eighty thousand in the safe-deposit box. Not for any reason. That was what you might call my retirement. So I had ten thousand. That's not so much, when you have to live and you don't have a paycheck coming in."

"Wasn't the robbery a terrible risk?"

"It turned out that way."

Lois, watching glumly, was dismayed by the ease with which Flint coped with Hornwood's cross-examination. His lies were lies Hornwood could not disprove. He did not evade. He answered every question calmly, looking directly at Hornwood. He gave Hornwood no opening for cutting interrogation. He had thought about his testimony for a long time, obviously. He had rehearsed himself.

Hornwood was annoyed, and he was unable to conceal it. The jury regarded him with skeptical curiosity, wondering probably when he was going to find a hole in the testimony of this witness and demonstrate to them that he had lied. He sat down. "Mr. Flint," he said, "do you mind if I call you Kevin?"

Flint shook his head solemnly. "Not at all. And—I guess then I can call you John. Okay?"

The jury laughed.

"Mr. Flint"—he had to pause because the jury laughed again—"you have committed murder. You admit that. You admit to several armed robberies. You admit to a lifelong career of larceny and fraud. We heard testimony to the effect that you sold untaxed liquor at one time. Incidentally, where did you get the untaxed liquor?"

"It wasn't untaxed, actually," said Flint. "It was stole. I bought it from some boys who'd broken into a bar and stole cases of liquor."

"You fenced it, in other words?"

"Yes, sir."

"Did you do that other times?"

"Yes, sir."

"You've been a dealer in stolen merchandise?"

"Yes, sir."

"Have you ever operated as a pimp, Mr. Flint?"

Lois started. "Just a minute," she said sharply. "I'll object to that."

The judge removed her eyeglasses. "I'm going to sustain, Mr. Hornwood, unless you can show some relevance for that question."

Teejay nudged Lois. "*Let him answer,*" she whispered.

Lois frowned deeply. "On second thought, I withdraw the objection, Your Honor."

Hornwood grinned. "On second thought, I withdraw the question."

The judge glanced back and forth between the two lawyers. "On my second thought, we're going to hear the answer," she said. "Mr. Flint . . ."

Flint looked up at the judge, smiling only faintly. "I have never been a pimp, Your Honor," he said. "I have never been mixed up in any way in prostitution."

"How about narcotics, Mr. Flint?" Hornwood asked.

"No, sir," said Flint calmly. "Ah have never been involved in any way with any kind of drugs."

Hornwood stood again and came around his table. He stood at the front of it. "Are you in love with the defendant, Tommy Jo Brookover?" he asked.

Flint frowned and considered for a long moment. "Well, I—it depends on what you mean."

"That's not so difficult, is it?" Hornwood asked. "Pretty common words, 'in love.' Most people know what they mean."

Flint drew a breath. "I have—a lot of respect for her."

"That isn't the question. The question is, are you in love with her?"

"Not in the romantic way," said Flint. He looked at Teejay. "I think awful high of her. I guess I love her in a way, but it's not in the romantic way."

Hornwood folded his arms. "If she is convicted in this case," he said, "she'll be sent to prison for a long time. Would you lie to save her from that?"

"No, sir."

Hornwood smiled. "You love her, but you wouldn't lie to save her from a long prison term."

"It wouldn't help her," said Flint. "If I lied, you'd catch me at it, and that'd do her more harm than good."

Hornwood's smile disappeared. "That's not the question," he said acerbly. "Would you lie if you thought it would help her?"

Flint regarded the district attorney with a calm, thoughtful eye. "Yes, sir," he said. "If it'd help her, I'd lie for her."

XXXVI

Thursday, November 30, 1978

The sun came up late at this time of year. It was dark outside the windows. She could not know what time it was, but she thought it was not long before dawn. She stood at the bars of her cell. She had stood there for a long time, maybe an hour. She was naked. When she slipped down from her bunk, she had tossed a blanket over her shoulders; but the blanket had been awkward when she lit a cigarette, and she had tossed it back on the lower bunk. Nakedness meant nothing in here. Anyway, it was comfortably cool; at long last it was cool, and she did not sweat. Her foot was on the lower brace. Her shoulder pressed between two bars. The bars were cool. She held a cigarette between the fingers of her right hand. It was burning, but she had only occasionally taken a puff from this one. It had been a long hour. It had been a long night.

If not for the federal charges, this could be her last night in jail. She could be acquitted in the next twelve or fourteen hours. Or convicted. She thought she would be acquitted. It looked good. Kevin . . .

If only she could tell him! Some way she would get the word to him. Whatever it might cost him, he had handled himself brilliantly as a witness, and she was grateful, limitlessly grateful. She wanted him to know also how very much she loved him. It was the mistake of her life not to have acknowledged from the first how she loved him.

Tomorrow was the last day of the first half of her life. After tomorrow she would be a convict with twenty years in prison ahead of her, or she would be a federal prisoner with nothing ahead of her she could not cope with. If in a year or so she were outside prison bars, she would not be a lawyer anymore; she would not be anybody; she would have the second half of her life to live, starting from nothing. Starting from nothing *again*. She had been thinking about that tonight. She had started from nothing, with nothing, and now she was back at the beginning. She was tired. She was hurt. She didn't know if she was able to make herself something again, all over, from the start. For one insane moment she had said to herself maybe it would be better just to go to Goree and settle in for twenty years: a prisoner, a vegetable. After all, she had had her initiation; she knew how to live as a prisoner. But . . .

It was the night to be philosophical.

She ran a finger down one of the bars. It was hard and cold. It was one of the many that held her in here, a human animal locked in a cage for humans. Really, there had not been a moment of it she had not suffered. All of it, all of what Earl Lansing called the trappings of imprisonment, was an instrument of pain. It was no better tonight than it had been the first night. You did not learn to live with it.

Christine McElhay was somewhere else. She was not in "B" Cage anymore. Maybe they thought she, Teejay, would attack her. More likely—from the talk she had heard last evening—someone else in the cellblock would have attacked her. They said they would; prisoners she did not even know had said to her they would like to do violence to Christine. It was a world in here, with its own rules and values. She had not bothered to learn them. She had been surprised the others cared anything about what happened to her, or about what Christine had done.

Earlier tonight she had wept. She was still afraid. You were alone in the end. She was alone now, more ways than anyone understood. She was afraid of tomorrow. It was all so irrational: that twelve strangers, with God-knew-what prejudices, what distorted emotions, would decide if she should be set free or committed to prison for all the middle years of her life. She closed her hands tightly around two of the imprisoning steel bars. If this was what they dealt her—twenty years of this—she would rather be dead.

Lois stood long in the shower. The first minute of hot water, with the first quick swipes of the soapy cloth, had rinsed away Bob's semen, which had dried on her belly and hips. Even a sensitive man could be insensitive sometimes, and last night he had wanted to romp. She had accommodated him. She would always accommodate him. Even now, in the shower, she ran the razor over her pudenda, keeping herself shaved, as he wanted. He had said he could steal her from the trial for a night. It had not worked. She had slept fitfully.

She was the poor little rich girl again. All who knew her and knew anything about the trial were congratulating themselves on the vindication of their longtime judgment; seeing her dancing at the ends of Teejay Brookover's strings, they could see she was a prominent lawyer, a partner and mover in a prominent firm, not because she had the ability but because she had had the connections. They were laughing.

Bob insisted no one was laughing. She did not believe it. He was trying to be kind. If they weren't laughing, it was because they were not shrewd.

Bob's kindness was condescending. No matter what he said, he had passed judgment on her conduct of the Brookover case, and his judgment was not much different from her own. Simply said, Teejay Brookover had seen the worth of the Farnham family name and had used it. Since it wasn't hers, she had used someone whose name it was; and she had wrung value out of it in a way Dan Farnham would envy. She had manipulated his daughter with a skill he—if it had not been his daughter—would have enjoyed watching. He would have enjoyed watching a woman prettier than his daughter exercising a cunning his daughter did not have. He liked a clever woman, he had often said. So did Bob Peavy. They had seen one in action. But it had been Teejay Brookover, not Lois Farnham Hughes.

Bob lay in bed and watched her dress. She wore the maroon silk with the pattern of white leaves, the suit she had worn the first day of the trial. He told her she was a handsome woman. She sat at the breakfast table with her children while he showered and dressed. He would be in the courtroom all day.

Norma Jean read every line of the *Post*'s account of yesterday's testimony. She liked the *Post*'s coverage of the trial better than she did the *Chronicle*'s—mostly because the *Post* only mentioned her name one time in this morning's story and had mentioned her only once or twice yesterday. Anonymity. That was the best she could expect from this trial. No credit. Anonymity. The less they said about her, the better.

She nibbled at a piece of toast. Hal was bustling around the kitchen, making the coffee, scrambling the eggs he never failed to eat for breakfast, every morning of his life. He was dressed. He would go to the office as he did every day, with the smell of bacon in his clothes. She was made up and her hair was done; her underwear was all in place and adjusted. All she had to do was slip off the quilted robe she wore in the kitchen and pull on her dress to be ready to go when Hal was. She stared at the newspaper as if she were reading it, to foreclose any essay he might make into breakfast-table conversation. The autocrat of the breakfast table he was not.

She scanned the story of yesterday's session again. The trial had been easy. It had required almost nothing from her, other than Lois's foolish demand for the meeting between Brookover and Flint. She'd had to rule infrequently; there had been few objections, little dispute. A few days ago, someone had handed her a quotation that might yet prove untrue. From Publilius Syrus (whoever in hell that might be), it said: "The judge is condemned when the criminal is acquitted." It looked now very much as if the criminal were going to be acquitted, but so far it also looked as if the judge might escape being condemned.

She was glad this trial was followed by the holiday season. She would have some time off. She was tired. She wanted to spend some time with her father and with the kids. (There was no point even in thinking of going somewhere alone. Too much fuss.) She had looked over her personal calendar for the next four weeks. In four weeks she had three nights left when she was not scheduled for a party, a dinner, carol singing, or duty at the Scouts' Christmas tree sale. That was the other half of the price of a judgeship. She had stopped thinking about that half: whether it was too much to pay. She had no alternative.

She looked up from the paper. She put on her glasses. Hal put her coffee, in a giant mug, on the table before her. She sipped, and the steam fogged her glasses. Jesus! Jesus, what a wonderful life!

For a moment the courtroom was silent, so silent you could hear the scratch of pencil on rough drawing paper: a sketch artist outlining with rapid strokes the posture and dress of the defendant now sitting in the witness chair. She, the defendant, wore a loose, long-skirted, sleeveless, cream-white dress, covered by an electric-blue textured linen jacket. She had sworn to tell the truth, and now she sat high and erect on the chair and watched her counsel confer for a moment at the defense table.

Lois stood. "State your full name, please."

"Tommy Jo Brookover."

Teejay had seen Lois step back to the rail and speak a word to an old man just before the judge entered the courtroom. He was sitting now in the second row of seats. She recognized Dan Farnham. Beside him was Bob Peavy. Beside Peavy sat a honey-blond girl. That was Lois's daughter, probably. And there was a cocky teen-aged boy: likely her son. All these people watched Lois put the standard questions: where she lived, how old she was, and—in her case—why she was called Teejay.

She spoke directly to Lois, answering her questions, but she glanced often at the jury. Once again, it was important to establish eye contact with each juror. So far the young woman married to the medical student had never met her glance. Teejay was afraid of her. She seemed to look away, through her heavy spectacles, to something beyond the walls of the courtroom. Her glasses distorted her eyes, but still she seemed to stare into space, vacant and vaguely sullen. The unemployed waitress chewed placidly on her gum and watched everything with the same detached interest. She met no one's eyes. The black woman who had nodded at Teejay the first day had nodded to her several times since. It was a cryptic nod. Teejay looked at her often.

"Miss Brookover," said Lois. She paused to glance down at Earl Lansing. "We have heard a great deal of testimony about the acquisition by Benjamin Mudge and his associates of certain stock in Futures Dynamic Corporation. I want to ask you if you, in your own mind, feel you did anything wrong in that connection."

This was what they had agreed to do. It was their strategy. Teejay nodded somberly. "Yes, I did," she said.

"What did you do wrong?"

"I took part in deceiving the stockholders of that company, to get them to—in effect—sell control of their company to Benjamin Mudge."

"Is that a crime?"

"Yes. It's a violation of the federal securities laws."

"Have you been charged with a crime?"

Teejay sighed and nodded. "Yes. I'm under indictment on federal charges."

Members of the jury frowned at her. They were surprised, as they were expected to be, to hear her testifying—in response to questions from her own counsel—that she was under indictment for other crimes. That was their strategy: to rob Hornwood of a weapon by bringing the federal charges out before he had the opportunity to ask about them.

"With regard to the sale of lots at Lago Aguila, did you do anything wrong?"

"Yes. I wrote property reports that failed to tell lot buyers some important facts about the lots."

"Is that a crime?"

"Yes."

"Are you under indictment for that?"

"Yes."

"Thomas Glencoe and Roberto Luiz are serving sentences in a federal prison for the same crimes," said Lois. "Do you expect to go to prison, too?"

Teejay nodded. "Yes."

"Do you expect to be disbarred?"

Hornwood interrupted. "Your Honor, the defendant can only speculate as to whether or not she will be sent to a federal reformatory or will be disbarred, and I see no relevance in this line of questions."

"Are you suggesting you wouldn't have asked them yourself on cross-examination?" Lois asked.

"The objection is overruled," said Judge Spencer.

"I expect to be disbarred," said Teejay.

"In his testimony," Lois continued, "Thomas Glencoe characterized his own conduct with the word 'fraud.' What word would you use for yours?"

"The same word."

" 'Fraud'?"

"Yes."

"Why? Why did you do it?"

Teejay looked for an instant at the jury. "I—"

"Objection," said Hornwood. "Why she committed fraud is irrelevant. The jury does not need to hear whatever speech she wants to make in self-justification."

"Overruled," said the judge. "We'll hear it for what it's worth."

Teejay, with her head lowered, glanced up from beneath her brows, into the eyes of Lois. They had arranged an accommodating judge. She looked at the jury again. "I did it for money," she said quietly.

"And for that money you are going to a federal prison and you've lost your right to practice law," said Lois.

"Your Honor!" Hornwood protested.

"Can we go on to something else, Mrs. Hughes?" asked Judge Spencer.

Lois nodded.

"Then please do."

Lois sat down and crossed her legs. "Miss Brookover, did you ever tell Christine McElhay you were in love with Kevin Flint?"

"Absolutely not."

"*Are* you in love with him? Have you ever been?"

"No," said Teejay. She fixed her eyes hard on Lois's, until Lois glanced away.

"What is the relationship between you and Kevin Flint?" Lois asked. She was looking at Earl Lansing.

"He's been a friend for a long time, pretty much the way he told it. That's all."

"Did you ever threaten to kill Benjamin Mudge?"

"No."

Lois pushed her note pad away from her, across the table. "Well, then," she said, almost casually, almost conversationally, "did you kill Benjamin Mudge?"

Teejay turned to her jury and spoke directly to them. "No," she said, simply and emphatically.

"The indictment in this case charges that you employed or procured Kevin Flint to kill Benjamin Mudge. Did you do that?"

"No. I had nothing to do with it." . . .

Hornwood stood tall and gray and loose-jointed in front of his table, and for a long moment he simply faced Teejay, with a skeptical smile and easy blue eyes. "Well, Miss Brookover," he said finally. "We have a lot of things to talk about."

She nodded. She looked up into his long, acne-marked face. He had the right now to question her as long and as hard as he wanted to; and he had the right later to call rebuttal witnesses to contradict anything she said. It was his chance to catch her in a lie. And he would try. He was a decent enough man, probably; she was ready to concede that. But he was frustrated and probably angry. Kevin had bested him. Some of his other witnesses had proved less persuasive than he probably had expected. Worst, he probably had guessed by now something of what had passed between Lois and the judge and had concluded he could have no confidence in Judge Norma Jean Spencer. He had been testy this morning in his objections; and now, she guessed, he hid a determination to destroy her behind the amiable smile with which he faced her.

"Miss Brookover," he said, "first, this morning, I would like to recall the afternoon of Sunday, March 5, 1978. Do you remember that you met with Benjamin Mudge and others on that day?"

"I don't remember by date. I remember there was a Sunday-afternoon meeting about that time."

"Mr. Glencoe testified about it and described it as a meeting at which you and Mr. Mudge became very angry at each other. Do you recall? Mr. Glencoe testified that Mr. Mudge called you a little bitch, among other things, and that you, when you were leaving, used some hard language toward him. Do you remember that?"

"I remember."

"I would like for you to tell us exactly what you said to Mr. Mudge as you were leaving that meeting."

Teejay licked her lips. She looked for a moment at Lois. "I recall it was just—angry words. I didn't threaten him, if that's what you're asking."

Hornwood smiled and shook his head. "That's not what I'm asking. What I want you to do is tell us exactly what you said to Mr. Mudge as you backed out the door."

"I believe I said I would get even with him."

Hornwood bent forward, toward her, and lifted both hands in a patient gesture. "In your words, Miss Brookover. Say again the words you said then."

"I said, 'I'll get even with you.'"

"'I'll get even with you,'" Hornwood repeated. "Were those your words, really? Did you say 'get even'? Are you sure it wasn't 'I'll get you'?"

Teejay frowned. "All right. It may have been that."

"'I'll get you'?"

"Yes."

"'I'll get you. . . .' And there was more of it, wasn't there? You said, 'I'll get you,' and then what?"

Teejay shook her head. "I don't remember anything more."

"Didn't you call him something? 'I'll get you, you . . .' something or other?"

"I don't know."

"Did you say, 'I'll get you, you son of a bitch'?"

Teejay sighed. "Probably."

"Probably," Hornwood repeated. He nodded. "And what else? There was more to the statement, wasn't there?"

"I—"

"*Objection!* This is pointless," Lois complained.

"No, no," Hornwood rejoined quickly. "The depth of her anger is demonstrated by the words she used. It is relevant and important."

"Counsel will approach the bench."

They conferred out of the hearing of the reporter and the jury—off the record. Teejay, watching them, was blocked out of the conference by Hornwood's back, but she could hear, indistinctly, what was said.

"What'd she say?" asked Judge Spencer. "What are you trying to get in?"

Hornwood whispered. "She said, 'I'll get you, you goddamn cock-sucking, motherfucking son of a bitch.'"

"*Oh, no!*" Lois whispered. "The only reason you want that in is to make the jury hate her. It's the most prejudicial thing I ever heard." Lois's quick anger was vivid in her whistling whisper. "The jury doesn't need to hear the kind of foul language she used."

"It shows how much she hated Mudge," Hornwood whispered. "I can bring witnesses, if you want to hear them, who'll testify she wasn't given to that kind of language. She used it against Mudge. She hated him enough to kill. It's *relevant!*"

Teejay could see the judge's pained, disgusted expression. It *was* relevant. She knew it was. And it was damaging. And she was going to rule it out. She, Teejay, had appeared before judges like this: where you knew they were going to rule against you, law or no, for reasons you could only guess at; and she knew how frustrating it was for a lawyer. Hornwood had to be seething.

"The objection is sustained, and the district attorney is directed to proceed to another line of questioning," said Judge Spencer aloud.

Hornwood smiled at the judge, and nodded. Grimly under control, he was more dangerous an adversary than he had been when his temper was showing. He ambled back to his table and picked up his yellow legal pad.

"You have acknowledged, Miss Brookover," he said conversationally, "that you defrauded the stockholders of Futures Dynamic. Is that not correct? You did acknowledge . . ."

"Yes," she said cautiously.

"How did you do that?"

"We didn't give them all the information they should have had," she answered.

"Oh, there was more to it than that, wasn't there?" Hornwood asked with a smile. "You lied to them, didn't you?"

Teejay nodded. "Yes. We did."

"You say 'We did.' *You* did. Didn't you?"

"Yes. I did."

"Yes. And the people who bought lots at Lago Aguila. You lied to them, too, didn't you?"

"Yes."

He picked up a manila folder from his table and searched for a moment for some papers. "You made certain loan applications, to banks, on behalf of Lago Aguila, Incorporated—did you not?"

"Yes."

"And those contained false statements, too, didn't they?"

"Yes."

"Lies."

"Yes."

"You knew all these statements—to the stockholders of Futures Dynamic, to the public buying lots at Lago Aguila, to the banks who made loans—were lies. Didn't you? Yet you made them?"

"Yes." She tried not to sound reluctant or sullen. She had listened to how Kevin had acknowledged lies and worse things, calmly, without embarrassment. It was not easy to do. She felt herself sweating. She struggled to control her voice.

"These were not small lies, either. These lies were crimes. You committed crimes by these lies, didn't you?"

"Yes."

He put the papers back on his file folder. He smiled. "Well, why, Miss Brookover? Why did you tell these lies?"

"For money," she said glumly.

"You had a motive to lie," he said. "Money. You have a motive to lie here, now, don't you?"

"Objection!"

"I have to overrule," said Judge Spencer.

"You have a motive to lie here, today, under oath—don't you?"

Teejay nodded. "I suppose I do."

"To avoid going to prison. Right?"

"Yes."

Hornwood nodded. "Yes. Did you lie in response to any of your counsel's questions?"

"No."

"Why not?"

"Objection."

"Sustained."

He had made his point. The objection didn't hurt him. Some of the sincerity returned to his smile. "Miss Brookover," he said, "you have testified that you are under certain federal indictments for violations of the federal securities laws and land sales disclosure laws. Did these frauds involve you in any other crimes, for which you have not been indicted?"

"Objection, Your Honor."

Hornwood glanced haughtily at Lois. "Miss Brookover," he said, "your attorney can advise you to take the Fifth Amendment, if you wish. You don't have to answer the question."

"I will answer," said Teejay quietly.

"I withdraw the objection," said Lois, closing her eyes.

"I am not aware," said Teejay, "that I could be charged with anything else. I suppose it is possible."

"Well, Lago Aguila made false loan applications," said Hornwood. "You signed the papers. That was a crime, wasn't it?"

She nodded. "Yes."

"Benjamin Mudge bought the best lots in the subdivision, for prices far below the selling price," said Hornwood. "That was embezzlement, in effect, wasn't it?"

Teejay drew a deep breath. "Yes. I think it was."

"You helped him do it. You signed the papers. Embezzlement?"

Teejay did not answer. She looked at Hornwood, blinking. She could not refuse to answer. But she did not want to answer. "I—didn't think of it that way," she said.

"Well. Was it not embezzlement?"

"It was embezzlement," she said quietly.

"At the time when Benjamin Mudge was killed, you had not been charged with any crime, had you?"

"No."

"Could he have been a witness against you?"

"Yes."

"On all these charges. Correct?"

"Yes."

"Did you ever consider volunteering to testify against Benjamin Mudge, in return for leniency for yourself?"

"Yes."

"And, of course, he could have done the same to you. Right?"

"Yes."

"In fact, he said more than once that he would. Didn't he?"

"Yes."

Hornwood was conspicuously satisfied with the way the cross-examination was going. It was hurting, and there was no way to stop him. She could see—or imagined she could—the attitude of the jury changing. Some of them were looking at her with expressions of deep concern, as if they were reluctantly withdrawing their sympathy. Hornwood turned his back on her as he walked around his table and, planting his hands, stared down for a moment at his notes. She shuddered. She looked at Lois and Lansing. They were staring blankly at the defense table. Hornwood looked up. He smiled.

"Miss Brookover, what was the nature of the relationship between you and Benjamin Mudge?"

"Attorney and client," she said.

"Were you friends?"

"I thought so for a while."

"Were you close friends?"

"No, never very close."

"You were not—*intimate* friends?"

She shook her head emphatically. "No, sir."

"He sent you gifts from time to time, though, didn't he? A case of wine one time. A case of whiskey another."

"Yes."

"How about your legal fees? Were they high?"

"I was generously paid."

"By Mudge?"

"Well—some of the fees were paid by the corporations."

"In fact, you were made an officer of both corporations, were you not?"

"Yes, sir."

"Did you have other clients who paid you anything like what you were paid, directly or indirectly, by Benjamin Mudge?"

"No, not really."

"How old are you, Miss Brookover?"

"I'm thirty-six."

"So you were thirty-five when you were doing this work. Would it be wrong to say you were paid as much for your legal services as the most senior partner in any firm in Houston would have been paid for the same services?"

"I really don't know what senior partners are paid."

"I'm going to make a statement. Tell me if any part of it is wrong. You were an attractive young woman. You had never handled any law business like this before. You were paid very generous fees, comparable to the fees paid the most experienced lawyers in the biggest firms. You were also given one hundred fifty shares in Lago Aguila, Incorporated—which would have been worth at least thirty thousand dollars if the subdivision had sold out successfully. Is any of that wrong?"

She bit the inside of her lower lip. "No, I guess not," she said.

"Benjamin Mudge was very much your benefactor, was he not?"

"Yes, he was, for a while."

"But you were never very good friends?"

"No, we never were."

"What did he give you for Christmas in 1977?"

"A wristwatch."

"Do you have any idea what he paid for that wristwatch?"

"It was an expensive watch."

"How expensive?"

"I don't know."

"Would you argue with me if I told you he paid more than four thousand dollars for it?"

"Would I argue with you?"

"Yes. Do you deny it was worth that much?"

"I can't argue about it or deny it, because I don't know."

"Well, does it surprise you to hear he paid that much?"

"No."

"You knew it was in that price range."

She sighed, nodded. "Yes. I knew it was worth something like that."

"He gave you a four-thousand-dollar wristwatch, but he was not your close or intimate friend. Is that your testimony, Miss Brookover?"

"I never slept with him, Mr. Hornwood, if that's what you're trying to suggest."

Hornwood smiled easily. "Im glad to have you clarify that," he said. "I didn't suggest you did. I'm only trying to discover the nature of the relationship between you and Benjamin Mudge. And I think that's all I have to ask you on that subject. Oh, except this—that wristwatch is the one you threw in his face on Sunday, March fifth, is it not?"

Teejay's face was flushed. She swallowed. "I threw it at him," she said in a breaking voice.

The jury was conspicuously incredulous. That she should have thrown a four-thousand-dollar wristwatch at Mudge . . . It introduced a new speculation into the case, one they had not considered. Neither had any of the spectators in the courtroom. The media people and the benches of spectators were silent: too stunned to snicker. That was as far as Hornwood could go—to suggest. It was far enough.

"Miss Brookover," he said crisply, injecting a new note of purposefulness into his cross-examination, "let's talk about your relationship with Kevin Flint. In the first place, did you ever sleep with him?"

"No, sir," Teejay said cautiously.

"He testified that he never stayed overnight in your apartment. Is that correct?"

"He never stayed overnight in my apartment."

"Did you ever engage in any kind of intimacy with him there?"

"No."

"I believe he testified he picked you up there to take you out to dinner. Is that correct? Is that the extent of his visits to your apartment?"

"Yes."

"He picked you up. He never stayed?"

"He never stayed."

"How many rooms were there in your apartment, Miss Brookover? Rather than telling me the number, would you describe them?"

"I—had a living room, kitchen, a—sort of dining area at one end of the living room. I had a bedroom that I used for an office. Two bathrooms. I mean, there was a bathroom opposite my office, and then there was my bedroom—the master bedroom—and the bathroom that went with that."

"Did James Rush sleep with you in your bedroom?"

Her face stiffened. She flushed. "Yes, sir."

"Used the bathroom there?"

"Yes."

"But it is your testimony that Kevin Flint did not?"

"Yes."

"Did he ever *go* into your bedroom?"

"No."

"In other words, was your relationship with him friendly enough for him to see your bedroom?"

Teejay shook her head. "I—no, he was never in my bedroom."

"Was he ever there without your knowledge, do you think?"

"Objection," said Lois quietly. "How can she testify he was there without her knowledge?"

Hornwood smiled and bowed slightly toward Lois. "Your point is well taken, Mrs. Hughes. I will ask the question a different way. Miss Brookover, did Kevin Flint ever wander around in your apartment alone, so that he perhaps went in your bedroom without your knowledge?"

Teejay was frightened. What evidence did he have that Kevin was in her bedroom? How should she answer? If she said yes, he was in her bedroom, she admitted more intimacy with him than she wanted to admit. If she said no, and he had some evidence Kevin *was* in her bedroom, then he had caught her in a lie. Kevin had testified he only picked her up there. She herself had just testified he only picked her up. What was Hornwood driving at? She didn't have time to think.

She shook her head. "I can't remember any time when he could have been in my bedroom."

"To pick up a wrap for you, for instance?" Hornwood suggested.

Teejay shook her head. *What was he after?* "No," she said weakly.

"Let's see now," said Hornwood easily. "I believe he testified he only picked you up at your apartment twice, three times at the most. Is that correct?"

"Yes, sir."

"So it is not difficult for you to remember those occasions, is it?"

"No . . ."

"How long did he stay on each occasion?"

"Maybe fifteen minutes. Once we had a drink before we went out to dinner."

"Did he ever use the bathroom in your apartment?"

"Not that I recall."

"Well, uh, if you remember the occasions—there being so few of them—can't you tell me if he used the bathroom?"

Teejay glanced at Lois. There was no form of objection that would stop these questions; yet she had a horrified feeling she was being trapped in something. He had led up to this, very carefully. He was cornering her, and she could not see a way out.

"I do not recall, Mr. Hornwood, if he ever used the bathroom."

"If he did, which one did he use?"

"The one in the hall."

"Not the one you could reach only by going through your bedroom?"

"I don't think he was ever in there."

Hornwood smiled tolerantly. "It's not really a matter of 'I think,' is it, Miss Brookover? You've been pretty emphatic that he was not in your bedroom, so how could he have been in the bathroom that could be reached only by going through your bedroom?"

That was it! Something in the bathroom! The search of the apartment had turned up something in the bathroom that told them Kevin had been there. A fingerprint . . . She had spent hours wiping things he could have touched—in fact, *had* touched. They had talked about it. She had wiped doorknobs, the knobs on the television set, the headboard of the bed . . . God, *everything!* Even so, they had found a fingerprint. In the bathroom. That was what he was driving at.

"Mr. Hornwood," she said carefully, drawing in a breath, drawing her lips tight, "you are asking me to remember exactly where in my apartment Kevin Flint may have gone sometime more than a year ago. I can't think of any reason why he would have been in my bedroom or in my bathroom, and I don't remember his going there; but I doubt if you could remember exactly what rooms in your home were entered by a visitor who stopped by a year ago, and I can't, either."

Hornwood planted his hands on his hips and glared at her scornfully. "A nice speech, Miss Brookover," he said. "That negatives everything you've testified to on this subject, doesn't it?"

"Objection!"

"I have no further questions of the defendant," said Hornwood, turning his back on the witness stand and returning to his chair.

Hornwood called one rebuttal witness. As Teejay had suspected, they had found one smudged fingerprint of Kevin's, on the wall above the toilet in her bathroom. A man, standing at the toilet to urinate, holding his penis with his right hand, had lazily put his left hand on the wall. It might be enough to send her to prison for life.

Lois and Earl stayed with her during the noon recess. She sat in the holding pen, frightened and depressed, no longer confident of her acquittal. "He had to have something, didn't he?" she said hoarsely, her throat tight. "Some . . . We had to know he'd spring something on us, something we couldn't anticipate. We wouldn't have been here if he hadn't had something."

"Don't exaggerate the importance of it," Earl Lansing said. He stood close to the chain-link wall of the pen. "It isn't so much."

"It's the kind of thing that turns juries against you," Teejay insisted. "They'll remember it more than anything else in the trial. Hornwood dramatized it so! It was obvious to the jury that I was squirming."

"Your last answer took a lot of the sting out of it," said Lansing.

"Or made me out the liar he was trying to prove I was."

She put her forehead against the chain link and closed her eyes for a moment. Lois stood beside Lansing, frowning, subdued, slack. Teejay looked at her. "*You've got to win,*" she whispered to Lois. "You've got to get me out some way. I can't stand it anymore."

"It would have helped if you'd told me from the beginning that you and Flint really did kill Mudge," said Lois quietly.

"What would you have done for me if you'd known?" Teejay asked blankly.

Court reconvened at 1:30. Hornwood made his final argument. He said he had no witness who had overheard the defendant and Flint scheming to murder Benjamin Mudge. It was in the nature of conspiracies, he said, that plots are made in secret; and one must deduce their existence from the results they produce. That was what the evidence was about, he said—the results of the scheme. "No one has ever seen a radio wave," he argued. "So how do you prove its existence? You cannot, ladies and gentlemen, deny that something exists, or has existed, simply because you can't see it, or hear it, or produce as a witness someone who has seen it or heard it. You must judge—and you *can* judge, quite rationally and quite fairly—from other kinds of evidence, that what you are talking about did exist, did happen, did produce the results that are so obvious."

He set forth the elements of his case: that Benjamin Mudge was dead; that Kevin Flint had killed him; that Kevin Flint was at the very least the friend, if not the lover, of the defendant; that Flint had had no real motive of his own for killing Mudge; that the defendant had a powerful motive; therefore, the only reasonable explanation for the murder was that the defendant procured Flint to kill Mudge.

He spoke calmly, trying to persuade with reason, not emotion. He talked at length about Flint being a liar and the defendant being a cheat and liar who had defrauded hundreds of people. "An attorney at law, ladies and gentlemen, licensed by the state to do other people's business and to solicit their trust for the doing of that business. She has admitted to you she lied repeatedly, consistently, to trusting people who listened to what she said and supposed they could believe her. And when I asked her why she lied, her only reason—the only reason she could give you—was that it was a way to make money. It was a way to *cheat* people, to take their money from them—dishonestly. And in this courtroom she faces you the same way she faced the stockholders of Futures Dynamic and the buyers of lots at Lago Aguila—lying once again, to deceive you, to cheat the law, to cheat justice."

Teejay never took her eyes from him as he argued the case against her. She had decided that was her most effective posture: not to hide her head, not to stare at her hands, but to face his words and solemnly defy them. She saw the members of the jury staring thoughtfully at her as Hornwood called her a liar and a murderer.

Lois argued for the defense. She reviewed the testimony of the many witnesses. "No one, ladies and gentlemen of the jury, not one of the witnesses has testified that this defendant killed Benjamin Mudge. Not one witness has testified that she had anything to do with it. The evidence—every last shred of it—proves only a group of circumstances that *suggest* she might have had something to do with the killing of Benjamin Mudge. The evidence proves it is not *impossible* she procured Flint to kill Mudge. The evidence is that she knew Flint, that he was a longtime acquaintance, maybe a friend. The evidence is that she had reason to hate Benjamin Mudge. From those two circumstances alone the prosecutor seeks to make you believe she joined with Flint to kill Mudge.

"But the law requires far more than that, ladies and gentlemen. Indeed, putting aside the law, *justice* requires far more than that. It is a fundamental principle of American justice, ladies and gentlemen, that you do not send a person to prison for life because the police and the district attorney *suspect* that person killed someone. If we sent people to prison only because officials suspect them, we would need no courts, no judges, no juries, no trials. . . ."

Lois's little group watched her somberly—Peavy, her father, her son, her daughter. Teejay glanced at them from time to time. Peavy was grim. Lois had told him, obviously, she believed her client was guilty, and he was watching her make an argument in which he knew she did not believe. That was a grim spectacle. Her father watched with self-satisfied cynicism. He knew, too—or suspected—but he didn't care. The two children were simply fascinated. Probably neither of them had seen Lois trying a case before, and they were seeing something of their mother they could not even have imagined.

Lois spoke thinly, as if she were on the verge of tears. Her voice did break twice. It was noted by the reporters. They would say, probably, that her forensics were of the old school. Teejay could see her fingernails digging into the palms of her hands. Teejay glanced at Earl Lansing, and his eyes met hers. Surely his thought was the same as hers: that Lois's genuine distress was the most effective note she could lend to her argument, and the jury would never suspect its origin.

". . . On Monday Mr. Hornwood told us he would prove this defendant murdered Benjamin Mudge. Well, he has not proved it. He has proved she hated him. In fact, he has proved she had some reason to hate him. He has proved she had dinner occasionally with the man who killed Benjamin Mudge, and that this man came to her apartment to pick her up for dinner and used her bathroom. On that evidence you are asked to believe she conspired with Kevin Flint to murder Benjamin Mudge. It takes more than that, ladies and gentlemen. It takes more than that."

Hornwood spoke for about two minutes in rebuttal. He said what he always said. "We are here to do justice, ladies and gentlemen of the jury. Let us not forget that justice consists of punishing the guilty as much as it consists of freeing the innocent. Society is entitled to justice, too. It is entitled to know, confidently, that we punish people who take other people's lives—when we catch them. Mrs. Hughes, for the defense, asks for justice. That's fine. The state of Texas will accept that gladly. Do justice, ladies and gentlemen of the jury. Do justice, and no one will complain."

Judge Spencer charged the jury. On the subject of circumstantial evidence, she said: "It is essential to the well-being, if not to the very existence, of civil society that it should be understood that the secrecy with which crimes are committed will not insure impunity to the offender. Circumstantial evidence is allowable because it is, in its own nature, capable of producing the highest degree of moral certainty. However, where a criminal charge is to be proved by circumstantial evidence, the evidence ought to be not only consistent with the defendant's guilt but inconsistent with any other rational conclusion. Where the circumstances are reconcilable with the theory of the innocence of the accused, the jury is bound so to treat them. It is only when the facts and circumstances are irreconcilable with the defendant's innocence that the defendant can be convicted."

She charged the jury that they could find the defendant guilty only if they believed the state had proved her guilty beyond a reasonable doubt. "A reasonable doubt is not a mere possible doubt, because everything relating to human affairs or depending upon moral evidence is open to some possible or imaginary doubt. It is that state of the case which, after the entire consideration of all the evidence, leaves the minds of the jurors in that condition that they cannot say they feel an abiding conviction to a moral certainty of the truth of the charge."

The jury retired to begin its deliberations at 3:23 P.M.

Teejay was locked in the holding pen. Earl Lansing sat outside. Lois went to speak with her family for a few minutes.

"What do you think?" Teejay asked Lansing. She shifted uncomfortably on the hard bench. "Am I going to make it?"

Lansing shrugged. "It's in the laps of the gods," he said.

"Whatever way it comes out," she said, "I owe you a lot, and I want you to know I appreciate it."

"Having an ol' country lawyer with you in court never hurts," he drawled with a smile. " 'Bout all I did was sit there, but if it helped, I'm glad."

"You know," she said very quietly, "if Hornwood gets his justice, I'm going away for life."

Lansing nodded. "I know."

"I guess the right way to say it is, I *let* Kevin do it. I could have stopped him. I—"

"Tommy Jo," Lansing said. "I've been tempted, sorely, in my time. It's just by the grace of God I didn't follow my temptation. I don't know what justice is. Certitude is a luxury of small minds. I want to see you get out because I think it's a waste of a young life to keep you locked up like an animal. If that's not justice . . . well, the world is full of things that aren't justice. I'd get a good deal of satisfaction out of this injustice, and that's good enough for me."

Lois came with cans of Coke—and a deputy to unlock the door of the holding pen so Teejay could have hers. Lois's face was flushed and she looked as if she might have been crying somewhere, maybe in the women's room. "If they just don't come back too soon . . ." she said.

Hornwood came. He stood in the door to the room, not all the way inside. "Nicely tried, Lois, Earl," he said, nodding, smiling. He looked at Teejay inside the pen. "Some kind of good luck to you, young lady," he said without embarrassment. "I can't wish you the kind that loses me my case—but all other kinds."

He did not stay long enough for her to respond, even if she had been able to, but ducked out the door again and was gone.

"The man has nerve he hasn't used yet," said Teejay bitterly.

After forty minutes, Teejay asked to be taken out to the bathroom. Two women deputies came and took her. When she returned to the holding pen, it was 4:12.

Lois sat with her. Lansing had gone out for a while, probably to have a drink. She and Lois had little to say to each other now. Lois sat in manifest discomfort on her wooden chair. The bench inside the pen was worse. Teejay sat, then stood until her legs were cramped, then sat again. There was no pacing inside the pen; it was too small. When Lansing returned it was 4:25.

"Have you thought about an appeal?" Teejay asked Lois.

"God forbid."

"We have to think about it."

"You're a lawyer," Lois said with a sigh. "What error did you see?"

"Insufficient evidence."

Lois shook her head. "Never reverse it with that."

"Will you try?"

"If we have to. Let's don't even think about it yet."

"That's right," said Earl Lansing. "Let's don't. Sour our luck."

Teejay settled on the bench. She could resent them. However this came out, they were going to dinner tonight—and somewhere fancy, too. However it came out, she was going back to jail. There was no point in cursing. There was no point in crying. There was not even any point in thinking. She bent forward, slumped, and stared at her hands folded in her lap.

They were called at 5:14. The jury had a verdict.

The jury filed in. They were downcast, unhappy. It was a bad sign, and she trembled. She looked at their faces. There was a myth that if the jurors looked you in the eye, they had acquitted; if they did not, the old story went, they had convicted. These jurors looked hangdog. They sat. The judge entered. They rose and sat again.

"Members of the jury, have you reached a verdict?" Judge Spencer asked. She had hurried back and was still adjusting her robe—or some part of her clothes under her robe—as she asked the foreman if the jury had reached a verdict.

The retired insurance agent had been elected foreman. He stood. "We have, Your Honor," he said.

"Hand your verdict to the clerk."

The clerk, a florid man who had not been in the courtroom except occasionally during the trial, took the verdict forms from the hands of the foreman. They had been given several forms: guilty of premeditated murder, guilty of unpremeditated murder, guilty of manslaughter, and not guilty. Frowning and deeply intent, he unfolded each of the forms and stuffed them one by one into his jacket pocket. He kept in his hand the one the jurors had signed, and this one he handed up to the judge. The judge glanced at it and handed it back to him to read.

Earl Lansing seized Teejay's hand and held it firmly. She watched the clerk, her mouth hanging open.

"State of Texas, county of Harris, ss," he intoned, reading every word of the form. It was his moment, and he wrung it out. "In the Criminal District Court. The state of Texas versus Tommy Jo Brookover. We the jury, being duly impaneled and sworn, find the defendant not guilty."

XXXVII

Twenty minutes after her acquittal, Teejay trudged back to the jail, handcuffed, led by one arm. She was stripped naked and subjected to the body search, put in uniform, and readmitted to "B" Cage, Cell 9. She had told Lois not to try to post the $50,000 federal bond but to expedite the federal procedures as much as possible. She wanted, she said, to spend Christmas in the federal reformatory, not in the county jail.

She remained in the county jail, nevertheless, for forty-one more days. She appeared in federal court on December 14 to plead guilty to two federal indictments; but the federal court remanded her to jail until January 11, so there might be a thorough presentencing investigation. She protested to Lois, but the federal judge would not be moved. She would spend Christmas in jail.

The second phase of Kevin Flint's trial was held on Tuesday, December 12. The jury that had convicted him of premeditated murder was reassembled to hear evidence and argument and decide if his punishment should be death or life imprisonment. The proceeding took two days. The jury deliberated for only ten minutes and decided he should be sentenced to life imprisonment. On Friday, December 15, he was taken to the state penitentiary at Huntsville. Teejay asked to see him before he left. Her request was denied.

December 12, President Carter announced an appointment to the Securities and Exchange Commission. His appointee was not Robert Peavy of Houston.

December 16, Lois Hughes and her children left for a vacation in New York and Palm Beach. Peavy would join them in Palm Beach on December 21. They would not return to Houston until January 6. Lois came to the jail before she left, to bring Teejay cigarettes and candy and books. No one would bring more until after January 6.

On December 18, the Houston Association for Women named Houston's Woman of the Year for 1978. She was Judge Norma Spencer of the Criminal District Court. She addressed the association's banquet on January 5. She said justice was the principal end of society, and justice was the sole concern of a judge.

On Monday, January 8—three days before Teejay was to appear for sentencing—Lois conferred with her at the jail. She suggested Teejay should speak for herself before the federal judge; it would be more effective than any appeal Lois could make. Teejay agreed.

The United States district judge was the Honorable Harry W. Hurd. Teejay had never before appeared in his court. She spoke for ten minutes, making an appeal for leniency. She said the time she had spent in jail waiting to be tried for murder was, in a very real sense, time served for her involvement in the stock and land frauds that brought her before this court now. She would never have been suspected of the murder of Benjamin Mudge, she said, except for her involvement in the Futures Dynamic and Lago Aguila frauds. She had been in jail since April 6, she told Judge Hurd, and it was doubtful the others sentenced in the Futures Dynamic–Lago Aguila frauds would serve that much time. Besides, she said, she was being disbarred—a penalty the others were not suffering. She wept at the end of her statement and did not quite finish.

Judge Hurd's decision was a shock. He did not sentence her. He granted her release on probation, on only two conditions: that she resign her license to practice law immediately and never seek reinstatement, and that she never again engage in any business that involved the investment of other people's money. After two hundred seventy-eight days in jail, she was free.